PLAGUING JAKE

BY THE SAME AUTHOR

FICTION
The Dying Detective
Omphalos
Missing Children
Exotic Dancers
Troutstream
Kisbey
One's Company

NON-FICTION
The One and the Many: English-Canadian Short Story Cycles
Stephen Leacock: Humour and Humanity

EDITED
Alice Munro's Miraculous Art: Critical Essays
The Ivory Thought: Essays on Al Purdy
Leacock On Life
Dominant Impressions: Essays on the Canadian Short Story
Sunshine Sketches of a Little Town, by Stephen Leacock
Familiar Ground: A Prose Reader
Short Fiction: An Introductory Anthology
The Canadian Essay
Bliss Carman: A Reappraisal
Prose Models
The Rising Village, by Oliver Goldsmith

PLAGUING JAKE
A Novel

GERALD LYNCH

Winnipeg

For Jo

The best lack all conviction, while the worst
Are full of passionate intensity.
— *Yeats*

And there's a mighty judgment coming,
but I may be wrong.
— *Leonard Cohen*

ONE

LEAVE TAKEN

"Excuse me, sir, but can you direct me to the Faculty of Arts, please?"

"The *what?*"

She'd known her mistake as it was spoken, didn't need his scrunched face like he'd whiffed a dump of sheep shit. It was all her father's fault! ... No, she didn't need any of this. She was dead tired already, from leaving home, which had been way more brutal than her worst imagining. Then the too-short train ride from Leitrim Falls to Ottawa, where the empty car had crowded her with its sweaty-sock smell. Then from the light-rail to the uBytown campus. Then from the long-haul walk in what was likely the wrong direction. To here, to this.

The campus had felt ghost-town abandoned—a tumbleweed could tumble by unremarked, a zombie could stagger from the shadows. There were no bustling kids her own age, no mature and studiously playful young adults, unlike the jackasses she'd suffered the last year of high school (not Jimmy, not Naomi). She'd felt cowed galumphing along. The big buildings were all greenish glass and steel, and already cold-shouldering her. Or it felt as if she were inside a bottle, displayed for alien eyes, exposed, like waiting for the dreaded examination in Dr. McKenzie's swank new office. She even wished she were back there.

She'd finally spotted some kids. A Black boy and a white girl were sitting in lotus position facing each other under a cedar tree's protective branches. They were doing the same thing as the stoner crowd at high school, passing a joint, which she could smell. There was only one Black family in Leitrim Falls. The guy leaned in and picked something off the girl's lip. Cute. She missed Jimmy something awful. She'd never liked the smell of marijuana and hadn't enjoyed the times she'd experimented with Naomi. Stoned, she was even more self-conscious, overly sensitive to remarks, and then just too anxious. And the smell made her think of the Canopy Growth operation, and so of her dad having to work there. Only oldsters carried on about how they just *loved* the smell of weed, puffing up their hipster cred against old age (not Dad). Who could really like the stink of that skunky shit? Forget what it did to your head. Who'd ever have thought she could miss the chicken coop? Because she wished she were back there too.

And now this, this tight-suited doofus with the gelled-up do. A mistake to stop him. But he carried nothing, he might know something. Was he checking her out? Hey, buddy, I'm up here. She turned sideways, away from his appraising gaze, felt her cheeks prickle warmly ... blushing? *Damn.* So she looked at her feet and ordered them to walk past him giving wide berth.

Time was still close enough to the most recent pandemic that Dean Jacques LaRoque could dismiss as habit a female student's swerve past him. Whatevs (as the kids say ... or do they still?). He wasn't offended, because Dean LaRoque could connect with students. He'd personally had a hand in bringing Nickelback to Frosh Week three years before. He'd introduced them to a mostly cheering crowd under uBytown's new Big Top, the high-tech tent that had cost the faculty's recovering budget a fortune, an amount equal to twenty-seven part-timers' salaries. Yes, and not only an expensive *initial* outlay, the Big Top, because continuing costly to put up and take down every September. But the bigger bread-and-circus had been paying off in recruitment PR! ... Sort of.

The glimpse he'd caught of her face encouraged him. He was a bit worried about the snap of his "the *what*?" response to her ignorant question. But "Faculty of Arts"? They'd been the Faculty of Digital Humanities for five years now (his doing).

And she'd jolted him out of contemplating the fate of the Music Pod's old building (some forty years old already). He'd not been musing again on whether Music should be incorporated into Communications, or even terminated (*did* it have a place in the twenty-first-century university?). He'd been wondering when the campaign could safely begin to have the old girl torn down and replaced. *Not* because he didn't appreciate antique architecture (he believed he did). But because the brown brick clashed in his mission—his *vision* to make uBytown's buildings uniform in an impressive steel-and-glass (silver and aquamarine). Clashed? *Crashed* aesthetically, like some Titanic berg, with the revitalization program he'd been overseeing for a good decade now.

Still, he worried that there'd been a sharpness in his tone, which would account for the lovely young lady's scampering. So he called after her:

"I'm sorry, young lady! But you startled me out of a reverie!"

She halted, still with face down. Her new shoes were pink and white runners, high-tops, with the bottoms of her jeans tucked under their fat tongues like they'd casually got stuck there. The shoes would have cost Dad a fortune. He'd found out about the retro-fashion for high-tops (from Jimmy of all people!) and paid no mind to her protests, or to her weakening insistence that the shoes be returned to the pricey Plutoria Footwear. She'd had her eye on a low-cut black pair at the new Walmart out on Highway15 . Dad had smiled as her resistance weakened, and she'd smiled back, for his proud pleasure in finding them, and for their connection to Jimmy.

She continued staring down as if seeking direction from the pricey new shoes. How do I get out of here? What am I *doing* here?

Dean LaRoque coughed into his right fist. "You wrong-footed me with your perfectly reasonable question. But we've not called our *Digital Humanities* sector the *Faculty of Arts* for over five years now. That would've been five years after I arrived here from Waterloo U, in fact. Are you an international student by any chance? Let me venture a guess: Wales? New Zealand? I reference them only because we've had a welcome influx from there. Perfectly lovely countries with a deep appreciation for tradition. The Chinese too of course! Always the Chinese, *most* welcome with their economically rising middle class and appreciation of our Western tradition of liberal arts education."

Still looking down she seemed to address only her own body: "I'm from Leitrim Falls. I'm not from anywhere else."

What an odd answer! But a small-town girl, if one got up like an ad aimed at "today's youth." Maybe even a farm girl, certainly rural. Should he bother mentioning his relationship with Nickelback?

He closed the distance between them in two steps. She flinched and slid away half a stride. He extended his right arm and splayed its fingers as if pleading: "You have no cause for anxiety on this campus, young lady, thanks to the campaign I myself initiated against sexual harassment in any form, if I may say so in all humility." He brought his right hand to breast-bone and tipped his head. "That initiative was enthusiastically endorsed by my friends in Nickelback. Do you know that rock-n-roll group? ... Are you registered for a residence?"

What did he say? She darted her eyes at him and returned to looking down. Should she be worried? Dad had schooled her in the sorts of approaches she might encounter. (Cute, Dad.) How could she be missing him so badly already? Anyway, this goof did sound like he'd know something. Her collarbone was hurting, so she unslung the bulging backpack and set it beside her pale blue suitcase. She massaged her left shoulder (books were like bricks). Still without looking at him, she answered:

"Joseph Brant Residence, my dad read that it was highest rated for safety and cleanliness." Idiot, *you*. Control your nerves, your gab. Thank him and walk away.

He couldn't make out her face. It was curtained in profile by mid-length black hair, blue-black as a crow's wet wing, if unkempt, likely intentionally tousled, which was a new style he'd noticed. ... "Bed head" it's called. Yes, though more likely she's already a year late for that coif's fashion peak. She was thin as a child if nearly as tall as himself, perhaps as tall (unlikely), and her clothing was either the wrong size or she'd shrunk in it. But the baggy yellow-and-blue plaid shirt looked like it was being worn for the first time for this momentous occasion. The blue jeans also looked new, no fading, and stiff as cardboard. They needed a few good washings, intentional fading, careful tearing above the knees, exposing some pale thigh. He imagined he could smell the musty newness of her silver-grey ankle-high runners, which excited him. He gulped, his Adam's apple a laggard piston.

She pivoted to face him and he was knocked back. Her smile was lovely, if likely put-on. But the face would have been lovely even had she snarled and spat at him. Not too wedge-shaped, high forehead, large navy-blue eyes, cheekbones like inverted commas for a perfectly perky female nose. The skin was so pale it was radiant (so *not* a weather-beaten farm girl?). And again those eyes as blue as … as blue as … as blue as blue to the power of two could be. Like dark azure sea reflecting … well, an untroubled azure sky. Whatever. A breathtaking beauty that fairly took his breath away. So Dean LaRoque took an extra moment; he had to, his next move could prove determinant.

She nodded: "Thank you" (for nothing). She picked up the black backpack, slung it, then extended the handle of her suitcase like a lady popping her parasol. "I'm sorry to have startled you and taken up your valuable time."

He patted the air with both hands: "Not at all, not at all, my dear. Coincidentally—*your* luck—I am Dean Jacques LaRoque of the *Faculty* of Digital Humanities. I was just out for a pre-lunch stroll and," he winked (which made her jig her head back), "to see what the start of a new academic year is bringing by way of fresh undergraduates. I'm *professionally* curious to see how many have chosen the in-person option over our perfected distance learning. Not too many, I see—present company excepted of course!"

He held his arms up, palms-facing, like somebody challenged to put 'em up. Steepling the fingers at his chin, he again bowed slightly like some monk wannabe. "I remind you that we're still not to touch, though I'd risk shaking *your* hand in a uBytown welcome!" He gestured to shake with his right hand and had to withdraw it awkwardly. "Though I will concede that *your* presence is an argument for the old-fashioned in-person class if ever I saw one!"

She didn't respond to any of it. He really is a doofus, and a flatterer, a sad old guy. Dad: *No one flatters but he wants something. Don't deceive yourself thinking that your hidden value has finally been recognized ... by anyone but me! And, well, maybe by ... Jimmy?*

"Sir, do I need to check into the faculty office before going to my residence, Joseph Brant Residence. My father didn't know."

"No, my dear. And in my role *in locus parentis*, I will personally escort you to Brant Rez. That will give my pre-lunch constitutional an even more worthwhile purpose."

She knew some Latin, the only student in Leitrim Falls to have had *any*. Her father had begun home-schooling her not long after her mother died, and madly had added Latin to the official grade-ten curriculum. This self-important goof, more *loco* than fit to replace anybody's parent, could *never* replace her Dad, never mind Mom, not in a million billion years of evolution.

"Your father also attended uBytown then?" He swept her ahead with a stagy flourish.

She knew why: he wanted to check out her ass—*her* bony bum! Guys were so sick. He hadn't offered to carry either of her cases. She needed more muscle. Jimmy had promised some weight training. August twenty-third it had been, a crisp morning of frost-feathered dew, the first day they'd baled together. He'd felt her biceps, squeezed jokingly, just right. She wouldn't cry in front of Dean Doofus. She thought instead. Her father never abbreviated "university" to *U*.

She smiled at Dean LaRoque and saw his weak chin tremble. Then saw the reason for his refusal to help with the suitcase. Without a word, he quickly drew a phone from the side pocket of his suit coat, like some futuristic gunslinger, and settled over it like a boy tickling a toad. She'd vanished.

So she may as well vamoose. She moved off the way he'd signalled with his ushering hands, moving at a fast pace back the way she'd come, self-consciously not wiggling. Hoping she was rid of him, she called back out of politeness: "Dad had wanted to go to university—and he'd won scholarships—but his father made him stay on the farm."

He hustled after. "Mm-mmm …" in the distracted way of texting addicts. "So you *are* a farm girl then."

Oh shit, here it comes. "We farm near Leitrim Falls. All my life. All my father's too. *His* parents immigrated from Ireland, off a small farm near a place called Oughterard in County Galway."

"And a noble way of life it is. Backbone of the country, salt of the earth. And the poor Irish have long suffered a nightmarish history. *Joyce*. Do you know James Joyce?"

She badly wanted to say *Fuck you* but never would publicly (except that one time to Fred Faucher at school, which was worth it, and then some). Instead she beamed up her phony smile: "That's a mixed metaphor, isn't it, Professor? I mean, backbone and salt? A thing we farmers learn to avoid?" She laughed falsely. "Coincidentally, Dad and I read *Ulysses* together a couple of summers ago, and it took the whole summer. We needed a guide! It was incredible. But I bet you've even read *Finnegans Wake*! Dad says, no way! It'd make us as mad as Joyce himself."

Caught up, he blinked a few times like he'd been cuffed near the crown. *What was that?* "Why, uh, yes it is, a metaphor … but intentionally mixed … more, uh, *synthesizing* imagery."

"Of course, that's what I meant too."

"But if I may inquire, what made you choose uBytown and the in-person option? I mean, other than your obvious intelligence and good taste." He snickered, pleased with himself for recovering and returning compliment for criticism. Oh, he knew how to work the insecurities of these freshman bitches. Or is that another mixed-fucking-metaphor, Daisy Mae?

What on earth was he going on about now? She took a moment to comprehend his meaning, a habit. Jimmy had once said he loved that about her, the way she reflected before answering. That was at the beginning of the summer, June seventeenth.

"As I said, my father had always wanted to come here, even after Granda died and the responsibility of the whole farm was his. Or *ours*, he always insists, his and mine … after Mom died too … though the work was mostly his 'cause I was a kid and in regular school. He'd always wanted to attend university part-time through the winters, but we could never afford it, even after he got the life insurance money … for Mom. He said those funds were set aside for me, untouchable."

Why oh why was she blurting private matters? Stupid. Fool. Idiot. *Born eejit!*

"My father has a collection of uBytown program calendars going way back. Every year he wrote away for a new one to … when it was still called the Faculty of Arts, I guess. But he gave up years ago, at least for himself. He used to write directly to your English professors too, and some would send him the … the *syllabi* for their courses. Professor Flynn, I remember. Dad read them all, I mean the works on them. Dad reads everything. We

have a library in our house that fills, like, two whole bedrooms."
Like like like, you babbling jackass!

"Ah, your father's an autodidact."

"What? I mean, pardon, sir? I guess so. I don't know. He *can* fix just about anything."

Not so smarty as our pants, are we, Little Mizz Mixed Metaphor? "So, in effect *you* are fulfilling your father's lifelong dream for post-secondary education here at uBytown."

Of, not *for*. Shut up, Mary. "My own dream too. I wanted out of Leitrim Falls. I didn't want to leave the farm. Dad wouldn't let me commute. But as far as I was concerned, it came down to a toss-up between uBytown and St. Paul University. We're Catholics." *Shut up, Mary. Stop it right this very instant or I'll make you eat lamb chops three times a day!*

He groped about: "As I said, farm labour is ennobling. Did you, by any chance, see the recent PBS documentary on farming post-pandemic? It was titled, uh, something like—he cleared his throat—*Agribusiness in a Post-Covid World*. A bit dated but still well worth it."

Such townie interest in farming always irritated her, mainly because she didn't know why she was embarrassed and pissed off. *Please*, do not be the same here.

"My father would never allow a TV in the house, or hardly ever." *Shoot yourself, McGahern, right here and now! Here comes a bus—throw yourself under it!*

Her father hated that word, *agribusiness*, said it wasn't a word at all. He'd spit out his witty play on it: "Aggra*vation* would be more like it." More and more he'd become quick to anger. He'd be alone now. If he'd sold to Canopy Growth when they offered on the land, we'd have been rich and living in town long ago, like Jimmy's family. Quick to drink too, Dad was, she worried.

Dean LaRoque blinked frustration. "I expect the doc would be online for streaming, or on YouTube. Its conclusion is that in future we'd best be prepared to pay much more for our agricultural produce—"

"*Or* a computer, not for *my* dad. But good point, Professor: food is important."

She glanced to see if her shot had scored. But this *Dean* was hopeless, full of himself and bullshit clichés. (Jimmy would have twigged to her irony; they'd learned each other's styles which, extraordinarily, turned out to be pretty much the same). He was checking his phone again. She relented: "And challenging to grow cash crops on a family farm, economically speaking, without sufficient acreage. Though Dad says it's more the bigger operations that are actually going bust—"

"Here we are!"

Where was she? Here she'd missed paying attention on her first walk through the interior campus, which she'd imagined would be like something out of an old novel, Hardy, Welty, or one like that. *Lucky Jim*? No, but she'd laughed her head off at that one, a Dad fave. Lucky Jimmy, off at Western University. Unlucky Mary Contrary (as he sometimes teased her).

The building before her, which would be her home for the next three months, looked like a greenhouse stood on end, more like Canopy Growth's Leitrim Falls head office than the student housing she'd imagined. One of the residence's inside walls was covered with plant growth like some post-apocalyptic place where moss had found purchase. She forgot the word for such eco-crap architecture, but it had one … "Living Wall" or something equally stupid. She could ask Dean Doofus, who'd likely skitter his tight pants in an hour-long lecture. Or no, he now looked finished with her. … But why this anger, Mary

Contrary? *Control yourself* (Mom's constant advice when she was a kid).

"I'll leave you to our competent resident administrators, then. You tell them Dean LaRoque of *Digital Humanities* says they're to give you the very best room available! And tell them I'll personally be checking up on that! Though I expect there are lots of fine rooms to choose from these dire days of post-pandemic absence and surplus … so to speak *paradoxically!*"

She could visualize the exclamation marks at the end of everything silly he said. He turned on his considerable black heels (for a man) and walked off, with left hand supporting right arm at the elbow, with thumb and fingers pinching the tilted chin, and with right forefinger tap-tapping his lips like he was entertaining thoughts that would stump Northrop Frye. He stutter-stepped away, toes repeatedly catching on nothing. Perhaps it was the forward pitch from the heels, on shoes as shiny as a little girl's patent-leather. The awkward walking made *him* wiggle a bit. He had a fat ass for such a skinny-legged geek.

He swung back as though a great thought had indeed struck him. "*I* know: why don't you drop by my office for a brown-bag lunch one day later this frosh week? I'd very much appreciate your first-hand *reportage* on proceedings."

She smiled small to herself. She'd had to endure this sort of come-on since turning thirteen, when her breasts had grown rapidly, her hair darkened to jet, and her lips gotten all puffy. Deal with it from boys and men from twelve to seventy. And grown hairy legs and armpits too. How lovely to be a woman.

"Thank you, Dean LaRoque. May I bring my boyfr—"

"Call my Administrative Assistant, *Ms.* Martine Marois, extension one-eight-one, and we'll find a day of mutual convenience for us both. This week of course, Thursday preferably, ideally thirteen hundred hours. Martine will be present the entire time just beyond the ajar office door. But just the two of us, no boyfriend, which is the most promisingly productive arrangement, selfishly speaking. I think of it as a wormhole into knowing what our best and brightest have to give back! Till then, then!"

He spun again and was off, sashaying a touch and gawking about like *he* was the rubbernecking hick from Leitrim Falls. Everything about the man was an act. Then he was bowed over and tickling his phone again. She'd known the moment he spoke that he hadn't a true thought in his head. Not what her dad considered real thought: a received idea that had been tested, owned or discarded. Comforting to recall Dad's thinking here and now: true literature, literary art, challenges what you think you know, most often makes you feel uncomfortable at first, makes you work hard thinking. Literary crap, popular shit, confirms your prejudices, whatever their stripe, makes you feel good about yourself. This Dean LaRoque, this academic leader, saw only what he wanted to see. He would be blind and deaf to anything that threatened his complacency. He heard only what confirmed what he already believed, what was needed to maintain his comfort.

Yes, Mary McGahern said angrily to herself, *I know all that already, after all of twenty minutes, I'm such a fucking genius! ...* But seriously, Mary, if you are *so* smart, why are you standing here like this, feeling more lost than a spindly newborn calf? (She flashed on Aoife; she and the cow had matured together; the reflection sank her; Aoife, pregnant at long last, now had no one to look after her either.) Yes, why are you here alone and Jimmy elsewhere, *if* you're such a big fucking genius!

She followed Dean LaRoque with her eyes as he grinned and nodded his way past the sparse number of students who were out and about. He kept gesturing with his arms like the

Pope or something. His odd-coloured blue suit shone in the late-summer sun. It was neither the deep blue of a late-afternoon sky nor the changeable blue of Big Pond, nor the colour of anything natural in between, though she *had* seen metal ashtrays something like. The pants were far too tight—a couple of times she'd had to look away—the jacket as tight and too short, its tail riding up like a duck's ass. Or maybe undersize for men was still the style? Her father sometimes used a word ... *infantilizing*, yes, something about sexism in the way women were dictating men's style. Nonsense, of course, a drinker's conspiracy theory, that downside of Dad. But this self-important Dean *was* like a gawky boy decked out for his first day of school. To think, she thought, some poor woman has to kiss that prissy mouth daily. *Maybe* some woman—don't be like that, Mary.

Yes, look at you! Here less than half an hour and already criticizing the Dean of ... the Dean of digital arses!

She'd been standing for five minutes outside the residence entrance, had rung the buzzer twice and waved dramatically. She was being pointedly ignored. So she rapped on the glass and waved like wonky windshield wipers, all the while grinning like an eejit (that all-purpose Granny McGahern word). Then waited another three minutes till noticed. The door buzzed and clacked open—she flexed backwards and had to get out of the way of the glass-and-metal monstrosity. It stalled at its limit. Began returning glacially—accelerated suddenly so that she had to lunge with her baggage and nearly fell over when the case wheeled up quickly and the door whooshed shut behind her. Advancing gingerly, already she was feeling even greater disappointment descend, like a lowering sky on hay day.

Her mother had taught her to get out front of depression. So Mary self-examined as she stood waiting forever for her welcoming package—the rules—and key card. Because getting out front meant confronting the cause. Certainly she had reason for anxiety and the sinking sensation. She was still missing her father something fierce. And pregnant Aoife with the infected udder, her teats fairly untouchable. Yet she *had* to be milked, and spared the machine, and Dad was just no good with her. She will call him right away and insist that Dr. North be brought in. Who would cook Dad's supper today? Who knew that he needed protein and had to be forced to eat more than just eggs and toast and raw vegetables? Who else but *she* knew how he loathed himself working at Canopy Growth when there was always farm work to do? Who would keep him from turning to drink?

And Jimmy. Of course. *Jimmy.*

He was probably already popular as all hell at Western University, where he'd gone the week before (eight days ago). Where he would meet someone else. Jimmy could mix; Jimmy would have conquered his frosh week. She sincerely hoped for his sake that he'd found more live bodies at Western than she had here (but *male* bodies). Why he had paid such surprising attention to her over their final year in high school she would never know. Well, she did actually: he'd told her that last evening. She looked okay now, she guessed. But *she* was no mixer, always only awkward, gawky. Didn't drink, didn't smoke weed, didn't … Well, they might have, the way they'd been going. And maybe even in as little as another week or so. Then she'd be rid of that burden, and in as romantic a way as any girl could dream. Not like Naomi and Rick Maclean—in the abandoned residential school of all fucking places! So to speak. Naomi had testified that it was great, that once you'd done it, it was all you could think about all day. Jimmy'd promised to visit her in Ottawa. She knew he was still a virgin too. The two of them freaks (now that the last known holdout, Naomi, had gone over to the fun side). She just knew it, from the way he kissed at first (banging teeth), from the clumsy way he touched her, at first (at the beginning of the summer).

She should have fought harder to go to Western. Her father's obsession with uBytown was *his* obsession not hers. In just about everything else he let her follow her inclinations. Jimmy couldn't hack the idea of his going away only as far as Ottawa (his alcoholic old man, his hopeless mother). For her he'd considered uBytown still, until she'd insisted he follow *his* best inclination. "Not my heart?" he'd joked, though by that late point it was a joke that choked them both for an awkward minute. They promised that they would visit each other every other weekend. But she'd known even as they were lying together on late-August's cooling earth out by Big Rock that she would need to go home to her dad whenever she could. Maybe she could convince Jimmy to go home those times too? Though London was a lot farther away. And Jimmy hated home.

Who wouldn't be depressed?

In the small stuffy residence room, she again felt like she couldn't breathe normally, as she'd been feeling since boarding the smelly train at Leitrim Falls. The first thing she'd noticed was the computer, big like the kind they'd used in art class, a Mac. She would set up her university email and write to Jimmy (she had the idiot-proof instructions, a good thing). First though she slid open the narrow slot at the bottom of the window and breathed deeply. She unpacked. With no good reason to be tired that early in the day, she lay on the soft narrow bed. She crossed her forearms on her chest and disciplined her breathing as Mom had taught her, belly breathing.

The room itself was so narrow she could reach to the desk chair and retrieve from the backpack the dated catalogue of English literature course offerings in the *Faculty of Arts*. Flat on her back she held it open above, but before she could read, her mind drifted to the day before. She'd been lying all by herself beside Big Rock and looking up at a mackerel sky whose scaly clouds were moving fast. She remembered telling herself to remember this: *This is heaven. And the heavens change too. We will always be here for you.* That was Mom.

Big Pond would always be hers. And the rock against which she and Jimmy had sat all summer, Big Rock, was her beach. "Ponder's Beach," she'd smirked that last day of summer holidays, for the first time sharing the name with anyone, not even Dad. "Singular possessive," she'd laughed poorly. Jimmy immediately had another name for it: "Lovers' Lane." That made no sense—there was no lane—and it was unoriginal, a cliché. They were death on clichés, the two of them. But she'd held her tongue for once.

Until she couldn't and did her ironic damsel-in-distress voice, batting lashes and touching her chest with fingertips: "More like *Lois* Lane, *my* Superman!" Which failed so miserably she dropped her face in a scowl.

Jimmy had watched her in profile, until at last she'd faced him with those eyes like blue pools. The rock seemed to soften behind them and in no time they'd slid to the ground and were making out like mad. It was all they *could* do. By that time, they were getting too soon to the point where they had to stop. Had to or not, they'd cease the rubbing and dry-humping mutually. Control their breathing. Then have to deal perilously with shared frustration. Early on she had startled herself by climaxing, first time with another. She'd known what it was of course, but was surprised when it happened making out. She'd not liked it happening out of her control like that. After that it felt unfair to Jimmy to carry on as they were. She knew he'd once come in his shorts, from the way he suddenly froze wide-eyed, with a bewildered look on his big handsome face. He'd continued looking away, gone home right away. In her room later she'd frowned for a long time. Then giggled. Then laughed and laughed so that she had to smother her face in the pillow lest her dad come wondering. She settled in some forced shame. *Poor Jimmy, guys were such runaway machines, I guess.* She'd felt so bad about her laughing at him that next time they hooked up she had to keep herself from apologizing.

In her residence room she wished again they'd done it that last evening, gone all the way, on the far side of Big Rock where the sun had warmed all day. All the kissing and rubbing and starting and stopping was maddening and exhausting. And afterwards it really hurt, being rubbed raw like that, and they could snap at each other. What was *wrong* with them? It was unnatural. They'd do it next time, for sure.

It seemed that already everything in her life was like that, remembered regretfully. Same as the way her father, when drinking after her mother had died, would begin talking . Wishing that things had been different, almost everything done differently, that *he* had been different. Do we really get only one shot at the most important things in life? Dad said so. She sighed, "It isn't fair." He saw where they'd steered themselves, poor Dad, and laughed falsely: "Fairs are for pigs!"

On her back she focused the English course catalogue held above. Dad and she had never thought other than that she would major in English, with a minor in Music, and maybe another minor in History. She'd have no piano, and neither of them believed she could live contentedly without one. As a registered student she'd have access to one in the Music Department. And English without History, he insisted, is like a pig without a pen. "Is that a pun?" she'd showed off. He'd slapped the kitchen table—"James Joyce was quite the pig!" She'd said, "With quite the pen!"

With two intersecting triangles like some satanic symbol her father had starred the English course offerings with such titles as "Literature and the Bible," whose required texts were a King James Bible and a book by Northrop Frye (Dad had said he was the best). She had a bible in her suitcase, which would soon be hidden in the desk's middle drawer, not that she was expecting company. Another starred course was titled "Great Books of the Great Tradition I," followed by "Beyond the Great Tradition II" (which made no sense). Starred also were a fall term's "Canadian Literature of the Colonial Period" and winter's "Canadian Literature of the Confederation Period." There were other courses titled Shakespeare, Milton, The Neo-Classical Period, The Romantics, The Victorians, The Modern Period. That's where dad's starring stopped. After that, the contemporary courses had such titles as "The Woman's Page" (he had written one word in the margin: "possible"), "Post-Postmodern Postcolonial Possibilities" ("here we go!"), and a raft of offerings prefixed with "digi," so that there was "DigiPastoralisms" ("Hot-diggedy, this could mean us!"), "DigiEcoFems" ("yuck"), "DigiAlterities in a Post-Human World" ("what the …?"), and "Systemic *Cyber-Racism* in a Post-Human Post-National Digitized World" ("Duh, gee, I dunno … a video game from NASCAR International?").

At the end of the calendar, his most recent, he'd carefully written up his own course on the blank inside cover.

ENG XXXX: Didger-Redoos

Course Description: In this course we will study, and so be privileged to associate with, three thousand years of the orature of the Aboriginal Peoples of Australia (unceded territory of Oceania) in an attempt to undo some minuscule portion of the colonial and techno violence of at least the past three hundred years.

Grading: To be determined
Attendance: Voluntary Online Distance-Learning
Required texts: None. Familiarity with the didgeridoo is assumed (available YouTube video)
Learning Outcomes: Dealing productively with postcolonial guilt. Restitution, not materially but of cultural value and pride (theirs).

She didn't understand all that he was getting at or where he, who'd still seemed to think that there was a Faculty of Arts, had learned such lingo. But then he read and talked and complained of much she had no interest in. On most such matters he could be as stubbornly *in*correct as a goat lining up a goat-whisperer's bum. She'd occasionally worried that he really might be racist and not just pretending for a joke. (Or is that racism too?)

She'd once broached the accusation, after her grade-twelve high school English teacher, Ms. Stottlemeyer, had replaced Mordecai Richler's *The Apprenticeship of Duddy Kravitz* with Richard Wright's *Black Boy*. Mary and Jimmy were the only students to have read both. She'd said that *Duddy Kravitz* was a better novel, and it was Canadian. Ms. Stottlemeyer had advised Mary to think about her expression of "systemic racism." On hearing this, her father had cursed. Mary had said that maybe all unaware *he* was expressing systemic racism too.

"Racist? Me?" He was trying to joke if off, but her face said *No*. "... Okay, serious time. But first things first: Honey, don't ever let anyone scare you from thinking honestly about anything. *Anything*. Or of speaking your mind by your best lights, *respectfully*. Either free speech means that or it means nothing.

"But okay, racism. *Systemic* racism. I like that. As I understand it, I'm racist without knowing I'm racist. I may think I love everybody but—surprise—I actually hate them. It's a perverse version of the old Calvinist *Elect*, where you're already going to hell or heaven whatever you do, whether you know it or not, and you don't know it. But, okay.

"Slavery has been a blight on humankind since forever, and it's not going anywhere any time soon. Just look at China, India, the Arab countries. Same for sexism—for all forms of bigotry, prejudice, and hatred. We should call them out whenever we smell them, as you're doing here with me, admirable girl. Apart from its stink and butt-ugliness, racism is an affront to human reason: faulty generalization for self-serving ends. *Duh*, I knew a Jew once and he cheated me. *Two* Jews in fact. Ergo, all Jews are money-grubbing shysters, so we have the right to confiscate their property and drive them out of the village. That's the *logic* of racism. Or I once saw some drunken Irishmen fighting ... well, maybe my sweet reasoning doesn't work for all stereotyping prejudices."

"*That's* what I should say to Stottlemeyer? That racism is illogical?"

"Good point. But you probably shouldn't say any of this to anyone. There's lots of *great* fiction dealing with racism, *Huck Finn*, *Black Boy* too, yes, lots. If racism is the subject of the book, or even just a part of the story—fine, then that's what should be studied. If doing so lessens racism and prejudice by as much as one hurt boy or girl—great."

"Then what's your problem?"

"*My* problem? It's not my problem, it's yours, and will be more and more. Reading and studying can and should change the ways we think and act … which sounds stupid to have to say. But here's my point, *my* problem: righting the wrongs of the world should not be the main purpose of reading literature or of choosing the literature we study. There's more and more machinery for trying to right the wrongs of the world, thank you Jesus and Marx, and good luck with that campaign, Mr. Inquisitor, Mr. Stalin. There is only *one* discipline that studies great literature in its own right: in high school English courses and university English Departments. Or there *was* one. From reading English Department course calendars over the years, I despair. *And* that makes me make fun for the sake of my sanity. And if it's a better world you want, and who doesn't, studies have shown that reading and studying great literature—not sociological-political hobbyhorse crap—makes readers more empathetic. *Of course.* Reading the best that has been thought and written would exercise even a lab rat's imaginative sympathies. And doing so could well be the only true hope for making the world better."

"I think I get it."

"And by the way, I agree with you and Jim: *Duddy Kravitz*, which also deals with anti-Semitism and class prejudice and English-French tensions in *our* country, is a better novel than *Black Boy*. As an English teacher, your Stottlemeyer has gone over to the dark side, so to speak."

"Glad I asked."

"Ah, irony, *there* is thy sting. Class dismissed."

She lowered the catalogue to her chest, still open like a fallen bird ... and fell asleep. Her fading waking thoughts were that she'd wasted an hour that morning giving her hair the dishevelled look, when she could have been comforting Aoife and trying again painstakingly, patiently, to milk her. The lowing—bellowing—was unbearable the whole night before the morning's departure, like Aoife had known she was leaving. It had continued even as they drove off to the train. She *had* to be milked, and by hand only, yet wouldn't let herself be touched for the infection ... she must be pregnant ... she saw her father carrying Aoife as a newborn calf to her, telling her the name was pronounced *Ee-fa*, making her learn to spell it correctly, what it meant, *Beauty*, and that Aoife was hers specially ... Dad couldn't do it ... the way she moaned even when so favoured to be hand-milked, still always kicking ... spoiled ... he'd turned old after Mom ... mad at the world ... never mean ... not Jimmy ...

She snorted like a throttling horse and bolted herself awake.

She's going home.

Dad should have let her continue home-schooling right through grade twelve. But no, nothing easy for Mary McGahern where poor widower Dad was concerned! ... Though without the final year done formally in the official school system, her application to uBytown would have been difficult, if not impossible, as Dad had known.

She couldn't go home. What was she thinking? And if she had continued being home-schooled through twelve, she'd never have met Jimmy.

Where is she? ... Oh yeah.

She rolled onto her left side and the catalogue fell to the floor, where it tried to close, but failed to, and sat like a tent over a germinating seedling. She draped her eyes with her right forearm and cried.

What was Jimmy doing? And with who? With *whom*?
Knock-knock, Jimmy.
Who's there?
To.
To who?
To *whom*...

TWO

PLAGUING JAKE 1:
A BIT ABOUT ME

My academic fields are early Canadian literature and Modern Irish. That makes me the only remaining Film&WordsWork professor to have traditional areas of expertise, whether national or historical. In thirty-five years I've published nothing on Irish literature and only a few short articles on Canadian. My last piece attempted to trace one of character Sam Slick's homey sayings to its original source: "A wink's as good as a nod to a blind horse." I found nothing, so was able to add it to the hundreds of original expressions of Slick's author, Thomas Chandler Haliburton (who was a formative influence on Mark Twain). On the potholed academic road to that scholarly sinkhole, I uncovered some interesting tidbits about the socio-cultural-gendered significance of winking. That was actually what made my squib publishable: it revealed early nineteenth-century instances of sexual harassment and prejudicial attitudes toward the visually impaired.

My passé fields of specialization and my perishable publishing record help explain why I assumed the Chair (as it was called back then) of the Department of English (ditto). Now, I'm officially *Leader* Jake Flynn, and my seventeen colleagues and I comprise the Film&WordsWork *Pod* at the University of Bytown. We're the world's largest English-French university, so we go by uBytown.

Here's how old I am: I was born the year the Beatles first appeared on Ed Sullivan,1964, which was a year after the release of their initial LP and the beginning of sex (as Philip Larkin joked in a poem). For a long spell after that, the Fabs owned the world's ears and collective cultural consciousness. Nothing was ever the same: boys' hair, decorative school lunch pails (not for me, I'm afraid, as such a possession would have required my mother to sober up); girls' hearts and skirts and pencil cases; from the way my father looked *to* me (my greatest misfortune) to the way he looked at me (a mistake). Also changed were the things buzz-cut politicians began saying to look like hep cats: "We must lower the legal voting age and decriminalize marijuana, yeah, yeah, yeah!" Everything changed. That's what the Beatles did, in every sphere of popular culture. Disbelieve as you will, but Leader Jake Flynn prophesizes: in a thousand years our bulbous-headed descendants will be looking back on the Beatles and their legends as we do on the pantheon of Norse gods. I exaggerate? Consider: how long has it been since "Love Me Do"? Yes, it won't be long till a hundred years have passed—and what's diminished? Exactly: they've grown. (Because I am yet a scholar, I must in good conscience attribute this theory/speculation to my local

Beatlemaniac, Crazy Ray; and by the way, "It Won't Be Long" is another Beatles song).

Jieun (pronounced _June_) says I scare our grandchildren when I raise my voice calling for a snack in my study. I hole up there even on Sundays to avoid, on the pretext of work, too much family socializing. I'm usually watching golf, that most perfect napping TV ever invented. No open-plan living for Granda Jake! As with fences and good neighbours, discrete rooms and solid doors make for a happy Flynn family. Consequently I am a good neighbour and happy family man, which are all I've ever aspired to be.

Jieun still has faith in academic me. She believes that my work-in-progress, the long-awaited, definitive critical biography of Thomas Chandler Haliburton, absorbs every hour in my study, and that the whispering TV helps me focus. Jieun will load my snack bowl with a mixture of the crunchy junk we call Kibble-n-Bits after some ancient dog food. She's given up remarking my spare tire, which is one of the few benefits of growing old together: mutually throwing in the towel on physical attractiveness. Knowing how socializing stresses me, Jieun leaves me alone after the rush of welcoming our three children and half-dozen grandkids. During the first pandemic, Jieun would joke to visitors: "Jake has finally come into his own—his whole life has been a prep for social distancing." Lingering traces of her Korean accent added to the joke's effectiveness; she was cuting-up the China doll bit.

Maybe she was faking everything all the time, my Jieun. … No, impossible. But she _was_ joking about my scaring the grandkids. They love me. Which is a very good thing, because Jieun and our family are my one true area of expertise, my real work-in-progress, the only field in which I excel all other scholars, my life.

With that bit of necessary bio context out of the way, I want to assure you that my story is not so much about me as it is a narrative record of what's happened to our Department of English in transitioning to the Film&WordsWork Pod. That's more important because the same has happened to every Department of English in the Western world (I know no others). They've all transmogrified from reading and studying the best that has been thought and written (Matthew Arnold) to appreciating movies and TV and various YouTube 'texts'.

A new literary genre has emerged over the past couple of decades, and my account here contributes to it. I call it "The Academic Lament." I concede up front that this may just be academia's version of any old man's insistence as he prepares for retirement that his profession has gone to hell in a handbasket. That the whole show will be closing with his departure for arid pastures.

Or think of it this way: picture my cantankerous former colleague, old Professor Oberon Stangle, out on Coriveau Hall's concrete porch shaking his fist at the Communications Pod's whippersnappers and yelling at them to get the hell off the great tradition's manicured lawn!

How have I managed to remain Leader of our Pod for fifteen years? I'm an agreeable, avuncular, non-threatening nonentity. It certainly wasn't for competency. Many are the times I've screwed up colleagues' applications in important career moves (tenure, promotion, sabbatical). It could even be because people have always thought me smarter than I am: intimidating height will do that for a mediocrity. But there's been more than enough time for all to know me for what I truly am. Yet I remain Leader.

My long tenure is likely attributable also to my avoiding confrontation like the Plague (if not clichés), my "leadership style." In private meetings with colleagues, I kid a lot. Then suss out the real reason for the meeting. Then affirm for my visitor my warmest support for whatever she or he wants. "Yes, John, Professor Turnbull, that *is* far too large a class—thirty-five you say?—though *you* would never complain, I know. We'll see if we can't have a second TA assigned. Dean LaRoque is a great admirer of your work, and of you personally."

"Oh, I'd ask the same for myself, Professor Abara, *if* I'd been only *half* as disadvantaged by systemic prejudice as you have. Half? One-quarter!"

"As much as I sympathize, Dr. Professor von Blüger, I'm afraid you cannot insist that students leave their laptops and phones in the hallway—our insurer would have conniptions! Now, why don't we try this: permit me to visit your class and have a little talk with the students. No? As you please, of course, the classroom is the professor's sacrosanct kingdom. One little thing before you leave, Bartholomew: *do* please try to employ *some* video, if not as part of your actual syllabus, at least as an item in your Suggested Further Readings. It couldn't matter less to me, but the Dean …"

"I do understand, I really do, Professor Kelly. Though we *have* made significant advances in our sensitivity training respecting the special needs of female faculty and students. I would be remiss, though, not to caution you that sleep apnea, and self-diagnosed at that, is not yet on the Student Services list of acceptable reasons for deferring the entire term's presenta-tions. It *is* a seminar course after all. Anxiety yes, sleep apnea nnn … Oh, it *is* on the list now, is it? And without medical documen-tation, you say? Fancy that! Dumb old Jake Flynn. Then off you go, Pat, and Bob's your uncle—or Roberta your aunt!"

Mine is a baritone voice, über-masculine but non-authori-tarian, non-threatening, softly rumbling like the distant thunder of a passed storm. Smoothly thumping when need be, this Leader's voice of mine, but mostly intoning wisdom (I trust). I like to think it suggestive of some reformed fallen angel whispering comforting advice from his experience of human suffering. Kind of like a golf commentator forever promising the end of a teeming rain delay at Augusta.

Jieun *cannot* be right about my scaring the grandkids! … Yet she's said so a few times, usually when groaning down to pick up the empty bottle of Bushmills from my study's oriental carpet. So who can blame her? Not I.

Nor, by the way, do I much mind if you don't give a red rat's arsehole about Canadian literature, or have never heard of Thomas Chandler Haliburton and his Sam Slick. You *should* know though: Sam, the original ugly American and its first deadly salesman, was likely the model for none other than Uncle Sam. And (as remarked parenthetically above) no Sam Slick would have meant no Huck Finn, at least not as we know him.

Everybody loves the Irish, thank God. Or everybody but the British. Just as everybody condescends to, when they're not laughing at, the sneakily ironic Canadian. But a wink really is as good as a nod to a blind horse.

Also as suggested, I'm tall, if again as non-threatening as a big old teddy bear. I stand to my full height, six-foot-six, only at formal university functions (to impress the public). Otherwise, I shorten, I slouch. When I hunch over colleagues who are sharing their troubles and gently cup a shoulder, they should feel like they're rolling in their sweet daddy's arms. (Whatever that feels like.) For example, I'm sensitive to that metaphor's (daddy's arms) having at least confusing reference respecting the father-son dynamic of the Professor formerly known as

Maksim Pavlov (now Professor Amari Abara; more to follow). With female colleagues my hand hovers as close as I dare without actual touchdown on the shoulder. Once I did hug one of our pod's four Jennifers, because one of her three cats had fallen from her condo's balcony. And I've often risked risqué humour with Pat Kelly (before our breakup; more etc.). I'm enough a man of my time to worry that such instances of systemic sexism could yet come back to emasculate me.

Another thing about me: it's come to the point where I scarcely believe half the things I hear myself thinking or saying. And this, I guess:

At sixty-five I'm already impotent as a football kicker amputated at the knee. Jieun swore it was a relief. I suspect a loving liar. I don't really know what to think about Jieun's performance or my own absence of performance anxiety. If I think anything, it's sadly also to recognize relief. When he got old, Robertson Davies claimed he was happy to be finished with sex. He said the male orgasm was no more important than a sneeze. I wish *I* could say witty things like that. Or something *about* Davies' saying. Perhaps the expression "blowing his nose" could prove useful? If it weren't so offensive.

My greatest weakness? My interpersonal style makes me a sucker for salespeople, and especially for young and pretty females (the true redundancy that). I'm a sucker for sales*men* too, and likely would be for anyone transitioning between. For example (of the young and pretty female), this morning at my bank, I agreed to purchase overdraught insurance. I've never in my life been in overdraught. But the teller, a recent graduate of uBytown, had recognized me. She had majored in Film&WordsWork, *mirrored* (as we now call *minored*) in Communications (perhaps with optional credits in bank-telling?), and had just started her job. She addressed me with a big smile and a "Good morning, Professor Flynn!" Right off I was rattled. I walked out of there with overdraught insurance that I'd not had the courage to cancel immediately following purchase. I am littler even than Stephen Leacock's "little man."

And that's enough about me.

In our pod of seventeen professors, I have, as remarked, four colleagues named Jennifer, two named Stephanie, and three named David. Of the three Davids, my favourite is Davey Swift, because, the most like me, he is the colleague who would be improved by a spine transplant from a jellyfish. Davey's female colleagues adore him, the males are bemused, and he has perfect student ratings for all his courses. More so even than Professor Pat Kelly, "Prof Davey" will accept any student excuse for a missed assignment. In a pinch he'll provide the excuse. The result is that only half his students show up for tests and only a few more than that for final exams. All are given automatic deferrals till whenever (I expect Davey says "whenevs," as does our Dean LaRoque).

Since Prof Davey instituted his policy of excuse-acceptance some five years ago, we have all followed suit. Many did so simply for the improved student ratings, which in these days of the student-as-client have come to play a larger role in tenure and promotion than the CV's publications section. Most did so because accepting any excuse without medical documentation was already the university's unofficial default policy. We can't be humiliating the little paying pipers! Consequently, in only a few years we went from accepting the excuse of "anxiety," to various permutations of "stress," to all manner of increasingly subjective (that is, unprovable) disturbances of the psyche. For example, the aforementioned sleep apnea has obviously moved up the excuse list with a bullet (Professor Kelly was well ahead of that curve, to the extent that envious Davey Swift counselled a few students to use the excuse of "dream-disturbed napping").

Not long after he'd arrived from the University of Waterloo, I took up this worrisome trend with Dean Jacques LaRoque. After outlining the problem, I blurted, "I mean, if this keeps up we may as well just sell our degrees!" Chin in hand the Dean appeared to ponder, then frowned worriedly at me and said, "Jake—may I call you Jake?—Jake? Professor Jake? Doctor Jake? ... Would it make sense, Jake, for a bank manager to turn away a mortgage applicant simply for being a financial risk? And please consider that I'm speaking here as a businessman, not as a scholar, academic, *Dean*, what-have-you. Would you care for an espresso, Jake? I'm dying to try out my new Vertu-Caff, a parting gift from Waterloo U!"

Our four Jennifers are all young (and not only as compared to me), so of course pretty by my lights, and all tall. In my thirty-five years here, females have grown taller and larger, with more and more of them reaching my chin (I could be shrinking, I'll concede). Jennifer Windsor never appears other than immaculately attired. She often remarks on my appearance with that passive-aggressive rhetoric of approve-and-disapprove: "That's a lovely shirt, Jake, the dun colour suits your complexion, if only ..."

Of the other three Jennifers, Jenny Orillia suffers from an eating disorder, though I've never determined whether it's eating too little or too much. Over the decade since her hiring, she looks neither to have gained nor lost an ounce: athletic, firm, intimidating in that irradiating way of exercise fanatics.

Jenn Sainte-Urbain, mousy if with a mind like a paper shredder, seems only ever concerned with telling me her one joke, that she's the real Jennifer. Jen number four, Professor

Sainte-Justine, is all scholar, which may explain why she laid claim to the most minimal version of the name, as a sort of Latinate abbreviation: *cf. viz. ibid.* etc. *Jen.* Or perhaps it was to soften her image, which is cutting edge in both her razor-seamed pant suits and academic field (French Feminist theory). Her most recent graduate seminar: "Transitioning Ecologies in the Vid-Age of Contingent Gendered Contextualities." I have no idea. I do recall that the course made much use of grainy YouTube videos (three students were excused from presenting on grounds that the videos triggered migraine, epileptic seizure and, yes, sleep apnea).

The videos were mostly of old travelling freak shows, as they were once called, if never in Professor Sainte-Justine's class, where they were "the exceptionally challenged on hegemonic patriarchal display." Regardless, the whole of that particular class petitioned an agreeable Dean LaRoque never to let that seminar be offered again. The grounds for proscription? 1) The videos disempowered and disenfranchised the differently challenged of their already marginalized socio-cultural status. 2) The videos made everyone uncomfortable (a student whom Jen and I shared told me in private that the operative word at after-class stonings was the highly uncritical "icky"). And 3) The whole seminar made mockery of the promise of campus safe spaces (though the same student informed me that after a few beers and joints the seminar group had concurred that caravan life actually looked "cool"). Otherwise, this student said, and I quote, No one really gives a shit about any of that shit, unquote. Dean LaRoque complied, as he would have been triggered to compliance on the "campus safe spaces" business alone.

For weeks after the unfavourable decanal decision, every time I talked with Professor Sainte-Justine her hands were trembling. It took a month to convince her that the whole matter had been forgotten and would never in a million years impact her contract renewal/tenure/promotion. Regardless, her most recent graduate-seminar offering was the more conventional "Zombies: Not that there's anything wrong with them!"

The three pods of our Faculty of Digital Humanities are housed in a five-storey building, the Digital Humanities Complex, which at twelve years old is now the third-most ancient building on the uBytown campus. Our edifice was stunted at five floors because it was prohibited from towering over the oldest building, the venerable Coriveau Hall at six. Coriveau is contiguous with us across a busy street by a glassed-in bridge like something an unpromising child might build during time-out on a rainy day.

The Communications Pod occupies our building's entire ground floor (and then some). It is booming through this long post-pandemic period of fiscal austerity. No one still seems to know just what Communications actually does, other than attract all the Faculty of Digital Humanities students and new professorial appointments. Philosophy and History, now one Pod, share the second floor like two old widower brothers crossing the threshold to the free fields of Parkinson's (Philosophy) and Alzheimer's (History). Our building has a retrofitted elevator to answer the accessibility "issue," thanks to the wheelchair-bound Amari Abara's campaigning—the professor formerly ambulatory and known as Maksim Kovalchuk. I've heard rumours that Amari finagled the Saudis into paying for it. The one-person elevator hardly ever stops at the second floor, not because philosophers and historians and their few students take the healthier stairs, but because no one goes there anymore.

I expect we're on-deck for that fate too, we of the Film&WordsWork Pod. We occupy the third floor, or three-quarters of it. The remaining quarter is being used for storage since the pandemics halved the number of faculty, and Digital Humanities' remaindered computers overflowed the fourth floor, which is all storage. We occupy our constricted premises like a venerable Japanese soldier on some south-east-sea atoll, the devoted soul who never got the news that the war ended long, long ago and the bad guys won.

It's intermittently rumoured that Communications will soon be given the entire building, and that we, Film&WordsWork, will be moved to the abandoned Athletics Facility. AthFac never transitioned to "Pod" status and has been virtually unused since the sex scandal. Some year-and-a-half ago, two members of the men's water polo team enjoyed a Bacchanalia lite with a prosti—a sex worker—over an entire Labour Day weekend. More likely Film&WordsWork will first be folded into the History and Philosophy Pod, and the three of us together will eventually be moved to the Athletics Facility. Or perhaps we'll all just disappear as distinct pods and be folded into Communications ... leaving not a rack behind. We are doubtlessly destined to become a shelved memory, fast fading, of what the study of literature once was, of what it used to do for one's soul and humanity itself.

Or perhaps we'll just be left where we are and the entire third floor designated storage. Setting is key in the study of literature, and that has been especially true of Canadian literature. We are where we were (just ask Alice Munro): a thinly civilized wilderness (just ask Margaret Atwood). We are what we came from, home place and nuclear or exploded family (and we don't get to choose). Not exclusively so limited, mind—we *can* change ... some anyway—but inclusively so forever. We are such stuff as the space-time stuff we were made from. We repress that ontological truth at our spiritual peril. Lose who you are, where you were, and you may as well end your life, because it's over anyway. May God guide, guard, and protect us (as my Irish Mammy used to say).

To wrap up this tour of my workplace. The fifth floor is yet for more storage, believe it or not, except for the glassed-in meeting room where we assemble for our monthly Pod Consult. I really have no idea why we require so much space for storage—some two-and-a-half floors!—why we're hoarding, for whom and when? What need will the post- post-pandemic denizens of the future have for our antique junk? There is of course an obvious irony in this, uBytown's neurosis for storing remaindered material: the chipped study carrels that signalled now-unfashionable privacy, the wobbly chairs for dangerously backward-tilting reflections, the Mac computers that now look like Sputnik, etc. And the irony? As we clear our institutions of so-called higher learning of cultural memory, as we deny the tradition of making meanings, as we sneer at the mission to pursue truth—as we do all that, we concomitantly hoard piles of broken old things … like some Kafkaesque dung beetle easing his ball of shit backwards down the slick hills of hell. No one but no one will ever want our old stuff again.

End of Academic Lament.

THREE

DOWN ON THE FARM

I made it to the end of September on my return to formal high school education before making a humongous blunder: I let Fred Faucher visit our farm. In my defence, he'd acted interested, and so I'd invited him. Faucher was very popular, quarterbacking and captaining the football team, cocky and good-looking, if also arrogant and with a kind of pimply facial puffiness, even a swollenness, and kinky fair hair on a high forehead that forecast a fat bullying adulthood.

Faucher had his posse with him always, a sycophantic mob: boys like himself, athletes, if not as shiny as Fred, and lesser hangers-on, and girls of course, cheerleaders both literal and Faucher's personal, and assorted sluts. The girls supplied the guys' merry-go-round girlfriends, the musical-chairs couples who were anchored by the enduring 'love' of boy-slut Dave Brun and loose

Lucy Legault, who was always hanging off Dave's shoulders. Faucher may have been handsome in a lesser male model sort of way, but in another way looked like a fattening Justin Bieber. So I don't know if "handsome" was ever the right word for Fred Faucher; maybe better is "temporarily passing pretty-boy." But those qualifications are vengeful hindsight speaking. At the time I thought Fred Faucher handsome indeed, quite attractive overall. When he broke from the posse that hung permanently at his locker and strutted the short distance to mine (thumbs tucked into belt, a bit bowlegged, like he was always about to thrust his crotch), all of a sudden I'm, like, all stupid girly-girl.

"Hi, you're Mary McGahern, eh? The new girl?"

I don't remember what I said, though I wouldn't have denied it. Probably something like "Not new, just returned after, well, my mother …" I kept my hot cheeks bowed and locked my burning eyes on Faucher's brightly coloured socks, one of his eejit 'signature styles' (garish: yellow with green egg yolks, or baby-blue with red stars, or purple with varicoloured crayons, he had different ones every day).

"Naomi says you were, like, home-schooled for part of grade ten and all of grade eleven, eh?"

I dithered mentally, then expressed this brilliance: "Naomi?" Even I knew that Faucher and cheerleader Adèle Pélletier were broken up again in the latest episode of the school's numero-uno soap opera. In the washroom I'd over-heard that Adèle had confronted Naomi in a cubicle and held her there till reassured that she and Faucher, far from serious, weren't even "only friends." Sweet Jesus, what was I getting myself into?

"And you, like, live on a farm, right? What's that like?"

His questioning wasn't so much like an overture to friend-ship or even—be still, oh stupidly tripping girly heart—romance as like establishing ground rules for a contest. I may well have been flustered and fluttering, but my "Carrie" antenna was rising and quivering. (I'd watched that old horror movie—true horror, not just the *boo* sort—one Halloween with Mom and Dad; this was long before Dad banned TV, obviously; after Mom died he started going into all sorts of rages against TV; of course the real reason wasn't the TV lying he suddenly couldn't tolerate, it was that Mom had watched TV all day when she was sickest, towards the end, another measure of *her* impending end; afterwards Dad just couldn't stand a TV's light and noise in the living room anymore, which was so unfair to me.)

"Okay, Fred, I guess. Did you mean the home-schooling or the farm, Fred?"

"I bet it's, uh, like great living that close to nature and all that, eh?"

The guy listened with all the sympathetic attention of a cop busting a bush party. He'd moved to scratch himself but checked the reflex. I'd often seen him scratching his crotch. Some of the other boys were always doing likewise but not with Faucher's apparent intense enjoyment. The girls pretended not to notice or, like Adèle, made crinkle-nose stinky faces, not for-real disgusting faces, because they might have thought Faucher was just doing a rapper's crotch-grab move. Fred wasn't. I'd actually once seen him bring a clawed hand like an oxygen mask to his face and smile self-satisfied. But he *was* a boy, a handsome popular boy, and I'd been thinking lately that, going on eighteen, it was high time I'd tried one of those. I'd been back at school only a week when I realized that the talk I'd been overhearing in the girls' room proved that everybody but me was now having sex. *Enjoying* sex. In couples, I mean. As in, two people, girl-boy, fucking. (Yes, Fred, we farm girls live closer to the soil.) And sometimes I was a senior overhearing juniors!

So how did I really respond to Faucher when I'd settled? I still can't believe it: "Why, uh, don't you, like, come out and have a look for yourself, like, Fred?" I'd spoken like a dolt intentionally, with an edge of irony (my default voice), which was all lost on Faucher, and likely would be on everyone but Dad for the rest of my life, I feared.

He brightened like he'd scored at the buzzer—"Great!"

"Saturday after lunch would be cool, Fred," said the newly minted cool chick. "One o'clock okay, Fred?"

Christ almighty, if I'd said "Fred" any more, people would have thought I was trying to sell him insurance. Dad would be in town Saturday working at Canopy Growth. I looked directly at Faucher and could see he'd not been prepared for that directness. His gaze dropped to my chest (I wished I'd buttoned up only to the third-last, not to the second-last as I'd wasted time deciding that morning), then slowly grinning back up to my face.

"Sure, I'll be there, one-ish."

He walked away—hooked thumbs, bowlegged … pretty good ass—already swaggering before he'd covered half the distance to his locker. There was some huddled whispering among the posse, some tittering, a cackle from Adèle, and I wondered if I could catch Faucher alone somewhere and cancel the invitation. I was getting that Carrie feeling all over, which I'd grown especially alert to since just before restarting school. I'd been fighting an urge to tell everyone I met, which had been no one so far, that I *chose* to be all the things I was and was perfectly happy with my choices. Which was a lie of course. I regretted all the stuff I'd missed, which was always coming home to me in the references I was missing, mostly musical, some movies, no books. Anyway, like I've been saying, Fred Faucher *was* a popular boy and sort of sexy, and I hadn't a friend in the world, and had never enjoyed even an inkling of a real boyfriend (cousins don't count).

"You're welcome," I said *sotto voce*.

"*Faucher?*" startled me from behind, especially as it'd been said like the other F-word.

It was the boy from my homeroom, Timmy or Jimmy or someone, who'd been paying me some weird attention that first week: he'd hurriedly shared his math text when I'd forgotten mine (the whole compulsive routine of regular school had struck me again like being at a kids' camp); the day after he said he'd forgotten the English anthology and asked to share mine (a few times we'd brushed shoulders); later I'd glimpsed the big book in his backpack; he'd been the only one who'd laughed when I smilingly said to Ms. Stottlemeyer that, I could be wrong, but I didn't think "Fern Hill" was in New Brunswick or (under my breath) that Dylan Thomas was "distantly related" to Nobel laureate Bob Dylan; he'd held a door for me and suffered some boys' and assorted sluts' "Ooooooo, Gentleman Jim." Then I'd vaguely remembered him from the last time I was in formal school, for half of grade ten. I think I'd even had a weird crush on him for a while—it'd been so long ago, in a very bad time—strong enough anyway to have mentioned it to Mom ... I remembered. But then Mom got sicker and he was put entirely out of mind, with everything else but life's unfairness to me. So *of course* he'd have had to be the one standing there when I invited Faucher out to the farm.

"Sorry to startle you, Mary. But *Faucher?*" He clenched his teeth, his cheeks jutted back and forth. He had big brown eyes like Aoife's, he was shorter than me, and he looked ... I don't know. Hurt? But I had nothing to say to him. His head kept wagging as he walked away. What the hell's he on about?

Yes: Jimmy Collins, which I remembered then only from homeroom attendance-taking. He'd corrected the teacher, saying

"Jim, please." Some guffawed, a slut's voice said "Ooooo, big man," that fucking Adèle Pélletier, Faucher's primo slut. Jimmy never corrected the teacher again. He simply didn't respond to "Jimmy," even when it was repeated for the third time, merely kept his eyes on the open book, which impressed me no end. At home and supposedly working on the simpleton math, I would think *Jimmy ... Jim Collins.* Thought it a nice name, just the sound of it, that's consonance for you. I thought I'd teasingly call him *Jimmy* and see if he'd accept it from me.

Jimmy was heading for the exit at the hallway's end. But when he arrived opposite Faucher's crowd, he stopped and faced them down, mainly Fred. He was also a good ways shorter than Faucher and most of the male hangers-on, all jocks. Jimmy would never make a basketball team, and likely no football either, though he looked pretty powerful through the shoulders and chest, and those shorter legs packed the thighs of his jeans and ... well. Faucher tried to stare back at Jimmy for about five seconds, then he and the posse started acting mealy-mouthed, which was not their style at all (aggressive, even violent, from what I'd already seen in their constant horsing around, that was their style, a.k.a bullying the younger kids). But what's going on here? What did I miss? My Carrie antennae were suffering seizure in a whipping wind.

Faucher turned away to busy himself with the combination lock on his locker, to which he addressed his question: "Whaddya want, Collins, uh, I mean *Jim-bo*?" Slut-queen of the cheerleaders Adèle cackled. Faucher swung the padlock against the metal door in a ringing slam. Round one: fighters back to their corners.

Jimmy said nothing, just proceeded towards the exit. He had a big head too, dark and bushy, a broad handsome face; he looked like no one but himself. I was surprised at *my*self for what I was seeing and thinking. There was something about him, something else, something different, and not just what I'd liked already in Stottlemeyer's class, that he too was a ferocious reader. And then (no hindsight bullshit), even then, I wished he was the one coming out on Saturday. *Then* I twigged: *Jimmy Collins* was the boy I'd noticed my last year in regular school, grade ten at Sacred Heart High. Yes: *the boy I'd told Mom about.* Only weeks before she'd died. I'd been resenting her sickness like a really bad brain sickness of my own. After she died, I'd spent every day sitting on the far side of Big Rock and crying and wishing myself dead. But it wouldn't have mattered which way I'd faced, Dad was nowhere.

Some months after that, well before Christmas break in grade ten, Dad pulled me out and began home-schooling. A full-time farmer! Part-time worker at Canopy Growth on weekends. For months he'd been insisting, drunkenly thumbing through my books and homework, that the whole school system was shit, as bad as TV. Then the pandemic got really serious again (people began saying *Plague*), and the schools shut down for an indefinite spell, and I was the only one getting any education.

Dad would set me a day's reading and studying, on top of the Mom work I'd slowly taken on, then interrogate me madly all evening, as he drank beer after beer (Harp Lager, or the version he'd begun home-brewing as we grew broker and broker). No more TV, of course. No TV anywhere, because he'd moved it to a corner of the barn (the cows would now be more *au courant* than I!). I'd continued mad as hell till well into the new year … And then I came to like it, the piled-on reading, our talks about it, no more aggressive interrogation. Both of us struggling as the math became more difficult. Hating quadratic equations, loving Shakespeare, the Brontës (him not so much, me mad for *Jane*

Eyre), *Sunshine Sketches of a Little Town* (him over the top for those silly stories about Pupkin and Pepperleigh and them all), Bertrand Russell's *History of Philosophy*, even a Latin grammar, and more, much much more as the advertisers say. I don't think he really knew what he was doing to me, or for me, maybe for us both. I was *so* relieved after Mom's death to sink deeply, obsessive-compulsively, into books and fiction and abstract ideas, lose myself. Later, this became one of our private lines: when a neighbour would look around at the walls and piles of books and say, "You *read* all these?" one or the other of us would answer: *Reading saved our lives.* Puzzlement in response. But reading might well have done so, and definitely did our sanity.

Once, about one of *his* favourite novels he asked, "What do you think the title means?" It was called *That They May Face the Rising Sun*, and I think he liked it first off because the author had the same name as us. Dad the teacher loved to explain: the title referred to an old Celtic-Christian way of burying people with their feet to the east, so that they'd be face-forward for the Resurrection. Then just like that we talked about Mom, for the first time since, remembered her in our different and same ways. And cried together till I went to bed still snorting snot, and he kept drinking. The next morning when he came in for breakfast I asked him if he really believed that stuff about facing the rising sun, and he, badly hungover, growled. Then he quit drinking for a long time.

Days when I bucked against his system, the whole home-schooling thing, he'd declare a holiday. We'd spend the day "arsing about" (a Granny McGahern expression), walking the fields and inspecting the stock, making plans. Or we'd drive around in the old truck. When schools were still in, we'd cruise past the yards, which all looked strange and spooky: slowing past Sacred Heart ("Not so slow, Dad," slumping, "Go go!"), I recognized no one inside the chain-link fence, because everybody was wearing a mask. The scene looked like prisoners at exercise time (I picked out Fred Faucher's gang) or like psych patients getting an airing (Adèle Pélletier *avec* sluts); many were wearing plastic face shields, so that the impression was a combination of banditry and welding school. I was overjoyed to be home-schooled.

The Carrie feelings were powerful again. As was my good angel: Oh, what's to worry, girl, it's your farm, your home ground. You're being silly. Faucher's just a big eejit (my good angel talked in Granny McGahern's voice). By lunchtime Saturday I was ashamed of how nervous I still was, such a silly girly girl. Dad noticed my condition too, and was pleased when I told him it's just because a new friend from school was visiting after lunch.

"A new friend!" (Okay, justifiable.) "Boy or girl?"

"Boy."

"Now you behave, young lady, you're on the honour system while I'm at Canopy."

The obviousness in that mock-voice just embarrassed us both. He reached for the frayed garnet-coloured cap that he'd ordered eons ago from the uBytown store, turned it over, smacked it once on the table (his gotta-get-back-to-work signal), tugged it onto his balding head, bent and kissed my head, and left. The muffler cracked like gunfire and I thought I heard it bang against the bump-up to the road. It hurt how much I loved him. Especially since Mom had died, or not long afterwards anyway, because for about a year I'd hated him. Then I hated that he had to work at Canopy Growth on Saturdays and Sundays to make ends meet. It hurt him to be working for the enemy, as Canopy was always trying to buy our remaining acres (some three hundred left of some eight hundred when Granda died). Dad never complained. But there I was, planning to go off to an expensive university in less than a year!

Faucher arrived on a slick bicycle before I'd finished washing up from lunch. At the sink window I saw that the thin wheels couldn't handle the turn-off drop from paved road to the gravel-and-dirt driveway that led to our house; the front wheel wobbled badly and he never regained control, like some drunk, which looked pretty funny; he managed to dismount without falling over and walked his bike up to the house like he'd meant everything to happen as it had. I smiled. I didn't want him in the kitchen—I suddenly knew I didn't want him in the house—so went to the door before he got too close and called hello and told him to have a look around, I'd be only ten minutes (which would bring the arranged time, not that I was compulsive about such things, it's just that Dad had taught me to be punctual: cows shouldn't have to suffer to be milked or fed, which was ultimately for our benefit anyway).

Big Faucher grin, like the cat that swallowed the crow. "No problemo, Mary!" He leaned his bike carefully against the washing line pole (still can't be beaten for airing), took a dramatic lungful of 'fresh country air,' and ambled towards the barn.

I guess Faucher's not so bad. His tight brown cords showed his high-riding ass to good effect, bum like a Black man's. Carrie calmed, settled enough to get dressed for the prom. I confess: I had designs on Faucher, at least through that smudged window.

Before going out to him I ran upstairs to my room and brushed my hair again. I was wearing my green-plaid shirt with rolled sleeves and yoga pants—too sexy, I'm no slut—so changed into my wide-legged green culottes that I'd got cheap at Lululemon just as they went out of style. I looked okay in the mirror, I guess, which gave me confidence. Then I looked dorky—but I had to go!

Before heading down I glanced out my window. He was over by the barnyard fence where the cattle went in and out. Only Aoife was out, standing very still alongside the fence, as if for added security, likely suffering again from the udder infection that had become recurrent with her. I don't get attached to farm animals (only crows), never named them, even the lambs, but I'd got attached to Aoife and worried constantly about her, ever since … well. Dad suspected she, still a heifer, was pregnant finally after the last covering (a waste of good money, he'd been complaining; I didn't like what he was likely thinking). Anyway, Aoife was looking at Faucher, mournfully curious in that bovine way, maybe seeking comfort, and Fred nicely raised a friendly hand to her as he approached. I *have* been wrong about Fau— then he dashed at the fence clapping his hands like a shot, which made Aoife leap backwards slantingly and big-eyed and run for her life to the far side. Faucher shook his head and swept his hands in front of his face. The smell.

But what if she was pregnant, and lost the calf? I'd kill Faucher. For sure the spooking would be enough to make her hell to milk that evening, which still had to be by hand, and by me of course. Dad was often kept late at Canopy on Saturdays, unless he'd be willing to work overtime Sunday to supervise the student part-timers, which he hated. But I had to allow that Faucher wouldn't have known the seriousness of what he was doing, it was just Faucher messing around with a cow the way I'd seen him bullying kids, nerds and the like (*my* peeps). Anyway, the animals themselves bullied each other all the time (chickens were murder for it). Dad had told me long ago that it was all about *dominance*, no big deal, though it could get serious when two males went at it. Made sense. I remember saying, "Is that where we get *pecking order*?" He said, "Smart girl, you. Okay, forget the Seton, start in on Roberts' animal stories for tomorrow."

As Faucher and I walked round the barn, going in and out, he kept up a silly patter about the advantages of living so close to nature.

I mildly jigged my head backwards: "You don't think it stinks?"

"Well, yeah, some, I guess, but it's not, like, real bad stinky." He tried to inhale deeply but didn't get too far, yet still managed, "Ah, clean country air!"

"Boy, have I got a job for you, Fred."

"Are you serious? I already work part-time at Canopy every other Sunday."

Jesus Christ, my shining knight, a born eejit. He was oddly nervous and growing more so by the minute. I thought of easing his silly anxiety with the sex joke in *Hamlet* about "country matters," which Dad had hurried past (I'd read the explanatory note on my own). But I'd never really have dared refer to it with Faucher; and anyway, there was about as much chance of Fred's knowing *Hamlet* as of Aoife's. The way he was acting and talking made me think of the way Jimmy had said his name, like he was a loser, a goof (I'd thought that was all Jimmy meant).

Despite Faucher's hymn to the joys of farm life, he was swerving and dancing all the time to avoid any contact with the animals, even the yearlings and cats. Our border collie, Towser, came up and sniffed at his hand and Faucher snapped it back and shook it, and Towser barked at him and took off. Faucher stepped extra carefully whenever he sighted shit, which he was looking out for like landmines, even when it wasn't shit or only very old bits of manure from the spreader, and he stopped repeatedly to knock his fancy runners gently against posts and door jambs.

I was again regretting everything, but I took him to Big Pond anyway, if only to view from some distance. I flirted with a thought about Big Rock, my beach, but thought better of it, as I didn't want to sit with Faucher, not this first time anyway. (Full disclosure: I'd determined to get some real experience before heading off to Ottawa and university, and I had less than a year to do it. I'd only ever sat at Big Rock with one boy, a second cousin or something from a failing farm north of Bellville, who'd spent a summer with us when his parents were splitting up. All we'd done was hold hands and kiss (no tongues, no "tonsil hockey" as I've recently heard it called in the girls' room); to say it was no big deal would be an overstatement. But yes, that was still the extent of my 'sexual experience.'

On the way back to the house I showed Faucher the chicken coop, explaining at runaway length in nervous pride that the chickens have always been *my* responsibility, even when my mother was, like, still alive. Stupidly, saying so made my throat tighten up. I threaded my fingers through the wires, imagined myself alone, shut up and just held on.

Faucher said nothing, showed no sign of discomfort about anything, not like with his fucking shoes. But good, good.

Until he wrinkled his nose and sneered: "Wow, what a lot of shit chickens make. Hey, chickenshit! So that's what it really means ..." His head bowed as his gaze traced a line from the scratch-dancing chickens to his own feet. "Fuck! It's all over my Jordans!"

Then I was absolutely nowhere for him, fine by me. On his desperate own he found the outside water hose and was dousing his precious Jordans (whatever they are, just overpriced running shoes of course). I came up behind him and asked if he'd like a pop or coffee or something. I wasn't hoping he'd say no, but I was definitely getting low and lower in hope of anything.

He startled, so intent he'd been on hosing his shoes. He mumbled maybe next time, turned off the water, and without a thank-you went for his bike, squelching all the way. He halted, looked down at himself with his arms spreading like a plump goose about to attempt flight: "Fuck!" In the near distance the chickens cackled.

I smiled, and for the life of me don't know why I shouted after him—the visit had gone too quickly and, for Faucher, ended in disaster, but I was now feeling quite superior to my school's intimidating hot boy, and even strangely, itchily affectionate, or at least a touch conciliatory and, okay, thinking too of future opportunities—anyway I called after him: "You could have one of my dad's homemade beers!"

"Sure, sure," he said without turning his head. "Maybe next time."

Such enthusiasm. He'd not even used my name again since arriving. Good riddance. Carrie was comatose at least.

On Monday morning after homeroom I paused at Faucher's locker where the usual in-crowd had collected, keeping back in the middle of the hallway. I really didn't know, and still don't, what I was doing, probably something like overconfidently expecting a hello. Or if a hi was asking for too much, at least some nodding acknowledgment that could pass for an invitation to hang out for a spell. I'd even steeled myself to pass some pleasantries: *How's it goin', Faucher? How'er they hangin', Freddy boy?* Not really. And there was nothing funny in the way the assorted sluts were whispering and tittering and stealing glances at me. King Fred said something to Queen-slut Adèle Pélletier, and I believe she spontaneously blew laughing snot into her hand.

But this is the welcome I got:

"*BOCK* buck-buck-buck-buck."

It wasn't from Faucher, at least not at first, but from one, then more, of his boys, and *then* with Adèle cackling in like the winner of Leitrim Falls' Chicken-Calling contest. The cunt.

Tuesday the same thing as I walked past as abnormally as a nun: "*BOCK* buck-buck-buck-buck." With cunty Adèle still crowing loudest.

This was hurled at my back: "Check your shoes for chicken shit this morning, Mary?" In a whiny voice of false concern. "I think I see some pasted straw!" It was from *the* cuntry matter herself, Loose Lucy Legault—whose own farm had just sold to Canopy.

"*Smell* it too." *That* was fucking Faucher's voice.

Ha ha ha …

Oh Carrie, dear Carrie, forgive us, now and at the hour of our death, which *is* now. I would have been happy to be dead and lying at the bottom of Big Pond, facing west, with Big Rock on my chest.

I couldn't tell Dad, though I wanted to (I would have told Mom right away). Then I did, because I knew in that sensible part of me that watches over me that I'd soon be in full-on anxiety-attack mode and heading for a real Carrie moment at Ottawa's Princess Diana Centre for Mental Wellness ("The Mental"): I couldn't think straight, couldn't read for beans, was madly mad at myself *all the time*, was crying myself to sleep.

"C'mere," he said. If I live to be a hundred and seventeen, I'll never forget his holding me, saying nothing, just his rough right hand on my back, and I pray to God I never have cause to cry like that again. I mean, loved ones die and you cry your heart out, but you didn't cause their deaths. I had no one to blame but myself for the many deaths I'd suffered over the past days and nights. I know how melodramatic that sounds, but it's the literal truth, or at least the figurative truth. So there is truth in melodrama. Is that why it exists? Discuss with your father in five hundred words or less.

With a lot of laughing and spitting of popcorn (the first food I'd kept down in two days), Dad and I worked something out. We practised it: "Just for fun," he kept saying. I don't know what he really thought. I did know that I could never actually pull it off, but the planning and rehearsals distracted me wholly back to my true self. I still cried myself to sleep for one more night, but dropping off calmly on the Thursday I focused on Dad's so-called plan—and suddenly there was light in my future, my life ... and then even in my room. I saw Mom at the foot of my bed, just for half a minute or so, and she smiled and nodded. Think what you want but, to put a twist on Dad's old Beatles song: Mary's mother came to me. Only then could I really see myself doing it, and I had to snort up some snotty laughter. Dream on, girl, I chided myself unconvincingly ... and did just that ... finally ...

... It wasn't Mom but Jimmy Collins. He rode a shining golden horse off the highway and right up to the front stoop. I was worried he'd break its legs and we'd have to put it down, and then I knew he'd never do that. Jimmy had grown up on a farm and was really good in English (as good as me—as I, maybe better, I didn't know yet), so I told him a white horse symbolized death. "Symbolized," he smirked. He reached down and helped me swing up; I was wearing my Sunday dress and the horse-hair was prickly on my thighs. I guess that's what a cliché my subconscious is. But the seeing-Mom part while awake was real, and it's happened since. Once when I was a little kid I was sure I'd seen a pet lamb that had been sent to the slaughterhouse, and Granny McGahern told me she saw ghosts and that those kinds of things happened to McGaherns, not to worry, pet. So I stopped worrying. She too died not long afterwards, of course. I've never seen *her*, not yet anyway, or only her features in Dad, in that way people see only their own family resemblance in babies. I've seldom slept so soundly as that night Mom's ghost smiled her old smile on me. I was glad to be a McGahern with the McGahern gift.

On the Friday after the Monday and Tuesday and Wednesday and Thursday morning gauntlets of cackling derision, I made myself stop in the hallway at Faucher's locker. The clucking stopped too in a trailing *bock* ... It had been Faucher himself about to crank it. I waited for complete silence. A locker door banged, and I knew it was Jimmy Collins' exactly five down from my own, which gave me additional courage. First with Dad and then in my bedroom mirror I'd worked on the bemused expression for when I'd take those two steps forward and be face-to-face with fat-faced Faucher:

"Faucher, just where *the fuck* do you think your fucking breakfast eggs come from? The Food Basics supermarket? Or your momma's ass? If the second, believe me, you're better off with chicken shit on them, you chickenshit." I'd got the silent shock we'd hoped for. I drew a steady breath and looked round at the posse: "Do you know, Mr. Tough-Guy here was scared shitless of the chickens! He hugged the fence when the barn cats mewed at him. And I *know* I smelled Faucher shit when our little milk cow Aoife stared him down and stepped towards him. Talk of a stink!"

No one moved or made a sound, till Faucher said lowly, in an attempt at that dismissive voice that assumes others' agreement: "She's lying."

"Bitch," spat the devil Adèle.

"Whoo-hoo, *burn!*" cried Jimmy Collins from down the hallway. "Fred Faucher, chickenshit of the purple sage! Bravo Mary McGahern!"

Faucher turned slamming his door—"You wanna go, Jimbo?" His face was flaming.

Said Jimmy normally, "*BOCK* buck-buck-buck-buck," and took a couple of steps towards us.

Faucher turned back to his closed locker.

There was a burst of laughter from some of the posse and other kids milling about, then one of the assorted sluts blew a bubble of snot when she couldn't hold back laughing. She failed to convince with flapping hand that she was laughing at me. Then, excepting Adèle, the entire posse dispersed, earlier than usual, disappeared, just like that, like they'd coordinated a vanishing act.

I stared at Faucher's back. The pale cotton shirt was showing shadowy sweat where Adèle touched his shoulder—"Eww, gross," she said, snatching the hand away and shaking it. I was silently begging him to turn around. *Turn around, Faucher*, I thought; *turn around, you fat fuck.* He straightened up but didn't turn around. I swear his ass had got fatter since Saturday, the back of his head balder. I worked to settle the adrenalin and walked away.

At first Dad wouldn't believe I'd done it, then kept pretending not to believe so as to make me re-enact the scene. Finally he mimed applause, lifted me off the floor in only our second hug since Mom had died and swung me.

"Inspired touch with the barn cats and Aoife! Bravo, Mary McGahern indeed! And here I'd been thinking the mention of his mother's ass would do it! Who's this Jimmy? Not Tom Collins' boy? Obviously *not* a chip off the old keg!"

It was easily the happiest we'd been since … well, that's enough of that. But both of us knew how I'd have finished that sentence, as well as we knew that neither of us need even hint at it. We'd been there, done that, the demonstrative mourning. Instead we continued laughing uncontrollably, in fits and starts and tits and farts (a Dad-ism), snottering unselfconsciously like toddlers draining a disease, then in some side-stitch pain for me. Dad held up an exhausted traffic-cop's hand. He shifted us out of that laughing madness by seriously explaining what a "Yo Mama" put-down was, how it came from American Black culture.

"That's *so* interesting," said mock-serious I. "I'll bet you learned that from … *TV*?"

"Okay, okay," he conceded. "We'll deprive the poor cows of their only entertainment; I'll put the TV back in the house and call Rogers. But you keep reading, young lady, and not just from the crap English anthology, and if I just once see you reading in front of the TV—Aoife gets her soaps back."

"Rogers offers a bundle deal for a smart pho—"

"No."

He began shaving every day again … okay, every other.

My little performance made me popular at school. Well, sort of, at least well-known for having severely dissed the school's number-one asshole bully, as I was surprised to learn. It made me some friends too, and one best-friends-forever girlfriend, Naomi, who was the one clued me in on Fred Faucher's true standing.

"*What*? Moi and Faucher?" she'd exaggerated *sotto voce* with right hand's fingertips to her chest, when I'd first awkwardly apologized because I'd heard she liked Fred. Naomi had replaced Jimmy Collins as my chemistry lab partner at that morning's rotation, and I'd been afraid that she'd manoeuvred to be with me. But when she did that TV-response to my apology, I was already thinking, please be my friend. "*Puh-leese* don't tell me that you, like ditzy Adèle Pélletier, thought that Fred Faucher and *I* were an item?"

Lied whispering I, "No no no, not at all. I could tell you were way too smart for Fred."

She'd winked at me with all the sympatico I'd ever imagined in a bosom companion and said too loudly, "Until *your* recent Oscar performance with Freddy boy—your Scarface mowing him down—I'd worried that adorable Adèle would be gunning for you as numero-uno competition for the affections of Freddy the pig."

"Ladies?" called Mr. Gaffney from behind his long green counter. "Do we have to do another rotation already?"

I should have learned to be careful with budding hope, but couldn't contain myself and whispered, "Where'd you get *Freddy the pig*? Did you read those books too?"

"Mary, my dear, I thought I'd die when I reached the last one."

She had her voices all right, her characters. And my undying love.

"Mary McGahern," lamented Gaffney, "I expect disruption from Naomi but I'm disappointed in you." He was just too nice to raise his voice, his beard would've fallen off.

I was gulping into my chest in that perfectly stupid way I have when I'm happily not in control. Naomi smiled like the sun come up on Big Rock: "Wanna eat lunch together today?"

"*Please* leave the room, ladies. Detention slips!" The beard itself had slipped.

Naomi visited the farm often that fall and helped me put up pickles and beets, which she learned to do. From out of nowhere others began asking if I'd teach them, but I was having none of it; Naomi was enough, and I wouldn't risk her best-friendship. Also, I didn't have time to find out who was serious and who was just titillated by the exotic attraction of the farm-living-close-to-nature bullshit. I even worried too that they could be agents of Faucher's planned revenge, which I fully expected. Jimmy Collins, who'd rung the bell with his slammed locker door and hooted brave Mary to her knockout of Faucher, was back in my corner, I hoped. What could go wrong? Sweet and sharp Naomi would turn out to be part of some new conspiracy to Carrie me? Jimmy would never forgive me for having invited Faucher out in the first place? ... Ah yes, I reminded myself, next September was still to worry about. Almost a year away yet already anxiously on my mind. I'd wanted to put off university for a year, didn't want to leave Dad, yet it was Dad making me go. At least let me go to Western University where Jimmy would be! And now Naomi would be off to Fanshawe College in the same London (Ontario). Only loser Mary McGahern would be going to Bytown University in Ottawa!

FOUR

PLAGUING JAKE 2: TENURED PROFESSORS IN THEIR PLACES

No false modesty, but I've always believed that every one of my seventeen Film&WordsWork Pod colleagues is smarter than I and engaged in more impressive research ('research' such as it's now practised in what used to be called "English literary studies"; as over the past few decades we've increasingly been 'reading' according to personal cultural-political agendas only). What I *am* better at than all others is being six-foot-six, easily the tallest member of our Pod, and likely of the entire Faculty of Digital Humanities, and maybe of uBytown itself. Or at least I *was* six-six at my tallest, for of course my spine's been compressing over the past decade or so.

I also play dumber even than I honestly am. Colleagues know I'm acting but also believe it, arrogant academics being what they are. It's complicated, my performance, our collective suspension of disbelief. Simply put, I am not as smart as my colleagues, play even dumber than I am, and we all have an understanding. That puts us at ease in our ersatz power relations and has the benefit of allowing me much room for excusable ironic zingers. "Surely old Jake couldn't have meant it *that* way?" Oh yes old Jake could have: "Professor Turnbull, just what is it that attracts you to the allegorical significances of the smaller fur-bearing animals in Modern British Fiction?"

John Turnbull must top out at five-foot-three-inches, four at a racking stretch, or at elevation in his considerable heels. He walks comically, scoots stiffly: head tilted back and stretched upwards, barrel chest going before him, little legs churning, always bumping into things and people (too often female students). His heightening spike of greying hair says would-be youth; the greying, not you old man. Don't get me wrong, I like John (I like all my Pod colleagues), we're oldest colleague-friends, but he *is* always carrying on about some fixation or other. The current *idée fixe* is his personal "war against cliché."

One of our legion of part-timers, the ingratiating Mohammed Abdulla, tells me that John stole that phrase from Kingsley Amis's son, Martin. I said, "You're quite the reader, aren't you, Mo? Better watch it or you'll give Film&WordsWork a bad name!" I don't know if his shaky command of idiomatic English enabled Mohammed to get the joke, because he frowned and said, "I will then be increasingly extra careful, Leader Flynn, thank you." It's always best not to pursue such misunderstandings, as doing so inevitably ends in a morass of cross-purposes risking greater offence. But John Turnbull is most truly at war with the cliché of himself: a short man with a Napoleon complex as big as the Château Laurier (clichés become clichés because they are useful shorthand, John: personally I do not fear the slap of the platitude).

To his credit, over three decades John has published some half-dozen novels and a couple of short story collections. He published them each with a different small literary publisher that no longer exists, all founded by John himself—"pop-up publishers," his colleagues call them when John's not present. As Pod Leader, I always strive to smooth such threatening internecine frictions. In John's case my collegial mission often proves to be an impossible task: one of his books, entitled *Haiku Min*, is a sixty-plus-page work with one word per page. Our resident theorist, Dr. Professor Bartholomew von Blüger, said dryly that the sequel would be one letter per page. I laughed a little just to temper Bartholomew. But von Blüger, always mentally abiding in fields of etymology, literary theory, and linguistic poetics, frowned ponderingly then gave his tag line: "I suppose so."

To be fair to Professor Turnbull, he has also published a substantial critical work with a reputable Canadian publisher, our second-best university press. John's study gained that degree of notoriety that can be won only among those who practise what someone (Freud? Pierre or Justin Trudeau?) called the "narcissism of small differences" (which means that no one in the real world cares a white rat's pink arsehole about your Brobdingnagian battles over which end of a boiled egg to crack open).

John's study was an eviscerating critique of the very idea of a distinctive Canadian literature (my field). He focused at wearying length, some third of his book, on the nineteenth-century satirist Thomas Chandler Haliburton (my guy), our first international literary star as the creator of Yankee clock salesman Sam Slick, who was not only the literary granddaddy of Huck Finn (as I've also already boasted Canuckily) but also the great-great granddaddy of Willy Loman *and* the model for Uncle

Sam himself. John, even then some twenty years immigrated from the poor side of London town, insisted that Haliburton would never have gotten published today; in fact, John argued generally in the book's introduction that none of Canada's writers up to the late-twentieth century were good enough to have been published outside the country, which flowering epoch, *mirabile dictu*, was right around the time John arrived in Canada. John: only *in Canada* could he have made such a well-paying career teaching at an esteemed university. From pre-publication to winning Canada's Social Science and Humanities prize for a literary-critical publication, John always went out of his way to insist that I was not to take any of it personally. I did of course. I still do, every sneering, humiliating word of *CanLit Can't: It Never Could*. Regardless, I take even personal attacks as cockroaches and street people take shooing: I always come back for more. John and I have remained supportive colleagues and friends.

What else is worth knowing about this irksome little man whom I nonetheless like? That he never visits my office but to trouble his Leader? Oh yes, I remember another matter now (that's irony for you, and *litotes*): I'm fairly certain John has begun an affair with our colleague Pat Kelly, with whom I'd been having an exclusive "emotional affair" (forgive me, Jieun, if it still matters; I'll gratefully endure added eons in Purgatory). I twigged to that revolting development at a reception for our most recent writer-in-residence, this one another friend of John's, who was published only ever *by* one of John's pop-up publishers. Said writer was your typical overcompensating unknown who throughout his inaugural reading repeatedly insulted his captive audience for their literary tastes, as one of the Davids complained next day in the coffee room (in Turnbull's absence). "But fair enough," said I. "After all, we *were* there to hear *him*." I got a surprised big laugh; as usual one of the Davids called, "Jake!" because, as said, Jake was supposed to be incapable of such put-downs.

Before agreeing to offer him the Writer-in-residence position, I *had* read one of that writer's books, *Up From Blood and Ice* (Bullish Press, proprietor John Turnbull), with its lavish hard-cover production in three-colour jacket and deckle-edge pages (thank you, Canada Council for the Arts). The epigraph was from Walt Whitman, something justifying his writing about himself because that's whom he knows best. Or it might have been from Thoreau. I read seventeen pages: the author wallowed in self-pity and run-on sentences, proving himself both a *witless*-man and *thorough* ly unreadable. (Jake!)

At the reception following his reading, just as Pat Kelly and I, clutching plastic glasses of rough red wine, were easing towards readjusting our emotional affair (I wanted out, honestly), John sidled over with his beer, in the bottle of course (a brandishing of his working-class bona fides, a British class-consciousness which no real Canadian had thought about for a century).

"Ah, the delicious Pat Kelly," said John, then smacked his small mouth. "I do love an androgynous name that makes for a complete sentence." He patted her forearm while pursing his thin lips. His patting caused a fat drop of red wine to hop to the rim of her glass, balance there, then defiantly hang on while skiing the underside of the cup to run down the stem to its base, where it paused again before proceeding along the sloping base to a second rim, where it delayed yet again, a ruby tear gathering its dissipated substance—before dropping onto Pat's expensive yellow shoes. She has elegant tiny feet, does Pat Kelly, though as a rule I find feet ugly appendages, alien-looking things, vestigial evidence that we must have evolved, like the clawed birds, from dinosaurs. Despite her aesthetically acceptable minimalist *pieds*, it was her new habit, when she'd grown comfortable with me, of kicking off her shoes that first urged me towards ending the emotional affair.

"And how's your lovely wife, Jake? *Die hausfrau* Jieun, as our colleague von Blüger would put it?" horning-in John asked loudly. There was no din at our poorly attended reception. And who could blame English professors—pardon, I mean Film&WordsWork professors—for not attending after the stereotypically anti-academic guest of honour had frequently derided them for not knowing some obscure kitchen-sink British novelist of the mid-twentieth century? The typically conversation-stopping Turnbull continued: "And all the wee Flynn bairns and grand-bairns?" For some reason in an inexplicable Scottish accent. "How many are there now, Jake? Six of one, a dozen of the other? Or so *you* say. But hoot, man, have you no consideration for the planet!"

Pat Kelly, who cared a great deal for "the planet," looked at me worriedly, *then* laughed. "I see, Professor Turnbull, that you do the police in different voices." She smiled guardedly if nonetheless encouragingly.

"Ah, what the Dickens, eh?"

"No," said patient-faced Pat, "Eliot, the original title for *The Wasteland*, appropriately enough, given the attendance at this event. Where did all the force-marched students go?"

"Ahhh …" Turnbull intoned like she'd stepped her stained foot on his equally small foot and twisted its heel there.

But what can one say about such an obvious tactician as is John Turnbull? Such aggressive testicular display is why the word "anti-social" has real meaning for me, *to* me. And explains why in that moment of one-sided male pissing-contest, I made no reply. I know it's not what Sartre meant by the phrase, but he was bang on regardless: other people are hell. The way people do blunderingly or intentionally stomp on one's toes, bludgeon one's sensitivities—*stick* themselves in and refer every conversational nugget to themselves. That's why I prefer never to leave my house, my home study, my room. Seriously, literally. Oh, retirement, where is thy refuge?

We were joined by Dean Jacques LaRoque—at one time himself the Leader of Waterloo U's Pod of Kinetics and Massage Therapy (not as fun as it sounds, he informed me), who had an impressive young woman in tow. I liked Jacques (I like just about everyone, as you may have gathered ... except Professor Oberon Stangle; more to come), a sharp dresser invariably accessorised by a different young lady. Dean LaRoque always had uBytown's future at his mind's forefront, or at least the Faculty of Digital Humanities' and his own climb up the administration ladder. That's all right. Alpha males are like that. Jacques is very good at what he does, and we all benefit in an administrative trickle-down of scant funds. A sharply stylish dean is such an asset to a cash-strapped faculty, even if Jacques' calculating head always suggested that it had just been withdrawn from a pencil sharpener.

"A highly successful event, Leader Flynn. I expect you are to be congratulated too, Professor Turnbull. As I was just saying to Felicia—"

"I thought it sucked donkey," said Felicia, her empurpled lips tightly confirming the assertion, her Goth eyes as walled as the Blessed Virgin Mary's in those primitive medieval depictions. She was still displaying a look that I'd been hoping had gone out of fashion (I thought of it as "virgin whore"), though I expect that some version of Gothic, like the poor and those of impoverished imagination, will always be with us.

"Well ..." said uncomfortable Dean LaRoque. "It *did* have an undeniable animal vitality."

"In fact, Jacques," said John, "Leader Flynn and I were just discussing advancing the timing of my next sabbatical leave."

Our dear Dean blinked. "But you're only now up for promotion to Full, John; an advancement high time in the making, I might add, I mean given your prodigious output and service to uBytown and the greater Ottawa literary community. Well, the English-speaking part anyway!"

Felicia smiled widely, in exaggeration, a frightful grimace actually, which accounted for her having some stained purple teeth. "Megalosaurus."

"Pardon, dear?" A note of impatient reprimand inflected the Dean's tone.

"This whole scene sucks Megalosaurus. That crap wasn't poetry! He's so out of it, it might as well have been in Mandarin! What that *poet manqué* needs is a good dentist. From where I was sitting his mouth looked like a bog of charred stumps. That and his typing fingers crushed."

"Yes, dear, but it *wasn't* poetry, was it? He was reading *fiction*."

John's attention had been attracted. "*I'm* a writer, Felicia, if I may so address you? You are too, I presume? Then let me give you some advice: outside the academy, real writing is not an occupation that pays, thus our visiting writer's dental woes. But I strongly disagree with you about his reading …"

She commenced an ironic curtsying, in plaid twill shirt and holy jeans, then stared daggers (another useful cliché) at Turnbull. "No, you may *not* address me so, fuckface."

Dean LaRoque hurriedly managed, "Well, this has been edifying fun! But we do have another appointment to keep, and miles to go before we sleep—figuratively speaking of course. Please convey my apologies to our guest of honour and give him my personal congratulations on yet another triumph! And, oh yes, congratulations to you too, Professor Kelly, and the entire F-and-WW Pod, on curtailing that other unspeakable speaker's spewing of hatred!"

He was referring to the leading role played recently by the Film&WordsWork Pod, led by Pat Kelly and including the four Jennifers, two Stephanies, and Amari Abara, in preventing a public address at our Grey Owl Alumni Auditorium for Free Speech, which had been sponsored by the Men's Water Polo team: "Laissez-Faire Sporting Masculinisms and the All-Too-Visible Invisible Hand of Black Privilege." As Pat had said to me, "Free speech is one thing, hate speech another." It would seem that the reactionary speaker, the notorious Jane Flamingo, simply hated the idea that white men were discriminated against in professional sports.

Bypassing the few students standing round the writer near the exit door, Dean LaRoque guided Felicia out with a firm hold on her upper arm, off to who knew what next appointment before they sleep (figuratively speaking, of course). He stared smilingly straight ahead, the only way to leave a party (I've heard it called the "Irish exit"), if our event could be called such. I suspect our Dean's planned performance for us had been short-circuited by his honest companion, as at every recent uBytown gathering he'd been pressing his campaign to reform our campus' reputation for "rape culture."

We had never actually been reputed so, or not until Dean LaRoque himself had introduced the brutal term as part of a damage-control campaign when, in celebration of the opening of our new Olympic-size pool, those two water polo players had been caught in the dressing room with a local hooker (sex worker). Because they never paid her, she'd complained to the *Ottawa Citizen* about "sexploitation" on the uBytown campus, and what with it being the slow end of a long winter, the story had gone national (and even got a brief mention on CNN).

Dean LaRoque, who'd been focused on being appointed the next Vice-Rector of uBytown, was roused in defence of his employer and had smartly exploited the media-attention. Too successfully: "rape campus" (his coinage) became uBytown's popular byword and continued as media local-colour filler for a bad few wintry months of administrative discontent. Spring-Summer session enrollments fell, another unintended measure of the success of our good Dean's campaign.

At the reception John Turnbull had watched the Dean and girl as they exited, focusing on the torn denim window in a lower left quadrant where a slash of Felicia's pale ass showed. I would wager, based on glimpses of the patchy evidence, that she wore no underwear.

John said distractedly, "We missed our chance there, Jake."

"What? *We?*"

"Down, boy. I was counting on you to raise the issue of my sabbatical application. I hope our fearless Dean has had—Felicia was it?—I trust he's had her sign a consent form—oh, I *do* apologize, Professor Kelly! How rude of me."

Pat Kelly reached and gripped John's forearm and prefaced what sounded like a prepared statement with a sniff up at me: "John, for some time I've wanted to talk with you about *your* writing, and even going only from what I've heard from Jake over the years, about your upbringing in merry old England! Or perhaps you could give a merry-old *Lucky Jim* address to the whole Pod!"

Pat's enthusiasm both worried and relieved me, like learning the lesser worse about a medical problem: not prostate cancer, 'only' benign prostatic hyperplasia (BPH). Hurt too, I'll admit, in humble pride, if only mildly heart-wise. I did still have a great fondness for Pat Kelly and cherished our relationship, though I knew full well that she, with an eye on promotion to Full herself, was interested in me, her Leader, mainly for that professional reason. So, okay, John could have his day, his nights, the rutting Turnbull, never one to settle for only an emotional affair, unlike his low-testosterone Leader. I've read somewhere that ambitious short men enjoy more sex than we of higher reach and lesser grasp. I wonder if they lie more too. The end.

Or not of course, for I want to give the core of my Film&WordsWork Pod colleagues as fair a bio thumb-nailing as is tolerable. Not only unknown writers, but the world is anti-academic and anti-intellectual enough without my pandering to popular prejudice. True, we academics are well paid for what we do, especially considering that most of us would do what we do without being paid (except for marking essays); and too many of us, Professor Turnbull for example, unceasingly sneer at the taxpayers who fund our sabbaticals. But, not to put too fine an elitist point on it, we *are* society's brains and keepers of its culture. And a society belittles its brains at its peril (see: the United States of America). So I will continue to be fair to the likes of Professor John Turnbull, with his self-serving pseudo-publishing ventures, his overreaching sexual adventures, his exploitative plans for "academic leaves" (a.k.a. sabbaticals), *and* his deep caring about the state of the English-speaking world's literary culture. My friend and colleague.

John spent the early part of his career teaching composition and public speaking in one of those Brit-twit private schools while working on something called an M.Phil. at something called "The Open University." I still don't know just what an M.Phil degree or an Open University is. John didn't write a thesis but something called a "Major Research Project" (MRP). The subject of his study was two obscure short stories by the novelist and poet Thomas Hardy, fictions that Hardy had not seen fit to publish. Yet still our Department of English (as it was known then) hired John, and at an advanced age for a new Assistant Professor, to meet the booming demand for writing courses, the only growth area any English Department has known for decades.

John had been publishing his own short stories and poems in British little magazines with such names as *The Shaved Stoat* and *A Royal Shagging*. He paid his own travel to Ottawa (one-way, I was to learn; we covered his accommodations). His willingness worried me, and to this day I don't know why he was so eager to leave his beloved homeland. Of course I suspected some form of foul play, either committed by or against candidate Turnbull (M.Phil.), but no one even checked his references, we couldn't afford to be picky. And we were still suckers for a British accent in service to a condescending attitude, that disparaging sneer for which I now actually have an affection; that, and even the way, some thirty years on, Professor Turnbull's British accent accentuates when publicly performed.

The demand for writing courses, and increasingly for "Creative Writing," continues apace. Yet fewer and fewer students still read actual books, and the majority can't write for beans. But more and more they want to *be* writers. To a girl and boy they prefer phone screens and laptop monitors to pages and books. But our culture has warped them to lust after fame, and they delusionally think writers enjoy such. Since they already speak English, well, the learning curve will be a slide, eh?

To his estimable credit, John did most of our writing-course grunt work for a long time. (God bless him, at one time seven composition courses per academic year!) He also played the role of famous writer for his classes, convincingly, in fact. But within a week of his achieving tenure and promotion to Associate, some ten years in, John scuttled into my office and announced that he was through not only with teaching creative writing but with all writing courses (before the boom in creative-writing courses, our bread-and-butter came from providing so-called "service courses" to the rest of the University, in packed classrooms with course titles such as "Business English," "Report Writing," "Lab Pro(s)," and the like, which eventually morphed into today's "Eco-Expressions," "Writing Back to Power," and—for a brief posting anyway—"Fuckin' Write").

I tried to talk John out of his refusal. But he insistently described his years of teaching writing as "refereeing the egos of illiterate yobs and yahoos" (he can turn a phrase, if always a nasty one). He complained that continued exposure to the horrid writing of today's students was threatening his epic plan to write a series of twelve novels on the subject "modern times," which would cover the whole twentieth century and circumnavigate the great globe itself. The first novel, "Slouching Towards Beijing," was already well under way, he'd explained. He planned new novels at two-year intervals, which would bring the series to completion when he was eighty ("eightyish," he actually said), and perhaps ready to retire ("perchance"). Although I had not contradicted him in any of this, he aggressively concluded that his plan was eminently feasible because, "You may recall, Jake, I do not revise my writing."

I recalled, smiled, and continued nodding, until he settled some, when I said, "That sounds *most* promising, John, and won't your many readers be fortunate! But what *will* you teach, then?"

"When I come back from my sabbatical, you mean?"

"But there is no sabbatical for you yet, John. Your application for promotion to Associate was only just approved. Next year."

He was nonplussed. Another thing I'll say for the little man, he could never be plussed. His applications for sabbaticals were repeated periodically, with the period frequency tightening up with the advancing years.

Again in my office the other day he struck his favourite pose: right hand holding his left wrist behind his back as he rocked back on his heels, chin tilted arrogantly, something of a Napoleon meets Mussolini:

"This time there can be no gainsaying, Jake. I must have the full sabbatical right away, or an *academic leave* if you will, and you must negotiate it with the Dean forthwith. Pat Kelly and I are planning to hole up in Cornwall for a year or so—England, not Ontario—where I will finish a draft of 'Slouching Towards Beijing'—the only draft—and she a draft of her long-promised history of the presence of the Irish Easter Uprising in Modern English bestiaries. Or rather she will be titling it *Towards* such a history, as I've suggested. I've always believed it a responsibility of senior faculty to mentor the junior."

Forget Napoleon and Benito, by then John's accent was clipping along in a kind of King Charles meets … well, himself. But this new plan was news to me. Pat and I had not spoken intimately since having *the* talk, though there *was* her behaviour at the writer-in-residence reception. So I wasn't shocked at John's news, if a touch nonplussed nonetheless and, well, hurt … if relieved. I *am* that craven, a veritable Gregor Samsa anxious for his day off to end.

Despite the bravado that getting his way was a *fait accompli*, Professor Turnbull nonetheless still trained on me a rhetorical elephant gun—*me*, who never objected to any request from a colleague short of complicity in a prosecutable crime. Then he appeared to remember to whom he was speaking, settled back on his soles, and lowered his weapon.

Yet still he carried on with the unnecessary legalese: "As you know perfectly well, Jake, the CA stipulates in Section forty-four, subsection D, paragraphs c through f, that creative work is now valued as highly as scholarly-critical work. And as you are also well aware, I have already published ..."

His rehearsal of his vanity publications gave me time to regroup. "But John, we *need* you in Creative Writing, especially over the coming term and the program evaluation."

John made as if to argue, then checked himself. "You're a music lover, aren't you, Jake?"

"Mostly opera, Jieun and I both. But where's this going, Professor Turnbull? Professor Kelly has an *appointment* to talk with me shortly; likely on this same subject, I now suspect."

"Do you know Twain's line on opera?"

"Yes."

"When the reporters caught him after he attended his first opera—"

"Yes, I know."

"—and asked him what he thought, he said he'd not heard sounds like that since the orphanage burned down." John slapped his stubby thigh like a dog bone and laughed heartily. He has a *schadenfroh* sense of humour, has John.

Yet further justification for my anti-social self. But I controlled myself, needless to say. "John, our only chance of securing one of the Faculty's new appointments depends on our showing growth in enrollment, and the only area where that is happening is our creative writing program."

"Don't abuse the word *writing*," John said. He sucked air, tipped back his head, and delivered to the ceiling one of the memorable utterances of which he, perhaps a writer after all, was sometimes capable:

"*As I was saying* … You love music, Jake, even if opera. Well, I love writing, especially fine writing of the kind we get from Martin Amis, micks such as William Trevor, *even* Canada's Alice Munro. For me to continue trying to teach our illiterate non-readers to write, for me to have to sit for hours reading their, uh, *challenged* prose, is the equivalent of emplacing an aluminum garbage can over your opera-loving head and whacking it the whole day through with a heavy chain."

Professor Turnbull then outlined for me that upon his return from a full-year sabbatical in Cornwall he would teach only Modern British literature, only in a series of team-taught graduate seminars with a focus on the allegorical use of animals (no challenge to guess the identity of his chief teaching teammate, who would of course be doing the lioness's share of the work).

"Surely *that* is a subject of some interest to Canadians with their fixation on fauna and flora? And just so you know, Jake, union President Isapoinhkyaki Narwhal—I think that's how one pronounces it—confirms that I have *our* union's unequivocal backing in this—in the event of having to launch a grievance from the bottommost—*you*, Jake—to the toppermost, President Montjoy and the Board of Governors. And next time you talk with LaRoque, Jake, you might whisper to our sensitive Dean that I am in touch, as 'twere, with a number of female grad students who are eager to join a class-action complaint for sexual harassment."

"That's the old Beatles, eh? From their Hamburg salad days."

"Wha—"

I'd nonplussed *him*—victory! "The toppermost of the poppermost. It's what John Lennon would say to his fellow Beatles when they were in the dumps. … A mutually supportive group, the Beatles, that also helped make them a cultural juggernaut. I must remember to tell Crazy Ray."

He watched me bemusedly: "Crazy Ray …?"

I continued wistfully: "Maybe we can learn something after all from popular culture for this island of broken toys we call the Film&WordsWork Pod. I don't mean what our colleagues—present company excepted—are fashioning from pop culture in their courses. I mean …" I didn't know what I meant. What the hell's wrong with me? I worried I was misting up.

"Wha … *Jake?*" John's deeper gaze was propped by a sympathetic little smile. *That's* why I could still feel affection for John Turnbull. He picked up on my wistfulness: "Yes, their Hamburg salad days, very good, Jake. That was when they separated the Beatles from the Sutcliffes and Bests. That was before my time, but my time and Carnaby-Street place still. … Jake, I need this sabbatical." He hung his head in nasal exhalation.

And you shall have it, old friend. Here's what made me love John Turnbull still: our lifetimes were coincidental, our aging sympathies channelled similarly, our nostalgia a shared delusion, our old-man regrets mounting concurrently. He compressed his lips and turned on his considerable heel (three-inches worth, I'd venture, with one inch hidden inside; my heart went further out to him). John paused in the doorway, turned back and half-raised his forefinger … aborted his forming thought and disappeared.

FIVE

MARY AND THE CROW 1

She'd not budged from the residence room's hard chair since sending the email, her first-ever, waiting to see if it would bounce back, then wait forever for an answer. It was stupid to just sit there waiting, she had lots to do. But for now all she could handle was to wait and worry every aspect of the sent email.

Jimmy'd know she'd only just arrived in Ottawa, so she would look desperately lonely. Which she was. But she could trust Jimmy. Couldn't she? The email's tone had been too straightforward informational. She should have been more jokey. Her second-ever university class, "Allegorical Manimals," online only, had provided much material for satire, before the whole system crashed, and she knew nothing, of course, about how to restore connection. There had been a good half-dozen students in 'attendance,' all in their little monitor boxes like the opening of the eternally rerunning *The Brady Bunch* TV show she'd loved as a kid. The professor's big talking head had monopolized attention: "Eden's snake, whom the writer may as well have named *Dick*, is, as 'twere, our original sin of allegorical speciesism" (she'd taken it down verbatim *for* Jimmy).

And the email was too brief, too text-messagey, like she'd forgotten how to write. She *should* have appended the yellow smiling emoji the program kept urging, but when she'd tried it the whole thing looked ... eejitty. It didn't matter anyway; he wouldn't write back, she just knew it. He was with somebody else already. How could he not be? She should have signed "Love" and used the animated pulsing heart emoji. Not likely. But "Your old chum Mary"? *What the fuck!* He'd probably sneer at the loud irony of "chum"! Or miss it entirely ... Yes, Jimmy had got away, mostly from his drunken dad, but he was finished with her too.

Breathing rapidly she opened the desk's middle drawer, took out the Bible and held it high like Moses about to smash the Commandments ... Thought better of it and merely cracked herself on the head, then set the good book aside. She tried slowing her breathing—snatched her stuffed backpack and hurled it at the door; it thumped loudly and dropped to the floor like a shot animal as the hallway echoed emptily. She waited for it, but no voice called to ask if she was all right in there.

What *was* she doing in here? Where was she? ... And Jimmy.

If she stopped monitoring the monitor, an answer would come. As her granny used to say, a watched kettle never boils (Granny McGahern who raved regularly about "born eejits" and "feckin' eejits" and the "eejity world" etc. ... and called her "pet").

So, forcing herself not to watch her little love life boil away, she lay down and stretched out on the bed again, with her feet just short of overhanging, and held her left fist in her right hand at her breastbone, pressing there. He wouldn't answer. Maybe. He would. He was still Jimmy, he had to be, c'mon, it was only a little over a week! Hope for the best … prepare for the worst. Dad wisdom. She *had* hoped for the best, yet here she was per usual: alone and out of place, feeling again like she'd arrived late to a party that was emptying out.

On the last day of high school back in June, with Fred Faucher and his crowd super-stoned (volume at eleven), I went into the alley to the side of the school to say goodbye to Big Al. It was late afternoon, lowering clouds, the sort of sky Mom had always called "the farmer's friend." Jimmy Collins—*Jim*, as he'd been insisting I call him since at least October, but I liked *Jimmy*, name and boy, because it contained *my Jim*—Jimmy had told me the word for that atmosphere: *crepuscular*. We both loved reading and gifted each other new words like treats. I'd said crepuscular sounded like an unseemly growth, it even has *puss* in it. Jimmy liked that but gently mocked, "*Unseemly*, eh?" and pretend-punched my shoulder. But Jimmy had skipped the whole last day of school (something with his drunken father and long-suffering mother), and I missed him. In a little over two months he'd be heading off to Western University in London, not the real London but in southwestern Ontario. I wanted to go there too, but I'd be heading to Ottawa, not the real University of Ottawa but lesser sister uBytown. Dad was so sad, I just couldn't argue with him anymore. He tried to hide it but that made the situation worse. It wasn't that *I* was leaving, it was leaving itself. We'd both already been left. I guess it was my leaving too. Anyway, I was on my own.

I found my spot on the far edge of the alleyway where the bushes helped hide me. There was a depression in the ground which had been molded by and to my bony ass. The dry winter and spring (which Dad was still cursing) had caused the packed earth to turn into velvety dirt fine as sand. Over the past months I'd kicked and heeled an excavation and picked out the stones. The rain that threatened (townies) would never come, another bad joke.

I sat and waited in my brand-new jeans in which, thinking of September entrance to university life, I'd cut two clean holes above the knees. But my fashionable tears looked like clean-cut smiley faces. "Eejit," Jimmy had smiled, using Granny McGahern's word, "they're supposed to look worn, not designed like that." Next morning I'd drawn teeth above my knee in one of the openings and a tongue in the other. Jimmy near shat himself in Chemistry. Adèle and the sluts took it as unneeded further proof that I was "re*tar*ded," as the girls liked to drawl it. But another bonus, my sitting in the alleyway's dusty dirt, as it would artificially age the stiff shining denim.

I didn't have to wait long. Big Al appeared from the brittle bushes a bit farther along and came hopping towards me. I'd not had to call, he'd known I was there, I know he knew, Big Al knows a lot, good and bad, crows are brilliant. I talked to him all the time and he listened. He was big as a chicken, but not squat fat like well-fed hens (mine), streamlined rather, built for flight and fight. Big Al would never fly again. If he'd been a better fighter he'd not have been in such shitty shape. He'd been made a joke, another bad joke, because any bird walking looks comical. Strutting roosters look comical too. Look at Fred Faucher always thinking himself cock of the walk (ha-ha … Okay, Fred's got a good ass on him, it's just that *he's* such an ass).

It was fucking Faucher who had hacked Big Al's wings—with garden shears! I'd heard from my new best friend, *girl*-friend, Naomi, the day after. She phoned and said she was sick about it. Then scolded me again because no one used a landline anymore, I needed to get a real phone (she meant a so-called smart phone, but my stupid dad still wouldn't get me a plan, *as he'd promised*). Next day in the library I'd googled the subject of wing-clipping. The flight feathers could grow back in a year, *if* the clipping had been done correctly. But fucking Faucher had destroyed Big Al's wings and nearly killed him.

It was all my fault. Faucher had done it as payback for my telling him off about the chickens in front of everyone last September, I just knew.

Faucher had always acted like Big Al was his personal property. He had some claim because he and his posse had tamed the crow and named him after an abandoned nearby residential school, Alexander Mackenzie's, which was known as Big Al's. Boys drank there and bragged of having sex with the sluts, but Naomi says it's all hand-jobs (does that count as sex sex?). We'd gone in once and there was human shit inside one of those old desks where the top lifts up, fairly fresh-looking. At our school, Faucher and the posse had lured Big Al with bits of their junk-food lunches tossed first at a distance, then reeled him in, till he was hopping about their feet like a pet. It had been worrying to watch even then.

Over a year they'd taught him to talk, or at least to caw one word: *Fuck.* So that our school, Sacred Heart High, had a mascot, this humongous crow hopping up and down the alleyway looking for Faucher's crowd and cawing "Fuck, fuck, fuck …"

And we're a Catholic school! One still with a few nuns and Brothers teaching. Once, a foreign-missions priest was visiting the school, and Big Al performed outside the classroom window. Our flustered Spanish teacher, Sister Georgina, explained to the deeply frowning man that the barking crow, *el cuervo* (nice touch that), was playing a game of cowboys-and-Indians that the children had taught him ("colonizers and Indigenous peoples," she'd splutteringly corrected), that it was warning a pretend Native child to "duck, duck, duck!" The confused priest had asked why *el cuervo* would call to *un pato*. A long pause, with Sister Georgina blinking like a wonky harrow. Big Al cracked the air articulately: "Fuck, fuck, fuck." The class broke up, Sister Georgina buried her face in her palms, and the priest turned smartly on his well-heeled shoes.

That story immediately became Leitrim Falls legend. Dad said they were still retailing it at Canopy Growth, which was dangerous when the workers had been sampling the product. He said the stoned would bring themselves to near seizure repeatedly calling across the lines, "Un pato! Un pato!" He himself would laugh just telling that story about the story, which was lovely to hear.

But that's the only funny thing in Big Al's story.

The wing-hacking had happened last October, by which time Faucher's gang had grown bored with the idea of a cursing pet crow. I'd managed to befriend Big Al over a mostly lonely September (it took a while for Naomi and me to get tight). I'd tried to un-teach him his sole word. I went to work on *Poe*, which went nowhere nevermore. Then diligently on *Mary*, but by then Big Al would learn no other word. Faucher and posse had succeeded because of their numbers and drilling repetitions of *fuck* over long lunch hours and skipped classes. I'd drift near the alleyway, not daring to go close. I was scared, yes, but equally just disgusted with what the sluts got up to in broad daylight, with their screeching and twerking about—not bumping with the boys but practising on each other!

One morning on his way to an unusual weekday's work at Canopy Growth (we always needed the cash flow), Dad had dropped me off at the mouth of the alleyway on Sime Drive. Faucher had gathered a crowd on the school side of the chain-link fence, posse and sluts pressed against it with claws gripping through its diamond spaces, even some poking beaks, with some troubling additions to the regular gang (semi-sluts and hopeful horny boys). But there'd been only weak tittering when I came along the gauntlet on the alleyway side (with screeching coming only from cunty Adèle Pélletier). I ran up to Big Al, who'd alarmed me at distance for his standing dead still by my place over by the bushes, not even hiding. As I neared I could see he was trembling and the closer I got the worse he looked. Dropped to my knees I saw that blood was dripping continuously from the tips of his wings onto the dusty dirt, then into my hands. Only Faucher stayed to watch when I sat and took the shocked bird onto my lap and, equally to hide my crying, bowed my head against its glistening blue-black neck.

I recognized Jimmy Collins' voice approaching quickly from beyond the fence: "What the *fuck*, Faucher?" Big Al stirred and croaked "Fuh" as weakly as a bird's last word. But I took faint hope from that.

When I'd got up the nerve to glance, there was no one at the fence, no Faucher, no Jimmy, no nothing but the world like a cage. I don't know where Naomi was, though I'm pretty sure it was she who had alerted Jimmy. Morning classes had started, I didn't care. It was October, all the grade twelves were already shitting bricks about exams and university applications (even Faucher, pretending of course, because that retard would be lucky to pass gas safely; he'd have been put *back* a grade if there was any justice in the world, which there isn't). I was alone with a dying crow. … I heard stony crunching, didn't have to look to know they were Jimmy Collins' knees level with my head. He stayed only a minute, said nothing, but before he left I felt his large palm on top of my head—no patting, no tousling, nothing but warmth and, weirdly, strength. I smiled small into Big Al's neck and shivered lovely through my whole body, and felt the good feeling go to my arms and hands and get into Big Al. I still think that could be called a miracle. Or maybe a first touch of love. Certainly my first brush with the real thing, which was miracle enough, I guess.

Big Al was having none of it, reviving some and struggling in what may have become my too-tight hold. So I set him down and backhand-brushed him, who was still too shocked to resist, into the bushes. At least the bleeding had slowed to nothing almost.

When I biked back that evening he let me cradle him. The butchered ends of the wings were crusted over like burnt plastic. But it got late; I still had bedding-down chores so I had to leave Big Al in serious discomfort, if at least seemingly no longer in shock. When I looked back he was pecking at the small pile of chicken feed I'd brought, so I knew he wouldn't die.

The next day I'd heard kids whispering during study period in the library, not about Big Al and me but telling excitedly how Jim Collins had kicked the living shit out of Fred Faucher in a fight that had begun in a murder-dodgeball game in the parking lot of Express Variety. The story fired my courage and I went to the Express hangout at lunch time, though it was way over on Main and I'd never been before. I thought again of Jimmy up against the bigger Faucher, steeled myself, went in and bought a bottle of iced tea. Outside I casually approached the fringe of the posse on pretense of asking the least-threatening slut where she'd bought the fabulous black lipstick. I glanced: Faucher's left ear looked ruby raw and itself freshly crusted where his spiral piercings had torn, and his face—his whole big fucking fat Faucher head—looked like he'd got way too much sun. I contained my joy, overjoyed. But walking away, I couldn't help myself and crowed a loud "*Bock*," and heard the howling behind, and the word *cunt*. Living dangerously, Mary my girl, I congratulated myself. Jim, Jimmy, my Jim.

A couple of weeks ago now, at our end-of-summer parting, Big Al was perched alongside seated me in the alleyway depression, looking kind of comical but for the one black beady eye that gave nothing away. What *does* the world look like when you're seeing it out of two differently focused eyes? What if one side looks lovely and the other all scary? Isn't it bad enough to have to hop about awkwardly without arms, all unbalanced like you might pitch forward onto your face, or beak I guess? Poking about like you're looking for some lost forelegs or something? What *can* the world in front of you look like without binocular vision? How can you see where you're going? When I was little, we had a horse, a Palomino that Dad named "Pal," sometimes "Pal-o'-mine-o." A big golden stallion, just for riding, a rare extravagance, gentle enough but I never got over being scared of his spooky bulbous eyes and jutting mouthful of ivory teeth. When I did finally ride him (forced by Mom), I was in terror that he couldn't see where he was going, just like Big Al. The view's better from the sky? But wouldn't you still have those separate eyes seeing two different worlds way down there? The so-called "birds-eye view" has it all wrong, because instead of seeing the bigger picture, you're likely still dealing with two views that can never agree. ... Though hunting hawks and eagles seem to do all right, predators of course. Faucher.

I had to smile, because Big Al standing there with regrown wings looked like some little professor whose gown dragged (at that time I'd imagined some of my imminent professors might still dress so). He flinched and only half-sidestepped when I reached and transferred him—his light weight always surprised me, like he defied gravity—to my lap. There, he showed nothing, kept his head poised and alert in that prideful pose that I simply adored. Until he stretched his neck and parted his beak:

"*Fuck.*"

"Don't say that, Al, *please*. Say *Mary*. Mary, Mary, Mary ..."

I'd again been trying over the summer to teach him my name. But Big Al would only always telescope his oil-slick-tinted neck as if issuing a call to arms:

"*Fuck.*"

In the library on YouTube I'd watched a documentary about crows, about how smart they are, how they communicate with each other, teach their young and remember across generations. If true, then Big Al must really be retarded. Anyway, I made crows the subject of my public-speaking assignment. Stottle-meyer gave me an A+, but after class she asked me if I knew why some of the girls, Naomi Munroe in particular, had been crying. *I dunno*. Jimmy Collins had smiled small and nodded once when he walked past my desk, tapped my desktop with forefinger. I'd seen sideways that his eyes were oily but he'd not looked embarrassed. That had been my second hint of love.

I pressed Big Al's sides gently—he squirmed uneasily—held him before me and tipped his beak towards mine: "Don't let fucking Faucher fuck with you when I'm gone, Al. Do you hear, don't—"

"*Fuck.*"

I inhaled sharply and screamed at his beady walleyes—"Mary!"—and was instantly ashamed. "Mary, Al," I said resignedly. "Mary Mary Mary."

I set him beside that depression whose dirt was as fine as some wandering moon's, got up and dusted off the cast-iron jeans. Waggled a hopeless forefinger: "I'll see you when I come home, probably not till Thanksgiving, I don't know, depends on how Dad gets along without me. Now stay away from Faucher, *please*, Al. Faucher's a mean—"

"*Fuck.*"

I had to puff through my nose, smile and shake my head. "At least you've got that right." Faucher wasn't going to university, of course; he'd already got a permanent job at Canopy Growth. I'd heard rumours ... okay, Naomi had told me, stories about Faucher and Adèle Pelletier. But can you imagine how dumb that guy is? I mean, after the Covid pandemic with every begging university refusing his tuition money? Had he filled out the applications with a purple crayon? For sure he *was* dumb enough to have put a bun in Adèle's oven.

I had to walk away quickly, eejit that I am, crying over a stupid—

"*Mary.*"

I turned, as bug-eyed as bad TV comedy: "*What?*"

But Big Al never performed on command, spoke only ever on his own terms, which had made Faucher come close to torturing him even before the wing-hacking.

"What did you say, Al?"

"*Fuck.*"

I waited, he waited. He blinked first (if not literally in the one beady black I could see), turned away and commenced hopping towards the bushes, his long strong tail feathers dragging some. So hopeless walking, birds, so graceful flying, which Big Al never would again. *Why not?* The flight feathers had grown out over the past year—look at that tail! Had the supposedly brilliant black bird forgotten how to fly? Or that he could? That's one thing no human can teach you, big boy, and certainly not me. ... *So* clumsy grounded, with only those claws for manipulating things. Imagine if Big Al had tiny arms and hands, like a dinosaur's, or a raccoon's, instead of wings, or, better yet, hands tucked under his wings—what a different life he'd have! It's credible that birds so armed and with hundreds of millions of years of evolution would rule! Especially if they'd grown bigger, and they *did* come from dinosaurs. Maybe at one time a long long time ago the girly arms and hands had been a good evolutionary trade-off for wings—and now Big Al doesn't even get that benefit. Thank you, fucking-Fred-fucking Faucher. If there was any justice in evolution, a man-sized and well-armed Big Al would tear off your fat fucking head and feed it ...

Big Al had come clumsily hopping from under the lowest-hanging bush ... with something in his beak: something pink, which was increasingly defined as he approached, a thing like a ... like a rat fetus? He hopped right on over and dropped it at my feet. I was too weirded-out to do anything but stare. Then I crouched. It was an unborn bird, or partly born, half-hatched, maybe even a baby crow whose egg had been broken open for ... I remembered something else from the YouTube crow show, which I'd omitted from my speech: crows are cannibals. *What on earth was Big Al doing*? Offering me a snack? A last supper together!

It hit me like a manure spreader's first spray of sheep shit. I'd been out here all this time playing I'm just a lonely girl and creating some Disney fantasy movie about my special relation-ship with a crow, which would have some dumb title like *Mary and the Crow*. *Special* is right, you feckin' eejit! You retard! Likely even hoping to draw Jimmy Collins' sympathetic attention. Big Al is an alien creature that eats the chicks of other birds! Even his own! He is as different from me as the pigs and lambs we seasonally send to slaughter!

I turned and ran down the alleyway … and running remembered something else I'd learned: that a tamed crow, like a cat, will sometimes bring dead prey to its owner. The barn cats did so; we had to break Panther of the habit of leaving dead leverets on the back stoop (and once through an open window to the foot of Dad's bed!). Nothing I could find convincingly explained why they did it, though one egghead speculated that the animal was not offering its beloved owner tribute but attempting to teach her how to hunt, so that one day she could look after herself in the big bad world. I picked up speed—

Sudden sound like the dull thump of wind on a window, black wings beating beside me. "Mary, Mary, Mary." He was alongside at about four feet aboveground, my wingman.

I slid to a stop on my heels and he flew on for a space. *Not only my name but Big Al flying?* I was dumbfounded for a spell.

He hopped after me when I shuffled back to stand over the aborted chick. Tiny red ants had already moved in on it. Its beak was moving, whether looking for food or mercy or attempting some curse against the universe—perhaps even trying to make, *if* Big Al's chick, a peeping *fuck?*—I sure didn't know. But I was no longer grossed out. *That's* nature for you too, Mom had always said. I slid my toe next to it and kick-flicked it into the bushes—Big Al hopped backwards. Then just stood still with that one beady black eye on me. What *would* this creature do next?

He permitted me to pick him up and hold him face-to-face.

"What the fuck, Al, you fucking crow you."

The beak in parting, "Fuck … Mary."

Startled I laughed. I can't say, though, that that verbal coupling hadn't been on my mind lately, my burden of pre-university virginity. I'd half-resolved to have a go with Jimmy, not at the abandoned residential school—yuck—but at home in my bed when Dad was working, even the coming Sunday.

I bowed deeply swinging Big Al back between my knees, like when in gym *Mizz* Muscles Miranda makes us throw the medicine ball, and launched him into the darkening yonder ... where he remained aloft—magnificent wings thumping the crepuscular air; he was soon but a shrinking dot. It bore left, kept on, turning, circling ... back? Growing, returning to a clumsy touch-down near me.

"Al, what the fuck?"

"*Fuck.*"

"Mary!"

"*Mary.*"

"Yes! Now this time don't come back, you dumb fucking born-eejit birdbrain! Or Faucher *will* torture you to death when I'm gone!"

I picked him up and again flung away with all the strength within me. I *didn't* imagine what I distantly heard: "Fuck ... Mary." Perhaps with a beady black eye on each word? Maybe bringing them together in a cross-eyed miracle? Ha! This time Big Al continued flapping away like a nun's black habit on a windy day, became a vanishing point in the distant dark.

SIX

PLAGUING JAKE 3: RAPE

From: Sureau Montjoy <smontjoy@ubytown.ca>
     Mon Sept 12 at 9:29
To: Sureau Montjoy
Cc: Sureau Montjoy

(French Version Follows)

Dear Department Leaders, Vice-Deans, Deans, and Vice-Presidents:

As Fall term is now under way, I write you on most urgent university business. To wit:

Training for Senior Administrators

Since these past months and weeks we held a series of mandatory training sessions for senior administrators, including myself and all the University's vice-presidents and deans etc., to enlarge our sensitivities to gender biases in ourselves and others, and systemic especially. I want to acknowledge up front that this initiative was spearheaded by Dr. Jacques LaRoque, Dean of the Faculty of Digital Humanities. Thank you, Jacques!

All personnel of vice-presidential and decanal selection committees, as well as members of all faculty hiring committees, must follow up also to attend similar anti-bias training workshops. These sessions are being expanded in the near future to include all University employees, professors, contract-professors, lecturers, part-time instructors, teaching graduate students, et al. uBytown will work tirelessly to uncover any sexist bias and root it out. That must be the mission of our university today, since how can we learn and begin to teach the pursuit of truth(s) if we know not ourselves, both conscious and unconscious *and* systemically, as participants in a campus of "rape culture," to use Dean LaRoque's ugly and apt expression.

Reaffirming My Commitment

Our work from this day onward going forward will represent only an important beginning, yet as we have been reminded so urgently in recent years, much more remains to be done, and more will be done, much more will, in future. Thus, one of our next steps for the present and immediate future, and sooner than that if possible we trust, will be to announce increased mental health supports for members of our female, minority, 2SLGBTQ+, and non-binary communities, et al.

There is certainly much more to do in these regards, there always will be where I am concerned. Here I wanted simply and modestly to reaffirm *my* commitment to you as **President and Vice-Chancellor of uBytown** to pursuing this needed and eminently just cause with compassion, determination, and a keen sense of our own inadequacy and privileged guilt.

We must stand together to do what is right, or we will all fall together in continuing to do what is wrong. We must band together to fight systemic sexism and reclaim our campus from the clutches of that prime sign of enduring patriarchy and white male privilege—**RAPE.**

To this/these end/ends I am today striking a uBytown committee of investigation, complaint, reporting, rectification, compliancy and restitution, one employing the ugly word itself as acronym and in that way, like Milton's God (or so I have been informed by our Anglo collègues!), bringing good out of evil: **R**ighteous **A**lliance **P**ro **E**quality.

RAPE

If you encounter, see or hear of, any form of sexual harassment (definition to follow), do, please do, report the offender to our **RAPE** committee on un-uBytown sexist activities.

Yours in the pursuit of truths,
Dr. Sureau Montjoy
President and Vice-Chancellor

Jake Flynn continued staring at the screen with crinkled brow and worried eyes, in a sort of bovine stupor, mechanically working his sugar-free gum as might a cudding cow watch the chinked barn board when she senses the cold hands of human need reaching for her teats. Jake thought to delete and then remembered the Borg directive: *Resistance is futile.*

From: Jake Flynn <jflynn@ubytown.ca>
        Mon Sept 12 at 10:00
To: smontjoy@ubytown.ca
Cc: Jacques LaRoque

Dear President and Vice-Chancellor Montjoy,

I write to congratulate you on our **RAPE** initiative, to thank you for it, to assure you that in this endeavour you have the full cooperation of the Film&WordsWork Pod, and to pledge my personal enthusiastic support.

Yours for a safe uBytown campus,
Dr. Jake Flynn, Full Professor and Leader
Film&WordsWork Pod

He read it over in a dull glaze of dissipating self-protection. Clicked SEND. Then himself imagined the cold fingers of self-loathing tightening on his old man's scrotum. As a man's spine compresses with age, his scrotum distends. Was God just to his male creatures? … Craven coward! Unearthly worm!

Despicable insect! Chisel them off with your own teeth and leave them for **RAPE** as a sacrificial offering, *castor canadensis!*

So Jake had no call to resist distraction when finally his mind drifted with his wandering gaze to the right corner of his office, where the windows gave on uBytown's only literal campus, the extensive lawn in front of neighbouring Coriveau Hall. It had been his only change to the Leader's office inherited from Oberon Stangle (when the title was still "Chair"), shifting the Leader's big desk to the right of the doorway, so that his back was to a wall rather than windows, and visitors actually had to come into the middle of the office and turn to face him. Which they did whenever the impulse touched them and would continue doing till he … retired. Ah yes. He smiled recalling again Kafka's story "The Burrow," which John Turnbull had importuned him to read. Sometimes, most of the time, Jake did not like that John knew him so well. But people whom one allows to get close *will* find one out. Sometimes there is just no getting away from it, Herr Franz.

He stood from his desk and moved to stand idly at the corner windows, as he'd been doing more and more, idling. Scattered students, the few, lounged in lush grass in groups of two or three, some isolated individuals, most smoking weed (no one smoked cigarettes anymore, and anyway they'd not be passed back and forth), under the many maples already dying back, and where some camping-out street people were always doing a brisk trade in marijuana. Jake suspected that the street people were tolerated by campus Security because university higher-ups believed their presence conveyed an impression of actual students still attending an actual uBytown in respectable numbers, an illusion of student activity (it would not beggar belief that the two currently flying a Frisbee were being paid to do so).

Jake himself wouldn't have minded a few tokes right then. He sometimes walked in the Coriveau field breathing deeply, hoping for a contact high, which he imagined he sometimes got. But of course he'd given up smoking long ago. Or only in his garage when Jieun wasn't … there. He was proud that he'd long since overcome his debilitating dependency issues. He had. At least he still had that, he had. … Jake sighed too deeply for a man alone and not performing for another, wishing yet again that he wasn't so old. He should never have let himself be cajoled into assuming the Pod Leadership. *Tempus fugit* incrementally. Retirement. Maybe just one more academic year—but with *this* one just beginning!

His gaze dropped to the windowsill, where a dark-green statuette of the plump and laughing Buddha rested behind a potted geranium that could use a drop. The Buddha's fat face gave Jake momentary contentment, but soon troubling puzzlement. He couldn't remember where the *object* came from. A gift from students? One of the many from their many foreign—*International*—students, who had a fetish for gift-giving (fans and useless book marks galore)? From Jieun? Unlikely, highly unlikely, for he'd not forget such a gift, as his wife had never forgotten the time he'd forgotten her birthday (it had fallen on a day when he was only just straightening out from one of his benders). He grew increasingly troubled that he couldn't source the Buddha … In fact, he couldn't envision it having been there before. He'd been increasingly worried over the past year about early-onset Alzheimer's (if it even would be early) and grown more and more anxious about it lately. He picked up the surprisingly weighty statuette. Was it expensive? A touristy thing? What was *he* doing with it? What *would* he do with it? Brow furrowed he hefted then turned it upside down. Its bottom was inscribed: "Your worst enemy is your best teacher. Buddha."

He raised his gaze to the window, past Coriveau's field and maples, drifting up to a clear sky of such a deep navy blue as would relax a rigid grenadier on Parliament Hill. If taken at face value, the Buddha's short statement of pedagogical principle—was it one of those *koans*?—would undermine his whole professorial career—his life.

Jake Flynn was no one's worst enemy. So no one's best teacher? Well, if he allowed it, he *could* see himself as the sneering Dr. Professor Bartholomew von Blüger's *frenemy* (as the kids say, if they still do).

SEVEN

PLAGUING JAKE 4:
DR. PROFESSOR BARTHOLOMEW
VON BLÜGER

And she left you when, Bartholomew?"

I addressed him so not because I'm turgidly formal, far from it. It was that Professor Bartholomew von Blüger would never permit his being diminished to "Bart," though that was what his colleagues called him when he wasn't there. It was that he occasionally even insisted on elongation to "Dr. Professor Bartholomew von Blüger." At least it wasn't "Herr Doktor" (which it *could* well have been for our very own Dr. Strangelove). Truth be told, Bartholomew von Blüger wasn't there even when he was there. To wit.

He answered me with his tagline: "I suppose so." (One could cue a laugh track.)

Which of course made no sense, which he very seldom did make. Bartholomew always paused an uncomfortable length before responding to even the simplest, most direct question (How are you doing, Bartholomew? *Pause*. "I suppose so." Laugh track). I suspect it was because he had to process the whole social situation anew every time he encountered it, with his unkempt head and hairy face held still while his eyes slid about looking for egress. Then he'd come out with *I suppose so*. When there was nothing to be said, Dr. Professor von Blüger, following the advice of one of those scolding German philosophers, supposed so and said nothing.

He had the oddest physiognomy too, Bartholomew, as if he'd been composed of left-over parts lying along the male assembly line in a rush to coffee break. All out of proportion, shortish legs supporting womanish pelvis and long torso, a head shaped like a football held for kick-off, with large flattened ears like tobacco leaves. The spare parts simile approaches literalness in the way his head sat: not as organically atop a neck but as set on a narrow shelf offset from the shoulders, awaiting fixing. Perhaps that way von Blüger could better watch out for himself in the confronting world into which he'd cruelly been thrown. With all that anatomical jigsawness, which would give any normal man a ferocious neurosis, abnormal von Blüger was a body of trouble and, like us all, yet "a parcel of vain strivings tied" (I believe Emerson or Thoreau said something like). *And* for all his unattractiveness of matter and manner, Dr. Professor Bartholomew von Blüger had married seven times—and recently been left by the seventh wife—and he but some fifty years old!

The head slipped forward on its shelf. "Jake, I'm being constantly harassed by HR. My academic freedom is being traduced, nay, violated."

Jesus. "With your permission, Bartholomew, I'll talk to Dean LaRoque again about an emotional leave. But don't get your hopes up."That possibility, the conjunction of von Blüger and rising hopes, was laughably impossible. Besides which, I knew beforehand that the Dean would refuse any such request. I'd said so only to remind Professor von Blüger of the professional responsibilities he was again attempting to shirk. "Okay?"

"I suppose so."

No "Thank you, fearless Leader," from von Blüger of course. If ever there truly was a thankless job, it was being Leader in that land of broken toys and demanding narcissistic children called the Film&WordsWork Pod.

In leaving my office that day Bartholomew left the usual cookie (courtesy of my stopping at Tim's) on the corner of my desk, also per usual for him. Did I mention that he always dressed in black? And that it could well have been the same outfit every day, given the unsavoury air that accompanied von Blüger everywhere?

In point of fact, for a bad year Dean LaRoque had been fielding complaints from students both undergraduate and graduate about Professor von Blüger's condition of hygienic ... Well, he stunk out the classroom, a situation that was exacerbated in the smaller rooms of graduate seminars and was only worsened by the professor's unpredictable dousings in undiluted colognes. I feared it wouldn't be long either before the Dean ascertained for himself the reliability of the other student complaints, those concerning von Blüger's living in his Pod office (Professor Pat Kelly had filed at least one work-conditions grievance through proper union channels; we could expect a resolution in three-to-five years).

In their emails to the Dean, students, grad students almost exclusively (if you don't know the breed, you know nothing of Pod politics, which you shouldn't want to know), itemized for the Dean the various articles of wardrobe stacked on Professor von Blüger's office window sill: the crumpled once-white towels with stiffened fringes, the evidently unwashed socks (ditto), the white jockeys (at least no one essayed *their* condition) crammed like marline calking amidst his ramshackle shelves of magazines and posters, with various decorative bottles of cologne stinking out in olfactory dissonance the even more confined office space. Grad students complained that meetings *in* the good ship von Blüger were impossible, while among themselves they shared the strategy that the only solution was to stand in the doorway and lean backwards into the hallway, hoping in that way for some ventilation. Such disgruntled grad students (not to be all redundant) had progressed to an official petition of protest to the Dean of Graduate Studies. Bartholomew's assigned Teaching Assistant had also lodged, through the part-timers' union, a formal grievance respecting work conditions (the plump boy, with round glasses thick as bottle bottoms slid halfway down his adenoidal honker, was yet another of our insistently declaring gay students, female as well as male, God bless 'em everyone; I couldn't care less, though I respect that it means a great deal to them). In all of these student complaints, I strongly sensed that I, if never mentioned by name or title, was always being implied as incompetent in my Leader's role.

Because Bartholomew von Blüger was in such mounting serious trouble, professional and personal, I had to find a way to help him. But how? Whatever I gently suggested received the reply "I suppose so." (And in my head the laugh track.)

"But surely your most recent wife—*Jasmine*, yes?—surely Jasmine knew that sending half your salary to her folks back in … Haiti, was it? Surely she knew that could not continue as sound household fiscal practice?"

"I suppose so." Absolute zero facial reaction!

But I feared that Bartholomew didn't really know what to suppose anymore. He stood just inside my doorway, refusing to come round and face me, so that I had to continue twisted to the left. He was a colleague who had just received an official request from his Dean for an interview. Jacques LaRoque should not have waited till Bartholomew had covered his Pod office door with an American Confederate flag. He did not have to wait so long to know that our only colleague of German extraction was fast losing his Canadian-born mind. Nowadays, students, and of course grad students especially, will tolerate any and all manner of deviance from the old norms, even encourage and applaud such, but absolutely nothing that leans radically to the politico-cultural right of the old patriarchal norm. Professor von Blüger was not being accused of sexual misconduct, so he was safe with the Dean and President Montjoy that way. But von Blüger's blog-inflected political deviance would have to be dealt with, and von Blüger himself as the expression of it, a professor who had crossed the border from fantasy Gucci fascism into publicly expressing political madness (Bartholomew had recently camped out all night with a militia-suited Confederate-flag-waving few on the steps of the Macdonald Library when it was first rumoured that John A.'s statue was to be violently assaulted with aerosol paint).

But any such process, the course of an official complaint against a tenured professor, takes years: with the initial address of the complaint aimed at discovering a mutually acceptable plan of action/resolution; union-lawyer involvement, with our union being as leftist as Marx on the road to communism at the British Library; drawn-out irresolution; mounting charge and counter-charge, further allegations, as the non-confrontational approach slips away like a snake's skin; with subsequent in-camera hearings and more public hearings taking at least three years (been there with other colleagues). By the end, the original complainants, if undergraduates, have graduated, leaving only the disgruntled grad students (see above: redundancy), half of whom never graduate, most of whom will hang around a Department for a decade before being cut loose into uselessness without the degree. A backroom deal is struck, the union is bought off with some such promise as more day-care spaces and the Professor is suspended with pay (a sabbatical by any other name). The whole process resolves finally in a letter of timorous reprimand for the Professor's permanent record, with the Professor him/herself welcomed back to full workload from the long and well-remunerated absence. By then, such dispositional malcontents will have long been up to something else distasteful, usually with a new spouse in tow, usually a something else loonier than the last. And fresh grad students will have arrived to re-revolutionize the Pod.

I was envisioning just such a stretch of painful administration as I watched Professor von Blüger's stiff back exit through my door as if on an airport's automatic walkway. Much could happen in the meantime, I hopefully thought, including my retirement (an aging boy must dream), with time enough for Bartholomew to recoup some vestige of common sense (it *could* happen; he'd already taken down the Confederate flag). But whatever would be the developments and outcome, a lot of university funds and administrative time would be expended wastefully, including especially mine. In that *mean-time* Film&WordsWork would have no tenured faculty to teach theory, or "pure theory" as von Blüger averred, that field of rabbit-hole mind games demanded by grad students (thus enrollments, therefore money). Such uncontaminated theorizing as Professor von Blüger provided had found most recent form in his graduate seminar "From *Young Werther* to Joyce's

Portrait of the Artist: Taking out the Modern Euro-Trash." And *that's* actually the nearest we come these days to teaching actual literature! (Excepting for my retrograde self.)

With whom, then, does one (this one) most identify, sympathize, and empathize: the occupant of Kafka's "Burrow" or his Gregor Samsa? Or Melville's Bartleby? Or just a Here Comes Every Loser? Answer: all of the above, my beautiful losers (*pace* Leonard Cohen).

EIGHT

PLAGUING JAKE 5:
BACK TO SCHOOL

July wanes like paling interest in a once-hot hobby, and summer lapses into its dog days of dry heat, a withering away everywhere, the dying back. In moderate northern climates, temperature and day-length diminish so gradually as to be imperceptible week-to-week. Jake Flynn always twigs slowly to the approach of mid-August's crisper mornings as a challenge to coffee on the deck, if more alertly to the chillier evenings as a handy excuse for uncorking a second bottle of the after-supper wine (Jieun always contra the additional uncorking, when she still cared), or a brandy, or two ("I'll have yours then!" Jieun would laugh at his standard joke, when she still cared, but even then would not sit on to watch him drink it, and the next one).

Watching from his front porch in this season, Jake will sense when the neighbourhood boys have grown tired of each other's play, picking on one other particularly (he, Jake, had always been that other, the boy from the trashy house). Soon the girls are less and less interested in cupping ears and sharing secrets about some little loser's parents (child Jake's, since he'd been ostracized by the boys). Adult Jake will notice that mid-August's helicopter parents look more and more worn from ever-present children (*his* MIA parents at any time of the year), with lessening energy to monitor, to correct manners, sometimes actually to enter the fray to break up belligerent forming sides. Decent suburban neighbours have grown just that much less tolerant of each other's dogs and street parking that encroaches even six inches into their driveway entrances. Gesturally their behaviour might be imagined as palms being brushed together twice like failing defibrillator pads, as if in signal: *We've had just about all we can handle of fulfilling the promise of another summer, the responsibilities of full-time parenting, and the strains of ever-present neighbourliness.* In the refuge of their backyards adults remain seated longer, languishing in still-warm late-afternoon sunshine, if in uneasy rest amidst tireless mosquitoes that know nothing of an enervated season, that actually get worse in August, that trap themselves in hairy shins and forearms and attack weathered necks needing barbering, plaguing even an old-man's bristly nostrils, making the buzzy best of it before the slap of death. While Plaguing Jake sits alone in shade.

With everywhere turned dry as rusty Mars, Jake wondered seriously: *Is* life finally just one damn thing after another? It seems only yesterday I was fearful turning sixty? Will there never again be anything new and exciting in my life? Not clichéic thrills but promising children, delightful grandchildren? Is there nothing truly new under the old sun? Some fresh learning in this stale schooling my life?

Jake: just when *did* you develop this mental habit of taking a pleasant thought—the lovely late days of the doldrums season, the street scenes of free play—and go all to hell with it? You're the very anti-Beatle for taking happy songs and making them sad. No wonder Doc Chan cautioned after the recent tests, "We'd best watch those serotonin levels, Jake."

So he would essay again, with his ass well cushioned in his habitual front-porch rocker, his long legs crossed at the ankles and heels propping to prevent slippage (and possibly attracting neighbourly attention), his half-mast eyes on the setting sun, his thoughts gathering as if forming a lecture from his reflections (professional hazard for the old professor).

Back-to-school time! Well into it already. The old teacher's vocational, social, and even existential salvation, at whatever school level. Story of our lives: back to school.

Back to school: a prime marker in the rhythm of most lives, *the* marker for teachers and students and young parents, if not recognized as such (thus my professorial expatiation here). Back-to-school is as deeply ingrained in our psyches and culture as any other anniversary, and more than most: marriage, children's birth, Dad's unattended cremation, Christmas, Mom discovered dead on the filthy kitchen linoleum, separation, divorce, and such. From the day school lets out in June, the advertisers try their best to ruin thoughts of September's distant return. But try as they might with their early-July back-to-school 'sales,' even the admen/women can only smudge the scholastic seasonal ritual of go forth and return, our pedagogical excursus-recursus, but never can spoil its true meaningfulness. Per usual, the sellers just make nuisances of themselves in the sacrosanct rhythms of human living and learning.

I suppose, being a professor at a great Canadian university, I should be using the phrase "end of term," and "lets out in April." No matter, the experience is essentially the same whatever the level: it's all still school's-out-forever and then back-to-school, and it happens for all teachers every fall: the elementary school's institutional odour of floor wax and paint, textile redolence of fresh dress, heavier clothing chaffing against the summer's breezy wear, the hopeful styles, hope itself, high school and university students' casing for potential friends and romance/sex, etc. As now.

For me, it's been a first week of wasted time, cooped up in an office after a summer on the porch, still with few post-Plague students bodily attending classes but with the noise of an extended Frosh Week much louder and cruder beginning *three* weeks of welcome. They parade past my office window in the colour-coded T-shirts of their Faculties, shouting the F-word with an abandon I'd not heard since my own student-drinking days (we *were* quieter, I'm sure). But my apprenticing binges then were shared only with other males; these carousing crews are abroad in daylight and equally composed of boys and girls—and all the etceteras! ... Jake old boy, *always* extra careful there these days, you do not want Dean LaRoque up your sexist ass! Regardless, I have often observed in recent decades that the liberated new girls have secured equality (and then some) as most obviously the right to act like bad old boys. Do I show my age in such musings? Very well: being "with it" is not always, or even often, the place to be. There's much to be said for being *without it*.

Dear Jake, what can ail thee, old knight at arms? Is it just that, age, *old* Jake?

I turned sixty-five last April. At one time I'd have been forced to retire then. Now, though I keep threatening retirement, I cannot bring myself to it: I'm just too well paid for doing so little. ("We don't *need* the money, Jake!" Jieun our keeper of the family finances was already crying *five* years ago; no, we don't, but there's something that I do still need more than money. Back-to-school hope? Because I'm hopeless.) Before the mandatory-retirement law changed, we lost many a good colleague with a lot still to offer, stalwarts to my way of thinking about what we're supposed to be doing here in the former Department of English: pursuing truth (don't laugh and I'll happily revise to the plural *truths*). They've not been replaced, that old cohort of mine. We're not hiring. So I must wonder if even this Film&WordsWork gig will survive in a digitalized AI world. We've shrunk by a good half of our one-time full-time tenured complement, which is the reason incompetent I am now serving as Chair of the Department—I mean, *Leader*—of the Film&WordsWork *Pod*. (Good God but there is such a fixation these days on that word, "Leader," truly a fetishizing; you'd think the working world could be all leaders and no followers! Personally I much prefer the role of follower but won't hold my breath for the LinkedIn posting "The Qualities of Good Followership: Flattery, Toadying, Realism.")

I really am so ill-suited for the position of Leader. I must devote all my energies to administration tasks, starting earlier than anyone ever did (9:00) and working much later (4:00), which leaves no time for my own research and writing (ha-ha, I'm joking; as confessed, I'm something of a scholar eunuch). A large portion of the Leader's duties is socializing, with various higher-ups and acting in their service (President, Dean, Vice-Dean, the U's Communications Commissioner, various PR officers), and too much with overly familiar undergraduates and delusional grad students (redundancy). I have always desired only to be left alone to my true vocation: reading, preparing my lectures, teaching. But my very most favourite thing to do is nothing. I reject the industrial production model that distorts all living (*pace* William Morris), and no living more than that of retirees ("Yeah young'un, I may be ninety-nine but I'm still productive!"). Me, I want to retire and produce nothing (hand me down my blanket, help me to my rocker). If you'll excuse my French: fuck your production line. Moreover, I truly am dispositionally anti-social. When I would say so, Jieun would cry, "No you're not, Jake! You just don't suffer fools gladly and you're uncomfortable with small talk." Thank you, dear, when you were so dear. Where are you now, dear, when I need you? … But the expression "anti-social," like the word "coincidental," exists because it does have meaning and applicability to some characters and events. Jake Flynn is *not* just shy; your grandkids' birth dates *could* win you the lottery.

It was for the sake of Pod peace and professorial prosperity, not mine, that I sacrificed my private life and the plan soon to produce nothing for the rest of my life. I believe *that* self-sacrifice has taken a heavy toll, as by definition sacrifice will (see: the crucified Christ). And I suspect that I've not yet paid the full cost. As harbinger, lately my bowels feel like a molten lava ball gathering for eruption. And my thoughts … my thoughts …

NINE

ONLY CONNECT 1

The monitor was full of messages from uBytown Administration, every one boldly titled in upper case: **CANCELLED**. All the in-person courses for the rest of the week, all but Professor Flynn's Canadian Literature I and his seminar in Irish literature. Mary had eyes only for the new email address she'd already memorized which, even without benefit of uppercase bold type, stood out like her own name called by a crow. Her finger slipped off the mouse as she moved to click on the message.

From: Jim Collins <jcollins181@uwo.ca>
Wed Sept 7 at 15:30
To: Mary McGahern
Cc:

Dear Mary,

Email? From the world's last-standing Luddite? ... Great!
We're connected again, as, you'll recall (from the summer
reading assigned by your dad), E.M. Forster advised
(though I don't think E.M. was thinking of email and texting;
you really should get a phone).

Back to school sucks donkey, eh?

Seriously (yes), Mary, I miss you so much already I was
afraid to write first, I didn't know what you'd think of
pathetic me. I am trying, a trying guy (ha-ha). I'm sure the
Ottawa university guys are all over you already and making
me look like the thick hick I am (which is probably why
I began with a learned reference!). I'm sending this in a
hurry, so don't judge my writing (and you are judgemental
about such things!).

Last night, lonely as Aoife, I went out with a few alright
guys. It's still like a zombie town here. We went to some
supposed legendary local bar called the Ceeps. They
got drunk and picked up a couple of drunken sluts (like
themselves, said your sensitive man!). I tried but couldn't
drink a third pissy draft (I miss your dad's homebrew!). I just
got lonelier and lonelier and went back to my single dorm
room and thought about you (like, all the time anyway) and
cried myself to sleep. Is it unmanly of me to admit that?
Let alone say it to you! Ok then, I just sniffled a bit, though
thrice (ha-ha).

Seriously (again): I miss you so much, Mary, and everything

about Leitrim Falls (except my old man, who got even crazier as my departure approached). What I really miss is the work with your dad and seeing you every day, miss it like I've been whisked away by aliens to another planet for observation (no probing please!). This place sucks and I can't see it getting better. Residence stinks, and literally so, like every locker room I've avoided, moldy, cheesy, moldy-cheesy. You don't sound too happy yourself (say more, please). What are we going to do, Mary Mary au contrary? I know we've really only just started university and how important it is, so don't tell me that, please. Just please keep writing, it's my lifeline. You can even call me Jimmy.

Love,
Jim
(comma optional)

Why in God's name had we not done it that last evening at Big Rock? I bet God was disappointed in me.

Breathing shallow, heart knocking, eyes brimming, she leaned in and hugged the oversized monitor, then felt foolish. At the beginning of her last year attending regular school, way back some three years, she'd hesitantly told her mother about a cute boy she'd seen in the other grade ten class, first time for such a revelation, *only* time as it turned out. *He's kinda cute.* Her mother, sicker by the day, had wasted no precious breath: "That's how it works, sweetheart—through the eyes to the heart. That's how it starts." Mom had taken her hand in a kind of supporting way she never had before, softly balancing it, as if this was a big deal.

"The first time I saw your father we were both only fifteen, same age as you are. He was standing in a group of popular kids. I was never popular. It was like I *had* to look at him, then couldn't take my eyes off him. He looked out from the enclosing circle, found me, and smiled slowly. And kept looking. Others might say your father was never much to look at, all hard edges. Me? *I* was amazed that those other kids weren't falling down at his feet. No one had ever seen him as I saw him that day, and I still do. For me those big McGahern blue eyes held all promise."

She closed her own blue-grey eyes, smiled tight-lipped, and squeezed Mary's hand like a shake, then just dropped it and herself off to sleep again.

Towards the end all Mom's talk had been more and more about herself only. Of course the boy *she'd* wanted to talk about turned out to be Jimmy Collins.

TEN

ONLY CONNECT 2

From: Mary McGahern <mmcgahern171@ubytown.ca>
Wed. 7 Sept at 16:00
To: Jim Collins
Cc:

Hi, Jimmy. Blue whale (the world's largest mammal), the best suckee for your back-to-school sucks. But speaking of optional commas, have you ever noticed how people always omit the comma in an address? I'll bet no one did when they wrote real letters. Omitting the comma makes of "Hi" a punning adjective; as in, Jimmy getting wasted at that Ceeps place is 'high.' Same rule as for your "Love Jim" ... I'm starting over. But deleting nothing. I want that to be our rule.

Dear Jimmy,

Sorry but I'm sticking with "Jimmy." I like the way it sounds as Jim + me. And, not to go all insecure-girly possessive, I also like the way it mirrors as "my Jim" (sort of). Does that scare you? I hope not. Or does it make me look needy dyslexic?

I think I'm going to like email, email with you anyway, and very much. (I'm trying to find Naomi Starling's email address. Do you remember she's also in London-not-the-real-London at Fanshawe College in something called a "Hospitality Program"? Funny Naomi, she was already calling it "Fanbelt," because of its reputation as an, uh, "industrial arts college.") Your first email to me was a lifesaver, Jimmy, I don't exaggerate (I won't add "literally"). Maybe a mind-saver would be truer. I would email you every day, twice a day! Only I want our emails to be like letters and not like the people who are always texting each other on phones, even across a table. Remember how Fred Faucher and Adèle Pélletier never looked up from their phones during Stottlemeyer's English class, with the phones held hidden in their crotches? Ok, their laps. I absolutely loathe that habit and hope they all end up with brain tumours or at least severe neck problems, or cancers of the genitals. If Dad hadn't banned all cyber-technology from our house, that image of Fred and Adèle alone would confirm me in the idea of NEVER getting a phone. But for your sake I will think about it, promise. I'll put the pressure on Dad, who *had* promised.

Anyway, I like the idea of our emails as letters ... with time between to think. Do you remember the word *epistolary*?

Stottlemeyer pronounced it strangely, making it sound like a computer with a bladder infection (ha-ha). But it once was a way to write whole novels. In fact, as I learned in my first Canadian literature class, it was the form of the first Canadian—the very first North American novel (suck on that, America!). I know you know things like that, Jimmy, and I know you write well, and I would never text "I M M-T, R U M-T 2?" Remember my 'joke,' that U R M-T would make a good rear licence plate? Dad laughed anyway. But seriously, if we email real letters instead of texting brain farts, then maybe our 'epistolary relationship' will get us through this first term. Or at least to Thanksgiving. Anyway, that's all I can offer for solace, sorry.

You *are* still going home for Thanksgiving, right? Not to get all dictatorial or anything.

But if you were to text me every hour in hieroglyph with emojis, I think I could tolerate it (joke: I refuse to use the fucking emojis this email program is always pushing on me; right here it's suggesting something that looked like the sun getting sodomized, and enjoying it ... I'm disgusting I know). (And in future I'll work at overcoming my new bad mannerism of parenthetical commentary; I order you to do likewise.)

... I miss you so much too much already, Jimmy, and wish only that I'd said it first in my first stupid email. (I hope my stupid second isn't too late.)

Your old chum,
Mary

Love
Mary

Love, (I hope that's ok?)
Mary XXOO (there: the original emojis)

ELEVEN

PLAGUING JAKE 6:
EX-PROFESSORS OBERON STANGLE
AND PHILIP BEST

I was drafted to be Chair during a rough period in the life of the Department (see above: Narcissism of Small Differences). Now-retired Professor Oberon Stangle—who was Chair at the time—had been refusing to offer graduate seminars in his area of specialization: Shakespeare. In those dark days of historical coverage, when an English Department was still an English Department, one not offering courses in Shakespeare would be the equivalent of a studhorse without a cock.

What's worse, Oberon Stangle was our only professor of international reputation. He'd earned his modest rep in part for six books with the esteemed publisher Macmillan UK, six monographs on Elizabethan "city comedy." (Note: mostly unintelligible old plays whose plots were all scam and trickery, stories that looked like high school productions, with characters chasing each other round the stage; and with the action's main trouble resolved by something like a plane crashing into the villain, what we in the business term the *deus ex machina*. A plane? Of course not, way too early for such. Okay then, a high-speed train. The point is, that's how existential threats were removed in those great works of early English drama. But just imagine *that* for plot resolution today! The writer would be hung, or hanged rather—lynched!).

Professor Stangle's dereliction of pedagogical duty (he refused to teach his subject) had been going on for over three years when I assumed the Chair he'd unceremoniously quit. His stubbornness and unreliability were in retaliation for some long-forgotten administrative slight that he and our union characterized as a "grievous professional insult." He'd been refused a third TA for a class of forty-five; but the man was as vain as a young Ali. The Graduate Program is where departmental vanity tries to justify itself, and enrollments had been dropping like the young Ali's opponents, and numbers were what literally counted most when our professors applied for 'research' grants. Without Professor Oberon Stangle offering graduate seminars in Shakespeare, applications to uBytown's graduate English program had hit historical lows.

Oberon, with a high-coloured visage and head-tilt as at permanent offense taken, always wore a green cape that looked like it was made of dyed potato sacking, and on the cocked head a ratty cap like something Sherlock Holmes might sport after a day of coking up. At first meetings with me as newly installed Chair he insisted on a/his small glass of dry sherry, which I'd learned he'd kept in a cupboard under the corner window, and which he would sip throughout the meeting like the stoners over on Coriveau Hall's front lawn their joints. When he would stand to leave, he'd slug what remained.

Professor Oberon Stangle played a character, even a caricature, perhaps one out of his "city comedies," or from a black-and-white comedy set at one of the stauncher Oxford colleges in the mid-nineteenth century.

Also, he was as litigious as a character out of Dickens' *Bleak House*, with his briefs and portfolios etc. In a jiff he could whip up an impressive grievance of some dozen single-spaced pages, and then argue your ears to cauliflower elaborating its nuances, its unexplored points and implications. Thus Oberon Stangle was celebrated locally too, for his years-long complaint against a Religious Studies professor, female, on the floor above him when the Department of English still occupied three old grey houses, a woman who'd introduced courses in "Wicken Studies" and refused on principle to bathe or use deodorant. It was the one time all were relieved when Oberon triumphed. Professor Wicken was golden-handshaked and retired to mind a cauldron somewhere in the bush of one of the smaller islands off Vancouver Island. Oberon came up smelling sweet.

But of course Oberon Stangle was *not* world famous all over Canada for his scholarly-critical work in Elizabethan literature but for his sort-of critical biography *Where Is There a Will?* In it he argued that Shakespeare wasn't really Shakespeare but an anonymous sixteenth-century writer who used the name "Shakespeare." Or perhaps even a collective of young geniuses that together had called itself "Shakespeare," with some purported William Shakespeare being their beard. We heard through the academic grapevine (via the younger John Turnbull, Stangle's lapdog) that the sickbed-bound Northrop Frye, upon hearing of Stangle's book, had rolled his eyes in a petite mal and breathed his last. Apocryphal of course, that story. By no means do I seriously imply a causal relation between Oberon's loopy narrative and the great man's (Frye's) demise. But the voguish book did make Oberon Stangle one of the academic firmament's shooting medium stars, and a small fortune, and so made feasible the early retirement which he'd threatened every time the administration balked him in one application or another. For the years of Stangle's starring turn, our graduate enrollments did increase, and consequently our funding transfers and the success of our applications for tenure and promotion and sabbaticals. And Frye did die.

As newly appointed Chair of the Department of English (still so named at the time), I'd promised colleague contemporaries (the first two Jennifers hired and feminist Pat Kelly mainly, who with me were still hopefully looking to the future, *at the time*) that I would try my darnedest to rid us of Professor Oberon Stangle and secure a tenure-track position for an internationally reputable Shakespearean, even one with postcolonial and feminist approaches to the Bard (*pace* Pat Kelly). I had no idea how I was going to do either, but Professor Stangle was duly called up on my carpet.

He dropped into the comfy guest chair, *requested* and was outfitted with a sherry (from that big bottle he'd left behind; assuming my ignorance he'd again wearily gestured at the cupboard below the window). I remained standing by his chair, my hand on its back, taking advantage of my height. Soon getting the drift of things, he refused to answer any question put to him without the union lawyer present, rejected mild suggestions about offering a graduate seminar in Shakespeare, or setting comprehensive exams in the area, or examining theses (forget supervising), and he was, or at least acted, aghast when I used the phrase "retirement incentive" (which I'd cleared with the then-Dean of the Faculty of Arts). Alarmingly Oberon then refused to budge from the chair until requested counsel was present to bear witness to this continuing professional crime being perpetrated against him. Oh, I tried to end the meeting, summoning up every placating, soothing, coddling, self-demeaning demon that possessed me. Stangle wouldn't budge. He did accept a refill of his sherry. Then he wouldn't talk—till suddenly he stood and commenced shouting, soon screaming at me about all the things I wasn't: a worthy professor, a true scholar, a real man of ... of "parts," yes, that was but one of his many spat archaisms.

To cut to the chase (literally), in the end I scooted behind my desk and called Security saying I was being threatened. Oberon jumped up and followed behind my desk and cocked his surprisingly big fist at me. Security *Emergency*, having already been called by our administrative assistant Peggy Dubois when she heard the shouting (God bless the most competent employee of the Department), was just coming in my door—not to witness Stangle's cocked fist but my gently knocking aside the whole arm.

The grievance brief was prepared that evening (likely during Oberon's après-dinner lip-smacking brandy)—he had now been *assaulted* by a uBytown official—served cyber-wise on the Dean before midnight, and copied widely, inclusive of the union and a few law firms. Stangle secured the services of a real lawyer that time, who negotiated the half-million-dollar golden handshake (three times what the Dean had approved, as for years afterwards he reminded me every time we met). Before we finally got shut of him, ex-Professor Stangle boasted tiresomely of his plan to spend eternity basking somewhere in the Canary Islands. But as far as has subsequently been discovered, he's not written (or at any rate published) a sentence in a decade, and rumours circulated that he'd gone over to the moneyed dark side in Kuwait or Beijing.

The temporarily enriching, pseudo-scholarly vogue of the immortal Bard's true identity passed, it having been consensually concluded that Shakespeare by any other name is Shakespeare. But of course any such literary issue is moot now, as no one ever teaches the miraculous plays and no graduate student has missed the Bard enough to request even a directed-reading course. And Frye, too, remains dead.

So you see better the situation in the higher learning of English literature. You get it: it's all just academic fashion, trends in post-secondary education, vanity of vanities, the small narcissism of smaller narcissisms, that sort of thing. And I do know that it really has ever been thus, things falling apart and the causes thereof: Wordsworth and Coleridge part company over whether poetry is emotion recollected in tranquility or tranquility excited by reason. Freud and Jung couldn't hang over whether dreams were a steam cock or a prophetic wet dream. Lennon and McCartney came to hate the sound of each other's voice. Entropy dictates that there's no going back. See you in court, Jieun.

Which brings me to ex-Professor Philip Best, briefly, promise.

Ex-Professor Oberon Stangle and young ex-Professor Best had a connection (so this is not non sequitur), and not, or not only, what the *ex* prefixes might indicate as per romantically. Inversely like the prolifically publishing Professor Stangle who wouldn't teach his specialty, young Professor Best had published nothing in his ten years with us (the "young" is meant ironically; he was forty when we hired him, which is common enough in academia nowadays); had never given a scholarly paper anywhere to anyone (though he had got in trouble in his first tenure application for listing as "published" in his c.v. handouts to his adoring grad students); had never even reviewed a book (that graveyard of the dying scholar-critic). But a brilliant mind, "a *quality* mind," Professor Stangle had argued mystifyingly, even mystically (since we couldn't very well see into Philip Best's mind and he'd shone forth no written evidence of its brilliance) in Best's favour in our DTPC (Department Tenure and Promotion Committee) when we were composing a response to the failure of Professor Best's first tenure application. Apparently, obviously as far as Stangle was concerned, Best possessed a mind such as Oberon had never encountered in his journeying through extensive fields of fine minds.

Following Professor Best's second refusal of tenure, Professor Stangle looked round challengingly at the DTPC, whose support was wavering. We had convened reluctantly at Stangle's request to plan a more aggressive defence of Professor Best, whose position was about to be terminated (within two-to-three years) by Dean Cheyne and his Faculty Tenure and Promotion Committee on basis of the two-strikes-and-you're-out clause. No one on our committee undermined Oberon's support of Philip, as no one on any university committee ever seriously questions anyone on anything. That's just not the way things get done in academia.

Despite Professor Stangle's championing his cause, in the end we lost Professor Philip Best (who had lied in his most recent cover letter that he was about to sign a contract with the University of Toronto Press, when all he eventually could produce as evidence was a form letter from an Acquisitions Editor saying she was willing to look at his proposed study of "*Temporalia* in *Piers Plowman* and the Aesthetics of Medieval Clock Faces"). What's worse, we permanently lost the tenured position in Early Late-Middle English, which marked the beginning of our shrinkage from thirty-strong to our current Pod of seventeen-weak. It also turned out that Philip Best was both a distant relative of Oberon Stangle and, yes, his sometimes lover. And there *is* something wrong with that, administratively speaking.

But ah those halcyon days of our monthly Department assemblies, when the full complement thirty of us met to settle the Philistines' hash (a Stangle-Turnbull expression), and we were still the Department of English offering the whole historical program of English literature studies from Beowulf to Seamus Heaney. Then, when we were most feeling our elitist culturally empowered oats (my expression), we would worry every comma in every insignificant text we composed like we were Lords and Ladies fretting and squabbling over the quality of the parchment for inscribing the Magna Carta.

"Let's break for tea and scones, or sherry and biscuits, as per your preferences," spaketh Chairman Oberon Stangle.

The tray would be wheeled in by the forever-young Peggy Dubois.

"Refreshed, I think we can now take a vote as to whether we adopt as Departmental style the Oxford comma. Motion?" (This had become a drawn-out issue mainly because our departmental prose style was partial to triples and series in our compound-complex grammatical constructions.)

Our ancient disputes were always of such moment, for we were once an intense illustration of Freud's oft-mentioned (by me, I know) "narcissism of small differences" (I'm not even confident now that it was Freud; it may have been Noam Chomsky on the discourses of late-capitalism, or maybe Robert Stone on the eternal high school that is Hollywood, or even Melania on Donald's dick; it hardly matters, of course, in any sense). Our former Miltonist (now specializing in Religious Texts and the Age of Silent Cinema, with his most recent offering being "Photogenic Jesus: What Silent-Movie Crucifixion Did for Christ's Six Pack"), our Miltonist thought that everything published after 1800 was trash fit only for book clubs, and so he disputed every claim to attention from our Modernist contingent. He now thinks that everything published before 2000 of the Devil's party, and at every Pod meeting he argues that we "chuck our vestigial colonial mindset and get with the program." I've yet to find someone to explain what program he means, but I gather it includes the genre of "adult colouring books."

Let that Academic Lament suffice for now. My head hurts seriously, which could portend migraine and even blackout. For I've arrived again at confronting how useless I am, my complicity in the whole academic farce; I am self-shoved face-to-face with the truth that my whole life has been, and continues, a lie. I needs must (a Stangle locution) break for a few Advil and a nap. Perchance *not* to dream, please, because encroaching memories of childhood—always a bad sign—have been threatening yet greater misery. Anyway, there you have us, more than enough: about me and the contemporary Film&WordsWork Pod, and sundry tenured professors thereof.

TWELVE

THE MYSTERY OF THE MISSING ULYSSES

"D ean LaRoque, Detective Gurmeet is here to see you."

"Detective! Welcome to Digital Humanities! How very *good* of you … to come …"

Over-the-top effusive, she judged. He was still looking past her, she knew why—being a *she* of colour—yet she smiled. "Just doing my job, no call for thanks."

He halted in mid-extension, not of his hand, as handshaking had been carried off forever on the second pandemic's wave, but in his body language he visibly withdrew and shifted down to a whole other persona. "*Are* you now?"

Wow, Detective Gurmeet reflected. As passive-aggressive as a sunning crocodile. Watch your step, Kiri dear.

Thanks to her demure smile only, they managed an awkward rapprochement and left the Dean's unimpressive offices (small, awkwardly arranged). They threaded their way through halls and stairs, crossed a glassed-in bridge like a kid's idea of Lego contiguity, to where an entrance like a door to an airlock bore the amateurish sign **Welcome to Film&WordsWork**. The odd word, the jammed coinage, was another disjunctive addition … though the dean believed it went well with "Digital Humanities."

Detective Kiran Gurmeet, runway model lanky and with a bowl-cut of jet-black hair, was taller than Dean LaRoque by inches, which obviously put him ill-at-ease, and subconsciously might have contributed to their bad beginning. Whatever, standing beside him in the Film&WordsWork foyer she refused to sympathize or slump.

"But the report this morning said the *Department of English*?"

Dean LaRoque sipped air and inflated with it, stretching. "I don't know *who* made that report, but if that's what it said, *that* is a gross, even an egregious, error. Our *former* Department of English has been the Film&WordsWork Pod for the longest time already, since at least two years pre-Plague. BTW, that exercise in discipline nomenclature, which I oversaw, aligned our *former* Department of English with current thinking"—he tittered against his forefinger—"while containing punning reference to the old Romantic poet—"

"I had to ask. I get it already, my partner teaches high school *English*." It was always better to maintain authority: no chumming, not right off anyway. But why restrain with this freely displaying creep?

"Is that right now? A *high school* English teacher? My my."

Yep. Buddy, obvious irony will *not* put me back in my place, wherever you think that is, or should be. LaRoque, LaRoque, LaRoque … Ah yes: *this* is the guy who's been going on in the media about uBytown and 'rape culture.'

"It is *so* refreshing to have a female detective, and, what's more, one of Asian—"

She nodded towards the wall opposite and said, "That's the case that held the missing book then?"

"Yes … why, yes. Quite the antique, I agree, a bit of an eyesore actually, I must apologize. On our homepage you can find a much more reliable current catalogue in PowerPoint of the published works of the entire *Faculty of Digital Humanities*. But not *missing* book, Detective, *stolen*."

She'd signaled nothing about the case's being antique, let alone unattractive. Her Meike would be quite happy to store her abundance of books in such a case … though she'd never be able to reach its top two shelves, Gurmeet smiled to herself. Then caught herself. This Dean had a habit of rhythmically tipping up on his toes. So start over and cut the little man a break, it could help later with the work. It's never been easy being a lanky woman, worse when a teenage girl, let alone one of 'Asian extraction.' Cut it, Kiri.

They stood together in a lobby of bright and shining red and green and yellow plastic chairs and sofas, where the seating formed a border around empty inner space. Perhaps the intended effect had been to create a "fun space to hang between periods of demanding study" (Pod Brochure), but to Detective Gurmeet the foyer or lounge or whatever it was felt about as comfortable as a police line-up. Of course there were no students present, and if there were they'd have to shout at each other across such a space.

Outside the elevator there had been two huge dispensers of antiseptic like hand-pumped water supply, and in the lobby four more which, with the atmosphere of abandonment, created the impression of a kegger party the morning after, or, better yet, of one that had never happened. The loneliness of English

Studies (did she have that right? or was it WordsWork work now?). She knew that the women's washroom would feel like an airport terminal's in the middle of a night of cancelled flights, all empty echo and stony dankness. But you're not at an airport or cleaning up after a party, are you, Kiri? Pay attention. Case the place.

Except for the glass-doored case against the far wall, which displayed brightly coloured book covers, the foyer most truly had the feel of a fast-food restaurant after closing and cleaning up: blindingly garish, scouringly antiseptic, a place for kids and their paranoid parents. Behind protective Plexiglas, an aunt-ish receptionist leaned forward dangling the requisite necklace of reading glasses and scarcely trying to hide that she was spying on them. Detective Gurmeet took mental note of her, though thought the woman's curiosity natural, if obviously frowned upon by the likes of dancing Dean Dweeb, who kept flicking a glance in her direction. Likely he was accustomed to being helped by female executive assistants (a.k.a. secretaries) but only after he'd exhausted his own incompetent means. He'll try to dominate you, Kiri, and he's no idiot—pay attention, Gurmeet! *Case.*

The case was filled with books and ugly scholarly magazines and stapled bundles of print and typescript; its middle shelves displayed CDs and what on nearer inspection looked like thick comic books. Atop the cabinet sat a sign nearly lost in the little space remaining to the ceiling:

SHIELDS
Never Fear When Shields Is near!

The name and motto of the security company were known to Detective Gurmeet, and as one of the better ones, though failed here obviously. Upon nearer inspection she saw that the case actually comprised five pieces in two sections: the top two shelves, were the more genuinely antique portion, with bevelled-glass doors that opened upward, with an oversized keyhole at bottom-centre of the second shelf (so it was the only part that could have been locked). Those two top shelves were an authentic barrister bookcase of dark-brown oak sitting on a four-shelf faux-barrister, likely of IKEA making, pressured pulp and glues, whose glass doors swung sideways. She tried the right door, which opened without resistance.

The topmost shelf was full, but the second had about an eight-inch gap in its middle. Or not a gap but containing a little black book stand, vacant, with the space a bit to either side filled as in the top shelf, with most of the books spine-out and a few displaying front covers. To the empty stand's immediate right sat a yellow slipcase with a brown book protruding an inch or so. Detective Gurmeet was tall enough to read its spine, which, leaning in, she did aloud: "*Finnegans Wake*, by James Joyce." Of course she'd heard of it, but was that a misspelling? *On the supposedly rare book's crinkled spine*? No wonder it was left behind. … Or wouldn't such an error make it even rarer, more valuable?

Without turning she said aside, "Expensive?"

Dean LaRoque raised both hands to his chest and gently templed their fingers for a little apex drumming against each other. "Oh, priceless!" He turned to the receptionist and, thinking himself unseen, raised his eyebrows like a nasal swab had touched his pituitary.

"Actually," responded the pleasant voice from reception, "it was appraised for insurance purposes at fifty thousand dollars?"

"Thank you, Peggy," he drawled while flapping his still-elevated right hand as if in bye-bye to a troubling child. Back to Gurmeet: "As *I* was saying, to we lovers of classic literature—priceless!"

Detective Gurmeet reflected that her English-teacher partner, Meike, was always correcting such over-correcting uses of *we* for *us*, or always corrected *her* anyway, even in company, the bitch. But she refocused on the job and continued peering into the case, observing that one author's name predominated on books and … well, whatever the comics were supposed to be … on display: *John Turnbull*. Note to self. And then remembered the term for the many bundles of stapled printed pages also bearing his name: *offprints* (thank you, Meike). Which would be the name of Commander Prints' handmaiden in Atwood's great novel. Remember to share that one with Meike, she smiled. *Where on earth have you got to, Kiri!*

By this point Dean LaRoque was fairly jigging beside her.

She relieved him: "The missing book was on that stand in the second shelf, of course, which was locked?"

"Yes!" the receptionist called. "The second shelf is *always* locked and was when I came in this morning. I unlocked it, I have the only key, and I locked it again. I shouldn't have touched anything, I know, tampering with evidence, and I'm sorry. But I *was* careful not to touch the glass and other surfaces, and I wore one of the rubber gloves I still have from Plague days."

Detective Gurmeet smiled at her. "How did you get up to it?"

"I had a little stepladder!" she laughed.

"Do you keep it in your office there?"

"No, Angus, Angus Daly, our custodian brought it for me."

"That was all very well done, Peg—Ms. …?"

Self-distracted, Gurmeet had turned away from them both and walked round to where she could enter the space inside the brightly coloured plastic furniture; she came across to where the Dean stood, now with his back to the case. There she did a very odd thing: dipped well down and with both knees tried to move a yellow couch; no go; she then jammed both hands against its plump back equally to no effect, it wouldn't budge. She returned to Dean LaRoque.

"What on earth—"

"Just casing the place," she said offhandedly. "The missing book?"

"Ye-ess, the *stolen* book, *Detective*. Peggy, Peggy Dubois, our sometimes *too*-helpful Administrative Assistant at Film&WordsWork"—he nodded towards the glassed-in reception area—"right away when she arrived this morning noticed that something was amiss, both literally and figuratively, and immediately did the right thing and phoned my off—"

"Thank you, very good. Ms. Dubois, if we could have just a quick word ..." Detective Gurmeet was heading for the reception counter but was beaten to it by a girl who'd stepped from behind the wall where the elevator's door had closed with a dull thump. The receptionist slid her glass window closed and looked with guarded welcome at the young woman, then past her with a smile for Detective Gurmeet, which beamed up as it travelled to Dean LaRoque, and the window was opened again.

The Dean stepped past Detective Gurmeet and, ignoring the hesitant girl, spoke to Peggy Dubois: "*Ms.* Dubois, this is Detective Karen Gurmeet of the Ottawa Police and she has a few questions for you."

The female student said with scant smile, "Good morning, Dean LaRoque."

"Ah ... why *Mary*! Fancy meeting you again so soon!"

Detective Gurmeet was alert to what sounded like a coincidence. She watched, her sharp head poised, only her eyes sliding from one to the other. Dean Dweeb had forgotten all about the crime and her and the receptionist and was grinning only at the girl. That girl, Mary, was a young beauty who, with that height, those legs, those breasts, that face of classic beauty (by Caucasian standards anyway) and those blue eyes, would grow more beautiful over the years and succeed big-time wherever she chose, and easily in what remained unstormed of the patriarchy. Lucky girl, Kiran Gurmeet reflected with inward sigh, because she'd had to fight for every inch of her way up ... She shook it off. As Meike was always correcting her, she mustn't indulge in sentimental second-wave thinking (feminist not pandemic). Truth be told, she had been helped up by various affirmative action initiatives, and more by men, white men, than by women of any colour, and most of all by the mentoring of her first Chief of Police, Frank Thu (also of 'Asian extraction,' Korean).

The Dean edged nearer to the girl. "Today would be a good day for that lunch we promised each other, Mary. One-ish?"

Mary smiled at him, looking slightly downward. "Actually, sir, thank you but I'm here to check again which of my courses are happening in-person. Right now the next is supposed to be 'Canadian Literature: Beginnings to 1920,' with"—she glanced at a paper—"Professor Jake Flynn."

The Dean actually turned out his lower lip. "Ah, Film&WordsWorks' inestimable Leader will have the pleasure of your in-person attendance but not your lowly Dean of Digital Humanities?" His head swung away like a turret, and as tactically. "Peggy, are we *still* offering *that* course? Unless I'm having a senior moment"—he scouted the possibility with flicking fingers, then resettled into his unsubtle irony, emphases, and exclamations—"I *do* believe enrollment these past few years has been slipping, not to say *tanking*, and not least because Leader Flynn *still refuses* to offer the distance-learning option!"

Mary poised herself further and smiled tightly at the Dean before swivelling to the receptionist: "Low enrollments? It won't be cancelled, will it, I sure hope not? By the way, I'm Mary

McGahern," she offered her elbow to the receptionist who, a touch surprised, met it with her own.

And a quick study, thought Detective Gurmeet, as this Mary already knew to address her question to the receptionist before returning to the needy Dean.

"But isn't that *our* literature, Dean LaRoque? I mean, we *are* here in Canada's capital?"

My-my, such a bright young woman, and bold and brave! If only I'd been like that.

But Dean LaRoque ignored or missed Mary's thoughtful questions, partly because his own querying of Peggy Dubois about "distance learning" had sidetracked him to his hobby-horse, which he was already mentally mounting. He figuratively clucked his tongue and dug in the metaphoric spurs.

Because it was Dean LaRoque's ambition to see all the salable buildings at uBytown's valuable downtown property, its "city-centre campus," sold. All but the original building from when uBytown was Bytown College, the gothically quoting, grand-entranced Coriveau Hall that housed his own Dean's office. As the buildings were sold off, he would commence realizing more fully his dream of renewal for the Faculty of Digital Humanities. Which was to make it wholly cyber-accessible only, which (if his ambitions for administrative leadership were realized) would open the way for declaring uBytown Canada's first bilingual university without classrooms or tenured professors—a truly virtual and open-access post-secondary educational experience! He envisioned himself as president and—an ambitious aging boy must dream—vice-chancellor.

The exceptional Coriveau Hall would be retained for recruitment purposes. On the university's website it showed to great advantage, and could be made to look even better in vibrant enhancement, even more like a humanist Luddite's retrograde idea of higher education, which was derived from images of southern American college towns in some splendour-in-the-grass 'classic' movie.

Coriveau's rough stone could be more pronounced digitally, the rougher the better; its trees multiplied and always in full fall colour (Adobe Lightroom); a boy and a girl also of colour, say a Black and an Asian (uBytown's future absolutely depended on registrations from the People's Republic of China), with the two standing atop the broad (broadened) entrance stairs and tossing mortar boards into the air (too dangerous?). And other such collegy stuff.

That was Dean Jacques LaRoque's vision, an as-yet seldom-expressed forward-looking plan that was still resisted by dinosaurs like inconsequential Leader Jake Flynn. *For the present*, resisted. Time and tide were on the Dean's side. ... Perhaps at the base of the broad entrance stairs to Coriveau Hall there could be an infant in stroller, gazing towards the future. Or no, that might be overdoing it. And maybe better that all personnel be female, with none younger-looking than, say, fifteen. Yes. How better to advertise the cyber-campus's transformation of its rape-culture rep?

"Yes," said Peggy Dubois, in full self-possession, if not quite knowing what she was assenting to. She knew well how Dean LaRoque could slip off into his own world in a sort of selfie-phasing-out. She spoke loudly and clearly: "CanLit One still takes place from 11:30 to 12:50. And yes again, Dean LaRoque, it is one of our few remaining offerings without a distance-learning option; in fact, there are only seven exclusively in-person courses still on our Pod's books. Three of the others are also taught by Professor Flynn, 'The Celtic Twilight,' one of our new first-year seminar courses, the only one in fact, and 'CanLit One and Two.' ... Dean LaRoque?"

"Pity … that. Ah, but here comes Leader Flynn now, accompanied by the equally inestimable Professor John Turnbull. Say, Jake, are you really teaching three courses this term, *while* serving as Leader? That's unheard of! Perhaps I could convince the governors to give you remission so as to drop at least one of those two in-person classes, if not both."

Ah, thought Detective Gurmeet, the prolific Turnbull. And this Flynn already sounds like a teacher after my own heart.

Arriving Jake Flynn crowed lowly for obvious irony, "A Faculty Council meeting to which I was not invited?" He had a baritone voice, mellifluously soothing as slipping into REM sleep. "But don't trouble yourself, Jacques: I'll enjoy my teaching just as it is: three courses over *two* terms. We'd never offer the historically consecutive sections of the Canadian survey in the same term!"

Corrected, Dean LaRoque was all business: "You know why we're here, Jake—I mean, Leader Flynn."

"I do, Jacques—I mean, Dean LaRoque."

It was impossible to tell if Professor Flynn had mocked the Dean or simply echoed him. Detective Gurmeet wondered if Flynn himself knew. Complexity. Regardless, she liked him all the more for the possibility.

The short John Turnbull stepped in front of Flynn. So self-conscious of his low stature was he that rocking up on tiptoes was not enough for him: he seemed to be extending his spine and neck, strenuously stretching his whole body, so that his back actually bowed from the effort. Only a gigantically vain short man would display himself so unselfconsciously, unaware that the effort actually drew attention to his low stature. Now he raised his eyebrows too, taking in Mary McGahern appreciatively (as *he'd* be thinking anyway), unabashedly pausing at her chest.

Thought Detective Kiran Gurmeet further: First the creepy Dean and now this sawed-off creep? She was beginning to suspect that what she'd remembered of Dean LaRoque's response to the water-polo players' misdemeanour with the, uh, sex worker—that Bytown University would work tirelessly to eradicate what he called its "rape culture"—might have legs after all.

John Turnbull turned to Dean LaRoque: "Have the police been informed? Or, heaven grant us favour, has the book been found, or recovered?" His colour ran high, he was sweating, and he grinned at Peggy Dubois to offload his inexplicable anxiety: "*You* didn't steal it, did you, Peggy? Ha-ha!"

Only Dean LaRoque laughed, nasally, sounding like a coffeemaker sputtering to a finish.

Hmmm, thought Detective Gurmeet, taking Turnbull's other measure. Hmmm? Welcome to the suspects' list, little man. "You must know a lot about books, Professor Turnbull, you seem to have written half the items in the display case. What can you tell me about the missing book?"

Turnbull's face cringed as if something prickly had also got far up his nostril. "Who is this woman?"

"Uh," said Dean LaRoque, "this is *Detective* Karianne Gurmeet; Detective Gurmeet, Professor John Turnbull."

Not bothering to correct the Dean's mistaking her name, Kiri Gurmeet stepped towards Turnbull and looked down: "Yes, Professor Turnbull?"

As ever, Jake Flynn intervened to draw fire, and as he spoke lowly and oh-so slowly, she relaxed. "It was a first edition of James Joyce's *Ulysses*, published by Shakespeare and Company in Paris in 1922. A rare treasure, Detective, our Department's greatest treasure."

"Oh, come-come now, Jake," said Dean LaRoque. "Surely our *students* deserve that accolade." He grinned at Mary McGahern like a basset hound awaiting a *good boy*. "*And* of course our esteemed professoriate!"

Peggy Dubois smirked and turned slightly away, to her computer monitor, to attempt work.

Jake continued speaking only to Detective Gurmeet: "It came to us long ago, first by way of a Jesuit priest from Dublin, who was visiting his dying cousin in Ottawa, a nun of the St. Joseph's order, an academic, an English scholar and specialist in Modern Irish literature, who'd helped found our English Department. Sister Mary Frances McMullen, a mentor of mine in fact." Leader Flynn paused a moment, as if to acknowledge a sanctity. "Our copy is number eight-eighteen of one thousand, signed by James Joyce himself, simply 'To: Frank McMullen,' mistakenly. Supposedly—"

Detective Gurmeet interrupted: "The great writer made his mistakes, then, as in the spelling of *Finnegans* on the spine of the other book?"

Jake smiled and found an even deeper register for his voice: "He *was* eye-plagued as a blind mole, poor Joyce, but that's not a spelling mistake or typo, Detective, which is not worth going into here. Sister Mary Frances was a professor in the Department of English for some forty years, Chair for some ten of those, ending a good half-century ago, I mean when those terms were still in use."

"Oh, Jake."

Detective Gurmeet helped them all ignore the Dean: "And this nun donated the missing book to the Department of English?"

Dean LaRoque *tsked*.

"Yes," said Jake Flynn. "She bequeathed her precious *Ulysses* to the Department, and not only it but that first edition of *Finnegans Wake* as well. Good old Sister Mary Frances. Rumour had it that Joyce himself was a fan of her critical writing, a rare honour for the genius to bestow on other than those who lavishly praised his work, which she didn't. Our great modern poet, Montreal's A.M. Klein, the first North American to write critically about *Ulysses*, by the way, actually borrowed some from the work of his exceptional McGill graduate student, Mary Frances McMullen. Perhaps it was the fortuitous coincidence—a synchronicity actually if ever there was one—of a Jew and an Irish-Catholic brought together at the *then*-racist, quota-bound McGill U—"

"Thank you, Professor Flynn," Detective Gurmeet said firmly. Dear God, did they all talk like lecturing? "What's the *Ulysses* worth then? As much as the mysteriously spelled *Finnegans Wake*, whose approximate price your receptionist has told me? Why steal the *Ulysses* and leave the more expensive *Finnegans Wake*? Or why not both?"

With opening mouths both Dean LaRoque and John Turnbull made to answer, but Gurmeet snapped, "Professor Flynn?"

"I've heard"—Jake Flynn winked at John Turnbull beside him—"that our first edition of *Ulysses* could fetch a very high price in a rare books auction, and on the black market—not that I understand the criminal trade in rare books, Detective!"

Why wink? Who *did* understand the criminal trade in books? Turnbull?

Dean LaRoque laughed like a mild fit of coughing: "Oh, *come on now*, Jake."

Mary McGahern had been withdrawing incrementally into a corner formed by the end of the reception counter and a jut-out. Kiran Gurmeet smiled at her: "Sorry, Mary, I didn't mean to cut in on you."

Mary smiled weakly at the detective and, if still unsettled and looking to make a graceful exit, had the presence of mind to wonder if she wouldn't enjoy studying Criminology as a second minor instead of History, maybe even as a major, seeing as how English was fast falling apart around her. Detective Gurmeet was much taller than herself, and *so* commanding, without a hint of awkwardness.

John Turnbull pressed: "Detective? ... Yes, as Jake has intimated, I have reason to know that a first edition of Joyce's *Ulysses*, in good condition, mind, numbered and signed by the author, as is ours, could fetch upwards of half-a-million dollars, *USD*. And I want you should know that I know that."

Gurmeet made no attempt to hide her impressed reaction. "Then, gentlemen, and ladies, we are dealing with a most serious felony indeed, grand larceny in fact."

Turnbull held the floor and held forth: "Did *you* know, Jacques, that Joyce, an overrated writer in my humble opinion, as witness the unreadable, not-worth-stealing, *Finnegans Wake*, had wealthy sponsors, patrons actually, so that he enjoyed the creative freedom of being on a version of permanent sabbat—"

Detective Gurmeet began topping his increasing volume: "*Then* such an expensive item as a signed first edition of *Ulysses* should cause a stir, drawing unwanted attention, when it comes on the rare-books market, no?"

"It would," Jake Flynn rumbled. "The poor man."

"Why poor, Professor Flynn? Sounds to me more like he'll be a rich man. *Or* woman. But let's not jump to *any* conclusions."

Leader Flynn looked lost. "I don't know. Yes, not poor literally of course; when and if the thief sells our treasure, he'll make a good penny. I was thinking figuratively: the poor man. Or woman, as you say. To be driven to such crime. And I must say, Detective, that Professor Turnbull could not be more wrong about James Joyce's genius."

Said Turnbull: "An obsessive-compulsive likely dyslexic nutter. Anthony Burgess was bang on calling him *palimpsestuous*. Because a pervert to boot, Joyce. If you'll excuse me, young lady."

Detective Gurmeet could see and hear in his sharply sipped breath and slight trembling of the right hand what disagreeing cost Leader Jake Flynn, and again she liked him all the more. She asked him, "But, Professor Flynn, why is *Ulysses* worth—what?—some *twenty times* what the other ... what *Finnegans Wake* would fetch? Is it the author's signature alone? Or does the typo on the spine lessen the other book's value? I'd thought such errors *increased* it, such as in a rare stamp's or coin's market value."

Dean LaRoque and John Turnbull exchanged blinks of mutual condescension.

Gurmeet took in their reaction and overlooked it. Peggy Dubois was doing much as Gurmeet was: watching the others for clues, if in Peggy's case as prompt to do some service for someone. Jake Flynn continued smiling to himself in a sort of sombre bemusement. John Turnbull, finished whatever he'd carried on about, swelled out his chest and looked too pleased to piss. Dean LaRoque momentarily bowed his brow into his hand, then snapped it away and did his defibrillator-rubbing-of-palms: "Well then! John, I too must take exception to your estimate of *Finnegans Wake*. Any book that could fetch that much dosh ..." Mary McGahern was trying and failing to catch the Leader's eye. She gave up and recommenced edging back towards the elevator.

Kiran Gurmeet said clearly, "Mary?" And held her back. "What do you think of all this, Mary? No damage to the display case, which was locked apparently, yet a half-million-dollar book stolen so easily? Where was Shields, who for my money is one of the best security services?"

Dean LaRoque reddened, a rarity. "Actually, Detective, Shields is no longer actively protecting the case. We have only the sign, an empty signifier, as 'twere." An appreciative snort from Turnbull. "We'd hoped the *appearance* of a security-alarm system would be enough."

Peggy Dubois leaned across the reception counter. "I worried about that right away, too, Detective. But I expect any bad boy—and what are the chances, really, it was a bad girl?—could pick that old lock with a wet noodle. No call to break anything! Though *I* didn't see any scratches around the keyhole."

Mary was breathing rapidly. "Excuse me, Detective, I'm sorry but I have to get to my Canadian Literature class—"

Jake Flynn heard "Canadian Literature" like his own name called to a lifeboat and gently smacked his forehead—"My class!"

"You still have ten minutes, Jake" Dean LaRoque said. "You really should be offering that course via—"

Detective Gurmeet turned from bestowing an appreciative smile on Peggy Dubois. "Mary?" she repeated quietly. She took a step and positioned herself facing Mary with her back to the academic assemblage.

Mary paused her breathing. Took a long one and held it briefly. Exhaled. And smiled genuinely, first round at the self-involved small circle, then beamed it up for Detective Gurmeet, who had slid yet nearer to her, enclosing them in a bubble of two.

Gurmeet asked, "Where are you from, Mary?"

Hearing the banal interrogation begin, the others lost interest and turned to their own concerns: Jake Flynn asked Peggy Dubois where again his Canadian Literature class would be meeting and she, frowning (in puzzlement not irritation), had to search; John Turnbull argued with Dean LaRoque about the "so-called value—whatever your definition—of writing that was a verbal mishmash of multilingual puns"—when he shifted suddenly to lecturing the Dean about revising the qualifications for and duration of full-year sabbatical leaves, since twelve months abroad was hardly time enough to make serious inroads on anything worthwhile—when he noticed past the Dean's elbow Professor Pat Kelly hurrying towards them down the narrow hallway. Or, he observed snidely to himself, was it because she was so stumpy that she appeared to be scuttling? At least he was taller than her. Or *she* rather.

Mary spoke quietly to Detective Gurmeet: "I'm from a farm near Leitrim Falls. I'm not from anywhere else." Here comes the townie condescension, God but she hoped not.

Detective Gurmeet smiled small at the odd locution. "University will be a picnic after that. What's your major, Mary?"

"English, with a minor in Music, and I'm thinking History too, or maybe, well, Criminology?" She blushed, dropped her chin. Where did *that* come from? Criminology? They stood almost eye-to-eye, or had before she dropped her chin.

"That sounds wonderful. But maybe too much. If you're curious about Criminology, I'd be happy to talk with you about it. I happen to have a Master's degree in Criminology, not from here but the University of Ottawa just down the road, where I expect uBytown's Criminology courses would be held too, the two universities have an arrangement. I mean, if you'd like to talk some time."

For the first time since arriving in Ottawa, Mary felt her spirits lift in the way she'd imagined university would affect her. "Thank you, I will. I hope you mean it too."

Mary smiled so surprisingly childlike that Detective Gurmeet, childless, was taken aback. "I do." What presence when her inherent self-confidence surfaces. What a human miracle will be emerging in this young woman over the next year, maybe even in as little as months: a fledgling finding its wings, and finding them powerful, and buoyed by an assured humility that will never leave her. How does she, Detective Kiran Gurmeet, know this instantly? Because she was Mary at one time, if without the looks and innate confidence, but essentially Mary. About the time she met Chief Frank Thu, when he guest-lectured in Criminology 101 and increasingly she'd felt like she'd taken a drug, which she must have taken to have gone up and shaken his hand. But I was never such a miracle as this Mary McGahern ... at least not till I met Meike. I'd like to meet Mary's parents on the farm near ... Leitrim Falls, especially her mother. I'd bet they locked the TV in a closet and banned all devices during hours scheduled for reading and study, the same routine cute Meike had immediately and boldly initiated when they set up house together.

Another professor, female and shorter even than Professor Turnbull, brushed past Mary and herself and joined the conclave at Gurmeet's back, where the discussion instantly heated up:

"Ah, Professor Kelly! I was just telling our eminent Dean here of our plan, supported by the union I might add, to take an at-least twelve-month sabbatical in Cornwall—"

"Colleague Professor Turnbull," interrupted the newcomer in an exaggerated formal voice that nonetheless sounded tinctured with helium, "did I leave, uh, something at your place on the weekend?" There was munchkin playfulness too: "Say, my pink flash drive?"

Detective Gurmeet refocused on Mary, and at this nearer range was confirming her recognition of a true beauty whose smile would one day enslave some lucky man, if it hadn't already. Since she'd determined that she was talking to someone exceptional, she proceeded without risk:

"What do *you* make of all this, Mary, but especially the missing book? Think of it as a first test of your aptitude for Criminology studies." She smiled and tapped Mary's upper arm in an attagirl gesture.

For only a second did Mary wonder if she was being patronised. No, not by this Detective Gurmeet, never; rather she felt an infusion of respect. So she spoke honestly to a stranger for the first time since leaving home: "I have no idea, Detective. I knew there were books worth that much—my father has collected a few, if *nothing* like a first-edition *Ulysses* worth half-a-million dollars, if I heard that correctly—"

"You did."

"Like you, Detective, I'm surprised to find anything that valuable so easily stolen, uh, *presumably* stolen. You'd think they'd at least have a working alarm. So, the *ease* with which it was stolen would first give me pause."

Wow. What is she, eighteen? "Yes, good observation, good memory, well-reasoned and expressed."

Mary blushed, though not as much as before, and she didn't lower her face.

Detective Gurmeet continued: "Do you think the thief will be dumb enough to put the rare book on the market soon?"

"I think criminals are stupid by definition, generally speaking—I mean, that's what this writer Nabokov—I don't mean—"

"I know what you mean, Mary. Criminals *are* basically stupid, too dumb and incompetent to make it by the world's basic rules, Criminology studies have shown it. Don't apologize when you know you're right, Ms. McGahern. ... Just a little advice."

Gurmeet was relieved to see Mary look only momentarily reprimanded, even like she appreciated the ambiguous compliment, and like she took teaching easily in her considerable stride, *and* that she was alert to the irony. Was Dad responsible? Mom? Or both? So she smiled and again gently cuffed Mary's upper arm at the shoulder, cupping it an instant, trailing away and patting near the elbow. Surely that was 'welcome touching'?

Mary's whole body relaxed in welcome. She said, "But I don't think it will come on the rare-book market any time soon. If you want top dollar for your produce, you hold back for as long as you dare. You get the best price for pigs when pork is in short supply. If you can afford to do so, you stay away from the meatpacking plant till pork is at its scarcest. And even hope for some African swine fever." She snickered. "I'm sure none of that makes any sense."

Gurmeet squinted at her. "You're no criminal, Mary."

"What! You suspected *me*? Is *that* what this is about?" She wasn't acting. And she was no shrinking violet.

Detective Gurmeet cautioned herself to go more slowly as she chuckled her companionable best. "I was joking badly there, Mary. I meant only don't pretend to be stupid, whether with me or the boys and men you're going to have to deal with here in the big city, and everywhere. I'm sure you've met enough such already in … Leitrim Falls was it?" She tipped back her head in another quiet laugh that quickly toned down to a warm smile. There, that was more like the way Frank Thu had always corrected her.

It was invitation to share a laugh, Mary knew, so she accepted.

Gurmeet reflected for a moment, watching the lovely face that would soon become more beautiful. "And if you wanted the price of your pigs to increase the maximum, it would help to buy up as many of the neighbouring pigs as you could?"

Poor Mary was fairly lightheaded, feeling now as if she'd been lifted into a space she'd begun to think existed only in her fantasies. She moved to fiddle with her black hair, then thought better of it (something she remembered reading about flirting sluts). Emboldened she said instead, "No farmer I know could afford to do that! But a criminal farmer might poison others' pigs. Or have them stolen and slaughtered and burned somewhere safe. But I've never heard of that happening either, I'm speaking only theoretically, if that's the right word, which it probably isn't. *Speculatively?*"

Gurmeet echoed, "Steal them or have them stolen ..." She reached into her breast pocket, one of many buttoned and zippered on the blue khaki shirt she wore, and handed Mary a card. "Mary, come by for a visit any time you like. In fact, I may well be here for the rest of the day, wherever they put me. Drop back or come down to the station whenever."

Mary closed her fist on the card and, in something of a Spartan salute, actually touched it to her heart. She left for the elevator.

Kiran Gurmeet watched her go. She was aware that she found Mary attractive ... and insisted that the attraction was professional and friendly interest only. She had a partner whom she loved, she loved Meike, for five years now, and thanked God daily (well, most days) that she had her. Regardless, after such a Mary, not much more than a girl, such a self-checkup was not out of order.

Peggy Dubois was speaking to her monitor: "I'm afraid admin has deleted the physical space for your course, Professor Flynn; the classroom you were assigned has been ... *cancelled without explanation?* That's a humongous mistake." She scanned the site efficiently. "The amphitheatre on the first floor is free, why don't you take it? I'll book it now. If you don't mind a little echo during your lectures?"

"Physical space," echoed Dean LaRoque as if a human turd had been floated under his nose. "Such waste, Jake," inhaling deeply in pique.

Professor Flynn betrayed mild alarm: "But how will registered students know we're meeting there imminently? Peggy, please check that the seminar room is still mine for The Celtic Twilight tomorrow evening, please."

"I'll message the class right away." Again she scanned. "Only five students have selected the in-person option for your CanLit Intro One."

"But I didn't offer distance-learning!"

Dean LaRoque blushed scarcely and murmured, "This term there's an improved default setting, one must opt out of the online ..."

Always attracted by the Dean's voice, Peggy had to return to her computer for a flourishing tap on the Enter key—waited—and the forefinger shot up in sign of success. "At least we can be sure you have one student in attendance at the amphitheatre, Professor Flynn: Ms. Mary McGahern here—where'd she go? Not to worry, she'll get the message on her phone."

Jake Flynn fairly flew to the elevator calling, "I'll catch her! She may not have a phone!"

And Peggy Dubois called after him, "And the seminar room *is* still yours, Professor ... Flynn ..."

Pat Kelly had been restless at John Turnbull's side, her pudgy arms slightly akimbo, shifting on her feet like a midget wrestler searching her opponent for a takedown opportunity. She turned her back to Dean LaRoque, knitted her fingers at breastbone and spoke in forced normality: "John, what was all that about an extended sabbatical? When did *I* agree to such an arrangement?" She was suddenly fuming, on the brink of eruption.

"Why, Sunday night, Pat, right around the third bottle of Merlot."

Dean LaRoque assumed that he was being addressed: "Professor Turnbull has provided me some most useful input, Professor Kelly, which, with your permission, I will throughput to the FTPC at our next ..."

John Turnbull said to Professor Kelly's back, "Pat, please, the Dean and I have all but confirmed sabbatical leaves for the two of us. Don't—"

Dean LaRoque frowned confusion, a state apparently stranger to his mug. "Professors, I do not think this the time nor the place for administrative disputation ..."

Detective Gurmeet moved closer to the reception counter and inquired after a private room she could use, telling why she wanted it. "You seem currently to have a surplus of unused rooms, Ms. Dubois."

"Space we have, Detective Gurmeet, and with few to interrupt you. But I'll have to get Leader Flynn's permission before supplying names and contact numbers of faculty and support staff. I'm sure there'll be no problem. There *will* be a problem finding all our professors in their actual offices; you may well already have met all the Film&WordsWork faculty occupying their physical spaces today." She didn't need to flag the last remark with an exaggerated smile. Detective Gurmeet returned a smirk. Peggy continued: "Will Forensics be visiting us, Detective?"

Gurmeet smiled a more intimate, if yet ironic, friendliness: "You've read a few mysteries in your day, Ms. Dubois. Or watched them."

Peggy grinned a broader ironic return: "I do love *reading* a good mystery, Detective, and I do often have time on my hands these days."

Gurmeet's face drew down slightly. "Peggy, you mentioned a key to the case's second shelf. Is there only the one key?"

"Yes, I keep it."

"Where?"

"Well, I have it in my pocket right now, but usually in this drawer." She touched the shallow drawer in the middle of her receptionist's desk.

"How many have access to your office?"

"*My* office? Oh, you mean the secretariat. Let me see. … One custodial worker, Mr. Angus Daly, who's been our maintenance man since before I arrived; Leader Flynn of course; and the Directors of our Undergraduate and Graduate programs, Professors Turnbull and Kelly, whom you've met. That's it. This feels just like a real detective story!"

"Yes, because it is, Peggy." That settled Peggy, and Gurmeet immediately regretted her tone. So said, "Welcome to," and lightened into a mock-horror voice, "the mystery of the missing *Ulysses.*"

"*Stolen,*" piped up the eavesdropping Dean Jacques LaRoque, who'd stood hidden behind Detective Gurmeet.

Gurmeet spoke in an enunciated sternness that only Peggy Dubois could see was put on: "Would Dean LaRoque have had access to the key?"

Peggy balked, then smiled falsely: "No."

"*What key, what key?*" said the Dean, who was answered only by both grinning women's turning away.

THIRTEEN

PLAGUING JAKE 7: PROFESSOR MAKSIM PAVLOV/AMARI ABARA

Professor Maksim Pavlov/Amari Abara was pretty thin when we hired him, which is when he *was* still Maksim Pavlov. Physically impressive at his interview, a handsome man of average height (before the wheelchair) in a glistening grey suit, with shaved head gleaming white as a roll-on, an intelligent brow, and soon expressing himself as if possessed of Cassius' lean-and-hungry look.

Just what we wanted: new blood, new brains, in that old national-historical area of literary studies: British Modernism. But even then we were being pressured to hire for greater diversity, by which was meant a professor of colour, preferably female. The committee hoped that the impressive Dr. Pavlov's heavy Estonian accent would satisfy our virtuous Board of Governors. I mention race without tincture of personal racism, systemic or otherwise (at least I trust and believe so, though I concede that one cannot always know these things about oneself). We were then still a "Department" of twenty-four white people which, since then (ten years ago), has shrunk to seventeen while hiring only one person of colour: an Indian woman (I refer to East Indian, of course).

Maksim Pavlov continues handsome some ten years on, if for the past few as Amari Abara, in a wheelchair, and having put on what I'd estimate eighty pounds. Also, Maksim has gone through various hair styles, first from shaved head to hair, with the first growth being a couple of inches of permed retro-Afro with a comb permanently affixed (like he'd forgotten it there, which I'd come close to pointing out to him once). How explain?

I don't want to insist that Professor Pavlov's adoption of his African identity and name, Amari Abara, was motivated by opportunism and raw ambition. But it was. Within months of his joining us, he sniffed the wind of higher-administrative disappointment over his hiring and began his researches, which amounted to one brief trip to Nairobi following his joining the ancestry site "TheCradle.com," which, having readily sussed out Maksim's desire, told him what he wanted to hear: he had a high percentage of African DNA. Under "Other business," Maksim told our Christmas Pod Consult that some millennia back he had ancestors in Africa, and that he was in fact Afro-Estonian. He had a document to prove it, which he passed around (a heavy-weight vellum thing attesting to the transition, with the pimply embossed stamp "#TheCradle"). Within two years he was tenured, within three promoted to Associate, and within eight was applying for promotion to Full, which wasn't granted the first time but assuredly will be the next (post the wheelchair addendum).

Our professor-briefly-known-as-Maksim-Pavlov does have a daunting gift for the learned, rebarbative gab. Professor Amari

Abara has read everything (it can seem) and does talk engagingly (intimidatingly) about anything. In Gatling bursts, in a constantly mutating accent that sounds most often like Borscht-belt stand-up comedy. Students love him. His attitude in any conversation with colleagues, though, is that of a dug-in soldier defending territory with both hands gripping his nest's machine gun, just a-wasting in panoramic swings all remotely suspicious, suggestively racist comers. When he's not talking, you suspect that Amari's thinking what a fool you are. Or that could just be me. As I used to say only to my Jieun, I never walk away from a chat with Amari but I feel both dumb and dumber. He is *always* proving himself, is Amari Abara, everything is always on the line. So he's a colleague of high maintenance, and I suspect on reliable evidence that his insecurity devolves not from whatever racial insecurities he may suffer but from daddy trouble (a little more a little below). I do sympathize, empathize, whatever, as I have good cause (more below on that too).

Exceptionally well-informed as he is, Amari has, unfortunately, no idea how literary-critical ideas connect, how concepts and insights fit together in a broader, a historically contextualized, perspective, or that such ideas need to be so fitted by the professional critic-scholar. Despite that failure of "the thesis thing," Professor Abara's undergraduate students continue to rate him most highly for "entertainment value" (now an official evaluation category, having at the union's insistence replaced "hotness") and availability. In the tradition of the bachelor academic, all Amari's time is his own to read and research and write, and socialize with students, which means no time for what I think a real life. And students do love Professor Abara for all that he offers: they check the course-evaluation box testifying that they would recommend his courses to friends, though, paradoxically, they also inevitably rank the handsome scholar low for having taught them anything. But a with-it entertaining lecturer? Amari performs, in everything from rapping a synopsis of *Paradise Lost* to staging and recording scenes from *The Rez Sisters* at Audio-Visual in budget-breaking 3-D. What illiterate student wouldn't like that in a university English course?

I very much liked it about Amari that in the middle of his own incessant rap he will stop suddenly and peer at me, his whole visage cringing, as if struck that I might be more than the complacent boob I've been acting. Then, either reassured or not caring, he's off again explaining his idea for a new seminar, and Shylock or Romeo is sellin' da bling to … Oh, forget it, I'd only date and embarrass myself further trying to mock the idiom, and make you wonder whether I am outright racist or just ignorantly systemically so. But Amari's rap is all done in a heavy east-European accent! And I should correct my earlier observation: I guess we do still offer some Shakespeare.

As implied, nowadays there's twice as much Amari as there ever was Maksim, and he now negotiates the conspiring world in a wheelchair and does half as much for Film&WordsWork as when he was half the size. A decade ago the Department could still argue its need for expertise in Anglo-American Modern literature, ideally a hire who'd bring along secondary interests in Culture Studies and (*gasp*) Shakespeare, and, yes, be available to teach writing. Voila Maksim Pavlov! He knew his W.B. Yeats, James Joyce, T.S. Eliot, Virginia Woolf, Gertrude Stein, H.D., Hemingway, W.H. Auden et al.

But over the years, Maksim/Amari has not only grown as flabby as a late-Victorian decadent (see: Oscar Wilde) but also relocated his academic interest to something called "CinePuke" (I seriously do not know what that means; otherwise I'd say so; it might be of Amari's own coinage, like Afro-Estonian; it's likely a play on something else I don't understand). With tenure and promotion to Associate, a militant union (not to be all redundant again), and academic freedom, there was nothing to be done about Professor Abara's field about-face (from W.B. Yeats to CinePuke?); in fact, to have breathed anything but *Alleluia!* at Amari's second radical switcheroo, this one in field expertise, would have been to risk official administration censure of *oneself.* I was reduced to pleading with him to design a course in standard Afro-American Literature, at least. From the look he gave me—much, I imagine, as a sunning croc half-liddedly eyes a careless bunny—I instantly regretted my "at least." By then, Professor Abara was taking instant action in response to anything touching his, uh, race, as sensitive to any such touch as somebody without a skin.

The upshot, though, is that Film&WordsWork not only no longer offers courses or supervises theses in Shakespeare but also in what will likely prove to have been the last period of great English writers, the Anglo-American Modern Period. And *of course* the seminars Professor Abara now offers attract three times as many students as their enrollment ceilings allow. I have seven in my Celtic Twilight first-year seminar, whose ceiling is twenty-five. On Professor Abara's behalf (at his insistence), I am currently petitioning Dean LaRoque to open up for the Winter term another section of his seminar "Traducing Tarantino with Semiotic CinePuke," to be taught by one of Professor Abara's many Ph.D. students. The Dean will agree, of course, though on condition that the course be offered online only and with no enrollment ceiling. Some seminar! Amari will also readily accept those conditions, and likely offer no graded assignments either. All will emerge satisfied.

Everyone but I. *I* will yet again solace my craven soul with thoughts of impending retirement, if in the pricking knowledge that my legacy as Leader will be to have graduated hordes of young people with no idea, for example, of the multifarious pleasures to be had from a close reading of *A Portrait of the Artist as a Young Man* or of Canada's own A.M. Klein's "A Portrait of the Poet as Landscape." Not to get even more lecturesome, but one cannot fully understand the second without the first, yet no one cares anymore to read or teach either, which is what the second laments not long after the ringing declarations of the first. A catch-and-release-22, "release" for the sake of one's sanity.

Equally problematic for me on the personal side of things, Professor Amari Abara doesn't seem prepared to endure any weekend unless late every Friday afternoon, just when I'm packing up work for home, he has cried in my office for a half-hour or so. Most recently I had to strain to hear him through the tissues snatched and bunched in his fist, with the next tissues so clumped together from the proffered box that the dispensing fold had ceased working, as Amari continued pulling them out in pieces anyway and tossing them about like a mad magician plucking broken doves from a packed sleeve.

Amari's current recurrent PTSD? (Yes, uBytown counselling has officially confirmed the diagnosis.) Some counsellor had recently helped him unearth a time when, *supposedly* (I'm sorry but I just cannot trust psychologists; psychiatrists yes, and only because they prescribe tranquilizing medicines), *supposedly* the then-Maksim's father had thrown the two-year-old child off their garage roof, in an attempt to appease Satan (who apparently has nothing better to do). I'd thought of reminding Amari (though it could well have been news to him) of the Oedipus story and how its deep archetypal narrative can destabilize the reliability of anybody's early-childhood memories respecting Mom and Dad. But I knew from experience that counter-narrative wasn't what was wanted for a quicker conclusion to Amari's self-renovating stories and the end of my week.

All that was wanted of old Leader Jake was his nodding away like a bobble-head Oprah.

So I jigged my chair alongside Amari's wheelchair like we were at the start line in some field day for the ambulatory challenged, lay my arm along his meaty back (could he be growing a hump? and a damp one at that?), and brought my whispering lips close to his ear. I spoke in my most foundational voice: "Were you hurt, Amari?"

"Yes, my ankles," he sniffed, then made a snorting effort to pull himself together manfully. "Permanently, as it turns out, though I didn't know it or express it at the time."

"Ah, thus the wheelchair mystery solved!" I caught myself: "I won't breathe a word. But oh such lasting trauma for you, Amari, when you were still little Maksim, I mean, and now of course continuing for the true Amari." I was fucking up. Maybe because *I* happen to suffer from *real* childhood trauma. Oh, I'm not claiming anything as dramatic as having been cast out by Satanic parents from off a roof, just ignored by them in their lengthy binges of full-system gin-rinsing, from before I began remembering.

Amari raised his face and gazed at nothing for too long a spell, perhaps twigging to the gentle irony in some of my responses, though likely not (irony requires at least some outward orientation); given his self-centredness, he was probably peering down in creative reconstruction at some long-ago newly mown lawn. Yes, as he finally said, "And I've had a severe grass-pollen allergy ever since." (I exhaled relief.) "I'd always wondered what—or *who* rather—was to blame for *that*. Now, thanks to regression therapy, I know for a fact."

"I see ... son." I couldn't bring myself to knead his plump shoulder like a cow's liver. "And what about your mother, Amari? Where was Mom throughout this ritualistic abuse?"

"Mom? Stupidly in the driveway *at the front of the garage*. I remember clearly that she was chanting, something in Latin or Armenian, or it could have been a Satanic version of glossolalia. We're still working through that. At least afterwards she gave me chocolate ice-cream with chocolate syrup."

"Afterwards ... of course *afterwards*, that's what matters most, Amari: what we make of the lives we've been dealt."

He sniffed. "No fucking clichés, Jake. Besides our lives aren't poker but solitaire."

"That's very good, Amari, may I use it? ... But what I'm trying to say, poorly I'll admit, is that it could indeed have been worse, Amari. Dad could have thrown you *off* the front end of the garage, and either killed you *or* Mom, or both! Grass and God's own soft earth broke your fall, Amari. Dad intended it that way, even if only subconsciously. Because off the front end of that garage roof and child Amari would have landed on paved driveway, with Mom reflexively ducking. That would likely have killed you, Amari. At best you'd have been severely crippled—not that the weak ankles aren't severe enough."

He frowned a touch. "Do you *think*, Jake?"

That emphatic *think* should have checked me, but not me, because I could not rid myself of the belief that we were talking so seriously about something that had never even come close to happening. "And who knows, maybe have inculcated an allergy to tarmac, even a lifelong reaction to any petroleum-based product. And that's pretty well *everything*, Amari, isn't it? You'd have been allergic to civilization itself! ... Uh, it really could have been worse, I, uh, mean."

He glanced in furrowed confusion, and I had to work *like* the devil to keep my compassionate face on. I should have shut up, but no:

"Mom *loved* you when you were Maksim, Amari."

Okay: he felt and looked calmer. His hunched presence visibly relaxed. But it was past four-thirty and he had to go. A little pissing-off usually worked. "But did you really *remember* that event, Professor Abara? From when you were two years old?"

Uh-oh.

He reinflated and shook me off. "How would you know if she loved me!"

That's always the way, isn't it? Give an inch of sympathy and they'll want the whole tape measure. Offer a course in "Sexting the Modern Transphobic Text" and the class will be picketed either for your presumptive appropriation, or for the glaring absences in your syllabus, or for both and more, much more. Become opportunity for the attention-grabbing of the marginalized. Colleagues have spent years, literally, fighting to salvage what remained of their professional husks after being crushed for hopeful, misguided attempts at inclusivity. One can never do enough, so do as little as possible. Jake wisdom.

But no one listens to the wise old Leader. More and more no one teaches anything identifiable (to me) anymore. The title of every Film&WordsWork course continues to focus on gender/politics/ecology/cinema, and combinations thereof, which is then coupled with all manner of confused subtitular concepts (involving race, gender, class, etc.), with most of those subtitles taking the form 'and the something-or-other text.' "Calling 'Timber!' on *Brokeback Mountain*: Eco-Cinematic Climaxes and the Allyship of the Woody Text." That one is straight from last year's grad-seminar offerings, and I have no idea what any of it means (though I liked the movie).

But our very own uBytown PR team (always a "team") is thrilled to promote such pop riddles to an innocently guilty public. And our students simply *love* such courses. Or so they tell us they *love* them (no student just "likes" in this loudly over-the-top age), for their "relatability," for their "relevance," for their "usefulness," for their "contemporaneity"—all those concepts that entail dismissal of anything cultural that happened before the enthronement of *caring* as the one thing worthy of worship. Even above true *loving*. In my best ambiguous voice I would say to colleagues and the eager Dean, "Then it must be the quality and not the quantity of student *love* that registers with them, because our actual Film&WordsWork registrations are half what they were when we taught the old-fashioned historically based program of English literature. Do you think it could be because these missing young people cling to the idea that English should be about reading and studying great stories and poems and plays?" I'm joking, of course. I would never really say anything like that, neither ironically, nor sardonically, nor satirically, and never seriously.

In my end-of-the-week office, though, I did badly want to say aloud to Professor Abara: 'Amari, I don't really give a red rat's hairy arsehole whether Mom loved you or loathed you. Because, Amari m'boy, I'm already delayed here listening to your recovered-memory bullshit when I should be home and cracking a brew or popping a cork—or just doing nothing! Don't you know that recovered memory was exposed as a scandal some half century ago!' But of course I let him carry on, I even encouraged him, as follows:

"But Amari, your mother *did* love you. Take heart: Achilles made out all right, even after *his* Mom forgot to dip *his* ankle! And please *do* excuse my intruding so clumsily into your personal space, Amari, but you need to hold on to that mother love. *That's* what will keep you *on* that garage roof, Amari, safe in your daddy's arms—keep you from falling into a life's living hell of bad ankles and grass-pollen allergy."

I could feel him reflecting, as he'd gone still in his rippling fatness and scrunched more deeply into his wheelchair, his chin pinched in his left hand.

With misgivings equal to agreeing to change a grandchild's diaper, I again emplaced my right hand on his left shoulder like a sweating ham. "Amari, parents are like kidneys," I said lowering my voice further in sepulchral whisper, believing I was ushering this little ritual to satisfying closure. "As long as you have one functioning, you can lead a normal healthy life. For you that healthier kidney is Mom. But I'm sure that Dad—"

He snapped his head and cranked it sideways to look up at me. "That's good, Jake. You steal that from … What's his name, the racist Haliburton? Or was it from his racist literary progeny Stephen Leacock?"

He compressed his lips, looking for all the world like I'd pulled his soother. I could feel his wet back through the shirt and let my hand slide away none too smoothly. I swear the man's very eyeballs sweat, perhaps from the added fat he now carries.

Pat Kelly pushed my always-ajar door fully open and advanced one small foot—"Oh." Fake surprise. Back leg advanced under her as she held the doorknob and smiled brightly. "Sorry, Amari. Maybe we could talk over the weekend, Jake. Remember: we need to talk about our winter term offerings in Eco-Psychologies. You'd said we could today." She sang it: "I'm gonna need more TA-ays!" And as she turned away she continued as if to herself but really to be heard: "Whoo boys!"

Amari pushed me off and, forgetting his condition (whatever it was), stood. The little happy Buddha statuette fell from his lap to the floor and gaped a crack. *How the hell* … In his pique Amari didn't even notice. But had my Buddha taken on a secret life of his own?

He said, "You pre-arranged with Pat to interrupt us, didn't you, Jake?"

At least he strode out after Pat; at least he whispered "Bitch" before fully disappearing. And at least I could think it was directed at Pat for her, uh, timely intervention.

I shoved the wheelchair out the door and shut it. It was 4:50. I went to the window and was setting down the cracked jade Buddha when it came apart in my hands, split neatly into two smooth pieces, perfectly incising Buddha's button nose. The attractiveness of Coriveau Hall's pastoral front lawn had waned considerably. I felt chilled, as if I were outside after sweating, without a coat and a cold wind blowing. I looked down at the broad grey windowsill in sad bemusement, if weirdly comforted by the schizoid chubby Buddha whose smiling presence I'd noticed only recently. Where *did* you come from, my waylaying friend? Such "senior moments" were beginning to pile up on me. I would ask Peggy if the two pieces could be glued (a pretense, as we both knew she'd do it). But personally I didn't really care about Buddha. If Maksim Pavlov/Amari Abara cared so much as to attempt stealing it, I'd give it to him. But *how* had he wheeled to the window without my noticing? For all I knew, he'd stolen it from somewhere else and forgotten it in my office the preceding Friday. Maybe Professor Abara was a kleptomaniac? … He *had* once been a Modernist. Our rare first-edition, the numbered and signed *Ulysses*? I'll have to inform Detective Gurmeet about Professor Abara, eventually. For the present I remained more worried about John Turnbull's culpability.

FOURTEEN

PLAGUING JAKE 8:
THIS AND THAT

At my age I should never have had an affair, emotional or otherwise. But what we do romantically is seldom governed by what we know to be best for us, never mind for others. Which is to say: it's not from lack of knowledge that people regularly and repeatedly screw up their lives. Forget the integrity of marriage vows, forget the sanctity and necessity of the institution itself, forget it—it just never should have happened. Even viewed from a purely self-centred perspective, it cost me too much, emotionally, nervously, at my advanced age. But it happened during one of my down periods—okay, I was deeply depressed at the time, about the Department of English I'd helped build going all to hell. And as I was feeling my age, dispirited over the transience of things, my own mortality: things falling apart, everything born dying, entropy, what have you. My Catholicism fully lapsed, I'd been contemplating the high possibility that everything was material, that everything would die, and that I would never know the answer to the most basic question of greatest import: Why is there something instead of nothing? In such mind and mood, I made the monstrous mistake of having a few drinks with Pat Kelly late on a Friday afternoon. Pat had been persistent, which, I knew, was motivated by her designated role to persuade me to accept the Department Chair.

Pat was sipping white wine, while I was beering like a would-be bad boy, already on my fourth Coors Lite (more than one beer having become a rarity with reformed me), with Pat making bemused eyes each time I signalled our waitress ("Is it that you find her pretty, Jake?" "Sexy, and her name's Marie." "Jake"). In trying to prove that I was not too old for a younger woman to consider romantically while insisting I was too old for the Chair, I gave Pat my Beatles timeline—"… their first Ed Sullivan appearance"—then recited/sang "If I Fell."

Instead of hearing what I'd wanted her to hear, she suddenly downshifted with downturned face: "Jake, my life is shit. Have I ever said that?" she quickly tried to recover.

"Wha …" I felt my very heart zigzag, and my head clear.

"I'm nearing fifty, Jake, unmarried, no children, no intimate friends."

"We're friends, Pat," I slurred, squeezing her forearm.

"I'm calling you an Uber, Jake."

"Uber-Jake, yes. *Pat*. I've always wondered: is that what they call an androgynous name? I need to know more about such things if I'm going to be Chair."

"Up we go, big boy. You *are* going to be our next *Leader*, Jake, or I'll have you professionally castrated for that crack."

"Castrated crack?"

She laughed. One thing that saves Pat from all the other loud complainers, she appreciates a joke and will tolerate one even about something correctly sacrosanct. And she never raises her voice. And that *is* only one thing, for there is much else in Pat Kelly to admire, to like, and even to love in a non-romantic way. She doesn't care that she's so short (radically unlike John Turnbull in that regard, though it is different for women; for women the big bogey is fat, and I'm sorry to say that Pat was putting on some pounds). She is admirably principled and humane, doesn't expect perfection in the flawed lot of us, demonstrates and encourages decency in all her colleagues. Or let me put it this way: if I were going into a dark alley, I'd want Pat at my back. As she walked out ahead of me, I noticed that her hips had indeed widened since last I'd looked. In a half-drunken swoon I thought: the poor woman, no wonder she's down. It was that—sympathy, compassion, even empathy—started my side of our emotional affair. On her part it had to be pity.

Pat was as bad as her word. She convened a department meeting on her own authority (Director of Graduate Studies), as departmentally we were drifting through an interregnum of leadership. She announced at it that I'd agreed to be interim Chair/Leader, and Dean Cheyne had assured her that the Board of Governors would be receptive to the proposal (anything to replace Oberon Stangle). I'd sat there smiling, failing to remember what had transpired between Pat and me at the campus pub, The Canal. I didn't want Pat defending her pronouncement by publicly referencing my having been alone with her in a bar. It wouldn't look right.

Since my appointment as Chair and titular transition to Leader, people, Department colleagues mostly, have taken to telling me I have a soothing voice. It's an odd compliment, but I'm content with it, though I suspect it's a way of not mentioning such traits as strength, intelligence, and the much-touted mysterious "leadership." Is that why they bring me their troubles, personal as well as professional, my mellifluous voice? Or is it because, lapsed though I am, I have something of the non-threatening Father Confessor about me, a hopeful sounding board of hushed Confessional compassion, prepared to forgive even the worst?

When anyone enters my office, I always come out from behind my new console desk and sit beside him or her on the couch that only the Leader's office has. I sit turned slightly away (non-confrontational, as I'd learned at a uBytown "Leadership Retreat"), elbow on knee and chin pinched in thumb and fore-finger (because I'm so tall that is *not* a comfortable sitting pose to hold for long). If my visitor has taken one of the two chairs, s/he will soon be induced to sidle it up closer to the one I've occupied, hopping it a bit. S/he will soon be holding at her/his mouth like a microphone one of the cookies Jieun used to provide me for these very tête-à-têtes, way back when (now Tim's business). Then the trouble drips, trickles, pours forth, as from some old-time crooner singing a torch song to his/her modified ambitions for professional success. No one but no one ever visits me to offer anything in the way of thanks or praise, or of course to enquire after *my* life and/or work. Lonely indeed lies the head of the Leader.

Our swank desks in our new Digital Humanities Complex (Marshall McLuhan Hall, MMH), which is jammed up against the venerable Coriveau Hall, are at least imposing: big L-shaped affairs in blond finish which take up half the office space. The whole transforming transgenerational Department/

Pod favoured the move into the spanking new steel-and-glass building with its so-called "suites of first-class workspaces" (a.k.a. offices).

Or not all favoured the move, because Pat Kelly complained, of course. Or not so much complained as made satiric fun at every turn. As I may already have observed, Pat is the shortest woman—person—I've ever had continuing dealings with. She has to be less than five foot. If standing and excited about something, she will dance up close to you and, with arms gesticulating, carry on like a mini-version of those balloon figures at car dealerships. Which she did for the whole crew the morning our Film&WordsWork Pod was given a tour of what would be our new digs, which were still under finishing construction, so with everybody wearing the requisite safety helmet.

"Are there any questions?" the bland functionary giving the tour asked.

Into the shivering silence Pat launched, saying that the whole proposed (though actually *fait accompli*) set-up would make everybody look like a secretary—"male as well as female," she chirped in that ironic way people use to pretend they're not obsessed with gender politics when they're obsessing over gender politics. "Perched at our *consoles* with our state-of-the-art computers and multi-function communication devices—a.k.a. *phones*—and War-of-the-World desk lamps, ready to serve the student-body *clientele*" (adding after the proper comedic pause), "which word has actually become more and more *truthier*." She addressed our guide: "Too bad you didn't get some media here, Fred: the public would be tickled to see professors in hard-hats—finally doing some real work!"

Only I laughed, Fred smirked, because he wasn't named Fred. Into the post-laughter silence came a grumbled, "I suppose so."

Unpredictable as a squirrel, contrary as a two-year-old, Pat made no bones about preferring the old grey-painted-brick houses the Department of English occupied at the time (so dilapidated that actual squirrels could be confronted in hallways, with both creatures dodgy about the unnatural meeting). Nobody's *au courant* fashionista, I nonetheless found Pat's complaints hard to support. The old Department had been scattered over three shambling houses built some hundred years ago, redolent of mould and sewer gas, impossible to keep warm or cool. No one could ever locate anyone in timely manner, and it was too easy to hide when need be. You'd think that one such as I would have appreciated those 'shortcomings'. And you'd be right.

But my view of our dispersed Department setup had changed significantly when I moved into administration and frequently needed people. "Significantly"? It amounted to an about-face, a common metamorphosis of rank-and-file soldiers promoted to command. It had immediately struck me as unseemly that the Chair/Leader had always to go looking for Department members for delegated tasks. The last time on such a mission to the last old house, I stood waiting in Dr. Professor Bartholomew von Blüger's office doorway. I looked up in the pause between having asked him if he would serve on our Hospitality Committee and his Lurch-like "I suppose so"—and was shocked to find not a squirrel but a bat hanging upside-down from the door's top trim and staring back at me with more interest than Professor von Blüger. I didn't scream, at least not outwardly.

I'd immediately gone and told Pat Kelly about it, and she said before I could finish the story I'd been polishing along the way, "Did you check Bart's incisors?" I laughed, which only encouraged her. "Or maybe the bat was moving out, couldn't stand the stink?" I toned down to only a compressed-mouth smile, turned and left her too. I'd been hoping to impress on Pat the advantages of our impending move into new Department digs. But of course I wouldn't insist with her (or with anyone).

One of my main goals since accepting the Leadership was to paper over old feuds and to encourage a true collegial atmosphere in Film&WordsWork. Respecting those goals I have failed, as do all. Not my fault. An academic department can best be understood as two things metaphorically: an island of broken toys, and poster children for a conference focused on the narcissism of small differences. Every member, smarter than your average citizen, is also more neurotic than an abused squirrel kit. No one in the real world cares squat about our so-called work. Yet our weirdly bent entelechies bring to any gathering of colleagues such a tiny-mindedness of academic punctilio regarding invisible disputes as would make the Queen's audience-manager blush (see above: the Oxford comma). With my brainy Pod colleagues, the intellect tops all other guidance—the emotions, the heart, intuition, gut, what have you—so that to a man/woman/non-binary they make a mess of their comparatively privileged lives.

And, by the by, I have no other "goals." Well, retirement.

FIFTEEN

PERSONS OF INTEREST 1

L eader Flynn, I hate to interrupt your work, knowing how busy you are preparing for your class and all, but could I please have just a quick word with you?"

Detective Kiran Gurmeet wasn't leaning in Leader Jake Flynn's open door with a hand on the jamb and grinning apologetically: she stood square, tall, and pleasant-faced. She retained respect for university education and still thought that she would like Jake Flynn better the more she knew him, and likely continue to do so whatever the outcome.

"You've rearranged your office furniture." Her grin turned to smile. "I like it, more direct, not to say confrontational." She laughed as she stepped forward.

Jake made his customary move to get up and come round the desk, was in fact already in a crouch when Detective Gurmeet held up her traffic cop's right hand to halt him, and then with both hands pushed on the air to put him back in place. Wrong-footed, he went from a crouching position to uncomfortably trying to stand tall between his chair and the desk.

Recovering, he spoke energetically, with a wide smile on his face as if grandkids were running towards him: "Come in, come in, Detective! Your work here is the most important event in the Department! The *Pod*. And yes, I—or someone—has moved my desk." He looked puzzled. "As for my seminar in"—he squinted at his watch, not digital but analog, and had to play phantom trombone with his wrist—"thirty minutes, don't concern your-self with that one little bit. I've been teaching George Moore for some thirty-five years!" He looked suddenly serious, if mock-serious and meaning to be seen as such: "Not that he's learned anything from me, the tough old Irish nut."

A good act, thought Detective Gurmeet. There would seem to be a lot of Irish in this De—Pod, which was fine by her (as much as Jews, the Irish had always impressed her as a distinctively messed-up-because-messed-with white peoples, thanks to the bully British). Only three professors of colour: an Indigenous woman, an Indian woman, and a Black man, with the Native and Indian being only part-timers. The Pod needed to play representation catch-up, which was likely a challenge for the likes of aging Jake Flynn. Get with the program, Jake: it's justice.

She smiled more warmly, getting over her irritation at having had to postpone these first interviews till today, the day *after* the crime. That was no good, not procedure, no good at all, and Chief Thu had not tempered his disapproval with the usual mutual teasing. Today she should have been moving on to select second interviews. But it had been like trying to herd squirrels yesterday getting the Department—the *Pod*, she reminded herself with less irony, as the dean was touchy about it—the full-time complement of seventeen, plus the maintenance guy, to show up on short notice; that is, getting them *to be at their place of work for a few hours. Christ* … She caught herself from blowing further on the embers of her anger. *And* there were four times the number of part-time professors! —*Whoosh*, a conflagration.

"Do you know Moore, Detective?"

"I'm afraid I don't. But I do know already that you are a modest man, Professor Flynn."

"Professor, yes, but please call me Jake; even my first-year students do, and without being invited to do so! But I'm not modest at all, Detective Gurmeet. Truth be told, I'm so vain as to crave a reputation for modesty." He stared without giving much away.

She grinned and shook her head: What an act. "You've used that line before, haven't you … Jake? And rightly so, it's a good one, I'll have to tell my partner Meike. What do they call that word trick, a *paradox*?"

Jake couldn't hide his vain pleasure. "I'm sure I wouldn't know. But our little talk here is *not* confidential?"

"It is, of course, for now. My partner is a high school English teacher, is all; I'd meant only to compliment your wit."

"A high school English teacher, very good; then I can assume the two of you share an interest in literature? Ask him about—"

"*Her*. But I don't want to waste any more—"

"Of course, very sorry. I was only going to say then that I think you and she would get great pleasure from reading Moore's *The Untilled Field*, a lovely little book of connected stories about rural Ireland at the end of the nineteenth century, which I *am* off to teach soon." (She thinks: He plays the fool yet is nobody's fool, a delicate balancing act that he's very good at.) "A little book, yes, but a big book too, in itself as good as Turgenev's *A Sportsman's Sketches*—do you know the Russian? ... No?—and also highly significant for—though this is something of a pet theory—for its influence on James Joyce himself and the first great short story cycle of the twentieth century, *Dubliners*. I expect you do know *it*? Or stories *from* it?" Professor Flynn was sweating and grinning in a way that would have frightened anyone's grandkids. His academic hobbyhorse had bucked them both into a ditch of discomfort. *Control yourself, Jake.*

Detective Gurmeet blinked first. For Christ's sake, where did this go wrong so quickly? Steadying herself from his possibly intentional attempt to wrong-foot her, she could say only "Yes, well ..." And they both waited out another awkward silence. Till again she was the one to continue: "This will take no more than fifteen minutes ... Jake, I promise." Something galloped to the rescue. "But James Joyce again, eh? I've never read him at all, but is *Dubliners* more important than the two books you had in the display case?" Whew, back on track.

"Detective, my time is your time, and we have all the time you need. Please have a seat." They sat, both relieved. "Now, we really do have all the time in the world. Business, the business of studying great books, has been very slow for years now. As for the comparative merits of Joyce's fiction, it's said that he wrote masterpieces only, four of them." He found his more natural smile: "I wouldn't argue with that estimate."

"You know him well then?"

"I've taught *him* too forever." Something clicked in Jake. "But only *Dubliners* and *A Portrait of the Artist as a Young Man*. I don't have the brains for *Ulysses*. Now, our Professor John Turnbull, whom you met and heard yesterday, *he* used to absolutely *love* that book"—he paused—"before going over to the dark side of a cultural studies approach to literature."

Jake smiled tight-lipped and again waited. Got nothing but blank patience from Gurmeet. While he'd been speaking, she had taken in his desk: compulsively ordered; even while talking he was linking up items, the pen and pencil cup just here, the papers squared, the lamp turned a millimetre—then actually nudging the desk to some fancied better position. Which made memorable the few new-looking ring-stains from coffee mugs, or glasses … or a bottle? She surreptitiously checked the shelves and windowsill; no more evidence.

He again tromboned his wrist and took in the time. "And anyone who works on *Finnegans Wake* develops a brain too addled to communicate sense to the likes of me and you! … Am I making any sense to you, Detective Gurmeet? We professors tend to forget that the real world doesn't give a red rat's bum about literature anymore. If you'll pardon my poetry."

Yes, she could like Jake Flynn. "*Kiran*, please, Jake. I have noticed the situation around campus: obviously your *business* has never fully recovered from what many are now calling the *Plague*, has it? That must worry a devoted teacher like yourself, one of the few who truly teaches an appreciation of reading—a *love* of reading and study; I mean, going from what you've said already. Meike, my partner, moans endlessly about the decline in reading and writing abilities. She says it's because *her* high school colleagues not only don't care either about reading and writing but that they themselves don't read and can't write for beans. So what can the high schools be sending *you*?"

Jake felt the shift he never liked, a sort of psychic slippage that no one would notice, because his controlled face was an old instrument he played with virtuosity. The shift was always triggered by a different kind of person's, a nobody's fool's, insinuating insistence that he be serious, speak from his true self, that he, as the kids say (or at least used to say), *get real*. And the shift was always precursor to uncontrollable trouble, with a capital T, a Trouble he could never identify or anticipate and so could do nothing about, like migraine, like black-out. What's worse, when the Trouble occurred, he couldn't remember it next day, like the day after when he used to binge drink, only now the cause was likely senility, its onset (no, not "early onset" anymore), the dreaded Alzheimer's. Jieun used to scout that notion, his number-one fear, as did Dr. Chan dismiss his fear with a few simple tests. Okay. Then what is it?

"Retire, Jake," Jieun had said oh-so easily. "The English Department you joined thirty years ago, where everybody shared the mission of reading and studying and writing about the best that has been written in English, that world no longer exists in your *Pod*, dear. And it's driving you crazy. You're your own ghost, Jake, vainly haunting a house where the new inhabitants don't believe in the spirit world." He'd smiled eagerly, sat forward and said, "Jieun dear, that's very good! Are you thinking of the old houses that used to contain the English Department? The best metaphors begin in material reality, Coleridge concurs. Remember when we had *two* display cases full of real ..." She'd slammed out of his study.

Sometimes, though, if rarely in recent years, the psychic shift triggered by such rare encounters as with a Detective Kiran Gurmeet *could* still make him get real.

"Thank you, Detective. I can see that you really *are* the great detective my quick googling revealed—oops!" Detective Gurmeet merely blinked modest acknowledgment. "The business of teaching English Literature—now the business of Film&WordsWork—is *all* business nowadays. Perhaps it was ever thus, but students *and* professors don't even pretend to care anymore about reading and studying *the best that has been thought and written*, as your old Victorian physician of the age

Matthew Arnold prescribed for what ails us more and more. Oh, I don't fool myself, *Kiran*—apologies if I've not got that right."

"You have it right." Fascinating, complex. Here was the kind of person she'd hoped to deal with more often in her work, but hadn't. Usually it's some dumb punk—of whatever age!—without the sense to know there are surveillance cameras everywhere. Jake Flynn was a complex suspect, and she prayed he wouldn't prove just another fucked-up criminal. But *was* he really a suspect, given the carnival of candidates coming into focus?

"I just soldier on, Kiran. If there were any honesty or integrity left in higher education, uBytown would have cancelled its classes till professors and students could meet again in real classrooms, in a true atmosphere of lecture, response, and discussion. Not this wholesale, wholly meaningless *distant learning*, which was promised as temporary and has become *the* platform, because the sky's the limit on enrollment. You'll thank me for not spitting, Detective." He paused, leaned slightly forward, his face a grotesque mask, and extended his right hand toward her, rubbing thumb and first two fingers like a tailor taking the texture of questionable cloth. "It's all about the money, Detective, as I suspect you do already know." He blew air. "As my Jieun used to say, it's fitting that the campus now looks like a ghost town."

"Used to? Your wife has also gone over to the dark side?"

Jake smiled blankly. "I said that? Don't tell her." And grinned.

But Kiran Gurmeet was feeling a sort of creeping apoplexy, or at least an arrested startlement, at the surprise of this brutally honest speech from the Department Chair—or Pod Leader, whatever. Yet still she was feeling confirmed in her expectation of coming to like him, more and more, as he revealed his truer character more and more. Unfortunately right now she needed to move him away from what obviously occupied him so deeply, disturbingly, and towards *her* present purpose. So she smiled small and nodded, hurrying towards a sighted bridge:

"Yes, your receptionist kindly supplied me with the current Film&WordsWork course catalogue while I was watching Forensics get started on the bookcase. They'll be finished soon, having found nothing, I suspect. But with the lone exception of your courses, Professor, I hardly recognized anything, or even knew what the subject was. It's like everyone is teaching the same thing: eco-this and toxic-that, the first *not* about nature and the second not about real poisons, right? All racialized and feminist and patriarchal and, well, no offense but a lot of it sounds more like Sociology or Political Science than English Literature. And can you or anyone enlighten me as to what is meant by"—she read from an iPad—"Sick Or-Well: All Al-Gorical Pig Shite"?

Jake opened his mouth to answer and opine ... clamped it and dropped his head in mock-shame. He looked up at her from under, mealy-mouthed; she sputtered, and they shared a real laugh that met like clinked mugs of first beers.

She was first to compose herself. "It's a play on George Orwell, right? *Animal Farm*? At least I know that much, and only because Meike regularly teaches it. And another play on *Al Gore*? The former vice-president of the United States, now the eco-warrior? I still don't get that part. But making fun of Orwell? Didn't *he* do enough either for your tinpot Marxist Professor Turnbull? I'm right about him, right?"

"I'm afraid there you'd have to look to Professor Turnbull himself for enlightenment. He's better on *Ulysses* too—or he was, have I said that? As you heard yesterday, he still can't forgive

Joyce for *Finnegans Wake*, yet his course titles—and *all our course titles* are similarly guilty, as you've just observed—are really just a poor professor's version of Joyce's brilliant multi-lingual punning."

She still needed to make something clear, which had been her reason for interrupting his prep time. "I like you, Professor Flynn, and I like you as Jake too. As said, you're the only one teaching anything I recognize in a way I know I'd like. Do all English—I mean Film&WordsWork—professors now hate teaching literature *as* literature? Are *they* the ones who gave up on it, and that attitude trickled down? Preferred self-importance in service to some social-justice-warrior revolution?

"My point is, Professor Flynn, what are students learning today? What are they not learning? History, context, the very continuity we all need in our lives, and never more than nowadays? They don't get to read and think about works that will give them pleasure and awe them? I noticed that even *Shakespeare* is persona non grata *in your English program*. Is it any wonder the kids stay away from your, uh, *Pod* in droves? I mean, Jake, you don't even *have* a Faculty of Arts anymore. uBytown administration acts embarrassed by the whole concept of humanities, never mind the arts. No wonder it's still like a ghost town out there. ... But of course, of course, as you say: it's all about the money. As if that excuses anything. The student-*client* calls the shots, right? The arsehole wags the tail that signals Rover and his pack that we're all *feeling good about ourselves* in our shitty ignorance. That's what counts, right? *Comfortable* students in their safe spaces. With *counts* being the operative word."

"That is incredibly good, Kiran, a real *apologia* that no one hereabouts would ever dare utter publicly, because no one believes anything anymore. If asked to defend what they're doing, they'd get all tongue-tied over what we"—here he minced—"*mean* by *good* and *literature* and, heaven forbid, *best*. Does continuing as old Jake Flynn teaches make *the planet* 'better'? Personally, Detective, I wouldn't argue with you, if humbly speaking only with your complimenting my own rearguard contribution to the good fight. You see, Kiran, I *am* vain about being humble."

She wouldn't lighten up. "Okay, the Plague devastated every budget, destroying everything from your grandkids' lemonade stand to Canada's fiscal future for decades to come, if we *ever* come back. So what chance a real English literature program could revive? None, that's what. But I bet a teacher like you, Jake, *was* in the rearguard position long before the pandemics. Don't get me wrong: I'm not saying that we don't need English courses with works by Indigenous peoples and whatever colours and orientations you like. I'm not, of course. I mean, *look at me*? It's just that, well—and this is from my Meike, who always inserts some LGBTQ reading into her teaching—it's that you've thrown out the tub with the baby in it, and all that's left is murky water running madly off in all directions."

"Hey, that's Leacock!"

"It is? Meike said it was Mark Twain."

Jake, deflated after such pumping up on a simpatico sensibility, actually exhausted his breath again and sat back in his ergonomic chair. He found his smile of genuine wise tolerance (he'd thought it was gone forever).

"Remember our prime minister back in early 2020 at the height of the first pandemic? The un-barbered bushy-headed Justin Trudeau, parading up and down Parliament Hill daily with a bushel basket of billion-dollar bills, casting fistfuls left and right, if mostly left? It was overdone, overkill, and everyone with the same hair-trigger excuse—emergency response to COVID-19 *pandemic*! But you're right, Kiran, we will never recover to what we were, not only the university but economically speaking, because eventually our dollars will be as worthless as pre-war Deutsche marks or Greece's old drachmas. And only true economic affluence makes everything possible, including the teaching of English literature, not this"—he paused to peer at her, confident he knew his woman—"this fucking student-experience-friendly Film&WordsWork bullshit, just give us your tuition fees, if you'll pardon my Irish, Detective Gurmeet."

She laughed. "I will, Jake. But good old young Justin, eh? Trudeau the younger, he just wasn't up to it, any of it really." It was her turn to peer at him. Then confidently: "Daddy's name, Mommy's brain."

Jake hooted with relish, which he'd not done in forever, leaned farther forward in an almost Japanese bow and clapped his hands once, which he once did all the time in appreciation. "Very, very good, that, Kiran. In return, here's my line on Justin Trudeau, the only decent joke I've made in years: *Endless deficits growing exponentially, if necessary, but not necessarily endless deficits growing exponentially.*" He peered again, waited, she didn't respond. "It refers to our longest-serving Liberal prime minister ever, the shape-shifting William Lyon Mackenzie King? You know, what he said during the Second World War to appease draft-resistant French-Canadians: *Conscription, if necessary, but not necessarily conscription?*" He watched again. She didn't know. "Never mind."

"Sorry, Jake. I must be showing either my age or my ignorance, or both."

"But, Detective Kiran Gurmeet with same-sex partner Meike, are *you* not concerned that your daddy-mommy Trudeau line is a tad sexist?"

She maintained her neutral smile. "No, Jake, I'm not, because *it's* not. Love him or hate him, Pierre Trudeau was a true Liberal and an original thinker, even ignorant I know that. His son, with his kindergarten-teacher manner, admirably represents the new model of über-correct Liberal, those of the twitter-purity tests. But Pierre married Margaret, a woman with the brain of a sixteen-year-old, the Rolling Stones' most famous groupie, remember? With a teenage crush on Fidel Castro too! The name *Trudeau* made their son Justin irresistible to the Liberal Party. Mommy's flower-child brain made his political blunders inevitable. Would it be sexist if the parental contributions were reversed? Or if it were Justine instead of Justin? Don't contradict your own best self, Jake, when you know you're right."

Jake is near free-associating in his mind, and unable to stop because he's enjoying himself as his buried self resurfaces for the first time in years. "Then would it be racist of me to observe that you're awfully tall for an Asian woman?"

"What! *Racist*? ... Okay, maybe. I'm Canadian, Jake, as are my parents, with family going way back in the Ottawa Valley. Regardless, their grandparents were shipped west and interred during World War II. That was racist, but not only racist, not only unjustifiable: in addition to much else suspect, the Imperial Japanese *had* torpedoed Vancouver Island, that's a fact. Meike researched the whole shameful history, yes, when we were in the first bloom of love." She smirked, Jake maintained a respectful gaze. "My grandparents' parents were from Taiwan, *not* Japan. You're just observing a racialist fact, Jake, and gender-wise, it's what you do with such facts that counts. I'm five-foot-eleven, which is tall for any woman from any background, excepting the Dinka, if still a few good inches shorter than you, Jake."

"The who? But I didn't mean to imply—"

"It's okay, Professor Flynn, I'm used to it. As I said, look at me. But speaking of height, tell me something: are all the Department of English professors—"

"Film&WordsWork," he grinned through his teeth, already reverting some to his guarded self, and finding there an honest ruse. "Tell me, Kiran, do you fish?"

"What? ... Well I ... No. I mean ... You are *some* adept at the surprise attack, Jake Flynn."

She was found out. She had underestimated him, had also fallen for the befuddled avuncular act. Still sentimental from her encounter with that Mary McGahern, she had let her antennae relax and let down her guard. She assumed a primmer posture.

"Professor Flynn, I am merely executing the preliminary stage of an investigation, an informal inquiry more than an interrogation. I would not characterize the process as *fishing*. However, should you desire legal counsel present ..."

Jake's eyes had fairly danced, showing that he was indeed quicker-witted than most assumed. "Dear God, Kiran, I was speaking literally! *Do you fish?* Do you get a rod and go fishing for fish? You know"—he leaned forward again, puffed out his cheeks, bugged his eyes and flapped his hands as gills at the sides of head—"*fish?* I was making small talk, not challenging your procedure."

Thinking was nowhere and Detective Gurmeet burst out in a noise like a curbed bus releasing its air brakes. She tried nonchalantly to dry her right hand on her thigh. Then she laughed easily, and Jake laughed genuinely. She confirmed that sure sign of companionship by returning a pleasant surprise to Jake:

"I do fish, Jake, with my father and still with my grandfather, up and down the Valley and wherever else we hear rumours of a lively catch. *Love* fresh rainbow trout; *love* a fry of perch too."

"Would you ever think of going fishing with me, Kiran?" He could be his own grandchild asking him to get right down on the floor to play trains.

She shook her head in mild wonderment. "I'd love to, Jake. We'll make a date for when this is all over."

"Not a one of my colleagues fishes, and neither would my Jieun, though she too loved a fresh fry. I don't mind fishing alone, as a lot of the pleasure for me is in quieting the mind and just letting it drift where it will. Do you know the old book, seventeenth-century, I believe, *The Compleat Angler*? It's … Oh, forget it."

"That's what I love about it too, Jake, the quiet, the bobbing of concentration, the not-thinking. But won't someone like Professor Turnbull or Pat Kelly or even Peggy Dubois go fishing with you?" She was digging, figuratively fishing.

"They say they've never fished, though Peggy will always take some of the catch, *if* already cleaned and filleted. Some others of my colleagues—you've met Professor Kelly?—they've made a big eco-deal about it, like I was dynamiting salmon farms."

"You're a teacher, teach them already."

"I've tried, Kiran, believe me. My best fishing line, so to speak: Anyone who can coax a tenacious gelatinous booger from deep in his *or her* nostril can fish." He watched her, and got what he wanted, and it was as good as landing a big bass or, he supposed, getting delightful squeals from that grandchild.

When they settled, she easily picked up. "But speaking of height, are all English professors—I mean of course, Film&WordsWork professors—either short like John Turnbull or, like yourself, Jake, very tall? Nothing in between? I couldn't help noticing the radical differences out in the lobby yesterday. The only person of average height is your receptionist Ms. Dubois, for a woman I mean. She told me she had to use a stepladder that morning to check those top bookcases." Wholly herself again, she watched him.

"And the eminently average and competent Ms. Dubois is the hub and pivot on which our Pod turns."

She smirked. "I again detect false modesty, Leader Flynn." She stood suddenly. "I'll take up no more of your precious prep time with my irrelevant chitchat. Thank you and have a good class."

Jake looked alarmed. "But didn't you want to question me about the theft of our *Ulysses*? I still have a little time before my Celtic Twilight seminar."

Taking advantage of his distraction, she leaned to her right and out the corner of her eye saw the blue container for recycling paper, saw a glint of glass but not enough of it.

"No third-degree, Jake. I had hoped only to talk with you just as we *have* talked. But where *is* my brain today? I also wanted to ask a favour. I'm interviewing as many of your colleagues as I've managed to get into the Department, very short interviews, no more than fifteen minutes each. Would you be willing to let me use your office for that purpose this afternoon? I *could* do it elsewhere, but I suspect your colleagues are most comfortable here. You have my promise that we will touch nothing."

"Of course." But he no longer looked wholly satisfied with what had transpired in the past ten minutes or so. What had he said? Already he couldn't remember, like when … he used to drink. Would Detective Gurmeet be interviewing Dean LaRoque? Would his loose lips and reckless talk land him in hot water? Jesus. To be thinking such thoughts at this time in his career. And mixing metaphors like some cliché blender!

He wasn't even aware of her. She edged to the right and looked down: *Bushmills* it said, an emptied bottle of … whiskey? She kept turning right as if naturally on her way to the door.

He managed, "And we have a fishing date?"

This time she *was* looking back from the doorway with her

hand lightly on the jamb and her winningest smile. "We do, Jake." Had that won him unreservedly, the cagey Professor Jake? She was almost out of sight when she made the move she'd learned from her favourite old TV detective show, the manoeuvre she and Chief Thu called a "Columbo." She turned back into the doorway:

"And you don't think it's worth my while reading *Ulysses*?"

He was not the man she'd just left. His head came up as if weighted, his eyes focusing as if from a drugged state, until they re-brightened. "Worth it, Kiran? *Ulysses*? If you were to read only one novel in your life, for the rest of your life's reading time, *Ulysses* should be it. Even from the little I know about you now, I can confidently say, you'd love it! Or come to love it, you and … Mackie? Read it together, a few pages at a time, a few paragraphs even. Don't be ashamed to use a critical guide, I had to the first couple of times. And this is what I tell students: *don't* read it like email or texting or the newspaper. Luxuriate in its sentences. Read it as you would look at a marvellous panoramic painting. Don't look through the words, look *at* them."

So he had been lying about his teaching *Ulysses* and his true estimate of the stolen book's literary value. She saddened, drooped within. But all Detective Kiran Gurmeet said, with a smirk, was, "Hmmm. You sound like Mee-kah."

"Meike sounds smart. Apologies for the *Mackie*."

"Thank you, vain Jake," she grinned, "you've been a big help."

And she was off, a Colombina in phantom dishevelled trench coat and with unlit cigar stub at her lips, if not even close to smiling satisfactorily to herself but blinking slowly as if done with the dirty work that someone had to do. Though only just begun, she knew.

Jake was troubled too, though he had no idea why. *I* was a big help? he worried.

SIXTEEN

PERSONS OF INTEREST 2

A Pod delegation of four professors led by John Turnbull and including Amari Abara, Bartholomew von Blüger, and a reluctant Pat Kelly met with Receptionist-Administrative Assistant (a recent budgetary doubling of duties, justified to the union as "financial exigency") Peggy Dubois to discuss the security breach.

The unlocked lower cabinet's six shelves were filled with irreplaceable Film&WordsWork faculty publications (some *were* first editions, if not actually value-enhanced for that because also the only editions of a heavily remaindered run). Disproportionately so, as Detective Gurmeet had already noted, seeing that Professor Turnbull's works took up the whole third shelf, the first below the antique top two shelves.

This had the unfortunate effect of making the remaining publications look like filler: Pat Kelly's permuting analyses in

Eco-Feminist Affective Psychologies (some in thick refereed publications from the end of the third shelf to the fourth, nonetheless supporting her fifteen-years' promise of a monograph on the subject); Bartholomew von Blüger's offprints on poetic-linguistics philology (most in German, some in Russian, none in English, all equally unintelligible, and also supporting a number of sabbatical applications promising a book-length study); Amari Abara's lone contribution (he *was* only ten years in the position), in black-plastic coil binding, *Black Academic Like Me: A Canadian Disgrace*; and various other publications of such as the Pod's four Jennifers, three Davids, and two Stephanies, literally spilling from shelf to shelf, or propped up and leaning against the glass as if looking for escape to some dreamed-of real reading world; and with the long-gone Dr. Oberon Stangle's six books on Elizabethan City Comedies relegated to recessed obscurity in a dark corner of the bottom shelf, where his best-selling monograph on the Shakespeare controversy, *Where Is There a Will?* lay face-down in dust balls and spider webbing.

The thing was, the delegation's *complaint* was, that only the top's second cabinet was locked (as had been known for decades); anyone could open the lower glass doors and pilfer what was there (the archaic word Professor Turnbull's). It mattered not that in the history of the Department/Pod on its journey from English to Film&WordsWork, until the day before anyway, that no stupid thief had ever executed such a pilfering. Fact was, unauthorized students only had ever *added* to the display: a destroyed sneaker blocking the incomprehensible title of one of Professor von Blüger's essays, a page torn from a (porno) graphic novel titled *The Wanking Dead* disfiguring the middle of Professor Turnbull's shelf, a condom still in its packaging (*deo gratias*) marking an unread place in a Professor Kelly offprint.

But that absence of actual crime didn't prevent Professor Turnbull from insisting with increasing vehemence that Peggy Dubois find a way to secure the lower case with reinforced "hasping" and state-of-the-art surveillance, which would mean getting funds from Dean LaRoque of the Faculty of Digital Humanities. Turnbull declaimed that, if necessary, he himself would pay and, when he wasn't contradicted by Peggy or the ad-hoc committee, qualified his claim by declaiming in a yet-louder voice that he would forfeit funds only on condition of the Dean's not ponying up for what was inarguably a Faculty responsibility. (Peggy knew to listen fiercely if she was to understand what her Film&WordsWork professors were saying.)

And in the "wholly unlikely event" that the Dean refuses funds, he, Dr. John Turnbull—or the committee rather—would grieve to the union before soliciting colleagues for contributions towards a cyber-enhanced security system.

"You do know," said Professor Turnbull to Reception-ist-Administrative Assistant Peggy Dubois, who did know because Professor Turnbull had told her so numerous times, "that the National Library of Canada would pay handsomely to have that shelf of irreplaceable Turnbull added to his NLC archive." It wasn't a question, as he was in something of a mid-level dudgeon, per usual.

Professor von Blüger leaned away from his own question and spoke sepulchrally from his shelved head: "Have you yet ascertained, Ms. Dubois, the liability of our insurer?"

"Yes, Professor von Blüger. But before she left yesterday, Detective Gurmeet said I should save myself the trouble, that, given the state of our security, or the lack thereof, the insurer would never pay out and that the university would be wasting its time and money litigating. You may recall, Canada Life had been only barely satisfied when we had the Shields equipment actually working."

Bartholomew von Blüger slid his head further back and said one word with noncommittal cringe: "Gurmeet." Then three more: "I suppose so."

Peggy Dubois sent them off to keep their scheduled appointments with Detective Gurmeet in the assurance that she would have the lower tier of the display cabinet secured before the day was out, her day, not theirs (she was already disturbed that so many professors *were* in the Pod that day). Which she did that very afternoon, with a baby-blue-felt-wrapped chain and small padlock of the kind lovers were prepared to waste to display their commitment by attaching them to the railings of the Corktown Footbridge across the Rideau Canal. She needed no Faculty funds or even Pod petty cash because, resourceful as good mothers everywhere, she'd soon found acceptable materials lying about the receptionist's large room of piled odds-and-ends, which was more her 'differently' organized mind extended than what administration called her "work space."

When he first saw the low-tech security, Professor Turnbull knocked hard on the Reception counter and, shaking pain from his knuckles, demanded of Peggy to know just *how* students relaxing in the Film&WordsWork lobby were to access a faculty publication to while away an idle hour or so?

"Are *they* to be given the key? And, if that be the solution, are they … *trust*worthy?" Again in high-blood pique, he'd said this with dancing eyebrows like he knew some secret and was semaphoring it.

Of course Peggy knew that no student had ever had access to the faculty publications (except to leave old shoes and unused condoms), as she knew also that Professor Turnbull's online class about animals had just crashed again and now had an enrollment of seven in a course with a ceiling of forty-five. So she replied only, "That *is* a serious problem, Professor Turnbull, but my solution *is* only temporary."

Turnbull suggested, or stated rather, that she should keep the padlock's key handy at reception only, ideally on the necklace chain with her reading glasses, and herself only ever to open the case for petitioning students, to monitor their behaviour closely, then gently to return the literary work and secure the case. "Problem solved then!" chirped Peggy, if worriedly high-coloured and nervously touching between her breasts.

Detective Kiran Gurmeet was receiving Department members in Leader Jake Flynn's office, planning to interview in short order (some three hours) as many of the incomplete complement of seventeen-plus-one who had obeyed her order and occupied their offices. She learned from Peggy Dubois that they'd not even tried to hide their resentment when she'd passed the order along, excepting the four Jennifers of course, and maintenance man Angus Daly whom Gurmeet had already spoken with about locked doors and key privileges and ladders and what he'd seen two days before: "Think now." Herself she'd seen right away that the empty whiskey bottle was missing from Leader Flynn's recycle container, and earlier Daly had attested that he'd never seen *any* such evidence in Professor Flynn's office, not in a decade anyway, and that Bushmills was little better than sweet piss like Bailey's Irish Cream. "Single-malt Macallan is the only—"

"Yes, thank you, Mr. Daly."

First up was Professor Dr. Bartholomew von Blüger, dressed in black from neckerchief to shining shoes, as he always dressed. Professor von Blüger held the recently established Nietzsche Chair in Teutonic Studies, a position he himself had proposed and secured funding for through the Austrian embassy. uBytown was thrilled to have the endowment, though neither Dean LaRoque nor President Sureau Montjoy were comfortable with the association.

"Nietzsche?" Montjoy had frowned, if only slightly. "Is he not the madman who thought he'd killed Our Lord and Saviour Jesus Christ?" LaRoque knew to nod assent, but to say, "Yes, that is somewhat unfortunate given our Catholic roots but, Monsieur le Président, to paraphrase our Lord and Saviour, the nihilists and atheists we will always have with us, and a funded Chair for the Faculty of Digital Humanities is a funded Chair." Montjoy appeared to understand, though his English was never the best, and LaRoque's French resided almost exclusively in his surname.

When von Blüger entered the office, he shut the door behind him with the careful manner of someone admitted to a star chamber. Detective Gurmeet immediately had to wrong-foot him by sending him back to open the door, not because that was protocol on first interviews (she flouted all such interference in her methods), though she told him that *was* the reason, but because he reached the chair in front of the desk trailing clouds of a cologne instantly as thickly sweet as that which wafted from a hair salon. She knew instantly that he'd not stolen the *Ulysses*, as she knew secondly that he'd provide nothing useful. Still, for formality's sake, because this was the first interview, for consistency and uniformity among the gossiping faculty, she asked,

"Professor von Blüger, I see from your narrative CV that you have spent a good portion of seven of the last twelve … *academic years*—whatever *they* are—in Vienna researching," she glanced down, "Teutonic Tonal Variations in the Definite and Indefinite Articles." She looked up blankly. "I'm hopeful that we can keep this initial interview short, *and* the only interview. So can you *briefly* explain your research to this layperson?"

"I suppose so." When he spoke, even while seated, he talked down his nose. His voice was as old sci-fi movies imagined a computer speaking, if lower and edgy from von Blüger and with an inexplicable ominous *knowing*.

"You only *suppose* so?"

It was like she'd demanded to speak with the demon possessing him. His head slid slightly forward on its shelf and he exhaled a long, mock-patient sigh.

"For all you'll understand it, *Detective* Gurmeet. To proceed then: I, Dr. Bartholomew von Blüger, am engaged in a comparative etymological poetic-linguistics study of the articles *a* and *the*, the indefinite and definite respectively, and the corresponding German *ein* and *das*."

She kept her eyes on him, which was easier because his had closed. "That's it?"

"I suppose so." Coming awake, or at least to greater awareness of the world around him, von Blüger looked almost sheepish, if somehow still in a wolfish way.

"I won't even pretend to understand, Professor von Blüger, but do proceed, please, it sounds fascinating." And duck before my nose hits you, buddy.

Then he did look directly at her and chuckled to himself condescendingly. Cleared his throat like he was hocking something up:

"In my research *towards* the definitive comparative etymological poetic-linguistics study of English and the Germanic branch of the Indo-European language family, the nonpareil Teutonic, I will demonstrate that humankind's rise from grounded snout to an erect posture—anatomically *and* figuratively speaking—itself demonstrates that evolution *hinged* upon the emergence of the *in*definite article, which occurred some thousand years earlier in German territory, or what would become glorious modern Germany and its language."

She'd been daydreaming (in her mind making up to Meike for their bitchy weekend) but just might have appeared to von Blüger as stunned by his brilliance. Mistake, stay focused, Kiri.

"I never expect one such as yourself to understand, Detective *Gurmeet*, so perhaps I may be permitted to sketch a scene so that even you can better imagine."

Go for it, Professor Dr. Herr Dickmeister, you miserable streak of black-clad prick. Later I may accidentally kneecap you for emphasising my names that way. "Yes?"

He's again closed his fucking eyes!

"Say aloud the definite article, Detective."

She wouldn't, she scarcely knew what he meant.

His head slid back on its shelf and he ordered the ceiling, "Say it."

"Pardon me, Professor?"

"*Thuh*."

Okay, since he went first. "The?" she said without commitment; in fact inflected as a question with undisguised puzzlement.

He startled her by springing forward as if he were Alexander Graham Bell hearing Watson for the first time over the first telephone. "You *see*? You *hear* it? Is not that interdental fricative digraph *the* most primitive phoneme ever uttered!"

He was staring without seeing her, so she could answer without worrying that he would detect irony, "My thoughts *exactly*." Patently as crazy as the skeleton of an umbrella, one that had provided no cover against too much sun. But go easy on him, Kiri, to whatever extent you can.

He sat back and lectured what soon became his only attentive class, the ceiling:

"*Think* of the very first human communication in language as we have come to define that code. A time when the miscegenating Neanderthal and Cro-Magnon were scuttling about dragging their knuckles in distantly potential sapience; say, those ancient hairy black Celts—the Scots, the Welsh, the *Irish*—and assorted Nordic specimens little advanced beyond the greater apes, unable to communicate what is wanted to bring about the selection of a truly superior race—*species* that is. Imagine if you will, say in *mittel*-Eastern and/or African habitat, a brutish Negroid and/or a Semitic specimen of similar dark complexion who wants something essential to life and limb."

"I'm sorry, Professor, but I'm afraid—"

"*Water*, shall we not say? But how does he signify so, his life's most basic need? He lies on a pelt pallet, on the threshold of his last desiccated breath, with the pestilential breath of natural selection hot at his tail, perhaps literally his tail. He raises his arm towards the distant watering hole where his tribe must compete for slurping privileges with wildebeest and hyena, points with hand drooping at the end of his wrist as if the dying *would-be* speaker were indicating with the stump end of a fleshy club: 'Thuh.' Of necessity his first human utterance: *Thuh*."

"I think I begin to—"

"The long-since further-evolved Teutonic on the other hand, so to speak"—von Blüger performed his own evolved demonstration of bemusement, a series of choked chortles that could well be mistaken as a cry for the Heimlich manoeuvre—"he stands erect and points to the well, his powerful *pale arm* (I cannot overstress that feature) extended straight as a spirit level true—*the well* I say! *Der brunnen*, rings a clarion call in the air, that articulation of *the definite* article in the language that would one day be the malleable medium of a Goethe and Heine! But only *then* follows the truer miracle: the *indefinite* article miraculously springs to mind and is singularly announced like the very spring of civilized culture itself: '*Ein glas wasser!*' ... Ein *glas wasser*. Need I say more?"

"No."

"The definite article, *thuh/das*, if inarguably a hobbled advance, was as yet semiotically indistinguishable from the physical object itself, much as an infant will at first not cogitate abstractly or self-consciously on its own reflection—*pace* Lacan—whereas the indefinite article leaps in obedience to the evolved ability to abstract accompanied by a particular linguistic sign. The—"

"No, *say no more*, Professor, is what I meant." She reached across the desk with open right hand and he, startled by both the gesture and what it signified, pulled back his whole body, as if avoiding a whizzing spear, and his head retracted yet farther onto the very back edge of the phantom shelf on which it appeared always to sit. He made a dismissive sound of fluttering lips, even more primitive than his demonstrative *thuh*.

"Yes, Professor, I'm sorry, I'm still always lapsing as regards handshaking." She made a fist of the yet-extended hand and knocked the desk with its knuckles. "But that will be all then, thank you, Professor von Blüger."

"I suppose so." His face changing kaleidoscopically like some trick of CGI superimposition, Bartholomew von Blüger stood ramrod straight. Then he appeared for once to suppose something more definite, and startled slightly:

"You have no interrogation respecting the pilfered *Ulysses*, Detective Gurmeet?"

"I suppose not. Thanks for your precious time, *Bartholomew*."

That scored at least in his facial response of squinting sinus pain, and she almost regretted her obviousness.

Yet he could still smirk: "You do know that Joyce's *Portrait of the Artist as a Young Man* is a plagiarism of Goethe's *The Sorrows of Young Werther*? And that in the plagiarized sequel fiction—I refer to his now *doubly* larcenous *Ulysses* (his textual squealing like a runt looking for a place at the trough among the tradition's bigger pigs)—*in* the Celt's *anti*-heroic story of a would-be writer, that Stephen Dedalus is in search of a father who will turn out to be of the Hebraic race or tribe—"

"I said thank you, *Bart*. That will be all."

With a phantom click of his heels, he took himself off.

Detective Gurmeet shook her head after him: Sweet Jesus. As his speech had progressed his *wills* had sounded more and more like *vills*. Encouraged in the slightest, it's highly likely he'd eventually have hissed "thuh Jew." Oh, it *is* still out there, ladies and gentlemen, and *in here*, this supposedly sacred place of merit. *Thuh* tenured Nazi. What must von Blüger be teaching his online skinhead acolytes? And of course in the event of any racist-based complaint, his professors' union will back him to the hilt, for anything short of his leading a broad-daylight *Kristallnacht* panty-raid of campus raping and pillaging. While two water-polo boys drinking with a hook—*sex worker* are expelled to their ruined futures. It's that self-serving idiot LaRoque's to blame, and what I know of uBytown's president, the Quebecois Nazi Montjoy, and, well, the whole fucking woke lot of them. No wonder Jake Flynn longs for retirement and fishing, and looks to be driven half-mad.

At least she now had a good ten minutes before the munchkin feminist Professor Pat Kelly arrived. She checked her tablet: some thirty messages, all marked urgent but none high priority, and none personal (which made her blink; she had said something hurtful to Meike the night before; she honestly couldn't remember the exact phrasing ... something about a too-revealing top; she used to praise Meike's fashion sense; was she getting fuddy? Possessive?). She tapped the screen to HQ, swiped to her profile, then slid to her Active Cases and accessed the report she'd ordered from MYCROFT, their AI crime computer. Go over evidence again and again and again, that was Chief Thu's prime directive.

So she read again that there were some eight hundred extant copies of the first edition of *Ulysses*. Only about half that number were in private hands, and few were ever put up for public auction or sold privately, as far as could be determined. The rare sale of the rare book had indeed been known to top half a million dollars USD, and one significantly above that figure most recently in New York. MYCROFT had managed to trace the provenance of seven-hundred-and-fifty copies, public and private, and as requested paid attention to North American territory, narrowing to Canada, focusing Ottawa. No first edition of *Ulysses*, let alone a signed copy, had ever been located in Ottawa. The nearest association was something called a "Limited Edition" reprint still on offer at Patrick McGahern Rare Books for a measly hundred bucks. ... *McGahern*, Detective Gurmeet reflected again, because she didn't believe in coincidence but did give heed to the divine dancing lessons of happenstance. Remarkably, MYCROFT had found no record of Film&WordsWorks' *Ulysses*, but then that copy had been a gift, not a sales transaction.

Nothing—but wait. What's this? Hello (she smiled). Left till after the end, where she'd not reached on first reading, and merely added by MYCROFT as "of further interest": one John Winston Turnbull had once acted as sales agent in the London (England) Sotheby's auction of a first-edition *Ulysses*.

The proceeds had gone to a publishing collective that included Turnbull among its aspiring writers. MYCROFT noted that there was some controversy about the transaction, and that Turnbull had immigrated to Canada, Ottawa, not long afterwards. The *Ulysses* had ended up back in Dublin in private hands, was sold to an investor in New York, who sold it to an international rare-books syndicate, which donated it (needing the tax deduction) to the backers of a James Joyce Research Centre in Dublin, after which it was never seen again. MYCROFT's secure communication informed her that signed first-editions of *Ulysses* could travel more than its eponymous hero (MYCROFT had been learning to make jokes, with the joking voice impersonating that of Chief Thu's old partner, the legendary Kevin Beldon). She said, because the computer processed voice better than most humans do, "You joke, MYCROFT?" Ignoring the question, MYCROFT informed her dryly that light-blue-and-white were the colours of the first-edition *Ulysses*, which were the colours of the Greek flag, and thus the highlight colour—

Kiran Gurmeet tapped out, as she always did when the crime computer pinned her with its prolixity (*so* unlike what a computer was supposed to be, intelligent or not). She would never understand why her mentor, Frank Thu, fairly adored MYCROFT. ... Hey! *Thu.* What would the racist von Blüger make of that! She now had a story for her Chief, who'd been looking like he needed cheering up ever since the beloved Kevin Beldon had finally retired for good, and was sick, she'd heard rumours. And now that she thought of it, Frank had told her that Beldon begrudgingly loved MYCROFT, and that he, Frank, would soon be following Beldon into retirement in the American southwest. And that Brigid Ertelle, whom Kiran had been admiring from a distance, would likely be her next Chief (Hurray!). "That is," said Frank, "if MYCROFT doesn't make us all redundant!"

When she again tapped the interview schedule, she saw that she'd misread, for next up was not little Professor Kelly but Professor Amari Abara, the Pod's one Black professor, she'd heard. Kelly wasn't till much later, just before the last, the (now prime suspect) Professor John Turnbull.

Professor Abara rolled in ten minutes late (when she later mentioned this to Jake Flynn, he told her with a wink that Maksim/Amari defended his habitual tardiness as being governed by "African time")—a heavyset *white* man? Literally rolled in, in a wheelchair, wearing something that resembled a Shriner's fez and a colourful orange-and-black tunic in the style old Nelson Mandela had made popular. And not only white but the whitest man she'd ever seen, who'd pass for albino but for the palest blue eyes (if the pink-eye thing wasn't a myth). She decided not even to gesture towards untangling the mess that sat before her, because she sensed he'd enjoy it too much and for too long.

She should have been more cautious, but in the aftermath of von Blüger she smiled and recklessly asked, "Professor Amari Abara. Has anyone ever observed that your name sounds like the Canadian motto *a mari usque*—"

"Your observation, Detective, is insulting and racist."

"I apologize, I'd meant no insult. Do you know why you're here, Professor Abara?"

"No. And here no longer without counsel and uBytown Human Rights personnel present."

"Okay. We'll talk later. Don't leave the city."

"Are you also restricting freedom of movement for my white colleagues?"

That had been a sneer. She *was* getting better but still sometimes could not restrain herself: "No, not *all* of them, not the whitest of the white, excluding yourself. Buddy, does your madness even allow you to notice whom you're talking to? Or do you need a lawyer present before answering that?"

"A self-loathing person of colour? You will definitely be hearing from our union lawyer and Human Rights officials." With impressive proficiency he spun in a wheelie and exited.

She tried to assuage her guilt for the unprofessional behaviour: he'd no more have been able to steal the book than was Inspector Gadget real. She smiled to herself, imagining the wheelchair rising on a scissors lift to the top of the bookcase, the attempted snatch, the extended chair tipping over. … If only this place had had surveillance cameras! Whatever, she'd be home early today and make up the real lapse with Meike.

After her blunder with Professor Abara, in short order Detective Gurmeet efficiently interviewed four professors named Jennifer, two named Stephanie, and three named David, and she was looking forward to Professors Kelly and Turnbull and making an end of a trying day's work. (Truth to tell, Meike had looked sexy lovely in the backless yellow top. She *had* been possessive, and jealous, because *she* was aging less gracefully. She would pick up a take-out tea, a Meike fave, at the Château Laurier on her way home: *home*, yes, Godspeed.)

The compliant Jennifers unsubtly complained—because it was *so* refreshing to deal with a female detective—of *feeling* compelled to be in their offices five days a week at least four hours a day, with doors wide open (of course a woman has to be *seen* to be working diligently). All four hurried to add, with instantly presumed familiarity and little variation in expression: *But no problem waiting for you, Kiran!* Like they'd talked about it. Detective Gurmeet knew with the certainty that approaches faith that none of them would no more have stolen the book than they'd steal the time of day (four whole hours!) or ever make any partner happy.

Ditto the Stephanies, who had asked if they could be interviewed together. They couldn't.

Contrarily, the Davids three were brazenly eager to get away, with none even faking concern that, were he working in a real office, he'd be quitting awfully early. After only five minutes one of them asked if they were done, peering at his timepiece the size of an antique sextant and mumbling that he had to get to Mont Tremblant to close up his cottage for the season. And these tenured professors are very well paid, Kiran Gurmeet knew, and would continue to be so whether they occupied their offices or walked away mid-afternoon, with benefits of the sort only politicians award themselves. Apparently no one really could compel professors to do anything, or only a bare minimum. Did the paying public have any idea what went on inside these walls? The Davids, unlike the Jennifers and Stephanies, at least showed marginal interest in the crime, the stolen *Ulysses*. But she had to work hard to keep them focused on what she wanted answered (perhaps she should have let them play with her gun?), so sent them off early, if obviously still not early enough for their liking.

Remembering Professor Pat Kelly's handling of the Dean and John Turnbull in the lobby the day before, Detective Gurmeet had looked forward to liking her but immediately didn't because the little professor, like all her female colleagues, immediately presumed to chat like they were two 'girls' conspiring in the ladies' room of some big bad boys' club. It would seem that disappointment was destined to dog Detective Gurmeet's day.

"Ah, we meet once again, the great detective and I," Kelly said loudly scuttling in. "The *tall* female dick—of colour!"

Why not, if those were Professor Kelly's ground rules?

"Have a seat, please, shorty."

That scored a little cringe that had wanted to be only a blink. Pat Kelly recovered face as she took the chair opposite, her feet not touching the floor. And went for it again: "It's Kiran, right? If I may. A lovely name. How's it been going with our tenured sexist pigs?" The last bit said ironically. But she meant it too. "That David Swift is something else, eh? Talk of your patriarchy, he walks around this place like he's permanently descending Mount Sinai carrying the tablets of the Ten Commandments of Patriarchy. And Davey—"

"Yes, thank you, Professor Kelly."

The round Munchkin face smiled smarmily, signalling that she registered the rejected offer of beleaguered sorority, or whatever she'd thought she was doing.

Detective Gurmeet gave a little ground: "But your Chair—*Leader* Jake Flynn doesn't impress me that way."

"Don't be deceived by that great deceiver, Detective: Jake is as sexist as the rest of them, though his is mostly a non-harassing expression of systemic sexism."

"Ah yes, *systemic sexism*, I've been reading about that for years in memos and the like from my own bosses, and recently in press releases from your own university. But just what is it? Educate me, please, Professor." And she smiled her winning smile, which scored a Munchkin grin.

Pat Kelly performed the same lip-fluttering exasperation that Professor von Blüger had before launching on his windy explanation of the evolutionary significance of the articles *the* and *a*, a sound as of a one-horsepower outboard motor propelling the ensuing lecture. "Who knows?" she said tossing up her open hands. "Nobody really knows. My feminist cred is impeccable," she smiled downwards in ironic bow, her right hand going to her scapula. Her face returned for some plain speaking: "But even *I* would say that the expression *systemic sexism* as pan-explanation of injustice is already as shopworn as the good old *patriarchy*. And same for systemic racism, whether that gets me arrested or fired or what. They mean everything—if mainly that you're sexist and racist but too dumb to know it—and so mean nothing—perfectly useful in academic argument!"

Good. So cut the little woman some slack. "That's refreshing, Pat; I hope you don't mind my calling you Pat?" Grinning Pat obviously didn't. "I feel I can be direct with you, Pat, cut to the chase." Pat Kelly looked as pleased as a half-drunk Munchkin to be cutting anywhere with this powerful woman. "What would make Professor Pat Kelly steal a rare book from her own workplace?"

The Munchkin, looking sucker-punched, transitioned to Wicked Witch. "*What*? ... Why, nothing would. You seriously suspect me of purloining the *Ulysses*?"

"No, I was being tactical," she settled her. "And I like *purloining*. Wasn't that the title of an old Edgar Allan Poe story, the very first detective story? Which I know thanks only to my high school English teacher partner."

Professor Kelly was further settled and thinking herself back in professorial control. "It is, and I wonder where such serendipity could lead us in this case of the purloined *Ulysses* which, unlike Poe's letter, was left out in the open *for* purloining. But seriously, why *would* I steal it?"

"*Or* have it stolen?"

"Hmm, I think I like this game." And she proved it by squirming into the chair. She made her cute thinking face, like she was looking for an answer inside her puffed lower lip. She came up seriously again: "I might do so to frame your new friend Jake Flynn, or Turnbull."

"Would you? Is there something between you and those two I should know about?"

"Not really. Jake and I had a sort-of thing going—oh, don't look like that! Nothing physical, I'd need a ladder to kiss him for God's sake! Too physically belittling. Standing beside Jake Flynn I'm perfectly positioned only for a blowjob."

"Jesus Christ, Pat!" Kiran laughed delightfully, if bringing her right hand to cover nose and mouth. On a case as she was, she didn't like giving such ground unintentionally.

Pat Kelly waited. "Really just a growing close friendship, especially over the past couple of years, and this last year more intensely as what's called an *emotional affair*. It was needy Jake who started it, and no one could have been more surprised than I, the way he's always going on about the saintly Jieun, his mysterious wi—partner. And it was Jake who recently ended it. So if you were to have heard about that from *someone* else, great Detective Gurmeet, not to name names"—round her hand she stagily mumbled "John Turnbull—you *could* seriously suspect my innocent wee self of something nefarious?" She sat up and flapped her lashes melodramatically, it was grotesque, if unintentionally appropriate to the gross story.

"I wouldn't worry, Pat, though this is of course interesting. But what *about* Turnbull? And you, I mean?"

Professor Kelly dropped all levity. "I have no real relationship with John Turnbull. He's always up to something. I say, watch him, though I seriously accuse no one."

"You also said *recently*, but when exactly did this—the end of the emotional affair with Jake Flynn—occur?"

"Uhhh … last Tuesday, in fact. Is that relevant?"

"How did Jake Flynn take the break-up?"

"Take it? Like I said, it was all his doing. He *was* upset the evening we had a drink and talked it over, of course, his colour high, his joking lame per usual, *and* his booze intake way beyond anything I'd seen for a long time. Understandable. It was a tense moment, despite my joking. We *were* involved."

"Jake's a drinker?" Had she successfully faked that? Because in her mind's eye she again saw the empty Bushmill's bottle. "I'd not have tagged him for one."

"Past perfect tense, Detective. Jake's not gone on a bender for years and years, far as I know, which is why I remarked his drinking last week. I've been sensing an incredible amount of stress there, mostly work-related, I think. Professor Flynn believes we're no longer a university English department if we're not giving a full-term course in Beowulf, *in* Old English."

"Okay, I don't know from verb tenses either, Professor. But you're saying you *could* have stolen the book, or had it stolen, to frame Jake Flynn or John Turnbull for the crime of, as I've said, *grand larceny*? That's no joke, Pat. Because he jilted you? And Turnbull because he's a sexist pig? Is that the best you can do, Pat?"

That took quick Pat Kelly a moment to process. Was the great detective serious or joking, or both? Fishing for incriminating information? Watch your step, girl, with this tricky girl.

"Well, no, you know that's not what I said, Kiran. But now that you've put the idea in my head … if I were to commit such a serious felony for the purpose of framing someone, that someone *would* be one of the Pod's two sexist pigs, John Turnbull or von Blüger."

"I see, the plot thickens." Detective Gurmeet gave her time to qualify or retract; Pat Kelly did not avail herself of the opportunity. "Would you elaborate, please, Professor Kelly."

Pat smirked. "You do know I'm joking, Detective, or at least half-joking? Forget Bartholomew, he'd no more steal a book than hit on a sane research idea. But Turnbull used to be absolutely head-over-heels in love with *Ulysses*, you should know.

I once, a long time ago, caught him gazing up at our copy in the bookcase—he could have damaged his neck, he's almost as short as I am."

"He is."

"Yes. He sensed me beside him and said something like, 'I'd give anything to own it.' He bragged that he'd once brokered the sale of a first-edition *Ulysses*. Out of politeness I asked to whom and for how much. He clammed up. Anyway, it'd be a lot easier to frame John than Jake, and a lot more fun."

"Why is Professor Turnbull a sexist pig?"

"You haven't the time, Detective Gurmeet, and believe me, that story would be irrelevant to your case. … Okay. John continues guilty of endless bad sex jokes and unwanted touching, not just with me but with every female I've ever seen him close to, colleagues and students, ask any of my colleagues named Jennifer or Stephanie. But now that you make me think of it: if any of my colleagues stole the book—or had it stolen—it would have to be John Turnbull.

"I'm no detective, but I strongly suspect it was an outside job, too obvious to have pulled it off from inside. *But if anyone*, Turnbull certainly had motive, and any of us would have had opportunity (you've seen our security). Though you'd never know it from what he was saying the other day, John once *loved* Joyce's *Ulysses* and taught it regularly with a passion. He went off it only because he's set on getting more sabbaticals than he's entitled to; thus passé Modernist Turnbull has turned strategically *eco-* and trained the pop guns of his great critical intelligence on the study of animals in literature. Maybe he's planning his autobiography, the sexist pig." Detective Gurmeet puffed a laugh of appreciation. "And b-t-w, his new field of study, animal allegories, is a direct offshoot of my work in eco-feminist psychologies. *Entre nous*, he's *stolen* some of my work, which, if different from snatching an actual book, is nonetheless an academic crime bordering on outright plagiarism! So: he's more than capable of all manner of literary crimes and crimes against literature." She caught herself and her breath. "But please, Kiran, assure me this will be kept strictly off the record."

"I can't do that, Professor Kelly. This *is* an official interview, as you knew, and as I've logged it, and as I'm recording it." She tapped her tablet lightly. "But it would only ever matter if Professor Turnbull were actually charged with the crime. In that event, you could well be called as witness, especially after what you've said here."

The munchkin eyes widened as though the Wicked Witch had appeared. "Then I will say no more without our union lawyer present."

"Good idea. We're almost done here, Professor Kelly, I hope. Would you please tell me something about your professional interests, and maybe that way I'll better appreciate the likelihood of Professor Turnbull's academic *crimes*."

Professor Kelly recovered in primness—tucked her skirt, even her mouth tightened—and commenced professing:

"Of course. But please stop me if I'm boring you, Kiran. ... As I'm sure you know, nature has always been gendered female, as in *mother nature*?"

Sweet Jesus. Once upon a time again. Do they all start back at the Enlightenment (thank you, Meike)? How do I head-off another runaway brainiac? Or better to let her run for a spell?

"The metaphor is useful, as it enables such accurate language for clear-cutting forests and strip-mining as *rapaciousness* and *violation*. And though I may have scouted the term *systemic sexism* earlier ..."

For sure: raping dear mother, a great metaphor, if not exactly making the unfamiliar familiar (as taught by Meike, *merci encore*). Kiri dear, cut across this shit before this disappointed Munchkin has big-daddy Greenpeace strategically—no, *systemically*—hammering spikes into the crotch of a weeping willow. Wait—there, she's paused for breath.

"Thank you, Pat. You've enlightened me sufficiently, though I'd love to have a coffee some day and talk some more."

"Wha … Well, uh, of course, Kiran, I'd welcome that!"

I didn't say *with you*, sweetie. *That* would be the day Juan Valdez is apprehended covered in clear-cut Amazon sawdust and wanking into your French Vanilla.

Brightened, Professor Pat Kelly stood, which strangely made her even shorter.

"And, Pat, as I've said to all your colleagues, don't leave Ottawa for the next few days."

"And David Swift sat still for that?"

"He has no choice."

"Then I expect I'll have to spend the weekend settling my six younger colleagues named Jennifer and Stephanie. I'm sort of their den mother. They'll have concluded that you think they stole the *Ulysses*. Next week they'll feel compelled to take up permanent residence in Pod premises, I mean twenty-four-seven, just to prove they're not afraid of the patriarchal law's systemic sexism. If you have no objections, I'll inform them that the Professors David are also under order not to leave town. Do you know that that Nazi nut-job von Blüger actually lived in his office for half a year, without official reprimand? That's another difference between—"

"Thank you, Dr. Kelly, and okay on reassuring your female colleagues that I have no such notion respecting their involvement in the crime. Or of you being implicated. This is mostly routine."

"*Mostly*, there's the rub. But who dunnit, Detective? In all seriousness, it had to have been an outside job. Peggy and I suspect—"

"Thank you, Professor Kelly."

She was in the doorway and turning back in her own Columbo:

"I'd like to say one more thing about Jake Flynn, Kiran, if I may, by way of correction."

"You may."

"Honestly speaking then. I did and I do like Jake very much, and I'm seriously worried about him. He is a deeply disappointed man, and a most admirable man, which is something I rarely say so gender-specifically. Jake overcame a serious drinking problem in my early years here, and that buoyed him for a few years. That and the love of his wife and family, I believe, as far as any of us could tell, which is not far at all. Jake Flynn is a compulsively private person. And at least equally Jake was saved by his love for the old-style teaching of literature he did and still does. The academic world underwent a revolution and Dr. Professor Jacob Flynn sat it out. Jake's been badly battered in recent years, professionally, as I expect you'd have gathered from talking with him, in his spirit, or his *soul* as he'd call it. He plays false modesty like an oboe, but his self-esteem really has been tanking like the Titanic. I've never seen him as … as dissociated as he's been recently."

"Poor man. But what's all that about, Pat, the professional sea-change and consequent stresses? Explain to this layperson, please."

"Well, *theory*. I'm sure you've heard of *deconstruction*, *postmodernism*, *postcolonialism*, *culture studies*, and such? Jake continued teaching, and tried to publish, like none of that ever happened, like what he took for revealed literary truth wasn't also a theory. To Jake, the literary text was still sacrosanct. Great authors still had something to teach us, blah-blah-blah. With *great* being defined, of course, by privileged white—"

"Thank you again, Pat, I *had* heard, thanks to my partner Meike. I had to ask but I'm not going down those rabbit holes with you. Meike is a high school English teacher, as I may have said, which is why I've been exposed a little to those critical practices. Meike doesn't like any of it. She too still teaches literature in the way you slight Professor Flynn for. *My* sense of Flynn from talking with him earlier is that he loves reading and studying and teaching, and that—"

"Oh he does, he does, and his students, the undergraduates anyway, love him for it. Because that's also still what the sweet dears think English literature should be about: reading and studying and getting lost in good books. Unfortunately for Jake, though, graduate committees stopped approving his seminar proposals, and tenure-and-promotion committees at all levels stopped granting his sabbatical requests."

Kiran Gurmeet kept her thoughts to herself, which weren't well defined in this area anyway.

Pat Kelly stopped waiting. "Sometimes I wonder if Jake even wants to live in this world anymore. He *should* retire, and I promise you here and now, Kiran, that I'm going to make a concerted effort to find and have a talk with the mythical Jieun about this, my purpose will be to have the two of us concertedly bring pressure to bear on Jake. Problem is, I've never been to our fearless Leader's house. None of us has! Even Turnbull, Jake's oldest colleague-friend, claims that Jieun's a rumour."

Detective Gurmeet couldn't help but grow grave too. "It's that serious?"

"It is. On top of which, I suspect a possible onset of Alzheimer's, though the symptoms I note could as well be the effect of the stresses. As I said, we were having an innocent thing, Jake ended it before any emotional damage could be done, in consideration of me, however mistaken, and, I must presume, of his love for the rumoured Jieun and extended family. Then next day he didn't even seem to remember having broken it off! And he's not mentioned it since!"

"And that was … last Tuesday, you said?"

"Yes, and as I also said, I'd prefer you kept our little talk—oh, John!"

"Time's up, girls, if I may address you ironically thus."

Professor John Turnbull stood in the doorway back of the now-standing Professor Pat Kelly, and even allowing for perspective, he couldn't have been but a couple of inches taller than the five-foot-zero Pat. Detective Gurmeet asked, "How long have you been waiting out there, Professor Turnbull?"

"Not long enough to hear you two lovely ladies discussing my various attractions!"

"Sorry to have kept you waiting, Professor Turnbull, and to disappoint—wow, look at the time! Professor Flynn will soon be wanting his office back. Come in, please. Professor Kelly and I are done. … Oh, Pat, would you do be a favour and remind David Swift that he is not to leave town, even to go to Tremblant to close his cottage?"

"No. John will."

Saying so, Pat Kelly waved at them both as to an infant—involving only the flapping fingers—as she turned away. She was heavily set, quite thick, from the absence of defined waist down, yet Turnbull was still ogling her rear. Men. Kiran liked the look of women from the back too but she never ogled, merely the sneaked appraisal. Could men not help the lingering notorious gaze? And if not, should they get sympathy or jail time? She always sympathized with those men jailed for non-violent crimes, because the law went lighter on women for the same crimes. Hey, call Pat back for discussion!

Professor Turnbull sat without being invited, with only the tips of his small shoes skimming the floor. He was grinning and swinging his head about like some stumpy lighthouse … the revolving male gaze? But he'd made no bones about being kept waiting past his appointed time, which seemed unlike him and made her like him some. Caution: MYCROFT *had* associated him closely with a first-edition *Ulysses*. He had a shady past and some suspect dealings in it. Both Jake Flynn and Pat Kelly, with no known cause to frame or conspire, *had* remarked his former fondness for the stolen *Ulysses* as literature and rare book of great value. Despite what amateur sleuths Peggy Dubois and Pat Kelly had deduced, an inside job was still as likely as an outside. Who outside would even have known of the book that had sat there for decades? Who better situated than, uh, *Pod* members to know? Who had greater opportunity? She would have MYCROFT investigate every professor's financial situation—shit, she should've done that already.

A mind-reader—or not, as that was why they were met—John Turnbull turned over his arms and presented her with his stubby forearms' pale wrists, and a shit-eater's grin. "Ya got me copper, I pinched da book."

She laughed mostly to relax him. "Then come out with your hands up, Mr. Cagney." He nodded and lowered his arms. "You did once broker the sale of a first-edition *Ulysses*, Professor Turnbull, did you not?"

His eyebrows rode up. "Very good. Was that the work of the famous crime computer MYCROFT? My compliments. But what of it? I'd steal the book thinking you'd never find out about that?"

"Just running my human polygraph, Professor. You passed."

He relaxed again, not that he'd looked worried. His roving gaze rested on the windowsill and he said, "I didn't steal the book, Detective, I wouldn't."

No? Why not? You could have ... if only by riding in a cherry picker. No, Kiri, stop that. Or you could have had it stolen. You could be doth-protesting me here, or purloined-lettering me, saying what is the truth in an up-front way that makes it highly doubtful. She must work diligently to put him at ease, off-guard, he's no idiot, none of them is, even that fool von Blüger. They are all smarter than me. Than *I* (thank you, Meike ... I think).

"I know that, John, if I may. And please call me Kiran."

He glanced and unabashedly appraised her face to waist; thank God she was seated facing him. He returned to the view out the window, boldly stood and went over. "Hey, where did this come from?"

"What?" *He'd* wrong-footed *her*. Damn.

"This little Buddha statue?"

She saw that he had his forefinger on the head of the statu-ette. "I have no idea. But if we could return to the sub—"

He leaned down to the statue, pinched an affixed paper and read: "*Newly glued.* Hmmm, quite ... poetic."

"What? What does that mean?"

He talked over her without apology, which also didn't surprise her.

"I walk to work, my morning constitutional, which I do for my health, since work stress accumulates and therapeutic sabbaticals are harder and harder to come by. I make it a point of walking through the lawn in front of Coriveau Hall. I love the smell of weed in the morning." She didn't get it, and it a popular allusion; are his references already betraying his age? "I've nurtured a nodding acquaintance with the vendors and street people. Rarely does one encounter a student anywhere on campus who has not ... excepting that lovely girl with whom you seemed to strike up a, shall we say, friendly relationship in the lobby the other day, Kir—"

"We shall not say, Professor Turnbull. Finish your point about the Buddha statue, if you have one, and please return to your seat."

"Yes. Two points actually: one, a few days ago, the dope dealer who claims the territory in the far corner of the lawn for his own vending stall—Crazy Ray, who, by the by, actually retails what *have* to be stolen books—accused me of stealing what I believe to be this very statuette. I also believe that the hirsute fellow is permanently deranged from ingesting his own product. But he veritably chased me across the field, shouting abuse and cursing, as if someone had deprived him of something of real value. Now, I'm not accusing anyone else of anything, least of all Jake Flynn, and I suspect such kitsch as this is widely available … but I will say that I do seem to recall seeing such an item on Crazy Ray's park bench. If Jake was gifted it from a student, which in all likelihood is the case, by one of our international Asians—no offence—then he should be informed that he may be in possession of stolen goods, even if cheap stuff."

Detective Gurmeet was at his side, which made him step away. "Can you point out which street person, please?"

Turnbull did.

"Thank you, Professor. You're free to go now. But as you heard, don't skip town till I give you the all-clear." She worried that her use of the lingo was either incorrect or lost on him, and likely both. She needed to work on her patter.

"And will you please inform David Swift of same?"

"Nothing would give me more pleasure."

He left fairly skipping out the doorway, the first time she'd ever seen a 'grown man' skip (excepting in that silly Olympics event). She needed to skip too, skip out, and pronto, as the last thing she wanted was to be there when Jake Flynn returned from his class. But first she turned back to the window and the pastoral scene of a traditional campus. She made a note in her pad to visit that hairy dispenser of stoned forgetfulness; there was something that connected, something going on in that corner of this whole unreal world. Or could Turnbull be distracting her? ... And then, apart from an official visit, the madman's (Crazy Ray's?) product had its attractions. She wasn't identifiable as a cop, could she safely score a joint or two for the weekend? No. It was only that her job really sucked when it was like this, at an impasse of possibilities and discomfiting probabilities. But what else could she do for a living now? Change fucking street lamps! ... Meike, please be home. Please be your old self. Please, love, tell me again that you love me *for* my beanpole figure, *for* my man's square jaw, for my almond eyes. Please, love, like we used to be. Even if none of that is as true any longer. Lie to me a little, love. Love, come lie with me a little. I still love you.

SEVENTEEN

ONLY CONNECT 3

From: Jim Collins <jcollins181@uwo.ca>
     Fri Sept 23 at 15:20
To: Mary McGahern
Cc:

Dear Mary,

Well, that's three weeks in the bag and I'm hungover again like a sick dog this morning after closing the Ceeps again last night. I think I could get to like that place (ha!). I go with a gang from my residence, who are all right when you get to know them, which I've been able to do thanks to the Ceeps. Like me, these guys (and a girl or two, it's a co-ed rez remember) couldn't wait to get away from home. Some of the guys have girlfriends here in London whom they sometimes meet at the Ceeps, so it's a great party every night. But seriously, I cannot believe how my old man lives all the time with the green sickness of hangover. Maybe that explains why he sold our farm to Canopy. Or did the money—which meant his losing a reason to wake up early and half-sober every day for real work—bring out the true alcoholic in him? I don't know why Mom stuck and sticks with him (I won't bore you with that whining story again, since you and the whole of Leitrim Falls know it already). At least they had no other kids but me. But enough about me. What do you think of me? (Ha-ha)

I still try to go to all my classes. I was honestly ready to quit after the first week. Anyway, it's neat that some of our courses are the same. My introduction to Canadian literature class is my favourite too (or did you say you liked the Irish seminar better? Sorry I forget, but your emails are getting like essays). Its professor is the only thing that keeps me here for now. It's remarkable we are both reading some of the same works! Or maybe not so amazing. But we also began with that silly *The Rising Village* poem, which seemed way too long and boring when I read it, and then the prof lectured on it. There still aren't many live bodies in any of our classes either, because if you want you can stay away and watch on computer. But this prof makes it worth attending. At first I was struggling to pay attention, till I really tuned in and realized that everything he said was actually brilliant or witty or both. Do you remember that part in the poem where Albert and Flora are falling in love? Albert is 'courting' Flora and it says, "and as his soft and tender suit he pressed"? Well this prof, Bewley, showing nothing in face or voice, said in this posh English accent that many of us might be surprised to read

that in pioneering Canada men routinely did their own ironing!
The others, of the dozen or so of us in this big lecture hall, just
kept taking notes. I coughed to control myself, it echoed, then I
sputtered and went into a laughing fit that made me leave the
room. I think it was partly from relief. I returned embarrassed
but the professor just grinned at me. Now, he mostly lectures
only at me.

My two other English courses don't have even one novel
or short story or poem on their syllabuses (is that spelled
correctly, Marm?). I'm serious. If the beardo and feminazi
profs were being honest, instead of pretending there was any
reading at all (I seriously do not even understand the titles of
the assigned readings), they'd just hand out those stupid Guy
Fawkes masks at the start of the course and tell us the final
exam would be our taking part in a storming of city hall. Hey,
Professor Gerta Suzuki, I'm here to read some great literature,
'relevant' or not to the mess we've made of the fucking world!
I'll take care of the activism in my own time—not. (Sorry for
that swearing I won't revise, Mary, because that's your rule.)

So Bewley's course is about it for real value for all my hard-
earned money, the summer earnings from your generous
dad, because my insane old man wouldn't give a penny. God I
miss the farm. Not ours, because I was actually happy when
Dad sold it last year and overjoyed to leave it and become
a towny. I miss *your* farm, Mary, working for and with your
dad, like last summer, and being with you every day, working
with you too of course. I don't know how long I'm going to
last here—I mean, what is this shit compared to what I did all
last summer? Maybe Prof Bewley will take an essay on that
question? "Great Escapes: From Worse to What?" Run away

from university back to the farm? Something like the reverse of what ironing Albert did. Will you be my Flora, Mary? Does that work? I'm losing it (seriously). I need a beer.

Sorry for going on here (I'm worse than you!). I'm just deep in the dumps again, and as said hungover. I think I'm actually depressed during the day, till the Ceeps (but no way I'm going to the counsellors they email us about at least twice a day). I seriously wish I'd followed my original plan and gone to U Guelph. I blame you for talking me into English (sorry, can I revise that?). Who ever would have thought that Stottlemeyer's grade-twelve English could be better than university? Prof Bewley excepted. ... But right now I do need a hair of the dog. It's Friday again finally and the gang's heading for the Ceeps soon. Bristle of the hog?

Miss you.
Love,
Jim

From: Mary McGahern <mmcgahern022@ubytown.ca>
        Fri Sept 23 at 21:30
To: Jim Collins
Cc:

Dear Jimmy,

Thanks finally for the longer letter. (I guess I do overdo it.) Your Professor Bewley sounds great, like my Professor Flynn, only funnier. But in their different ways two such teachers should encourage you and me that a meaningful university education *in English Literature* can still be had, and is worth the time and tuition money. (Did you already forget what Stottlemeyer did with your essay on that short story "One's a Heifer"?!). Prof. Flynn is also the professor of my Irish seminar. The first book we read was a great collection of short stories titled *The Untilled Field*, which made me homesick in a good way. I'm going to get Dad to read it. My point being, Mr. Collins: all's not lost in university English studies (half-joke).

That said school-marmishly, here's the flipside. In one of my other English courses, this one focusing on "animal allegories" (with a title neither of us would ever understand), and all online, we were introduced to the term "Manimals," which is meant to signal the ways in which animals in literature are really just projections of (are you seated?) *patriarchy* (the dreaded). But I guess it is a pretty clever term. Still, in the stories we read, one about a randy Bull Moose in New Brunswick who was traumatized as a calf and so suffering bovine PTSD (ha!), another about a wolf way up north, I couldn't exactly see my or anyone else's daddy (and I know that's not what patriarchy means); well maybe my dad *is* a sort of Lobo and yours a bull—ha ha. The thing that got me, though—the stories were great! But we never analyzed them *as* stories! Only as anything but. And another new word, though I think this one's a real word: "speciesism." That's the eco-sin (*my* word!) of something like preferring Towser's company to Pluto's. The guest lecturer for that particular class, a short fat woman with a big voice (body shaming, I know, like *you* would care, Collins!), has never mucked out anything, including her head. She and the regular prof, also short and fat, obviously have a thing going, but it's kinda gross to imagine that even in an email to your gross self.

Thus spaketh the Virgin Mary. ... I think you know I'm still a virgin, Jimmy, but I've wanted to get it out of the way—I mean, saying it to you. But who knows what a girl means! ... I'm being too cute, I know.

I miss you too, too much, Jimmy. I don't want to come off as your mother, but watch the drinking, please, for your own and my sake. But your every email now contains a reference to drinking at this Ceeps place. I need to justify my presumption, so let me say: my father was drinking too much too when I left. He first drank too much after Mom died, got in trouble, maybe saw what I was doing to keep things going on the farm and in the house, then got control of it. That's Dad. But I noticed it was starting up again as our glorious summer wound down. I blame you (joke), as the two of you drank more and more of his homebrew Harp as September loomed (remember the number of times you had to sleep on the old couch in the porch?). At least that drinking was after a hell of a day's work. But seriously, Jimmy, watch it, please, for me, even pretty please.

Love (no punctuation joke goes here)
Mary

From: Jim Collins <jcollins181@uwo.ca>
        Sun. Sept 24 at 16:30
To: Mary McGahern
Cc:

Dear Mary,

I know you warned me, but boy have I got a fresh bun on,
just getting up in fact, way too much pissy beer two nights
in a row till closing time. I'm going to quit, promise, though
I don't know what I'll do for friends then. I sure miss your
Dad's homebrew. I sure miss you, Mary, and the summer,
and the farm etc. etc. etc.

Later: back from Ceeps
Hey, wait till Aoife hears about speciesism! Hands off my
teats, human! (just like us at first out at Big Rock all those
steamy eves, eh? Sorry sorry sorry, it's the beer talking).

Later still: back to Ceeps and back again:
It's just that I miss working on the farm with your father,
God I wish my old man hadn't sold our farm, Mom says
he's drunk all the time now and she's gonna leave him. I
don't want to be here. But where can I go? I hate Leitrim
Falls. I hate university.

I'm still a virgin too Mary, like you didn't know, what with
all my smooth moves out at Big Rock those same sweaty
summer evenings before your dad would come close
and call and lure me back to the house with the offer of
a second brew, which led to a third, and a fourth and ...
sleep because, as you so sensitively remember, I'd fall

asleep on the porch, I loved waking up at your place even hungover. I'm dozing here again. Later again. What a joke I'm the only male 18yr-old virgin in all of Western U! The guys are always trying to make me hit on some slut, and when I won't they say I'm gay. So I pretend to be gay, which grosses them out. But now, coincidentally, they've taken to calling me the Virgin Jim!!! I'm hitting send because if I leave this as a draft—hey, another draft! I'll not send in the morning and you made me promise no editing emails Jim my Jimmy-Jim-Jim love the Virgin Mary

From: Mary McGahern <mmcgahern022@ubytown.ca>
Sun Sept 24 at 23:30
To: Jim Collins
Cc:

Dear Jimmy,

I must try to keep this short. I have to write an essay on *The Untilled Field*. The library is too depressing for serious work. Now's my window.

But how often *do* you go to this Ceeps place anyway? Sounds like you live there. What's so special about it? Anybody special I should know about?

Jimmy, listen to me please, and carefully, whatever fog of alcohol I'm talking through. I'm sure what I'm about to write is also in some two-bit Psych 101 text somewhere, but it's my own honest thought. You're drinking too much not *like* your dad but *because* of him. Clear your head, sober up, and think—use that great brain I so admire. I mean, couldn't you be all subconsciously *becoming* your dad? That happens to a lot of people. Think: Fred Faucher's father is a bully supervisor at Canopy; Adèle Pélletier's mother was a high school slut too (my Mom told me they had to get married). Whatever your father was and is, however much you hated and hate him, he had and still has all the power in your home. Power is very attractive when you have none and especially when you find yourself lost in a strange place (where they call you the Virgin Jim!). Please, Jimmy, I'm serious, and worried for you (and me), and I love you too much not to say this.

Please keep writing—my lifeline—but please try to do so sober. I'm dying for Thanksgiving weekend and seeing you again and talking (even if about our burdens of virginity! But talk is cheap, and I'm not!!!)

Love you forever,
Mary XXXOOO

EIGHTEEN

PLAGUING JAKE 9:
PALLIATIVE MARY

Detective Gurmeet was gone by the time Jake Flynn returned from his senior seminar in Irish literature, "The Celtic Twilight." It was four o'clock, an acceptable time for the Leader to go home to a well-earned weekend, and to do so quickly before Maksim Pavlov/Amari Abara showed up for his weekly—too late.

The tap-tapping on his door jamb—"Come in, please, Amar—" The smart pretty girl from the seminar, who's actually in both his classes. She was already blushing before she spoke, and Jake had to speak a serio-comic warning to himself: *Be still, my aging heart.*

"I'm very sorry, Professor Flynn, I don't know if it's okay to bug a professor right after class, I know you have posted office hours, and late Friday afternoon and all that. But I ..."

Jake was up and round his desk and, forgetting caution, taking Mary McGahern by the forearm and leading her to the desk chair, the small couch being for colleagues only. Talking continuously in that voice like the smoothest single-malt scotch: "Not at all, not at all, Mary—it is Mary, isn't it? Mary McGahern, a lovely name—I'm *so* pleased you've come by, I've thought of talking with you after class, as it's a rare treat these days for the old professor to have a student offering such informed comments and asking such challenging questions. Now, sit right down and tell me what's on your mind, and I'll just scoot around to the captain's chair there." His brow stretched upwards: "Can I get you a coffee or tea? Here, please have one. Jieun makes the best oatmeal-and-raisin cookies West of Avonlea!"

Charmed to instant relaxation, Mary took one of the big cookies from the round porcelain container. She held it near her chin like presenting a badge ... it still smelled of fresh baking, and, unlike just about everyone who'd ever accepted a cookie, she took a healthy bite. She managed through some crumbling: "Thank you, Professor. If you don't mind I'll save the rest for later. My dad makes peanut butter cookies to die for." She'd never mention that the campus Tim's made a cookie that looked and tasted remarkably similar to the Professor's wife's.

She merely smiled and blinked the big deep blues, her pouty lips were plump and shiny as Cupid's spanked bum, and Jake swooned inwardly. He wished he had his life to live over. "My favourite cookie too, Mary, peanut butter—but don't tell Jieun! Now, what can I do for you, dear?" That was all right, he was sure.

She blushed. "Nothing really, I mean, I wanted to say that I love your classes, so you've already done a lot for me, thanks."

She had more to say, but Jake was already wondering if he'd slipped into some other dimension, some parallel universe where professors and students still related so. He caught himself. It was too much to believe. He was being set up, by Turnbull, even by Pat Kelly, or Turnbull *and* Kelly. Or some coalition of the student malcontent and professoriate disaffected. ... Oh, surely not. Be willing anyway to risk future trouble for the present prize. He beamed up his smile.

"Yes, dear, if I may address you so again, which I'm sure I shouldn't." Now Jake blushed. "You won't report me to Dean LaRoque, will you, Mary?" And smiled the paternal smile that had defused a thousand student (and Pod colleague) complainants.

Remarkably Mary found herself relaxing, and reflecting: Granny McGahern, who called her "pet." He was like Granny. And so identified the other thing that had distracted her during his lectures and discussions. But she always paid attention, when she wasn't being waylaid by her not having received email from Jimmy in days.

"Actually, Professor, I came here to apologize." Can she *not* control the fucking blushing! "I shouldn't have asked that question in your Canadian literature class Monday: it was smartass, if you'll pardon *my* language."

The professor strained to remember whatever she could be talking about, and Mary saw the effort in his frozen small smile. She dropped her gaze.

Thank God, thought Jake. *Old* Jake, he reminded himself. But what is a man, however old and innocently intending, to do these days when presented with such blushing youthful female beauty?

"I should never have asked if all Canada's early writers were so dour and guilty and afraid of everything."

Dour? thought Jake. And correctly pronounced, given that she'd probably only ever seen it in print. He had indeed entered strange territory here. He'd not talked with a student in years who spoke in more than three-word fragments, and one of those words would be *like*. So his pedagogical mind had to work as it seldom had in a long time. I'd *better* think, thought Jake. So far in that course they'd covered only the first quarter of the early Canadian syllabus, Oliver Goldsmith, Thomas McCulloch, and Thomas Chandler Haliburton … Ah, he remembered her question, yes, as she'd just rehearsed it. At least it hadn't caused him to have a stroke (as happened to a questioned old professor in one of Leacock's stories) but it had stopped him, stumped him actually, and to cover he'd simply agreed with her, then asked if she'd not found the first two sketches of *The Clockmaker* entertaining. She'd said she had, and especially Sam Slick's way of talking. But even there, she'd added, isn't there an undercurrent of Canadian envy, even anxiety, *even* fear, of America? That was when Professor Flynn had thought to have a chat with the beautiful, promisingly brilliant girl—young woman. He'd not realized that he'd stalled till another student, per usual presuming familiarity, said "Prof Jake?"

Scattered laughter.

Now he said, "Not at all, Mary, absolutely no call for apology. Please never feel that you should not raise any question in our classes." Could he risk it? Yes. "For me, the classroom has always been a sacred space for that very purpose, and *not* necessarily a *safe space*: *that* is still our whole *raison d'être*. And by the way, that's also the extent of my French."

She tittered onto her first knuckle like a tinkling Christmas tree. Jake had to hurry: "They *are* a dour crew, I completely agree, those old Canadian writers. Goldsmith was afraid of his own shadow, and McCulloch would have found fault in Michael the Archangel. But they had to be that way, they were pioneers not only as Canadian writers but many of them literally so. *They* had to be their dour way so that we could be this way, here today in the country's capital, comfortable, talking about them and what they wrote. They are what we come from, what makes us who we are. I believe that's something like what you were implying to Dean LaRoque out in the lobby the other day way back, if n'er so well expressed by me."

It was Mary's turn to feel overcome, for this dreamt-of meeting of minds between student and professor—and his remembering something she'd said! She recognized nudging joy in what was making her dizzy with delight, something like she'd felt meeting Detective Kiran Gurmeet that first day (she *must* go see her). But she soon felt that she was losing control in strong conflicting waves, danger signals which she recognized from when her mother had died. "It's just ... I'm ... I don't want to ..."

Jake forgot himself and every regulation in the harassment book ("for his own protection," as it affronted him). He moved round the desk, placed a hand on Mary's shoulder and spoke from an impenitent heart: "There-there, pet, things are never as bad as they look."

But of course that, the *pet*, wasted Mary, with vivid thought of Granny McGahern and her floury perfume ... entraining Mom, Dad, Jimmy, and rounding back to this incredible professor, his touching her too like that. Nobody touched anybody anymore. Jimmy knew how to touch her now, in lots of ways. There *were* many ways to touch, which made zero-tolerance a stupid joke. So there was no reason even to worry that she should stop crying like a big girly baby. But she had to, she was losing it.

Jake knew to let her cry it out. Which she did in short order. Snorted unselfconsciously like a child and dabbed her reddened eyes with the sleeve of her plaid shirt. She *was* hardly more than a child. She came back to her adult self: "I'm so sorry, Professor Flynn, its's just, well … I think it might just be homesickness, forgive me please. I'm ashamed of myself." One last sniffle and unladylike snort for good measure.

Jake patted her shoulder in parting and returned to his chair behind the desk. In the half-minute he let pass he wondered: Should I offer something about the tyranny of hormones at a woman's time of month? … No, too risky, like asking a fat woman when she's due. Instead:

"There's no call for apology, Mary, I won't hear it from you, and certainly no call for embarrassment. These days I'll cry over nothing myself, an old song that I didn't even care much about when it was current, something bathetically obvious on TV, it makes no sense. You're welcome to talk, if you'd like to, but something tells me you wouldn't like, not at present anyway. So, whenever you do like, Mary, please drop by and we'll chat about whatever, books or being away from home for the first time? … Or boys—they're all pigs, aren't they, as I'm sure you know," he scowled comically and glanced to confirm that he'd judged her correctly. She giggled like a breeze passing through chimes.

He said seriously, consciously shifting direction, "But you've been quiet in the Irish seminar, Mary, unlike your participation in the Canadian course. I hope that changes, because something tells me, Mary, that you have much to offer in that smaller group of, uh, young scholars."

Mary was continuously smiling again, and Jake saw her as he once saw his youngest daughter, Rosie, or just Rose now because already thrice Mary's age … his Rosie who was as sweetly alert to irony as Leacock himself. "So tell me, Mary, what do you think of *The Untilled Field*?"

Mary was surprised, and buoyed. "Oh, I just love it! I love the characters and the settings and the writing and, well, it reminds me of home ..." She deflated in a kind of self-alarm. "Uh, I guess that's not very critical."

Jake gently slapped the edge of the desk. "It isn't, Mary, and it is, the very best critical response! Where are you from, if I may ask?"

"I'm from a farm near Leitrim Falls. I'm not from anywhere else."

Jake was taken aback at the expression, though not visibly or for long. He leaned forward, as if literally wanting to get closer to her again. "Lovely, I know a lot of people from up the Valley, some of them farmers, great place, wonderful people, the real thing. And you know, the name *McGahern* rings bells for me. What's your father's name? Your mother's maiden name?"

"Séan. Mom passed away, was Carol Fleming."

"Sorry, Mary, for being the reminder of that hurt. ... What about the name *Collins*? Do you know an old farmer, about my age, named Tom Collins? Or he's probably not a farmer now. Last I saw Tom, couple of years ago, was at a high school reunion. In my day Leitrim Falls had no Catholic high school nearby and Tom had to come to St. Patrick's here in Ottawa, boarded with us his senior year, grade thirteen then. We needed the money. ... I heard Tom was thinking of selling the family farm to that big marijuana operation that moved in, then retiring, God bless him. Strictly *entre nous*, Mary, he had a little too much to drink at the reunion and by the end was—now never breathe a word of this—well, he was crying in his beer over the prospect of selling the farm. But any of that ring bells for you?"

What on earth was he going on about? That was Jake's thought.

Oh, my, God! And that staccato thought Mary's, confused by the mention of Jimmy's surname and his email silence, by her reticence over divulging personal matters, and by a creeping physical unease. Though these were her spoken words:

"No, can't say that I do know any Collinses, Professor. But I *do* appreciate George Moore's stories. I'm going to tell my dad to read the book. He had me read a similar book of short stories set in the Canadian West during the Dustbowl years."

"Hmmm. Was it by a writer named Grove?"

"No."

"Ross? Sinclair Ross?"

"That's it! I really remember loving one story about a young boy out searching for the poor family's lost cow, a heifer, in a blizzard. But the whole book was great!"

Book. When had he last heard that word from a student? *Or* a colleague? It's all *text* this and text that. "Very good, Mary. Would you like to do your presentation assignment on a few of Moore's stories? Say, the first one, one from the middle, and the last?"

"Thank you, Professor, I would like that. Can I come and talk with you about it, please?"

"Of course, and if my regular office hours are inconvenient, just say so and we'll find another mutually convenient time. Heaven only knows what hell has planned: but there are few students competing for time during my posted office hours!"

Mary continued feeling charmed down to her toes, but anxious about overstaying, she laughed gently and asked as she moved to stand, "Was that yours?"

Jake was puzzled. "Pardon? I don't understand …"

"The *heaven only knows what hell has planned*? Did you just come up with that, Professor, or is it a regular expression? I mean, if *I* may be so bold?"

Which only continued Jake in his chaste love. He side-stepped her complimentary question with fallback irony: "Mary, you obviously have a fine ear for poetry." They both guffawed. "Have you noticed the posters advertising our undergraduate English's—I mean, our Film&WordsWork Pod's poetry contest?" He'd already picked the sheet from his desk's corner and was handing it across to her.

Puzzled, she read aloud quietly: "Double trouble! Student-Poets of the world unite! You have nothing to lose but your reputation for serious scholarship! Instructions: In a short poem play with the contest title, *double trouble*, and do so as nonsensically as you can! The world needs more nonsense! Never more than now!" She pinched her mouth: "Thank you, Professor, but I'm no poet."

"No? Who is until she tries? I think you might be, Mary. I have a sixth sense for this kind of thing. Did you notice the prize? Bottom of the page?"

She hadn't till then, as her gaze dropped to where in bold at the bottom it was given: "Five hundred dollars!"

"See," said laughing Jake, "I knew there was a writer in there wanting to get out!"

She exhaled through her nose. "But I don't get it. What would they be looking for, Professor?"

"Nonsense verse, Mary. Do you know the *Alice* books of Lewis Carroll?"

"Yes. ... Oh, I get it."

"There you go then. *Double trouble*, doubleness, though I'm not confident either that *I* know that's what they want. Maybe *duplicity* or some such, served up with *double entendres* and *puns*? But I expect you're licensed to interpret the theme as you see fit. Here, I'm going to jot down a couple of names, Edward Lear and Ogden Nash. Have a look, there'll be lots online. You'll come up with something, I *am* confident, and something good." Jake put a hand over his heart and intoned mock-seriously:

"Shake and shake the ketchup bottle, none'll come, and then a lot'll."

Mary shook her small-smiling head: "What?"

Jake elevated his large forefinger: "Ogden Nash … I *think*. Nonsense poetry."

"Thank you, Professor. But what's a ketchup bottle?"

"Dear God, Mary, but of course! Condiments used to come—"

"I know, Professor. I was making a stupid joke. Though nowadays we *do* squeeze and squeeze the ketchup pack, first comes none, and then—splat!"

"I knew it! A poet! I want half the money as finder's fee! I caution you, however, that rhyming *pack* and *splat* is not in the best tradition of Canadian nonsense poetry!"

They laughed together. Mary was rising again and Jake wanted to delay her again. He was confused as to why. He knew that he'd again experienced the psychic shift, if in a different way from with Detective Gurmeet. But, then, it was always different. He *should* check himself with this female student, but he didn't.

"It's such a pleasure talking with you, Mary." Mary sat back. "My most recent seminar, last winter, was in Canadian humour and satire. We began with some of the same books, uh, *texts*, as in our early Canadian course, McCulloch's *Stepsure Letters* and Haliburton's *The Clockmaker*. About halfway through we reached *Anne of Green Gables*. Do you know it?"

"Know it? I absolutely love it! Read all the *Anne* books, then turned to the *Emily* books, which I loved even more!"

Jake could not believe what he was feeling: delightfully charmed, in a way he'd thought impossible anymore with a student. "A writer you are, *see*? But if you will indulge me just a little longer, please, Mary? Yes? Whenever I come across an exceptional student, one who has read widely already and who writes so well—no, no modest objections; I have the evidence in your respectful classroom questions and comments, and already in your short essay on the love story of *The Rising Village*. But whenever I encounter the increasingly rare student such as yourself, I like to ask her—and it's just about always a *her* these days—how she was brought up?"

Mary was confused, as she knew neither how they'd got where they were nor where this was going, nor how she could feel so unburdened after feeling so miserably put upon and crying in front of a veritable stranger! Her professor! So she didn't have to counterfeit gratitude to smile and say, "Okay, I'm game—I mean, yes sir, please."

"Well then, what was different in your home compared to ninety-nine-point-nine percent of your peers'?"

"Oh. That's easy. My mother and father made me read every day from the age of three till they didn't have to make me anymore. Nowadays, if I don't read every day I feel, well, like I forgot to put on my pants or something." Was that a gush? Jesus Christ! I *knew* it.

Jake laughed and felt actual pain in his chest from restraining the urge to howl. He managed, "Did they restrict your watching television and time on the computer?"

Mary smirked in some unease. "You could say that, Professor. When my mother was alive—"

"Oh, I'm so sorry to again—"

"Thank you. I was allowed only one hour of TV a day, no cable. Mom and Dad watched with me. They read all the time, even in front of the TV, hardly ever the newspaper, which is all my friends' parents ever read, those who regularly complain to teachers that their kids never pick up a book. As for computer time, no computer whatsoever. No ironically named *smart* phone.

I had nothing to do *but* read, and eventually that was all I wanted to do, like I said." She was again worrying about overstaying when Professor Flynn cut in.

"Please, Mary, tell me more, I'm not just idly curious, teaching has been my life, please, I'm interested."

She compressed her lips, looked down, looked up. "Not long after Mom died, Dad put the TV out in the barn and home-schooled me for grades ten and eleven. Dad actually went sort of nuts about TV, going on and on about how it was all lies lies lies, saying that for a hundred years now the main thing people watched and heard was all lies. He meant the ads mainly, but not only. He was death on canned laughter, laugh tracks for him being one of TV's biggest lies, to quote him, 'in so-called comedies about as funny as a pig pissing.'"

She paused till they'd finished laughing.

"Dad said that to fake laughter is as bad as faking love. He said that false TV laughter was why people laugh at everything nowadays, after everything they say or is said to them, or at nothing at all! They will say nothing funny and cue themselves as the laugh-track. Dad called it laugh-track living. He said that when everything is funny, nothing is serious, and when nothing is serious you can be more easily convinced by the lies that you need to buy everything!"

"Wow. Did your father write?"

"I think he did when he was young, but not otherwise. When he was still letting me watch my one hour of TV per day, he began making me pick out the lies. After a while it was easy, because just about everything on TV *does* have some version of a lie in it. From the lying laughter to the lying threats that if you don't buy this right away today, you don't care about your children's safety. If you don't buy this, you don't love your wife. You're not using this? Then you're a fool. You don't think this is funny? Listen to that laughter! All fathers and husbands are idiots—born eejits, as my Granny used to say. All that lying—"

"Eejits! I've not heard that word since my own mad father died!"

"I'm rambling, Professor, I'm sorry."

"Not at all, Mary, quite the opposite. And *I* asked *you*." He mimed tiny applause: "More! More!"

Mary wondered, worried, but carried on. "Dad has this theory that three-quarters of a century of TV has made people blasé about lying, so accepting of it in fact that they've become unable to distinguish truth from lies, and no one cares anyway. He says that politics and advertising have of course always been about lying, but it got way worse with TV, and now with social media it's the Apocalypse. And that all that lying is what made straight the way for crooked Donald Trump ... uh, I mean, my dad says."

"Remarkable. To return the compliment you paid me, is that line, the play on John the Baptist the truth-sayer as being somehow like TV preparing the way for Trump the anti-Christ, is that your dad's or yours? ... Okay, I might blush too if I were a poet. Mary, I don't know why I'm telling you this, but to finish my *Anne of Green Gables* story, which I'm more certain than ever you'll appreciate. That particular meeting of the seminar concluded that Anne Shirley may well have been—and it's a good thing you're seated—a lesbian!"

Mary frowned, smiled small, nodded, and Jake knew that he could finish, though why he did so he never would know.

"And not *only* a lesbian but in her kind of natural religion very close to Judaic philosophy, or theology—its *beliefs* respecting nature anyway. Do you follow me, Mary? Or should this old white man just shut up?"

"No. Please continue, Professor." Though she *was* creepingly worried now about Professor Flynn's state of mind, as she'd seen the same excitability in her father after a full-flight presentation of weighty evidence against TV: a sort of nervous exhaustion, yes, but also something more enervating, a frightening dismay wearing a grin, finished with the world and his own future in it. She felt a twist, a grip in her guts, the foreboding cramp. She needed to go.

"Oh that's all of it, I guess, *more than*. Canada's literary sweetheart, Anne Shirley of Prince Edward Island at the turn of the last century, is actually a Jewish dyke—forgive my French, Mary."

Mary didn't need to forgive anything. She rejoined lamely with the line she'd heard on her favourite TV show: "Not that there's anything wrong with that!"

Jake recognized the line (Jieun had loved *Seinfeld* in endless rerun), and himself added lamely, "And there isn't. I swear to God I'm neither anti-Semitic nor homophobic, it's the fashionable *il*logic of it all!"

Then they settled in the strangely shamed awkwardness that results from sharing TV preferences and unpopular prejudices.

"Thanks for, uh, *sharing* your story, Mary." She responded again with an ironic nod of affirmation, which encouraged him to continue. "But it all makes sense: your literary intelligence, your fine writing, more of which I very much look forward to, your appreciation of *Anne* and *The Untilled Field*."

Could she go now? She'd better, she had to go. *Please*. But he wasn't done!

"You know, Mary, I used to fish up Leitrim Falls way, I even did so with Tom Collins a few times, a long time ago … though what we mostly did was drink beer all day! … Imagine that: such a drinker named after a drink!" Jake lapsed, his smile waning, his head tipping a bit.

Thought Mary: *Wha* …? But if I don't go right now I'm going to bleed all over his chair and floor! What'll *that* do to him!

But she recognized a more pressing human need, so had to tell her body to relax (sometimes that worked). She took a deep breath and spoke clearly to him, and more loudly. "I fish too, Professor, in our farm's Big Pond, mostly just carp and other garbage-feeders, though Big Pond *is* spring-fed. Dad says he once caught a rainbow trout, but I'm almost sure he's lying just to tease me. Or maybe I'm just not a good enough ... *angler*. You'd be welcome to come up and try your line, Professor—if I'm not being too forward, I mean. I mean, I'm sure Dad would love the company, *and* the fishing."

Jake lifted his gaze to Mary's face and seriously wondered if he was experiencing not just the psychic shift but something of an angelic visitation. He *was* still a believer, though he'd be hard put anymore to articulate what in. He even spoke in a prayerful whisper: "I've fished with some success hereabouts, Mary. All over Canada, and most rewardingly in Ireland too; *brown* trout there, delicious, in Wicklow, in Connemara, all over ..." And then lapsed again in something of a wide-eyed apoplexy.

Mary continued to sense growing serious trouble, the whipsawing, though knew it to be of a sort she could not relieve, and not only because she was feeling seriously crampy again. "I've taken up far too much of your time, Professor, I should go, I have to in fact."

She was up and at the always-open door when Jake said normally, or with the low resignation that had become typical only in the last few months: "Do enter that poetry contest, Mary."

"I will, I promise, and thank you, Professor," she said taking a step. But stopped in the doorway, paused, and turned back:

"Do you know, I think I do know the Collinses, if your old friend is the father of Jimmy Collins."

Jake shook himself and snapped up his head. He instantly found his Professor Flynn persona: "That's the ticket, Mary! I look forward to seeing you in class Monday!"

"Thank you, bye-bye, Professor!"

He called, "And Mary, next time remind me to give you a copy of *Sarah Binks*, iron-clad guarantee you'll love it!" Why on earth was he shouting into the empty hallway about the so-called Sweet Songstress of Saskatchewan? He waited for Peggy's voice. ... Nothing. Good. Home. Home?

And Mary, in some menstrual distress now—*Where is that fucking washroom?*—thanked Mother Mary that she'd at least packed tampons in her rucksack (Dad's word)—Mary was able to hurry off with her opinion of herself partly refurbished, having acknowledged Jimmy, if at the expense of having serious Jimmy worries again. Had she used—abused—yo-yoing Professor Flynn? Was it all just hormonal? ... Fuck off.

NINETEEN

THE DISCONNECT

From: Mary McGahern <mmcgahern022@ubytown.ca>
Mon. Oct. 4 at 20:01
To: Jim Collins
Cc:

Dear Jim,

You don't answer, so I'm guessing you're not going home for Thanksgiving? Poop and shallots (my genteel version of Dad's "shite and onions," which he attributes to James Joyce). If you're not going home, I wouldn't go either only that it would disappoint Dad so much. I know that's no concern of yours, I mean, what *your* father would feel. Or maybe that you care what I care anymore. But what about your mom, Jim, don't you want to see her? She needs your support. But I can't go on making small talk, even this big small talk, not with you. Because what I mean is: What about me?

What's going on, *Jimmy*? If you want to do something else, I'll do it with you. Quit university? I'm down for that. Leave, go to Europe? That too, only I love my father. But what's happening, Jimmy? Do you think maybe you're drinking too much? Is there someone else? Don't you love me anymore?

Love,
Mary

From: Jim Collins <jcollins181@uwo.ca>
        Mon. Oct. 6 at 02:29
To: Mary McGahern
Cc:

Mary Mary quite contrary. ... I don't give a fuck about my mother. She's the enabler, that's the word, and that's what she's been my whole life, making things easy for my old man and to hell with me. What's going on Jimmy? What's happening? Is there someone else? What about you and Fred fucking Faucher? Yeah!!! You said nothing happened between you and him because he was such a prick about your fucking chickens. But what if fucking Fred had been real nice like? Then wha

From: Naomi Starling <mar171@fanshawe.ca>
Mon. Oct. 6 at 14:00
To: Mary McGahern
Cc:

Hi Mary. Thanks for emailing me first. I wasn't sure if I could find you and didn't think you'd ever use student email, I'm glad you do! You're my only real friend from Leitrim Falls that I want to keep in touch with. You don't say much but you don't sound happy, girl. Are you still not going out? Isn't uBytown right in downtown Ottawa? You're not still carrying a torch for Jim Collins, are you? Me and my new friends go only to this really cool student bar called Ceeps. Now don't climb all over my ass about this next part, you know I'm no slut but I met this really nice guy named Mike Brown. He's from Sarnia not far from here, he's doing a diploma in Student Counselling. One night we were left alone at Ceeps, I couldn't keep up with him, he drinks like a fish. Guess who else is a regular at Ceeps? Your old flame Jimbo. I go maybe twice a week and Jim is there every time, so he must be there like all the time. We only wave to each other, and he's always still there when we leave. His crowd looks pretty wild, not the old Jim we knew.

I had your strawberry jam on toast when I got home tonight. Delish! My courses in Hospitality are ok but like a bird sanctuary. I didn't puke your jam at least.

Your friend,
Naomi

From: Mary McGahern <mmcgahern022@ubytown.ca>
      Mon. Oct. 6 at 14:15
To: Naomi Starling
Cc:

Are there any girls in Jimmy's group? With him? Will write decently later.

Thanks.
Mary

From: Naomi Starling <mar171@fanshawe.ca>
      Mon. Oct. 7 at 16:00
To: Mary McGahern
Cc:

Hi Mary. That was to the point!!! I'm hungover, only just out of bed. Last night Mike and me ended up throwing up together. Must be love, eh? He passed out in my room, nothing else. I like him and I think I could a lot. But boy can that boy ever pound the brewski! ... I'm avoiding your question cause I think I know what you're getting at, I didn't mean to joke about you and Jim. I didn't see much of you over the past summer and I know Jim worked on your farm. Something happened, right? So, BFF to BFF: there are some girls in Jim's crowd and slutty, same crowd always, some of them look more like biker chicks than your run-of-the-mill posh Western students. And I hate to say it but a little blond is always sitting beside Jim and hardly drinking at all (yes I keep an eye on him, and she can't seem to take her eyes off

Jimmy boy). He looks like he's carrying on the great drinking tradition of the Collinses, just a-pounding it like his old man. I don't know what else to say but I hope this doesn't upset you too much. He doesn't look like he's having fun if that helps. Right now I need to hydrate and eat real food.

Your friend, hoping we can hook up in the Falls over Thanksgiving!
Naomi

From: Mary McGahern <mmcgahern022@ubytown.ca>
    Mon. Oct. 7 at 16:10
To: Naomi Starling
Cc:

Thanks, Naomi. You're a true friend. Sorry you're not feeling well. I trust you know I'm being a true friend to you when I say: watch the drinking. You're too smart to drink just to impress a boy, you don't need to. I remember your experience with Rick Maclean: try sex with your Mike Brown. It may be just the (sober) distraction you both need! Think of it as field work in Hospitality! (ha ha). Seriously (or more so), please think of this as just an unnecessary word to the already-wise woman!

Thanks again, Naomi. I'm a bit in the dumps. Very much looking forward to seeing you over Thanksgiving.

Your BFF,
Mary OO

TWENTY

ANIMAL HUSBANDRY

It had rained all night and was threatening more, which was way welcome with a hundred acres of soybeans just seeded and rolled, but no good for a planned first cutting of hay. This had been back in late June and we needed at least three days of good weather to cut, ted, ted again, rake and bale. And, late in the season as it already was, eighty acres still had to be seeded with corn. And another hundred acres of planted soybean had to be rolled. But Dad and I were trapped mucking out the sheds, the shit work for such shitty days, with Dad using the loader bucket to scrape the floor, and me keeping the cows back, which was made worse by the pigs who'd again got their gate open, smart buggers. We were both irritable as all hell.

Dad had left the little Deere idling and come over to help me, and probably also for a break. I'd mentally been preparing for him to ask me how I liked *Jude the Obscure*, since he still sometimes acted like he was home-schooling me. I liked his thinking that way, I liked the novel so far, and I liked breaks in the shitty work. The black pickup turning of the road distracted us both from jokey talk of the aesthetics of pig bladders as tokens of love, kicking up gravel and mud. It parked to the side of the front porch and he was out of the cab before I recognized Jimmy Collins. That would have been his father's black pickup.

Even at a distance he looked shy and awkward, though he was really neither, and I was remembering how much I liked his smile as he got closer. Then I panicked: *I* looked like something that had been dragged through a byre, because I pretty well had been, in my screaming-pink shit-splattered wellingtons (not even turned down), unsexy overalls (*way* oversized and thick as tarp), maybe Dad's first-ever cap (black-and-red and fuzzy—with ear flaps!). My face was going all space-heater on me. Dad may have noticed and said normally, "Isn't that Tom Collins' boy?"

Before I could answer, Pluto, our big old boar, went thundering past us and Dad after the pig. I did nothing, I expected Jimmy to turn tail and run for his life. He'd grown up on a farm himself so would have known you do not want to fuck with a boar, whether guarding his sows or one in rut (which is just about any time for pigs). But Jimmy stood his ground spreading his legs and arms like he would actually block Pluto, who bore down on him (I can joke about it now!) in what looked to be shaping up as a contest of chicken—it was the pig swerved if not without clipping Jimmy and sending him flying into a paste of mud and soy-straw cuttings. Pluto stopped a few yards past and turned as if coolly surveying the damage he'd done, with his heavily lashed tiny pig eyes fairly indifferent to whatever.

Dad stamped a foot towards Pluto—dominance—got behind him and booted his ass, a signal Pluto never disputed. He helped Jimmy up and, still holding his hand, was slapping the plentiful dirt from his tan cords. Pluto, his dignity intact, trotted blithely past me like I didn't exist and on into the fenced pen (I half-expected him to turn and shut the gate), where his harem had gathered admiringly for the show of porky defiance. He moved off proudly on those nimble legs, a pig prancing, and the sows eagerly followed him to their corner.

Forgetting myself I went to Dad and Jimmy. "Are you all right, Jimmy?"

"All right?" said Dad, who continued to hold Jimmy's hand, which looked kind of funny. "When was the last time you saw anyone stand his ground with a charging boar?" He laughed, encouraging himself. "This young man deserves ranking with the heroes and lesser gods of Olympus, Valhalla, and Tír na nÓg!" He was acting and serious, at once truly impressed but overdoing it as he pumped Jimmy's arm like a jack.

Jimmy didn't blush, he never did, I realized. He just smiled at Dad, then stayed on me. "Where's that?"

I said, "What are you doing here?" That was too direct, so I tried, "Are you sure you're all right, Jimmy?"

"I'm fine," he continued to smile. "But *Jim*. Do you know, I can't believe it but I forget now why I came out. I hope it wasn't to show off my new cords! My dad said ..." He looked like he was truly failing to remember. Perhaps charging Pluto had rearranged his brain.

Dad kept looking from Jimmy to me like it was tennis, and finally after a pause of grinning at me said, "Never mind, we're glad you came, Mr. Collins. How would you like to work for me this summer, Jim?"

"What!" That was me. Though Jimmy looked only slightly less surprised.

Dad continued: "I can't pay you much, say, five hundred dollars a week? Monday to Friday, at least ten hours a day, and some weekends too. It's been a bad spring, lots of catch-up, we're still doing corn and soy and with a first cutting to be done, and a lot else all at the same time. Whaddya say, young man?"

Eloquent as ever I again said, "What?"

Jimmy didn't fumble. "I'd love to, sir. But that's my dad's truck. I borrowed it today because Mom said I could if I was coming out here to see if … well, I guess to see if Mary wanted to go for a ride over to Perth."

For the first time I knew what it meant to feel weak in the knees. *Why did Dad have to be there!*

"There *was* something else, and it involved you, Mr. McGahern, but the old man was in pretty bad shape this morning … maybe 'cause he banged up the truck last night." Jimmy glanced at the truck, whose rear left corner did look freshly scraped. "Anyway, he didn't argue with Mom for once." His mouth turned down and he looked down. He talked at his fancy black runners, now muddied: "Wait: Dad said he'd run into you, Mr. McGahern, at Matty O'Shea's and you had said something about a few days' work … or something." Now he *was* blushing a fine rose, which was a great relief to me standing there like Anne Shirley the morning after sleeping all night in the White Way of Delight following a bush party.

Dad took my hand, reeled me in then pushed me towards the house. "Go go." He winked at Jimmy and did his hick voice: "She cleans up real good, son, you'll see. You can hardly expect her to be lookin' quality when she's been mucking out a stable."

"I … but the sun's been peeping, what *about* the work—"

Jimmy blinked like he knew he was watching an act, so kept quiet.

Dad took on a different mock-tone: "Your father said go, young lady, now go."

I went.

I looked out my bedroom window and couldn't have been more surprised than if Pluto had been driving the tractor, to see Dad with a brush cleaning of Jimmy's pants again. After some serious face-washing, hair-brushing, and slut-conscious clothes choices, I guess I looked all right in my second-best sundress and cleaned white sneakers. Were the baby-blue ankle socks a bad idea? Probably. At the front door I snatched my straw hat with the pink ribbon, which I'd left hanging there on the antique mirror for decoration and hadn't worn in, like, well, ever. Before stepping out I listened through the screen to Dad and Jimmy standing by the truck discussing future work to be done, talking seriously, if also teasingly on Dad's part. He couldn't help himself; as with Granny McGahern, teasing was a form of affection with Dad, and I expect Jimmy knew that. It wasn't just the Irish in them but also a farmer's way. Whatever, I was again much puzzled about the whole deal. I heard a tap-tapping then Dad say seriously, "Billy O'Shea will be in trouble with the law if he lets customers drive home in the condition your dad was in. The risk to your father is one thing, but he could kill someone else."

As I came round the end of the porch, I realized that the tapping had been Dad knocking the crinkled fender of the truck with his brush; my held hat was now tapping my pelvis bone as if reminding me there was still time to run away and hide. They looked at the same time and under that heavy sky smiled like dual suns.

I looked at the sky just as the sun was blown of cloud cover, there was more blue than before. I said, "It's clearing, we'd be losing a day, Dad."

He said, "You'd better get going then before the day clears and I make you both stay to work!"

And then he did one of the oddest things, for him: passing me he paused to kiss my cheek like a goodbye, then rubbed the small of my back, and continued on towards the barn. Jimmy's next move may not have been that strange, but it was the first time anyone ever did it for me: he hustled round to the passenger side of the cab, opened the door and sweepingly gestured me in. I should have said thanks but didn't. It was a whole new world for me and, unlike Jimmy, I wasn't able yet to be ironic about it.

I had one of those rare great days, the best time in a long long time, the kind I'd forgotten existed since Mom's death, though nothing special happened and the sky continued patchy. Well, something incredibly special happened, but nothing anyone else would notice, including Jimmy.

It was Perth's Spring Fling, no matter we were into summer by then and nothing much was flinging in the overcast little berg (with three-k more population, we Leitrim Fallers are the big city—and don't we know it). Jimmy and I walked up and down the main street a lot, Gore Street, just "arsing about," as Granny McGahern would say. We quietly sneered at some pathetic store-window displays—leftover Christmas stuff still!—but also smiled in recognition—a ten-year-old poster for "Take-Out Lasagnia Dinner" at the Legion (neither of us needed to point out the misspelling). We had lunch at a place called Martha's Table, which was nice; arsed about some more (even visiting The Mammoth Cheese!); a slow walk through the park by the Tay River (no handholding but our upper arms and shoulders touched when we leaned against a rail to watch a flotilla of ducklings; neither of us pulled away; and it felt perfect that I was taller, just a little, for once). We'd both been in Perth hundreds of times since before we could remember, and yet it was like seeing a new place—"The Canal locks really are impressive!" observed effusive Mary—of course because I *was* seeing it with someone for the first time.

The visit began to end around four with a good hour spent at some used books bins, with the slow flipping-through working to keep Jimmy and me distracted from what we were actually doing: ending a first date. At least I was assuming-hoping it was the same for Jimmy (and, well, he did ask me). He picked only one book, something on cosmology, *Black Holes* it was titled, an oversized book full of pictures. I bought some half-dozen books, showing off, giving two to Jimmy, refusing his paying me but making him promise to read them and tell me what he thought.

"Hey, I love reading, you don't have to coerce me, school-marm McGahern."

"*Coerce*," I mocked. "Shame if all the pictures in your *big* book there are already coloured," I nodded, having got back my irony chops. "Of course you'd have needed only the black crayon anyway."

He frowned ... then burst out laughing. "But black's so obvious, I'd use the purple, perfect purple!" Oh, Jimmy Collins knew from teasing all right.

One of the books I gave him was *Sunshine Sketches of a Little Town*, in a pretty green cover with a stout and menac-ing, if also colourful, Josh Smith on the front. "The future Ted Faucher, bossman of little Leitrim Falls," I turned it for Jimmy, but this time he held the frown (he didn't like any mention of Faucher), so I hurried to press on him the twenty-five-cent used paperback of *Breakfast of Champions*. I'd picked up a couple of old and pretty hardbound novels for Dad by authors who were already on his shelves, Ralph Connor, and a more expensive Kurt Vonnegut, *Time Quake*.

For myself a deluxe edition of *Jane Eyre*, which I would never tire of rereading, and two bargain hardcover Alice Munros also for rereading, *Lives of Girls and Women* and *Who Do You Think You Are?* The girl working the cashbox paused in her totting up to admire the lovely cover of the second and read its title aloud: "Who Do You Think You Are?" And I knew I was pretty well risking it all with Jimmy right there and then on our first date: "We're Mr. and Mrs. James and Mary Collins-McGahern, we're from Leitrim Falls, we're not from anywhere else." It was a line I'd stolen from a story by Mavis Gallant (thank you, teacher Dad). The salesgirl made a stinky crinkly-nose face as she was making change, and Jimmy and I laughed together turning away, scatting whatever awkwardness had been snuffling between us.

On the short drive home the late-afternoon sun suddenly came out fully behind us and kept Jimmy from glancing again in the rear-view mirror that had instantly sparkled the cab with iridescence. He squinted ahead, exhaled a kind of delicious exhaustion, and seen even in profile was wearing a plain face of near oblivious contentment. He said more to himself than to me, "We'll be cutting that hundred acres tomorrow, then, tedding Saturday and Sunday if the weather holds, if we're lucky, then raking and baling Monday." He hitched his head towards me but didn't look: "That's when we'll need you in the field. Do you feel lucky, Mary? The weather, I mean."

I didn't have to look either: *that* was the face of the boy I'd talked to Mom about two years before. I squinted away from my side mirror at the stubble whizzing by close to the road. "We need *you*, Jimmy."

I knew he smiled small. "*Jim*, Mary-Mary quite contrary."

And that was the singular instant that I, Mary McGahern from nowhere else but Leitrim Falls, knew that I'd fallen in love for the first time forever. The McGahern gift, as Granny called it.

Dad was happy with his books, but he pretended that they were from Jimmy and wouldn't hear otherwise than that he was staying for supper as payment. Jimmy went along and complained that he'd tried to get the money from me and that I'd said Dad would add it to his wages. Dad did a double-take: "*Wages?*" Jimmy rewarded him with laughter. Dad was soon bragging about his homebrew, how it was based on the Irish Harp Lager but better than, and that real visiting Irishmen had attested so. He didn't have to press Jimmy to have one while he barbecued the steaks and they talked more about plans for the summer. Dad had another brew with supper, but Jimmy refused saying it was so good he didn't trust himself because he was driving. It was so great seeing Dad come back to such fine form. For that alone Jimmy Collins was a godsend. But there was more, much more, as the advertisers say.

After that first day he always biked out, worked hard and had supper with us. At first I walked him only as far as the road. Even in open air, after such a day and no showering, he gave off an odour that can only be called "Jimmy." Do I need to say I liked it? I began walking him farther and farther and standing closer and closer. He kept urging me to turn back before we'd get too far. One of many jokes that developed between us over that summer involved his growing pretend-anger with me for not going back home. He'd pick stones from the road and throw them near my feet: "Go home, Mary! Home, home." It didn't matter that it happened every day, because every day I walked back smiling. Or it did matter that it happened every day. Dad would notice and say, "Young lady?"

He arrived at five every morning without fail. He remembered a farm's routine well enough, knew that the work demanded a strict methodical approach and attention to detail. On his own Jimmy would begin jobs they'd talked of at supper the day before, the mornings Dad had a bad hangover. But those mornings, whose slow increase had had me worrying again, soon lessened and eventually disappeared, *because* of Jimmy's work habits and the stepped-up demands of peak-season.

With Jimmy doing the work of two regular hired hands (as Dad complimented him over suppers, for my sake, I suspected), I was needed in the fields less often. Of course I worked at least as long and hard a day, though, because with steady Jimmy, Dad needed to hire no other temporary help. On my own I looked after the Holsteins, some twenty for beef and thirty for dairy, and the dozen milking machines; the endless feeding of hungry pigs; the chickens that had once seemed quite enough chore for me when school was still on; and using the small Deere to move forage and silage, filling the troughs, filling them again. And again.

I soon shrugged off most of the feminist nonsense I'd picked up in my reading (like, a farm can afford that?) and brought Dad and Jimmy water in the fields and had dinner and supper going when they came in. But only *most* of that raging adolescent feminism. Two things I noticed in the fields, one admiringly, the other needling me. Dad, fifty years old, had been moving more slowly the past few years, but I could never remember him ever moving like Jimmy: stripped to the waste and leaping a dangerous gap from the wheel of the big Deere to the seeder, dumping in bags of corn seed, springing back and landing on the big tread and on he went, all in about three minutes, always waving grinning acknowledgement of where I'd set the ice-filled plastic container of water. Dad had never let me drive the big Deere, which I'd wanted to do but would never ask, and I'd worked as much with him as Jimmy was doing, and as hard ... well, close enough. The big Deere, new, probably still having to be paid for into *my* old age, had A/C and could be GPS controlled, doors and windows tight as a space suit, and a radio whose quality was as good as a headset, monitor with cameras back and sides.

Pre-Jimmy, when I'd be following behind the rollers on a day that could melt roads, picking up rocks and hustling to throw them off to the side, Dad would be in the big Deere's cab still with his plaid jacket on—reading a fucking book! When he'd look up at me, I'd dramatically do a waving wilting faint, sometimes dropping right to the ground. He'd smile big and wave, then point pointedly at me and make a drinking motion with his hand. At first I'd thought he meant that I should drink more water, but he was asking to be *brought* a drink. Watching Jimmy move off in the big Deere I could smile remembering Mom's refrain: "That's your father, dear, we have to work on him." I said, "We could start by hiding the homebrew kit." And she: "It would be all my life was worth." Dad had instructed that I always bring two beers to the field toward day's end, and he and Jimmy would sit in the shade of the big Deere, clink bottles, and guzzle the first third before pausing. I felt uneasy about feeling uneasy about ... something. Maybe my small jealousy of their bonding? Then thought it might be the relished beer, which was soon followed by more back home. I never liked the taste of beer.

On wet days the three of us found enough to do about the barn and yard, more than enough, and sometimes all three of us herded the animals morning noon and evening. It seemed all our conversation consisted of counting and compulsively checking each other's counts, and describing and rehearsing the next day's work to be done, and the day after that, and the four good days needed for a second cutting, still more planting to be decided, when and how (with seeder or without?), the work owed to neighbours for borrowed choppers and seeders and such. Just about everything was rented or borrowed; we owned a fairly new cultivator, which others borrowed in barter, and a new Tebbe—still being paid for of course. But everyone had got their chicken-manure spreading done in late April that year, when hope ran high, as it will for farmers, when Dad always complained about the cost of crop insurance (his view had shifted by July and August).

When mucking out came round again, we all pitched in. With three of us, we were able to do the straw-chopping for fresh bedding for the heifers while the scraping was being done because I'd watch the rented chopper and Jimmy would do my old job keeping the animals out of the tractor's way. I did *not* like that Dad switched off driving the small Deere with Jimmy. I did *not* like that we chopped only soy straw, which was so dusty it made me look trashy comical, which was not the effect I'd aimed for (more slightly slutty farm girl). But getting that job done in less than a working day (if sunrise till set) saved us badly needed time and funds, because of machinery rented by the hour and of days borrowed from a neighbour (which meant payback in lost days' work). It was high season for farming.

After suppers Dad and Jimmy would drink at least another beer (having had the one before and another during), and while the days were longest Jimmy was in no hurry to head home. He never looked even tipsy, which I thought a good thing, till I remembered Mom saying that the macho "holding your liquor" was *not* a good thing: it made men think they could drink without damage. She'd said that Tom Collins had already been famous in high school for handling his booze, and look at him today. But with Dad and Jimmy all the work and food seemed to counter the effects of the booze, and they drank more water than anything. I'd often have a chore to do after supper (reminding Dad to do the kitchen clean-up), and Jimmy began accompanying me for the egg collection or whatever. I don't think he was trying to avoid another beer with Dad, but maybe.

More and more around Jimmy I felt what I'd known in the car on that drive back from Perth, but I showed nothing, needing him to come to me, or it would never happen the right way. Then it did happen over the first couple of weeks of July, almost imperceptibly. This will sound silly, like a movie "meet-cute," but fuck silly. The first move was when I stepped out of the barn after him and caught the ledge and his grabbing my arm, steadying me up close to him, and his hand sliding down to my hand, which he held for a long moment, and we looked at each other and smiled then stopped smiling. He felt as I felt, but (call me what you want) that still wasn't enough.

After one of his "Young Lady?" half-jokes at my daydreaming, Dad looked all serious. He shook out his farmer's paper and quoted his favourite Shakespeare character from his favourite play (mine too), pretending like he was reading it from *The Farmer's Almanac* or whatever: "Lest too light winning make the prize light." He knew that I knew what he was talking about, because we'd argued about that scene in *The Tempest*, so he didn't need to elaborate. I turned away from Dad pretending more insult than I felt and walked heavily upstairs.

Sitting in my room and watching the place in the road where I'd left Jimmy only half-an-hour before, I thought some more about Prospero's line. I wasn't some "prize" to be won or lost, I wouldn't be a *thing* traded between Dad and Jimmy. *I* wanted a part in winning too. And I didn't want to be either slut or tease. Feminists made things sound so cut-and-dried. I'd have asked Naomi for advice, but I suspected that her way with Rick Maclean could never be mine. I'll also admit I didn't like that I was beginning to believe Shakespeare's sentiment—*some* things don't change. So I continued to wait for Jimmy to declare himself first.

After supper one day in the third week of July, the subject of fishing came up naturally. Jimmy had never fished. "*Never fished?*" Dad exaggerated. "There are fish in Big Pond, right daughter?" Jimmy ventured half-jokingly: "I've still not been there, Mary's very possessive." Big Pond was visible only if you left our working fields and passed through a stand of trees that bordered the field we rented for … well, for nothing useful as far as I'd ever seen. The trees were ours (Dad used them for fuel in his work shed's rusty oil-drum heater, which had been a constant worry to Mom when he was drinking), as was Big Pond. Third-beering Dad trotted out his fish story of catching a rainbow trout in Big Pond, then turned to me mock-accusingly: "You've not shown our Herculean labourer the sights? I'm ashamed to call you daughter." Big Pond was my place, as only Dad knew (I was still ashamed of myself for having let Fred Faucher even within sight of it).

"Feel like a walk, Jimmy?"

"Yeah, I'm stuffed." He pushed away the half-finished supper beer, which wasn't usual.

Picking up on the vibe Dad said, "I'll finish this then, *and* I'll clean up, *again*." Which he began doing.

With only a bit of trouble hiding our self-consciousness over what Dad was up to, Jimmy and I went to collect the eggs, after which we walked out to Big Pond about five-minutes' distance. The ground was soggy with the welcomed rain, but the fields still sere from the long dry spell. The stubble raked our ankles where we'd impatiently gone ahead and done a poor first cutting: Dad and Jimmy had argued mildly over whether we should have waited, Dad for, Jimmy against. But now the late-day sun was at our backs and when we came out on the far side of the woods the scene opened up like a different planet; it really was like we'd passed through a membrane into some new dimension. I think Big Pond had once been a gravel pit, though Dad insisted it was the site of a meteor impact in ancient times when Leitrim Falls was smaller than Perth, arranged by aliens to cover up their visitation, when he and Mom were a-courtin' and had bin abducted (his hick character). But not-*so*-ancient a gravel pit: its deep sides were still bare and light-brown, if spottily filling in with weedy growth, burdock and such, some Queen Anne's lace. Only I had ever swum in Big Pond, and come out covered in leeches from skinny white thighs to gawky whiter feet, and developed a rash like measles for weeks. No matter, I loved Big Pond. Noticing the frilly white flowers as we drew nearer, I said all stupidly,

"This is my Green Gables place, so be careful what you say, Collins." I tittered all girly-girl silly as a puffy-sleeved dress. I wasn't me, it felt like I'd left me on the other side of the woods.

He ignored my unease. He took my hand. I walked him round the perimeter, stopping at Big Rock.

"And this is my beach, Big Rock."

Now he laughed lightly, let go of my instantly cooling hand, and placed his freed right palm on the east side of Big Rock. "It really *is* a big rock, look at the size of it! Maybe it broke off from the meteor." That was pretty good, gently making fun of Dad and me both. Though neither of us laughed.

I sat on the bare ground facing east, my back against the warm stone. He sat up close beside me. He plucked a blade of the tough grass and put it in his mouth, laid his head back against the rock. The silence got awkward. With head still tilted and eyes closed he seemed to address some other sky: "I don't believe in God, Mary, do you?"

It didn't startle me or even much surprise me. "No. Not the way religious people do, the so-called believers. I don't have anything smart to say on the subject. I believe I'm sitting here with you against Big Rock and wish I could do this forever."

He took my hand and held it in his lap.

I watched our hands. I held my breath. "I stopped believing in anything when Mom died."

"I know what you mean. I don't believe in anything either, so I guess I believe in nothing. I wish I'd known your mom, she must have been something else to make you like you are. And your dad too, I can see of course. But I bet if she were still alive, likely I wouldn't be here. Definitely we'd not be sitting here alone like this, against Big Rock, beside Big Pond. Ironic. Or is that *paradoxical*, Ms. McGahern." He was also making gentle fun again, but he held my hand more strongly, so I didn't mind the things he was touching on. "If there *is* a god, he, *or* she, created irony on the eighth day."

"That's pretty good, Jimmy, you should try that on Stottle-meyer." I teased too: "You're smarter than you look, which still isn't saying a lot." He puffed a derisive laugh from his nose. That made it easier: "Mom would have liked you too, Jimmy, a lot, I know."

He slouched some and lifted my hand to his muscled stomach, which was warm and moving a bit quickly. "You're lucky, Mary, which I know must sound funny, like, insensitive funny, which is not what I mean. But I envy you your memory of your mother, and your dad's great. I hate my mother and father."

"Oh, Jimmy."

"No. She's what they call an enabler, *his* enabler. And he's pure fucking psycho, almost as bad sober as drunk, and that's *really* saying a lot. But sober he loses his excuse, so he drinks, a coward too." The next words came out of him like pulling up a string of smashed Christmas bulbs: "He's never said a kind word to me in my life. ... Big boohoo, eh?"

I looked: he was dry as Big Rock itself. "Jimmy." I started crying, and couldn't control it, just snorting and snotting away onto the back of my left hand.

He turned my right hand in his and brought my palm to his mouth and kissed it. "I know it's soon, Mary, but I'm pretty sure I love you. Is that okay to say?"

"I love you too, Jimmy."

Before he kissed me, he grinned and said "*Jim*." Then we banged teeth.

I whispered in hot breath close to him, "We need practice."

We were still really kissing (we got real good pretty quickly) when the sun was fairly sunken behind us. I pulled back and said "Crepuscular." He was approaching again, which was the only thing I wanted, when a familiar sound started up like the evening itself was moaning for the day to stay.

"Shit, Aoife!" I jumped up. "And hearing her at this distance that loud? She needs milking by hand and badly, and Dad's no good with her at all! And if he doesn't hear *that* he's half-drunk and asleep."

The rest of the summer got pretty hot and heavy out at Big Rock, maybe every other evening, but we never actually did it. Dad never came out and interrupted us, and he could have. Twice when I returned from walking Jimmy up the road a ways, Dad shook his head over the paper or the sink (he'd taken over the dishes fulltime) and said half-jokingly, "What would your mother say? What sort of father am I?" Both times I said, "I'm a big girl, Dad. That's what Mom would have said." And he said, "That's what worries me; just be careful big girl." We were both embarrassed as all get-out. Before flouncing out of the kitchen I said without resentment, "Don't worry about it." But I was worried about "it."

Jimmy and I had been taking a blanket on our walks to Big Rock, which made life more comfortable. A few times we came so close we almost did it, our shirts open and with nothing between us but hairy chest, hard tingling nipples, and our underwear (much to Jimmy's embarrassment that other time). After a very short while, most times we were managing to get each other off and, once we made sure to have tissues handy, that seemed to satisfy Jimmy (but what did I know?). I wasn't. I wanted to go all the way and couldn't have resisted had he taken me further into that place I'd never been, had heard only detailed descriptions of (Naomi), and wanted to go to. He'd got a condom and kept it in his wallet (I was impressed), but still he wouldn't do it. And we didn't. I began obsessively worrying why not. It wasn't the sort of thing we could talk about though. I sadly began to sense some deep-down refusal on his part, some ultimate withholding, which soon had me mad and hurting worse.

My only experience of sex had been TV and movies and reading and BFF Naomi's retellings of her escapades with Rick Maclean—regularly in the graveyard now, or in his parents' Honda Civic (ouch), or in her bedroom once, and only once because her kid sister blew off day camp and showed up when they were both naked and Rick was putting on the condom, etc.—and from Naomi it had impressed me as a very interesting activity I'd like to try some time.

Of course there were the animals, Pluto and the rented bulls, but I never thought of that as sex sex, as in romantic, just "rutting" and having the cows "covered." *That* had nothing to do with me and Jimmy (or: that too-real language was not fucking with my romance). With Jimmy out at Big Rock those long summer evenings, both of us getting all hot and bothered and grinding away as if to pulverize the little clothing remaining between us, I knew a longing for sex as the deepest bodily desire to join with him, part to part, soul to soul. Besides which, Naomi was always bragging that it felt awfully good. But Jimmy either didn't feel the same as I or for some other reason—his old man? his belief in nothing?—wouldn't act.

On our last night together at Big Rock we were too wrought up to proceed past kissing to our usual dry humping. We just held and kissed a lot and promised to love each other forever no matter where we were. I would visit London and he'd get to Ottawa and we'd meet at home every chance we got. By that point I was talking through a real blubber of crying. He couldn't look at me for long; he'd put his lovely face in both hands and be crying too in little jerks and puffings.

A week later with Jimmy gone I was still crying at the drop of a … well, anything, a fork, a window blind, even Dad's hat. When he put me on the train Dad whispered while hugging me, "It'll work out, sweetheart, I promise you it will." I made to break but he held me tight. "I should have told you this before, but your mother knew Jimmy Collins, I think because in high school she'd dated Tom a couple of times. When she got sick she suggested I should hire Jim to help out. She said you knew him and liked him. And she didn't think he was the kind to go off to university. Do you know, Mary, the way he works he could run this place without me."

I was too shocked to get emotional, let alone think straight. Then I remembered telling Mom about Jimmy before I knew he *was* Jimmy. I responded softly at my articulate best: "Wow."

"It *will* be okay," was all Dad could manage, as I think he feared he was about to shame himself (in his view) with tears (which always threatened at any reference to Mom, especially if his own). I was fine with his just turning away and leaving.

Thus ended my summer of love, as Dad sometimes referred über-ironically to one of his and Mom's teen years. But no irony here.

TWENTY-ONE

DOUBLE TROUBLE

TIDINGS
Newsletter of the
Film&WordsWork Undergraduate
Student Association

As president of the Film&WordsWork Undergraduate Student Association (F&WUSA), I can report that, despite the never-ending need for social distancing, our **Twister Night** with professors was a touching success, so to speak, with Professor Turnbull winning hands-down, so to speak. I am equally pleased to announce the winners of our nonsense poetry contest, **Double Trouble**. Third-place prize and $100 goes to Billy Rubin (nom de plume) for his nonsensical gender-bending 2SLGBTQI+epic "Nigel Nigh Gel"; second-place prize and $200 goes to Wai Wungchou for her politically risky and riskily silly "Justin Just Out"; and the first prize of $500 goes to Mary McGahern for her unintelligible (bravo!) "Adèle a Devil," which we print in full below. The other winning poems, including those of the five (dis)Honourable Mentions, can be read on our web page. A big thank you to contest judges Professors Turnbull and Kelly, and to Leader Jake Flynn for sanctioning the contest. Dr. Flynn assures us that all three winners are near relatives of his. Have a Happy Thanksgiving everyone!

– Spencer Mellon, President, UF&WSA

Adèle a Devil

I met a devil named Adèle
who just adores the door to hell.
Her mother was a midnight moth
vis-à-vis a Visigoth.

Adèle's not just a silly pill
who once fell up a hilly hill
and bumped her bum against a cloud
(but a boom that loud was not allowed).

We went skating, she ate the ice!
And a cake all icing, which wasn't nice …
Hey, where's the tale I was about to tell? …
Oh that devil, that Adèle.

– *Mary McGahern*

TWENTY-TWO

ONLY CONNECT 4

From: Naomi Starling <mar171@fanshawe.ca>
        Mon. Oct. 11 at 08:00
To: Mary McGahern
Cc:

Hi Mary. I near peed my pants when I read your poem. Congratulations! Five hundred smackers is nothing to sneeze at. Thanks but if you send any more poems like that you'll have to pay for the Depends. Where *did* that Devil Adèle poem come from! I still remember your excellent crow speech in Stottlemeyer's class but who knew you were a talented poet too! I immediately taped it to our little fridge but I don't think my roomie likes it, when she goes for her like tenth diet Pepsi that day she always looks at it and crinkles up her nose like she just walked into your piggery! Critics, eh? On the other hand my Mike blew a bubble of Molson Canadian from his nose. But speak of that devil Adèle! Rumour from home (Mom) has it that Adèle and Fred Faucher are getting married!!! And sooner than later because the devil is pregnant with their very own little demon in the oven!!! But they're only like 18! What is this the Middle Ages or something? ! Will we be invited to the wedding? I should fucking well hope so! Is it really Break Week already? See you next Friday. Sorry for going on here. I know why you're coming to London, I should have kept my big mouth shut about youknowwho. Take the airport bus to Fanshawe, I'll meet you at the Tim's in the first building you come to. You don't even have to pretend you've come to see me but I'm glad we'll be seeing each other anyway.

Your bff
Naomi

TWENTY-THREE

THE DARK: UNDONE IN LONDON

I had no plan, none other than to talk with Jimmy and to stop crying when I thought about him and me.

There was a nonstop flight from Ottawa to London, which was expensive and left early but saved me from a stopover in Toronto. The ticket cost more than half my prize money, which I'd been planning to keep for Christmas (Dad badly needed clothes, and I'd picked out a pricey jade ring for Jimmy, his birthstone, at Burns Jewellers). I bought one-way, planning to return on the cheaper VIA train. It would be long, but I had course work to occupy me.

From the shiny little London airport I bussed along Oxford Street keeping an anxious eye for the Fanshawe College stop. I waited for Naomi in the campus Tim's. She was beaming as she approached me sitting alone at the table, was saying "How do you like Fan ... belt ..." but beamed it down when she sussed my condition. I will love her forever, my BFF, for saying, "We can talk later, and only if you want."

She cut class and we took a bus to her apartment on the upper floor of an old house on a street called Dundas. I'll love her twice as much for leaving me alone while she went to buy some stuff. "You look tired, McGahern—if as lovely as ever. Seriously, you can use my bed to rest, Mary." She shut the door quietly. I lay back on the couch and stared at her stippled ceiling, was drawn to a buzzing, and in a corner saw a big fat fly unable to break the hold of spider webbing. Where was the spider? Killed? Who cares? I think I dozed. When Naomi returned I said, "I'm not staying overnight, Naomi. I should have said so before you left."

I couldn't touch the croissant she'd brought back, just sipped the good coffee. Eventually, with the silence being broken only by her own forced chatter and my lame noises, she reached and without apology began eating my bun. "I can't believe McGahern passing up a chockie croyzie! ... Hmmm these are delicious." As she stuffed her face she gave me directions: "We'll get off at the corner of Richmond. I'll head back to Fanbelt. You take the Richmond bus north and tell the driver you want off at Western's gate. Then walk straight towards the old-style building with the tower. Continue past it, ask someone for directions to Wawonosh Residence. I've been there but only at night, though I kinda remember that it's well off to the right. After you're ... well, afterwards, you can find your way back here, right? All done!" (her chockie whatever). I wanted to kiss her, I wanted her to hug me.

We took the bus back along Dundas, all the way through London's downtown core. *This* is the big city? Its downtown was more haunting than the empty campus of uBytown. Truth is, the main streets of Leitrim Falls and Perth were livelier than that graveyard of shut stores, with staggering bickering street people, plastic bags and fast-food junk containers blowing about. A ragged stout woman flailing and pulling at the arm of an uncooperative companion. A crooked stick figure of a man pissing in a doorway. Compared to downtown London, Ottawa was the Emerald City. We got off at Richmond, where Mary waited to put me on another bus, with this parting advice: "Take no shit, Mary. Stick it to the prick!" BFF or not, I'd always suspected we had very different attitudes in matters of the heart.

The walk up Western's Grande Allée provided some relief. So *this* is what a university campus should look like? Lots of lawn and bushes and trees, students walking purposefully and milling about, boys and girls throwing footballs and flinging Frisbees, some still wearing masks, most of the girls still cutely hopeless at the sports; old and new stone buildings set back; a bridge across a river, to a slow-rising hill topped by a building like Disney's Magical Kingdom (a showpiece, of course, like Coriveau Hall, if situated much more attractively). I made my way around it, asked directions, walked some more, got lost again, asked again, and found the front desk at Wawonosh Residence.

"Are you a relative of Mr. Collins?"

Yes, we were married one day in Perth. "Just a friend from home."

She cocked an eyebrow of lascivious implication and buzzed me in. Cunt.

Jimmy's door wasn't locked, it wasn't even shut all the way. Breathing rapidly I tapped lightly with forefinger knuckle, speaking into the crack like it was a mike: "Jimmy, it's me, Mary."

Nothing.

"May I come in?"

With fingertip I pushed open the door, it squeaked, like in a horror movie. The room was too dark to make out anything. But my nose was working fine: the stink was worse than the chicken coop on a hot day, way worse, because I knew it was human stink, from cleaning hungover Dad's room even after he'd been out of it for an hour, the nostril-stopping rot of beer farts. Remarkable still that one drunk body could exhaust so much gas while sleeping. I prayed he was alone: *Please God* (I who claimed not to believe), make it that there'd been a party in his room and only guys are passed out on the floor. As my eyes adjusted, with help from the hall light behind me, I made out the complementary visual mess: a dump, like a careless recycling plant for beer cans and bottles, coloured (wine) and plain (vodka? gin?). On the narrow bed in the left corner lay a body curled away towards the wall. One body. *Deo Gratias.*

"Jimmy?" … More loudly, firmly: "It's me, Mary."

Only a low rumbling noise like the impatient cows make when they sense I've come into the barn, but *they* at least know I'm there to relieve hunger or swollen udders. Then, like the occasional uncooperative cow, or a dead frog whose nerve is touched, his top leg suddenly kicked out, followed by a curling farther into the wall. I went to the window, raised the blind halfway, and managed the little window slot. I bowed and breathed deeply, turned back to the bed, and in doing so banged the inside of my right knee against something hard, which echoed distantly and rocked still. A silver cylinder like a … a keg.

"Jimmy!"

"… Jimmy?" He rolled over to look, eyes at three-quarters-mast, groaned, closed them fully and rolled right back into the wall. "Why are *you* here? Or is this a nightmare?" It didn't even sound like Jimmy; likely he'd been snoring his throat raw. One thing for sure: no amount of soy-straw dust had ever done that to his voice: how an open grave might sound if it could speak ... which it can, I had reason to know, its memorable words of forever despair. Each of Jimmy's words had been articulated at some volume. His hair was longer than when I'd seen him last, clumping like ropes about his face; to excuse it as bed-head would be generous, more like unwashed for a long time. I hoped the chunky pinkish soup clumping back of his head near the edge of the bare mattress was only vomit. I gagged, fearful that I was going to add to it.

"Go away. Go home." Unslurred, which made it worse.

And stopped me for a spell.

"Jimmy, may I turn on the light, can we talk first?"

"No." Clearly enough again. "You don't even know my fucking name—get out."

"Okay, I will. You know I've never wanted you do anything you didn't want to do. ... Jimmy?" He might have dozed off, though I couldn't really believe that. If so, I was dead.

"Good. Then go."

"I will, promise. Will *you* answer one question for me before I go? ... Is there someone else?"

I knew that he wasn't sleeping through the silence.

"Yes."

"Do you love her?"

"I'm going away, by myself."

I gritted my teeth. "Where?"

"Anywhere, I'm never going home or back to Leitrim Falls, that's where."

"Why are you mad at me? Why do you *hate* me?" Don't start crying, don't cry, don't cry, don't.

I didn't just imagine it, he'd somehow moved closer to the wall, he must have had his nose pressed against it. "What part of *fuck off* don't you understand, McGahern?"

"You saying it, Jimmy."

"Clever, *as usual*. Well here's more for free: get, the fuck, outta here, right now!"

My answer was an involuntary childish gulping: "I just, I don't, I mean—"

He twisted, his shadowy face some mad artist's vision of hellish torment, showing a Jimmy I could never have imagined existed let alone known about, and shouted at the ceiling: "Who asked you to come here, McGahern! What *the fuck* do you want from me?" The words worked me over like bitch slaps, punches to the gut, then the knockout: "I am not your fucking mother!"

Leaving the room at least without staggering, I nonetheless literally bumped into a girl in the hallway and we both came up short in surprise. She was a blond who came to about my chin, but solid, as I was the one who'd bounced off. "Oh," she said. "Jim's awake now?" She was raking me up and down, while I dazedly watched her eyes. "I'm impressed he's alive!"

"No, Jimmy's dead to the world."

"Jimmy?" she sniffed. "Who are you?"

"His sister from Leitrim Falls."

"Oh yeah, the home he hates. Which sister? He says he has, like, ten brothers and sisters, then other times he'll say he's, like, an only child. *And* that he's from *Ottawa* and, like, *from nowhere else*." She didn't do much of a Jimmy, or not the Jimmy I'd once known. "He's a real head-case, your brother Jim." She was instantly as casual, even as presumptuously familiar, as the girls from high school who hated me. "I'm Ava."

"Jimmy's been drinking a lot ... eh, Ava?"

"Jim sure can pound it! Like, every night and sometimes all day down at the Ceeps! Talk of holding your booze. I've never *seen* anybody go for so long, and I didn't just fall off the turnip truck! How did you guys put up with him? Though don't get me wrong, he can be, like, *awfully* sweet too."

Can he now? ... I made to walk around her, but she said, "Wait, wait," and was fumbling in her sack. "Now don't be ratting him out to mommy and daddy, but look: Jim's our floor's new champ of the keg stand!"

She turned her phone sideways and held it up close to my face as though I'd asked for a makeup mirror. The video quality was okay but the scene was lit poorly, the volume high and tinny. It took me a while to take it in. The room could have been the one I'd just left, but over-crowded as a mosh pit, as the view of the held-high phone camera moved like a periscope towards the point of attention. Cacophonous, yes, but what the crowd of them was chanting soon came clear enough: "Jim Jim Jim ..."

The crush parted for the camera, many turning to grin into it and salute with their bottles. I made out two boys, no three, and one girl, fair-haired. The boys were each holding an ankle and thigh of the upside-down third, who was also supported on his own stout arms over a silver tub, a barrel, no, the keg of course. He wore only white jockey underwear. It was Jimmy's room. The blond girl looked at the camera—it was she who stood beside me, Ava—who then returned to her work squirting beer from a looping tube into Jimmy's mouth, mostly into his mouth. She paused and patted Jimmy's ass, glanced back again and said low in a scowling scold: "Don't you drop my fucking phone!"

I turned away and moved off at a clip. She called laughingly, "Hey, I'll have to remind Jim you were here, he'll forget for sure. He's a black-out artist, your *Jimmy*! What's your name?"

"Aoife."

"Lovely name! Come back later, Aoife, or meet us around suppertime at the Ceeps! I'm sure Jim will be just thrilled you're visiting. He should be back in fine form by then! It'll be like you were never here!"

It was the second-most-frightening sight I'd ever seen, that Jim, and I knew I could never un-see it. It's not that I'm some innocent prude and death on partying: it's that it was Jimmy not-Jimmy, dehumanized, inhuman, monstrous. It really did remind me of a painting in one of Dad's art books, a vision of hell by an artist named Bosch, where I'm pretty sure one of the figures literally has his head up his own ass. And what Jimmy'd said to me, I will never forget. I was chased from that residence with hand to my shocked mouth like that other painting, *The Scream*. My *most* horrifying sight was of course Mom in her coffin like some horrible practical joke life was playing on me. I can't say for sure how real the thought was, but crossing the silver-metal bridge I did wonder about jumping into the unreal London's unreal Thames.

Back at Western's front gate waiting for the bus, I struggled to pull myself together into some semblance of myself. Jimmy Collins has daddy troubles? Boohoo. Boo-fucking-hoo! "I don't even *have* a mother anymore!" I said that aloud? ... Too loudly, causing the two grannies standing a bit along to move farther along. "Who's afraid of Fred-fucking-Faucher! I'm gonna find Fred over Thanksgiving and fuck the fancy socks off him! Thanks be to God, as *my* Granny-fucking-McGahern used to say!" They decided not to take the bus after all.

In that altered state of consciousness I got off at York Street and lined up in the train station. Quickly feeling sick. Then a too-long layover changing trains at Toronto's Union Station, all lonely echo and cold and people garbage. I was sicker than sick, sick of what I'd shouted at those poor women that I was going to do with Faucher, and stupidly sick at the thought that

Fred and Adèle-fucking-Pélletier were getting what I was being denied.

Into the washroom and throwing up. Mom in her coffin had sent me into the funeral home's washroom, where I'd emptied my bowels to shame a sow. Till I could think again: That's not Mom in there. I moved my hands from face to chest: She's here, forever.

Back waiting on the antique wooden bench, my bony ass gripping itself like pincers, I finally thought sensibly, if still dead to the world: Had the summer meant nothing then? ... Yes: it had meant nothing to Jimmy. Remember? He'd made a point of announcing that he believed in nothing, and like a born eejit you'd concurred, believing he couldn't possibly mean you too, you and him together. You should have taken him at his word, McGahern.

Then I was back in the station's can puking and crying into the same filthy toilet till I had nothing left. I have nothing left. I have left ... nothing. Jimmy. A big zero. A black hole.

My next waiting stint on that hard wooden bench in Union Station was spent shamelessly crying my eyes out, *publicly*. People looked but no one cared. And who could blame them? Except for one bedraggled old man who stopped and kindly said, "There-there, child, nothing can be that bad." He was temporarily down on his luck himself. "All things must pass, as Beatle George sang, eh?"

I felt an urge to stand and hug him, maybe people weren't so bad. Could I spare a little money so he could feed his little grandkids, whose parents died in the first pandemic? I gave him the toonie in my coat pocket, which he looked down at in slow bemusement; he tossed it on the bench beside me, where its clattering drew more attention than my crying had. "Shove it up your ass, girly, if it'll fit in that stingy orifice."

I couldn't help myself, the shock of it made me laugh and blow snot. And, miracle of miracles, I felt a little better. Something or someone had helped me. Mom? Thalia (goddess of the funny, thank you Dad)?

I arrived at our sad little Leitrim Falls train station late Friday night, wasted another hour waiting for Dad—*as we'd arranged the pickup time*—and ended up Ubering out to home, worried all the way. Snoring like a chainsaw, Dad lay sprawled across the kitchen table, or the near half of it anyway, because the other half was covered with his oversized Big Rock bottles (as he'd named his home brewery). I woke him none too gently. I don't think he knew who I was at first or that I'd been away. Before bumping off to bed, he managed to ask me if I'd look after the livestock. He wasn't paying attention when I said, "My pleasure," which was strange to say that way to Dad, though warranted. But going from the two of us, it looked like we now had livestock and deadstock.

He didn't get up till late Saturday morning, then drank through the lunch and supper I made and he didn't touch. Sunday he slept till mid-afternoon, when he recommenced drinking. At least he was always a quiet, peaceful drunk. We said next to nothing to each other the whole Thanksgiving weekend; in fact his bleary bloody eyes never met mine. I didn't care and he didn't notice that I didn't. I cared only about my own troubles. With him it was no more complex than the return of his bingeing alcoholism. That was always a danger this time of year, when most everything but continuing care of the stock—some shipping to the slaughter yards, machine maintenance, maybe tillage ploughing if it looked like an early winter—was done for another year. Of course he'd been living totally alone for the first time; when Mom was alive she'd kept him off fall's fall into indolent boozing. He'd stayed pretty straight when home-schooling me too. So what? I had no sympathy to spare.

Gratefully returned to caring for the stock, I spent Saturday and Sunday wondering what I was to do with all the newfound freedom: no one to love me but, surprise-surprise, nobody to worry about loving either. Yet it wasn't long before I was wondering why the frequent unbearable lonely sadness had been greeted by … what? I can only call it peeping *exhilaration*, strange to say. I wouldn't go near Big Pond to test my weird resolve. I wanted to return to Ottawa, so as to explore this new me and the road ahead, but forced myself to wait a little longer and took the train back early Sunday afternoon. I was to have spent the whole of Break Week at home, with Jimmy, hooking up with Naomi, comparing notes with both. *Losing my virginity*. But I was finished with home and knew all my planning to be the cosmic joke it was. If the old saw is true, that God smiles when humans make plans, then I must have put the Creator in stitches.

Back at uBytown I couldn't fall asleep in my cell. I got up and turned on the computer and emailed Naomi my apologies both for not returning to her place in London and for leaving Leitrim Falls early. She didn't email back. I didn't care. Back in bed and tossing and turning I was flipping back and forth between a sorrow like death and that scary new elation … whose attractions were lessening every time *its* turn came. The whole empty residence, echoing in shots its every contraction and expansion, was likely responsible for the nightmare about being a little girl again and losing Mom in a big empty place that I knew to be Union Station. Talk of bereft. I woke up crying, a few times. I went for a walk through the campus at three in the morning.

No one tried to rape me (ha-ha). In fact I didn't see another living soul. I thought how little different it was from any day and what would be the rest of my life.

TWENTY-FOUR

ONLY CONNECT 5

From: Sureau Montjoy <smontjoy@ubytown.ca>
Thu. Oct. 31 at 9:05
To: Sureau Montjoy
Cc: Sureau Montjoy

(French version follows)

Dear Department Leaders, Vice-Deans, Deans, and Vice-Presidents:

As we are all refreshed from our Reading Week, I write you on most urgent university business, to wit:

Training for Senior Administrators

Over these past months and weeks and days, as part of **RAPE,** we have been holding a series of wholly and completely voluntary training sessions to increase our sensitivities to sexism in ourselves and others, and systemic. Those colleagues who have not attended the sessions, or at the very least subscribed to the webinars hosted by HR, are strongly encouraged to do so. Others have suggested that attending be encumbrance on a member's workload or s/he face penalties such as official Letters of Reprimand (LOR) in their files or worse. Your union objected, though it was quick to agree that we do not want sexual abuse on our uBytown campus (Rape-free that is).

That unneeded unpleasantry said respecting **RAPE,** now we must turn our communal attentions to the equally grievous transgression of **racism**. In fact, the two go hand-in-glove.

As many of you may know, or have heard, or read in the extensive media coverage (unfortunately), earlier in the Fall term uBytown Security stopped a young Black man/Afro-Canadian who was traversing campus. Security alleges that he was smoking a marijuana cigarette, broadcasting sexually offensive music loudly, and carrying a skateboard. The young man revealed that it was a regular cigarette that he had rolled himself, ditto his skateboard. Security alleges that the young man had no business on campus, not having a student or employee card. The young man offered no resistance physical or verbal, and handed across the skateboard he'd been carrying under his left arm altogether innocently, revealed that he has been thinking of enrolling as a Communications student. We accept his word on these matters, as all should. Security allegedly produced statistics showing that a rash of vandalisms had been committed on campus since the very first COVID-19 pandemic, and that in every instance the damages (minor) involved a young person of colour, or numerous such, many with skateboards. The young man's lawyer has brought a suit against uBytown alleging racial profiling, which we are nonetheless confident of having dismissed.

I must regret to say though that our Security Officers, *and so we*, is/are guilty of this paramount injustice of prejudicial racialized behaviour, and that it is now up to us—*all of us*—to do something about it. Which is to say: *to stop it.* Since though, we must first educate ourselves as to the hidden extensiveness of the issue.

All uBytown personnel of vice-presidential and decanal selection committees, as well as members of *all* faculty hiring committees, must attend training workshops in racism, which will involve the studying of many texts on the subject from our library of systemic racism texts which grows even as I address you (merci Dean LaRoque of the Faculty of Digital Humanities). My President's Office is currently planning a weekend study retreat and looking into reserving a resort at Mont Tremblant to that purpose, soon since it opens for skiing. These weekend sessions will eventually be transferred to campus and expanded to include all university employees, professors, contract-professors, lecturers, part-time instructors, teaching graduate students, et al. in the old Coriveau Hall gymnasium. Moreover, we will be installing a series of book clubs, which is after all the way we learn.

By these and other means (sub-pods, teams, town halls, informal chats at water coolers, etcetera), uBytown, which already since my arrival has overcome its reputation as "Boytown U," herewith pledges itself to work tirelessly to uncover any and all racism and root it out. *That* must now be the primary mission of our university today, for how can we learn and begin to teach the pursuit of truths if we know not ourselves, both conscious and unconscious and systemic, as participants in a campus that not only tolerates racism but practises it? Still sexism too.

Reaffirming My Commitment
Our work going towards will represent only an important beginning spearheaded by me, yet as we have been reminded so urgently in recent times with the various killings of innocent young Afro-American males, much more remains to be done in Canada too, and more will be done also, much more, in future, here in the nation's capital at "Canada's University." Thus, as part of our next step into the immediate future, and sooner than that if possible, we trust, will be to announce increased mental health supports such as counselling for members and students who have experienced racism capaciously defined, anticipate it in others *and* themselves, or all systemically perpetuated it (no guilt!). We must be inclusive. Funds have already been set aside for this purpose. Feelers are forthwith out to Mont Tremblant for a Racist Weekend Retreat for senior administration.

There is much to indeed do in all these regards, and there always will be. Here I wanted simply and modestly to reaffirm *my* personal commitment to you as **President**

and Vice-Chancellor of uBytown to pursuing this needed and eminently just cause with compassion, determination, a *de*racinated sense of our own inadequacy and guilt, and fairness justice.

These are dark days for uBytown, and we must stand together to do what is right, or we all fall together in continuing not to rectify what is wrong. Enrollments for the winter term are far down. We must *band* together to stamp out systemic racism and reclaim our campus from the bigoted clutches of that prime sign of enduring Anglo colonialism—RACISM.

To this/these end/ends I am today striking an empowered University committee of investigation, complaint, reporting, rectification, and restitution, one employing the relevant ugly word as acronym and in that way, like Milton's God one more time, bringing good out of evil.

Definitely **A**gainst **R**acialist **K**nowing = **DARK.**

That is who we are, and me and uBytown without question.

Yours in the pursuit of truths,
Dr. Sureau Montjoy
President and Vice-Chancellor

Dean Jacques LaRoque had kept his teeth clenched as he read, if grinding them periodically so that it looked as though a small animal might be trying to exit his mouth. He swallowed hard as he finished the president's memo. *Fucked again.* He had been royally *fucked* yet *again* by Montjoy! Following the earlier memo on sexism and "rape culture" (his baby!), he had stupidly presumed to talk freely with the president, on the pretense of thanking the Québécois racist for even acknowledging that the initiative, like the striking phrase "rape culture," was his. LaRoque's. He had segued to discussing the sensationalist media attention over the recent arrest of the Black boy, and tactfully suggested that uBytown should now initiate an anti-racism campaign.

President Montjoy had widened his eyes, then squinted sagaciously: "To show that we're against it?"

Mais fucking oui, mon fucking capitaine: to show, that we're, *against it*—you dumb fucking pea-souper you! No wonder: the idiot *had* crawled out of some Catholic backwater in the remote-from-everything northwest of *la belle province*. But just look here again—royally fucked again! If this isn't outright criminal, it's at least plagiarism! ... Well, anyway, if it isn't, then he's not the Dean of Digital Humanities. And *he's* also the one who'd told MontFuckjoy that they were being called Boytown U! ... Okay, it was a line he'd got from Professor Pat Kelly of F&WW, who'd probably made it up. And, well, at least Montjoy had mentioned him in his illiterate memo, if only once.

He went to his expansive window and looked out on the near-empty parking lot— there was still some way to come back from Plague—which usually reassured him with the sight of his new BMW in his private Dean's spot. Nor did the focused view help calm him as usual, because two boys, white and Black, and a white girl in tattered clothing were standing close to his personalized wheels (10k for the robin's-egg paint job alone). Street people most likely, not students, though it had become impossible to tell.

The girl approached the hood ornament, which was toward him, attracted no doubt by the custom bling: triangular golden leaves surmounted by the maker's standard blue-and-white emblem. She wasn't going to touch it, was she! Pull it off like, well … She must be cold in those tight denim shorts cut so high that her pale cheeks herniated considerably like white inner-tubing. She (a Boytown U student probably) was likely being forced into the criminal lifestyle by those young thugs, feeding her just enough … *smack* (*crack*?) to keep her dependent—her pimps?—and up to all manner of hanky-panky in threesomes and such. He would go out to her, *unto* her, as the Bible might put it, minister unto the … *ho*! It was only the right thing to do.

Exiting his office with an affecting nod to Executive Assistant Madam Marois—"Martine, write an email to President Montjoy endorsing his DARK campaign, you know the drill"—he did feel better. So much so already that he hummed and sang softly to himself: "My faith is strong but I need proof, I see her bathing on the roof, dum-di-di-dum-dum Hallelujah …"

Nor could Leader Jake Flynn read the president's latest memo with equanimity, stabbing the delete key before finishing. He'd cracked a nail. On his way to his Celtic Twilight seminar he at least didn't instruct Peggy Dubois to send a *pro forma* response to President Montjoy. He was helped to that unintentional prudence because wholly occupied mulling over—actually obsessed with—the lovely Detective Gurmeet's recent disturbing insinuations. Oh, there'd been insinuations all right. What else could she be thinking? Could allegations be far behind? Wholly unfounded accusations! As he passed through the foyer, scene of the crime, he brought his right palm to his brow, as disturbed as he'd ever been over Pod matters, and that was saying something about anxious Leader Flynn. His moist palm was moister than when he'd raised it. He forgot to smile and wave at Peggy Dubois.

Who watched him pass as she often observed Jake Flynn, with a look of bemused affection, though it had once been more. But years ago, when her gaze had been of a waning love, she'd finally grown tired of waiting for the ballyhooed Jieun to leave Jake, and she'd married custodian Angus Daly's son, Harvey, which had worked out. There had never been anything romantically reciprocal between Peggy and Jake, all one-sided fantasy on her part, based on an affectionate simpatico that never left the office and continued still in a minor key. Jake *did* used to complain about Jieun, though, and seriously, which had suddenly ended, as had Peggy's dreams. So that now she watched Jake Flynn with cooled affection, as might some time-travelled paleontologist track the passage of the last Cro-Magnon into the Alps. Then the smile disappeared entirely from her pleasantly plump face, as her antenna told her that Jake was disturbed, and deeply so, which had the renewed power to disturb Peggy so that she watched him out of the foyer blankly. She admitted she still loved him … and still more than Harvey. Which was yet more disturbing. So she got back to work.

TWENTY-FIVE

DULCE ET DECORUM EST

In Professor Flynn's Irish literature seminar, Mary McGahern finally spoke up; or rather she'd 'intervened' in another's presentation, as their academic politesse called interrupting. She'd gained confidence from the success of her own seminar on *The Untilled Field* and was puffed on the celebrity of winning the student poetry contest (the group had applauded her arrival at this latest meeting, the first following the announcement, or all but one participant, Evander, had clapped). The day's subjects were William Butler Yeats and John Millington Synge, with focal texts the poem "The Second Coming" and the drama *The Playboy of the Western World*. Mary had liked neither. The first she thought cynical and horrifying, and the second simply silly.

Professor Flynn had provided the introductory context: Yeats' discovery of Synge, his encouraging and promoting him as "authentic," and supporting him through the violent response to his play (at its debut the author and actors were vilified, chairs had been thrown at the stage, Yeats scolded them from the apron, a riot ensued in the streets of Dublin).

Professor Flynn said, "Shameful, true, but also testament to how much literature mattered, once upon a time." He failed to shame a dozy boy whose head was permanently bowed over the phone in his crotch by asking him if he had found something to share relevant to Synge's play (that was okay, as this was the new first-year seminar and some students still needed such elementary scolding from *his* professorial pulpit). The distracted boy, Gary, glanced up: "Yeah, I mean no, like, no one cares about this shit anymore, Prof. Stuff like that only happens nowadays on wrestling shows, knowwhatImean?"

Professor Flynn smiled small and said, "I do know what you mean, Gary, it's not as if you're glossing *The Playboy* with cultural-anthropological theory." A laugh? … Ah, Mary McGahern and Alice Pham. "But I do wish you would stay with our discussion, Gary, as you illustrate my very point: who indeed cares about literature anymore? These days audiences are inspired to throw chairs only when Dr. Phil tells the abused wife that *she* must forgive the alcoholic sexually abusive husband." He was surprised to see a few of them smile. Mary again, the pretty girl who'd come to his office, already upping her participation grade, as he'd encouraged her to do. *Hope*, Professor Flynn? Get thee behind me, Hope, or I'll cut thy throat.

Only student Gary, having remained in attention, frowned the bewildered "Wha …?" and returned to tickling the phone in his lap.

The seminar on the poem was given by Alice, a girl of Asian heritage, who to that point had proven to be the group's best performer, if not its noisiest (that was Evander), whether making shorter presentations or talking with Professor Flynn. An excellent student and seminar presence, Alice; in answering the fair question-comment from Mary, she had not tried to make the poem less cynical or horrifying, but had explained fairly well how it fit in Yeats' larger vision—amazing! Could these new first-year seminars, which he'd fought for, be the beginning of a way back to sanity? ... Do get thee hence, Hope.

In proof of Despair's strengthening rule, Evander, the boy making the second presentation, on the Synge play, immediately focused on the word "Playboy" and talked of the sexist, the *misogynist*, implications for Irish women and "Western" women and non-binary people. It was doubtful he'd read the play, as he observed nothing whatsoever about its subject or characters or setting, and he'd momentarily looked baffled when an accommodating Professor Flynn asked him what he thought was the point of Christy's macho bravado. Evander had begun an answer with his usual "My partner and I felt that Chris Maloney's—"

Her heart going like a compressor, Mary McGahern spoke up for the second time, interrupting again as Professor Flynn had encouraged them to do, "intervening":

"That's very interesting, Evander. But do you think it was better or worse for Irish men *at that time*? I mean, to pick up the professor's earlier point, only that Christy *Mahon* acts awfully confused about his identity, even unbelievably so, even, well, sort of silly?"

That brought Jake Flynn to sharper attention, because it *was* Mary McGahern again, pulled him from his manic thoughts of Detective Gurmeet and concern for John Turnbull and the stolen *Ulysses* and worry that his own old problem was starting up again.

Evander, who at every meeting so far had let it be known

that he was gay, at first by referring repeatedly, and irrelevantly, to his "partner" (though most all did that, personalized every work before Professor Flynn could turn them to a more objective criticism), then simply by prefacing many comments with "Being a white man of privileged status, *if* a gay man ..."

At the first meeting of the seminar, he'd also stiffly reminded Professor Flynn that uBytown—"or *Boy*town U, as my partner and I have been calling it lately"—protocol stipulated that every meeting on campus begin with acknowledgement that they are occupying unceded lands of the Algonquin-Anishinaabeg Nations. He himself had made that acknowledgement at length to begin his seminar on Synge's play, spending some ten minutes on the atrocities that had been done to the Indigenous peoples of the region, devoting five additional minutes to eviscerating Ottawa's Duncan Campbell Scott and the enduring cultural trauma for Native peoples of the residential school system. No one argued, as who could. But empowered Evander would not leave it at that: "I do not think *genocide*, cultural and racialist, an inapt term. My partner—"

Alice, who always sat just down-table from Mary, had intervened: "But weren't the Indigenous nations continually at war with each other before the arrival of missionaries and soldiers? First the French, then the English? And didn't the explorer, whatshisname ... Thompson, I think, didn't he even record their practice of *cannibalism*?"

Evander had sniffed, and sniffed again, self-stereotyping as a gay man who unapologetically, even aggressively, presented as flaky effeminate, and unfortunately aligning with the sort of gay man who asserts and celebrates his identity and rights by cavorting in a Pride parade wearing only a thong. "Alice, I'm surprised, *and* disappointed, to hear such an expression of systemic racism from you especially."

"Me especially?" said Alice, genuinely taken aback, so sitting back.

Alice's withdrawal relieved Evander from having to find a bridge back to Synge's play, which he'd never really left because never begun with. He had simply turned again to the word *Playboy*, anachronistically limiting its associations to Hugh Hefner's fallen empire. As irrelevantly, Evander had proceeded to champion the socio-cultural value of authentic sex workers. He had just again prefaced whatever next point he was about to make with "My partner Don and I—" when Mary spoke up again on the importance of context, of maintaining some historical perspective.

To her he said with exaggerated prissiness, "I'm going to choose to ignore that intervention, *Ms.* McGahern," and moved on to how he and his partner had been detained on suspicion of *being* sex workers at a fireworks display at the Casino du Lac-Leamy in Gatineau, which was also built on unceded Algonquin-Anishinaabeg lands, needless to say. "And so what if we *were*?" He glared around at the intimidated or baffled lot of them. "Dare we—*lest we forget* the ugly incident with the sex worker in our *Boytown* U sports complex?"

Somewhat baffled Mary, encouraged by the professor's earlier response to Gary's dumb comment about TV wrestling, Mary who was having as bad a day of distraction as Professor Flynn, rejoined: "What? Excuse me, Evander, but what about Synge's play?"

She looked round the table of nine, who were as well spaced as university protocol still insisted they be and as the seminar room allowed (one empty seat between, which created an oddly hollowed-out atmosphere). Those six or so paying attention wore noncommittal if expectant looks, with Alice's still a touch cowed. Mary's gaze came to rest on Professor Flynn. "I mean,

I'm only just learning about this subject, and I had difficulty understanding just what *The Playboy* is about, but if we're jumping outside the work right away …"

"*Yes?*" grinned Evander, obviously fearing nothing.

Mary, after one good inhalation and exhalation: "At this time *in history* weren't the Irish, women *and* men, themselves still struggling under British rule? Is that a part of Synge's play, the question of what it means to be authentic Irish versus British or even stage Irish? Which was, as Professor Flynn has told us, also behind Yeats' whole revivalist program? I mean, given the subject of our seminar, *the Celtic Twilight*, shouldn't we be talking about *that*, or something related to that, whatever we think it means? At least to begin? My Granny McGahern—"

"Oh, your, uh, *Granny McGahern?*" presenter Evander fairly sniffed again. "What has Granny dearest got to do with *our* subject … Mary? You *are* Mary McGahern, right, the nonsense poet?"

She stared at him, struggling to keep at bay—forget understanding—the anger that was boiling over in her head and guts. Why was this twit making her so mad? But she wouldn't be passively-aggressively shut down, as had little Alice.

Evander misread an advantage gained, and authoritatively pressed forward into familiarly irrelevant territory. "Would you care, Mary McGahern, to enlighten the group as to why you're the only one here who hasn't signed our petition to President Montjoy, Dean LaRoque, *and* Professor Flynn here in his role as Department Leader, asking that *Boytown U* permanently post on its home page the statement—which I co-authored— acknowledging our historical failure respecting the rights of 2SLGBTQI+, Black, Indigenous, and peoples of colour everywhere and in all times? *Why*, Mary McGahern, nonsense poet? It should be obvious to anyone with eyes to see that the

Film&WordsWork Pod has *no* full-time faculty of coloured non-binary orientation, Professor Abara notwithstanding. I—"

Alice Pham interrupted to say quietly, "I didn't sign it either."

And Phil Latour, who sat one seat over from Alice at the opposite end from Professor Flynn, spoke up at normal volume: "Nor I."

Evander blinked strenuously in attempting to ignore the two. "I discussed *your* refusal with my partner, Mary McGahern nonsense poet, but this now goes for you other holdouts too, and Don and I both felt that unanimity could only strengthen ..."

Mary let him finish this time, scarcely listening. She again looked round at the group and wondered if she should bother responding truthfully by her best lights (as her dad had once insisted she always do), risk it. There *was* a risk of being publicly shamed if she said aloud what she wanted to say, as she knew already from the social media sites she'd been following alone in her residence room (she now had her own Facebook page). Feeling the waves of Evander's continuing melodramatic outrage, she gazed round the room, coming to rest again on Professor Flynn. Seeing how deeply distracted he was, she turned to Alice at the end of the long ovular table.

What was she doing? Do it. For Dad. This was *university.*

"Alice, Professor Flynn told us that in this seminar we should talk freely, disagree, argue, politely. So please forgive my spotlighting you like this—I know I'd hate it! But I'm curious to know: do you agree with Evander's approach to our second reading for today?"

She felt her groin tingle, but knew it couldn't be another period starting. It was fear, she recognized it, having had much practice lately, and it instantly shot into her throat. But again, it was also strangely exhilarating.

"*Oh*," drawled Evander. "So now *Mary McGahern* is running this seminar, *my* presentation? Professor …?"

It was Alice took the considerable breath of one who had been waiting and hoping for just such a moment, an audible inspiration which seemed to propel her off the chair's backrest. She leaned in: "No, Mary, I don't agree with Evander's approach, and thank you for asking me." She smiled and drew another substantial breath. "I chose to major in Film&WordsWork because I love reading and good movies. I did well in English in high school, and I wanted to study works of literature and film more deeply. But except for this seminar I've got neither good books nor movies. So far, it's all been theory and cultural studies and zombie flics."

Evander tried a dismissive jocular tone: "Oh, Alice, that's *so* retro. Conservative politics, anybody? … Though I don't mean to impugn the whole of Chinese culture! Ha-ha. My partner—"

"I'm Canadian," she stared pleasantly at him. "Of Vietnamese heritage. And more, we suspect. You know nothing about me, Evander. And anyway, my subject position is irrelevant to this question, to our study, as Mary suggests."

"Of course you are!" said Evander, creepingly nonplussed. "And we're *so* lucky to have your *different* p-o-v in our seminar. But seriously, I ask you, who really cares about the writings of these dead white guys? Victimized Irish or not. These silly writings—as nonsense poet Mary McGahern herself at least recognizes—are meaningful only as they can be made relevant to our lives today and the issues that affect *us*, such as the incredible wrongs continuing to be done to Black and Indigenous and 2SLGBTQI+—"

"I agree with Mary and Alice," said quiet Phil. "I'm not going to say *being a gay man*, though I could, because I am." He waited. No one, including Evander, appeared to care. So

Phil continued: "I sympathize with the struggles of oppressed peoples everywhere and stand up to be counted where I can *when it's appropriate*. But, like Alice, I didn't take this English seminar to right the wrongs of the world, or even to think much about such issues, unless relevant to the work under discussion, which they usually aren't. I enrolled in this seminar to read and study Irish literature. *That's* what we're supposed to be doing here, and should be doing, Evander, uh, no offense."

Evander pinched his mouth and looked directly across at Mary, who thought, *Oh fuck*.

"Well then, if that's the way you *all* feel ..."

Only three of the nine had expressed views, if thinking rather than feeling (with three others continuously tickling crotch-hidden phones). The remaining three looked like spectators enjoying a show. But the three speakers had been unanimous.

... "Then I'm finished here. And I trust that Professor Flynn, in assigning my earned grade, will take into account that my presentation was terminated prematurely by my reactionary fellow seminarians. I would not want to have to appeal my grade."

He had continued staring only at Mary, who was increasingly feeling good about herself, the very thing her father had said true literature was *not* supposed to encourage.

"But you should know"—Evander looked more penetratingly round at each of them—"all of you, that the way you're behaving is the reason the old English Departments, like Alice's high school book club, exist no more. And I *don't* say so prejudicially but in sadness. Do you know what Professor Kelly told us in Eco-Psych? That *WordsWork* is retrograde as a term and facing extinction as an academic Pod. *Why?* Because we spend forever arguing about what a stupid play like this one means. Even as we meet here and now, Professor Kelly is herself preparing a petition to have the Pod's name changed to *Flics and Eco-Texts*. I support Professor Kelly's initiative and encourage you all to do the same. What's important is how we use old books *today* to effect real change in our disgustingly white-privileged society!"

His clarion calling was causing him to tear up, then he was sniffling for real. And Mary was feeling horrible. The other two speakers, Alice and Phil, didn't appear affected sympathetically; they were even smiling just perceptibly. It was sentimental Mary spoke again:

"No. I'm sorry to have to disagree with you again, Evander, because you are obviously sincere in what you say. But so am I. What you think we should be doing here is the business of sociology or something; maybe Communications, whatever their business is. But it's not our business. *We* contribute most and best to solving the legitimate problems of the world that concern you by increasing understanding of the world's complexities, not by radicalizing or simplifying every problem. And we do that best by reading and studying great works of literature which, as scientific studies have shown—or so *my father* told me—nurture empathy. Did you know that, Evander? That reading great fiction in its terms increases empathy? And *that*, the exercise of empathy, compassion, makes us most fully human. *That's* what the world needs now: imagining ourselves truly in the other's shoes, not more bullshit about *caring*, not competing over who *cares* the most about wrongs that very few people will ever really try to right. That sort of *virtue-signalling* costs no one anything. If that's what you want to do, right the world's wrongs, great! Then go do it. Just not here. … Though I don't mean, uh, to get, like, all preachy like." She hoped she'd acted the last bit of street stutter convincingly.

Professor Flynn had long since come fully awake and was breathing hard, and now he caught his breath. Students needed him. He too nodded round at the frozen scene. "Do you know, this is maybe the most rewarding discussion I've ever had in a seminar. And I'm talking senior undergrad *and* graduate seminars. For a first-year seminar to have come to this level of—"

"Oh for fuck's sake!" When he'd stood and finished gathering his undistributed hand-outs, snatched up his backpack and turned for the exit, Evander added with impressive haughtiness: "Your reactionary attitude *is* just about all we text about following *your* classes, Doctor Professor Luddite, some of us anyway."

It is? wondered Mary, knowing there likely was something and she was left out of it. Could she ask Alice? Probably not, she regretted. But the rude little prick, whatever the facts, to address the professor like that. She glanced at dismayed Professor Flynn then back to Evander. "That's a lie, Evander."

He halted in real surprise but quickly made his prissy dismissive face at her, like she was something he might yet snort up and spit out. "Oh, kiss my ass, nonsense poet."

But she recognized in his attempted breasting a tactic of the sluts from the early days of her return to high school. Except for when she'd fallen in love with Jimmy, she'd never felt so settled, so full of herself. She said, "*Póg mo thóin.*"

His face was so like Faucher's among chickenshit that Mary nearly burst out laughing. But Evander was nothing if not gifted in his own sort of self-possession; he shook his head in a feigned shiver of disgust, was moving haughtily to the exit door.

"*Ma-hone,*" Mary enunciated with an authority that arrested him again. "Sound at all familiar, Evander?"

"No." He looked irritated, at least genuinely so. "Enlighten me, *s'il vous plait*, and pronto, I have a real life to get to."

"My father's mother, Granny McGahern, used to say it to us kids when we were a nuisance: *Puh ma-hone*. It's the Irish for your *kiss my ass*. Could it be that Synge the playwright thought his character *Christy Mahon—not Chris Maloney*—an ass?"

"Your point? Oh, who gives a shit—shove it up yours." He stared at Professor Flynn. "You should know, Professor, that this meeting has made me uncomfortable throughout: *no* recognition of unceded Indigenous lands, *no* trigger warnings for sexism, and *no* opportunity to present my seminar as I had prepped it. *That's* what I'll be communicating to Dean LaRoque in my appeal." He was gone.

At least there was no chance of his following Granny's order literally, not respecting her ass anyway. Oh, that's bad, Mary, you should be ashamed. Yet she wasn't. Instead she was feeling better and better, and ... what's that? Inexplicably hopeful—surprise! Another miracle.

She looked at Professor Flynn, who burst out laughing, as did she in snotty sputtering answer, which seemed to license the others, or most of them, to avail themselves of a wounded community's surest balm, laughter, administered judiciously.

Alert then, the anxious group didn't know what to do next. Collected, Professor Flynn yet offered no guidance. He was still processing the other miracle, of their having gelled as a group, as an English seminar, in such serious discussion. He sensed also that their next move could not be at his instigation anyway, if this secular miracle were to continue unfolding naturally over the rest of the term. But in that pause began increased squirming, their shuffling possessions and touching backpacks, with six now returning to phone-checking. With Evander, one of the day's chief presenters, having gone, impending break-up tinctured the air of the seminar room. It was Alice stilled them when she began in a different, a commanding, voice:

"A sudden blow: the great wings beating still above the staggering girl, her thighs caressed ..."

She recited the whole poem without glancing at any of the books she'd brought for her formal presentation; in truth she simply spoke the poem to the group, meeting each in turn, reciting almost as naturally as conversation. Into the strange silence that ensued she shifted register and whispered, "That's poetry, and sometimes that's enough. That's why we're here, as some of you obviously know."

Mary led the applause wondering feverishly, *A friend?* The clapping tailed off and died, and Professor Flynn, his eyes actually brimming, stared straight ahead and began easily from memory, as he thought he remembered reciting it to Jieun over their dying pit fire:

"When you are old and grey and full of sleep, and nodding by the fire, take down this book …"

When he finished there were shallow tears on his cheeks. That made no one uncomfortable. This time Alice led the applause, during which Phil came to her place, picked up a book, soon found what he wanted, and read the whole of "Sailing to Byzantium." Professor Flynn spoke huskily, barely above a whisper, to the relaxed gathering: "This *is* a class after an old professor's heart, thank you, Phil, Alice."

Phil passed the book to Mary like a torch in a relay and took his seat. She found her poem and remaining seated began: "I walk through the long schoolroom questioning," and read well to the end: "Oh body swayed to music, oh brightening glance, how can we know the dancer from the dance?"

She gestured with the book to the others but no one took it, all looking pleasantly satiated, fewer now tickling phones. The meeting dispersed a little late, in a continuing silence reminiscent of reverence. Even the few students waiting outside the door appeared solemnly a bit puzzled; they'd been waiting for a while in mildly impatient surprise, some straining to hear the singsong talk, as if eavesdropping on secrecy. As the seminar group moved off down the hall, it broke into chatter, which dispelled the atmosphere at the door. A secular miracle will do that.

TWENTY-SIX

PLAGUING JAKE 10:
CRAZY RAY

Back in his office Jake wondered if the Irish seminar would continue at such a level, and worried about the boy's, Evander's, threat. Mary McGahern's performance would have taken a lot out of such an introvert, though he was beginning to think she was tougher than even she likely knew; also, she had received considerable support from ... Alice Pham and Philip Latour, yes. And she'd grown stronger as events unfolded. Those spontaneous recitals of Yeats had lifted sinking Jake's spirits. Mary's "Among School Children" had thrilled him, then filled him with longing, the true nostalgia for a time that never was....

He snapped to and cursed his craven self for not having spoken up in support of Mary's and Alice's and Phil's positions *contra* Evander. He was ashamed of himself—tenured, Full Professor, protected by academic freedom and a militant union (redundancy) just this side of organized crime—ashamed for not professing what he believed, for not doing the job he was *paid* to do and protected in doing.

But to have spoken out, however diplomatically, would have had Evander run immediately to Dean LaRoque with a petition demanding the immediate cancellation of Professor Flynn's tenure, his sacking, and ... what else? What could they do to him really? Return his office to the Algonquin-Anishinaabeg nations? Unnecessary, such a move, as the Natives would settle for reconciliation, restitution/compensation, a.k.a. *money*. His mother used to call Natives ("Indians" in her expression) "smoked Irish." He never did know why. Perhaps a conflation of two racist stereotypes, the drinking Irish and the drunken Indian? Catholics in Northern Ireland should refer to that territory as unceded traditional Celtic lands. The fighting Irish could learn a lot from the smoked Irish: England owed Ireland big time, from the depredations of sub-human Cromwell through the long gauntlet of Black and Bloody Sundays. That was no joke. And neither, Jake old boy (privileged white man), was what was done to Canada's Indigenous peoples. Okay: but what's to be done now? ... And no joke either was the situation with Detective Gurmeet. He must protect John Turnbull, he owed him as much. He must cease this mental rambling and do his job. Such schizoid talking to himself was always a bad bad sign.

He went to the corner windows, but this time with no interest in the expertly glued Buddha statuette (thank you, Peggy) or in Coriveau Hall's front lawn of grass needing cutting, and only a little in the fast-falling leaves. Jake was searching the lounging weed-smokers and enterprising street people. But the homeless seemed all to have gone home. Or not quite all: the one he was looking for remained, obscured in his far corner of darkening maple trees. Jake knew him without being able to see him clearly, because he passed him daily when he couldn't avoid him: the streaky thinness that made him appear taller than he was, the bare feet in sandals whatever the weather, the thick blue wide-legged sweatpants like a gown, the bulky green cardigan, always the same one, forest-green and covered with refuse (fallen leaves for the season), the long sparse beard like a shovel, the thickly matted head hair like something even a Rastafarian might wash, the thin face forever mournful, the pointy noise like a complaint and accusation, the ever lively (drug-addled?) eyes. A ranting madman who could go from zero at your approach to ballistic once he understood that you had nothing for him. Then would erupt with insane accusations. That was Crazy Ray.

So then, what was the attraction that drew Jake to and through that corner every day? Beatles music. It was all Crazy Ray played on his ancient big old boom box like a Cadillac's dashboard. Beside it sat a long rectangular cardboard black box of digitally remastered complete Beatles. Ray would begin each day with Paul counting them in on *Please Please Me* and play all the way through to the end of *Abbey Road*, then start over: "One, two, three, four: She was just seventeen ..." As the day passed he increasingly boomed the music, till the daily police cruiser pulled up along the fence around two. Soon after they left, Ray would repeat the cycle, at volume. Students sometimes sat at safe distance, many never really having listened to the Fabs before. Occasionally a campus group—The Young Conservatives, Caribbean Canadian Youth, Young *Men* on Campus, and such—petitioned the authorities, and Crazy Ray, who would never play Bob Marley or Billie Eilish or anything else, would simply shut down the show. Then start up again three days later. Jake loved the Beatles too. Their music and they themselves were maybe the only thing from his youth whose remembering didn't make him nauseous, just tolerably nostalgic, and often delighted in the mystery and miracle of art.

God but he could use a scotch before drinking from this unavoidable cup—a confrontation with Crazy Ray. Yes, he must go out to him, he had to, for John Turnbull's sake if nothing else … and he could not shake the feeling that there *was* something else. But what else? He knew what was coming with Crazy Ray, if still he never knew what was coming with Crazy Ray. And the Bushmills was all gone, somehow.

He gazed left past the castellated Chateau Laurier Hotel to the Gatineau Hills beyond, beyond Ontario, across the Ottawa River, beyond Gatineau, into the Quebec wilderness. *Behind the Beyond*, he was able to smile small recalling one of Leacock's books. It wasn't his memory at least. … Then what was it? … John Turnbull had stolen the Buddha statuette, most likely from Crazy Ray, and he, Jake Flynn, must return it before John got into more serious trouble. Jake did not like putting his worries into words, but he did: *Ulysses. Theft. Grand larceny.*

Only a few weeks ago the Gatineau Hills had been in full autumnal glory, the tourist-luring "Cavalcade of Colours," a riot of strokes in yellow, red, auburn, brown, and bleedings thereof, with lingering patches of shrinking green, all draping the hills in Group of Seven arboreal impressionism. Now the world was sere, as if a great fire had passed through closing down all hope of avoiding bleak winter. Ottawa's Archibald Lampman, the late-nineteenth century poet and dear friend of Evander's demonized D.C. Scott, had written numerous verses about walking through such local landscapes in consciousness-altering high-summer heat and melancholy shutting-down autumn. The latter never ended hopefully, at best stoically. And now he, Jake, must take a walk.

TWENTY-SEVEN

QUITE UNREQUITED

She considered going to the only open cafeteria, but Mary wasn't really hungry even a full hour after the seminar, just figuring it was suppertime and that she shouldn't waste her prepaid meal ticket. She was losing weight, she needed to eat, she couldn't. She walked to the light-rail station about midway along the campus' western border, where the empty trains rolled in and out, and their wheels scraped along the tracks like failing to brake. Who's afraid of Alfredo the Train? She smiled, and wondered if she was losing her mind. Good riddance. Anyway, nonsense *was* her poetic métier.

She turned further inward and, as on her first day, returned through a campus like a sci-fi movie where everyone's been whisked away to a real world. Or like a now-too-real virus-pandemic flic. Zombies could lurch from doorways no longer knowing they once were students, professors could stiff-leg it like Frankenstein's monster searching for his creator, or administrators patrolling alone with magnifying glasses, searching out acts and thoughts of sexism and racism ... Not that nice Peggy Dubois though. Nor Alice nor Phil. Not Professor Flynn either, whatever was obviously troubling him, which was increasingly apparent to Mary: once he'd seemed to fall asleep in the middle of a presentation; awake he often looked ready to cry—as he'd actually done that very day reciting his Yeats poem. Perhaps she should go to his office to talk with him again, for his sake.

She stopped, came out of herself some and looked around: spindly leafless trees that would not make it, everything grey, sidewalks unnaturally clean, dimness everywhere, *crepuscular*, as ... She'd not even think his name. An abandoned place, sterile, where it appeared and felt that the only humans who remained were administrators in lifeless glass and steel towers. A place that had forgotten what it was. What was that poem on her CanLit syllabus? ... *The City of the End of Things*, "Where no thing rests and no man is." No man.

Turn further inward then, turning and turning, the falconer (female) no longer hears the falcon ...

Would anybody ever write a poem for her such as the professor had read? Would she ever love someone for life with a love that would inspire *her* to write such a poem? Not that she could, but she could have. Though it was looking more and more unlikely, impossible even. And did she really want that? *Why* was unrequited love so attractive to poets and moviemakers? ... Because lost love is too much to bear in real life, that's why. Distanced in poems and stories, it's someone else's problem. Yeats's. And at distance, loss can safely be examined, analyzed, internalized, shelved? ... Also, face it: the unrequited are such losers finally, and losers make us feel good about our winning selves, our wise decisions not to love madly, but to stay home in Leitrim Falls … like that devil Adèle and her fucking Faucher.

No real reader really loves requited love, or not for long anyway, which is why it comes in only at the happy ending. Because in the end requited love makes losers of us all; we lose the longing for what we can only dream. … Had Yeats made the gigantic mistake of confusing art and life? Had he *chosen* to live literature's great theme of romantic dissatisfaction, frustration, the unrequited … and maybe even so he could write about it? His picture showed him with a tiny pair of glasses perched on his nose, beribboned. What real woman *would* love such a nincompoop (that Dad-being-silly word)? "Yes, William, you may write poems for me, but as to fucking, fuck off. What part of fuck off don't you … understand?"

Had foolish William lived his life to fit that bill? If so, it worked! If only in brilliant pathetic poetry among school children. No real writer bothers with lovely love, or at least not for long: *bo-ring*. Look at Alice Munro, where, love is hellfire, and who in real life abandoned her young family so she could write. The lovelorn live forever in literature and imaginations, the suffering Romeo and Juliet, or they are immortal because they off themselves. Paradox, anyone? as Evander would put it. That's literary love and immortality. Maybe she *could* be a writer, having now gained some requisite experience for the job. Could unrequited love be done in a nonsense poem? … Who's afraid of Alfredo the train? Not I, not naughty I! … Hmm …

Fuck it, I'm switching to Criminology.

TWENTY-EIGHT

PLAGUING JAKE 11: CRACKED BUDDHA

Jake was running, which he'd not done in decades, from the far corner of Coriveau Hall's front lawn to about its centre, where he had to rest for breath and calm his thumping heart. He felt scorched, from belly through sternum to throat, acid reflux. That was *not* how he liked to remember his body working in full flight, with the parts moving so out of synch, with lungs burning after only ten metres, with head aflame and face prickling like damaged nerves, till huffing and puffing against a tree trunk like a big laughable wolf. But thank God he'd taken flight over fight!

He waited, glanced back, then leaned his whole body against the maple's trunk, fairly doubling over again with his left hand against its rough bark, sucking air. And here he'd thought that he and Crazy Ray were becoming friends. I really am old now, which reflection was almost amusing him when something crashed the tree trunk right beside his hand, exploding bark and—no, not shrapnel but ... stone?

The familiar voice seemed to boom from the sky: "I was *aiming* for the tree, Judas! Next time it'll be your traitorous fucking head!"

It was the Buddha statuette had supplied the missile, and now instead of the previous manageable two halves, it lay in three large and many small pieces; a yet intact half of the head was face up, showing but a half-smile of wise Buddhist contentment. Jake, a much-lapsed Catholic, could not have been more surprised had it been a broken bust of himself.

Without thinking he picked up the largest piece and moved off, back towards his side of campus. He congratulated himself again on at least not having fought further with the madman—who *had* intentionally displayed a machete on the park bench that served for his storefront. Maybe he was robbed a lot. He was clearly insane and, like the surprisingly mad, probably capable with that machete. Where *were* the police? Where was Detective Gurmeet, who'd been told about the suspicious madman who also sold weed on campus—on the very lawn in front of our showpiece Coriveau Hall! Or wait, that *had* been the initiating cause of his confrontation with the madman. Gurmeet had visited Crazy Ray, he'd been falsely accused, not of stealing the statuette but respecting the missing *Ulysses*. He'd been ordered to pack up and leave permanently or be arrested. The madman blamed the university for that trouble, and so Jake. All of which just proved his madness.

All the madman had to go on was Jake's returning the happy Buddha statuette John Turnbull had stolen! Which Jake had repaired! That the stolen statue *was* the madman's originally Jake had deduced after Turnbull had drawn attention to it in Jake's office. John had stolen it and stealthily managed to deposit it on the sill of Jake's window. That was clear now.

But *why* had Turnbull done so? That remained a mystery, yet another. Perhaps John was subconsciously crying out for help (John in his "war against" would never use such a cliché, Jake smiled to himself inappropriately). Most likely John was a kleptomaniac. He exhibited many of the symptoms. Jake had Googled the subject: a difficult childhood, a drinking problem, marital difficulties (divorced three times, Turnbull), poor impulse control (he seemed unable not to sexually harass every female he met), and, maybe most tellingly, his refusal to own up to, to take responsibility for, his recurrent crimes and misdemeanors.

Jake had approached the dim distant corner of Coriveau Hall's front lawn, where the ground was bare of grass (no sun) and leaves (the madman was neat), and where the roots of the biggest maple broke the surface like something left over from Halloween decorating. The scene had everything but a black cast-iron pot simmering and steaming with whatever the madman fancied: eye of newt, hair of dog, bum of bum. The corner *was* defined by black iron fencing spiked with fleur-de-lis, possessing the only gate, narrow and long-wedged open in inches of dirt. The entire small field was surrounded by the same fence, except of course for the open top of the lawn, so that parents scouting with prospective students could saunter freely this only organic space of uBytown's otherwise postmodern campus, this lone piece of grassy campus before the only antique building that, as Dean Jacques LaRoque knew, answered to parents' dreams of the college education they'd never been able to afford.

Standing there earlier in his garnet-coloured windbreaker with the uBytown logo (a kicking mule), with his left elbow tight against his side, Jake had briefly had second thoughts about what he was about to do. He forgot those thoughts … and proceeded with all the considerable good will he possessed, fronted by his big Jake smile of wary forbearance, the happy Buddha statuette held slightly forth in his right hand like an offering. He was uneasy, too, maybe because "I'll Get You" was playing at moderate volume; it was a nauseatingly nostalgic 'fave' of Jake's from the time when—the early years of high school actually—he'd been pining forever for a girl who wouldn't give him the time of day (literally: he had only ever spoken to her between classes to ask what time it was, and she'd sneered, "Fuck off, Flynn"). Funny that song had never made it onto a regular Beatles album. The harmonies were exceptionally lovely.

The madman had been tending one of his orderly piles on the park bench but sensed Jake's approach and looked back over his sloping blade of shoulder. He didn't grin madly, he looked worried, severe, then more so as he straightened and turned around. Jake continued his guarded smiling as he surveyed the madman's latest salvage: a rubber-banded collection of pens, a computer keyboard, one pink rubber boot, what looked like a crushed mortarboard (the kids still rented them for tossing high on Coriveau's photogenic lawn, when uBytown still had held physical convocations), and four smart phones; the usual row of books spines-up, some dozen currently, old hardbound books of various sombre colours, auburn, brown and black, books that would never be called *texts*. They simultaneously reassured Jake and ramped up his anxiety. His left ribcage was hurting worse from the elbow pressure he was applying.

He looked away in sudden strange shame. He had to remind himself of his mission, as his distracted gaze began to wander further. He made himself concentrate till his head felt splitting. The corner tree provided a tie-off for Crazy Ray's pup tent, whose other line was tied to the back of the bench. There was an additional hoarder's pile on the ground behind the bench covered by the blue plastic of what once had likely been part of another waterproof tent. The madman was meticulous, as the compulsive mad can also be ...Something else John Turnbull was, obsessive-compulsive, OCD, and another trait of the kleptomaniac. Those thoughts returned Jake fully to himself and urged him on in his mission to save his old friend and colleague.

The madman stood his ground, would not step forward in greeting but waited for Jake's nearer approach. At Jake's next sliding step he flailed his hands. Jake knew that the madman flailed at everything and nothing all the time, because he already knew him, at first only in literal passing, distantly from his daily walks through the park. He knew him by name too, Ray, "Crazy Ray," only because that's what he'd heard other street people and students hurl. But he *had* talked with him, more than once. Jake's walking route from home made it best to enter by the corner gateway, then hugging the fence along one side so as to avoid Crazy Ray. But the madman seemed preternaturally alert to Jake's ruse, and he'd managed to engage him once, then did so every time.

Crazy Ray wasn't so mad as to have forgotten that everyone—and no one more than professors—liked to talk about their interests, themselves. He knew Jake was a bigwig professor, that his field was English (Jake had almost missed the joke in Crazy Ray's affected hick voice: "This is *my* field, *Perfesser*"), and even that his specialty was Canadian literature. He knew too that with increasing ease Jake could be engaged in criticizing the university, what and how his colleagues taught, the ill condition of the students the high schools were sending him, and the state of literacy generally. More than that, the madman would sometimes display an impressive knowledge of books, the greats and many of the also-rans. He knew, Crazy Ray did, that with Jake he would not have to remain sole for long in his roaring flailing complaints against the world, especially if that world could be contained to academia.

But they had not been on the friendliest terms of late and he wouldn't smile, the madman. "What do you want here, *Per-fesser* Flynn?" He could sometimes use the title with remnant respect, but most often resembling what was customarily said patronizingly to old codgers on the threshold of senility, or as one might address an ex-con or the garbage collector: *Right you are, Professor*.

Jake wanted to get the business over with quickly. "I wanted to return this." He held out the Buddha statuette in his right hand, his left elbow crushing his side as if failing to relieve a runner's stich.

"*Return* it? That's never mine."

"It's okay, Ray, I believe a colleague of mine, a short man with spiked grey hair, took it from your bench of goods when you weren't looking? Likely you didn't even notice or had forgotten it."

The madman demurred, ignored the proffered bait and instead frowned like some hoary prophet at Jake's other side. He squared-up against him, spoke angrily, his usual style, though they had no argument with one another. "I know Professor Turnbull. He's a regular customer of mine." He piped air to signal what it was John Turnbull was buying from him. "Weed may be legal now, but John knows where to get quality, and not be seen doing so. Isn't he up for another sabbatical or something? He's always yammering on about his rights and privileges." He squinted meaningfully at Jake: "But *he* didn't take nothing else from me, not *Perfesser* Turnbull."

Jake knew the bad grammar was intentional, part of whatever act Crazy Ray was now performing. "Well, I'm leaving this here all the same," he said carefully, and as carefully leaned in to set the statuette on the foremost slab of the bench. "We don't want any more trouble with the police." It was already taking too long, and he had that hospital-gown feeling with Crazy Ray at his back.

"Hey, whatcha doin' there, *Perfesser*? Them books ain't for sale, they's *my* personal lie-berry." Ray then proved he really was crazy by radically changing register from the mildly alerted to the sarcastic: "But yeah, that's right, *Jake*, who was it sent the fucking cops over here to interrogate me about some fucking book anyway! That Detective Gurrr-meet! Or *hur*-meet or no-man's meat! Was it you, Perfesser Flynn?"

Jake already knew that the madman could explode, get physical and start flinging things about. And now Crazy Ray was leaning past him to the bench and brushing aside a collection of pink plastic plates to reveal a large knife—no, a machete! He didn't pick it up, thank God, just looked at it, then looked meaningfully at Jake, and back-and-forth one more time. He again shifted vocal register and said like a normal guy in normal surprise, "Hey, what the fuck …?"

As suddenly, and as insanely, he grew calm. "You know, Jake, you were right: that Turnbull doesn't know his arsehole from a black hole, not as a reader, not as a teacher, not as a scholar, not in his life." Then roared: "But *he's* not the one who stole my old happy Buddha!" He leaned in, as if with that high white forehead he might butt Jake on the bridge of his nose, knock him into unconsciousness, or maybe some higher consciousness.

"But I thought you denied that it ever *was*—"

"*I* denied? *I* denied?" He was once more flailing in full flight. "Turnbull denied! You deny every day of your fucking life with every fucking breath you take, *Perfesser*! You deny the purpose of your entire fucking professing! You betray your vocation! You deny the mission of seeking truth! Turnbull and you are embarrassed by the whole idea! I'm right ain't I, *Perfesser*? You deny the value of your whole fucking raison d'etre *as a teacher*! You deny these idiot kids, like that Mary who was just by here, you deny them even the *hope* of a meaningful life made beautiful by art! *I* am that truth, Jake, I am the way back! I speak only the truth! Singular! I—"

Jake knew well the danger of riling him further, which *was* yet possible, and so he backed off literally, talking loudly and normally: "Ray, I'm leaving it with you, Ray, and asking you not to press charges, that's all, though even if you did you wouldn't succeed, so why bother, eh Ray?" Student Services advised using the student's name frequently when confronted. "I did want you to know, though, Ray, that John Turnbull suffers from a psychological disorder, an obsessive-compulsive mania, probably *klepto*mania, and I would have thought that you, with your own troubles—"

"Psychological disorder my concord-discordia asshole! Everyone nowadays makes some psycho-social excuse for their failures, failures of *will*! Crimes!" He suddenly calmed again and did a mincing voice: "My mommy breast-fed me with a pickle, my daddy was disappointed in me, big Uncle Willie took too long changing my diaper, woe oh woe is poor wee victim me when I was wee. Turnbull's an egomaniacal idiot, that's *his* disorder! *I* know I know nothing, but I know more about Orwell and Camus and Kingsley Amis and John Osborne and that whole kitchen-sink lot than that Gucci socialist thinks he knows!"

And as suddenly again the air seemed to go out of him. "I'll give you this, Professor Jake: at least you *did* try … at least you did, and you still do, sometimes, if we can go by your lovely student Mary's admiration. I'll give you that much, Professor, which is the only reason I'm not slicing and dicing you with Señor Machete there! ... *No Man's Meat*—ha!" And madly calmer: "Do you know that other title by that Callaghan you urged on me? Not as good as *Such Is My Beloved*, you're right there. But not bad for a Canadian, if light years from James Joyce. But then who isn't, eh perfesser?"

Jake had slowed some at Crazy Ray's calmer madness, but picking up his backpedalling retreat at reference to the machete, was near to turning and running, if now at least conscious of relief from the pain in his left side, which puzzled a part of him that for the present he could not fully attend to. He dismissed his confusion as anxiety over what he'd just had to do, replace the statuette. Which was over, thank God.

Crazy Ray noticed Jake's hurry and permitted himself a smile before returning to earnestness. "You'd better keep on trying while you still can, Professor—repent! *If* you still know what that word once meant! *Pace* Leonard Cohen! Because the dark day is nigh when the hardworking parents of these children, *and* the kids themselves, are going to twig to the confidence trick that's being played here! *What a racket!* Four years of an expensive distracting party with nothing to show in the end but a monstrous morning-after of debt and no prospect of a job, while all the Gucci socialist perfessers spend year-long sabbaticals in Saint-Tropez.

"The big bogey Plague made the situation only plainer, just as the pandemics revealed much else that's gone all to hell, from those morbidly obese—those disgustingly fat— Americans who can't stop stuffing their faces with processed shit and so have no defence against little ol' viruses—to starving Indigenous children whose parents waste their funds on booze and building casinos and drugs and all manner of crime—including their army of lawyers! *Repent!*

"This whole fucking joke of a university will shut down! Like is happening already right before your eyes! Good riddance! Because all I hear from you per-fessers is shit! Your so-called higher learning has become only a bigger and bigger pile of shite stinking to the very nose hairs of the Almighty! *Repent*! And you English *per*-fessers are the worse of a bad lot, giving up on Shakespeare and Joyce and Munro because *you* know better! *Repent*! If it weren't so patently ridiculous, you'd go back and improve Mozart and the Beatles! Thinking you're Martin Luther King fucking Junior whoring after cunty Mother Teresa and Karl kiss-my-ass Marx! *Repent*! *Repent*! *Repent*!"

Crazy Ray's mad eyes were rolling and bugging and glaring in finest frenzy as he turned and reached for the machete—when Jake spun about and ran for it. But Ray had been reaching only for the happy Buddha statuette; and who knows, had Jake not run, Ray could well have been planning only to settle down suddenly and make a wise point with it, weighing the plump smiling demigod in his hand. Crazy Ray *was* capable of quieter wisdom, if also obviously prone to radical mood shifts. Perhaps in a way, and not only from his own cracked point of view, a demonstration of wisdom is exactly what he did in throwing the statuette—a precisely powerful pitch that would have done the Bodh Gaya cricket team proud.

As shocked Jake made his way back towards the business side of the campus, mindfulness slipped from him with the evaporating sweat; he felt the welcome cool on his forehead first; then commenced a familiar phasing out, he didn't resist, he couldn't anyway because he never knew how it was happening. He ended up somewhere but for a long spell had no consciousness of where that was or how he'd arrived. Wherever, whatever, he felt more and more settled—perhaps inevitable after escaping such an encounter with frantic madness—if soon an increasingly disturbed peace. He wanted to sleep, just a quick nap. Here? Why not? ... Half in a dream then he remembered Lampman's poem about being led to a better place by "some blessed power." Maybe that's what was happening here. He squinted at his feet with somewhat becalmed visage and, head deeply bobbing and bowing, continued draining the artificial heat ... more mindless by the minute.

8

TWENTY-NINE

A MEETING OF MINDS

Mary McGahern was sitting on the cement steps of the grand entrance to Coriveau Hall. Were she observed from a distance, she'd have appeared no more than a dark dot in an expanse of grey concrete, which is how she felt. From her vantage point, she had squinted with interest at the performance played out in the far dark corner of the front lawn. It had looked pretty funny: the street guy, Crazy Ray, who'd just finished talking with her, had screamed and flailed and boomed at Professor Flynn. Then the gawky professor was running like a newborn giraffe and hiding behind a tree—the thrown rock just missing his head! ... Which wasn't funny, she supposed.

When Professor Flynn walked dejectedly from the field of battle, she'd sat on. She thought of asking a passerby to take her photo. Dad would love a picture of her on the steps of the old-fashioned 'college' building he'd dreamed of for decades. But how to get it taken, then get it to him? Someone with a smart phone could email it to her. Then print it somewhere and mail it to Dad, I guess, she thought. No use waiting till she'd go home again. Or forget it. Besides, there were no passersby. Per usual there was no one. I'm getting a smart phone and that's that. I've never taken even *one* selfie!

On her wandering way to Coriveau Hall's grand-entrance steps, she too had encountered the madman in the far corner of the front lawn, whom everyone but her (it seemed) already knew as Crazy Ray and a reliable source of marijuana cheaper and better than at the government-run stores. *Seemed* because she'd only once overheard Evander praising the supplier to one of the smart-phone dolts before the start of their seminar: "Be careful, though, Gary, he's crazy mad, anti-academic as all hell and likely a sexual threat. But the best weed to be had, *if* you can tune out the boomer music. Just pay and go. It's sort of like the Seinfeld Soup Nazi, if you know that ancient boomer show in endless boomer reruns, of course."

In her dawdling (*arsing about*, thank you Granny McGahern) after class, too early for her meeting with the Dean (who'd insisted on the late-day time), and unable to stomach the thought of something to eat, out of curiosity Mary had ambled past the corner's stuck black gate and paused to observe the madman. She liked the music, her dad's Beatles ... she recognized the beginning of the *Let It Be* album, their last.

She'd read that marijuana was an appetite stimulant for cancer patients undergoing chemotherapy. In the afternoons of high school, with the lot of them stoned, fat Faucher, his protruding eyes bloodshot as pinkeye, was always going on about having the munchies. Alone with Naomi on the porch at home, she'd resisted the persuasion that a little weed can cure what ails you, even when nothing's ailing you (and then Naomi, toked up, would laugh too much at her own stupid jokes, dissuasively, and brazenly ask for a snack). She *had* tried it, twice, and the second time felt more anxious than the first, like a squirrel that's forgotten where she's buried her nuts. But desperate times require ... So, halted in her idle wandering she was still worrying the idea of an illegal purchase when the madman turned to her, or rather *on* her.

"Whaddya want, girly, sneaking up on me like that? You're not another cop, *are* you? You sure don't look the Mary-Jane type." He turned down the volume on his black boombox, quieting "Dig a Pony."

He didn't scare her, and she'd picked up the irony in his old hippie name for marijuana; so she smiled, tried signalling a twigging that could hold promise of mutuality. "I don't want anything, just taking a walk." She wouldn't budge. "I'm a student here. You don't own this place, *do* you? My name is Mary McGahern, from Leitrim Falls, I'm not from anywhere else. I like the Beatles."

Despite its strangeness, and likely because of it too, her aggression and declarations calmed him. He smiled tightly and seemed to be accepting her further, then grinned widely, his mouth looking like a fire had long ago passed through a poor stand of birch and poplar, leaving only blackened stumps where nothing had grown back. He abruptly demanded, "What's your major?"

She thought she should just walk away, but that thought was immediately followed by *Why not?* There was something fascinating about the way the madman alternatively—even simultaneously—spoke like a dumb boy and an educated bum.

"Film&WordsWork, do you know what that is?"

"No, and neither do your *perfessers*."

She snickered involuntarily, and he responded well, appearing willfully to lengthen the frequency of his vibrating frame. He reached and turned up the volume just a touch for "Across the Universe."

Yes, there was something intriguing about this guy ... Dad! *Dad* was something like, a self-taught man who would play the ignorant hick to entertain, to divert, to trip up, and with her to teach. And when he was drinking sometimes play the Beatles on what eventually sounded like an eternal loop.

The madman swept an arm at his park bench. "These are *my* study books, some maybe for sale to the right buyer. I have *other goods* for purchase too, if you get my drift, girly." He mimed sipping a joint and cleverly followed it with a softly sung "Gur-url ..." and sipped again. Then shifted radically: "Cops think I stole some book, *but I don't steal.* Books are left all over the place around here, abandoned! Do *you* take things that don't belong to *you*, Mary-Mary quite contrary?"

"Don't call me that. ... But yes, all the time, big-time crime." Which froze him, till his head jerked back in appreciation. She was calmed and encouraged: "Those look like library books to me, Mister, the call numbers on the spines? All but one anyway. Maybe that's why the police are after you."

He thought about that, then smiled like pain. "Your library's not long for this world, girly, least not under its current name, *John A. Macdonald.* Who owns a book, Mary?"

She was fully engaged then, because her father had asked the very same question more than once, usually when the evening's home-schooling was over and he was easing into his second homebrew Harp. So she had at the ready her father's answer to his own question: "The reader who knows the book intimately owns it, especially if she loves it. I don't currently have a copy of *Emily of New Moon*, yet I still own it."

His eyes widened, he flicked the tip of his extensive beard, then widely smiled his foul approval.

"Well, if that's the case, then I already own the book I'm accused of stealing! If not that particular edition, which is neither here nor there. In evidence of my claim to its ownership, m'lady …" He struck a mock-military pose, holding saluting left backhand to forehead. He sputtered over some wordless private joke. Returning to ease he gestured with both arms raised and hands turned outward like some sermonizer on his mount. Yet he recited in a lilting rhythm: "I'm the queerest young fellow that ever you heard. My mother's a Jew, my father's a bird." He jabbed both hands, still with palms up, and wiggled the fingers towards himself in the manner of a ham-performer soliciting appreciation.

Which he got when Mary beamed. "My dad recited that poem too once! Isn't it from …? Who wrote it? I love poems like that."

"You do, do you, Mary-Mary? Then according to your own terms, you own *it* too! It was an Irishman penned that little gem, a mick as mad as me! Some doggerty-goggerty fellow or other. But he's no one now, and anyway he's not how it came to mmm …" He frowned deepening puzzlement at his book collection on the park bench. "What the … where'd that come …?"

He turned from the bench and caught her smiling brightly, and was stunned by a young loveliness which, even from such a bum, could be called beauty harassment. He squinted in growing interest and dreamy forgetfulness, or maybe only in natural reaction to her having lit up his shadowy corner of the world. He pouted briefly, then said, "Your turn, Miss Mary, a poem for a poem is only fair!" He turned the boombox down further.

"Oh, I don't—"

He stepped into her likely path of departure and spoke harshly in what she prayed was but more mock-madness: "A poem, Mary-Mary-quite-contrary, or *you shall not pass!*"

That was a fair impersonation of the actor in the *Lord of the Rings* movie, which helped her see through the angry pose. He was still clearly mad, but his eyes weren't *that* crazy, not really. She looked the madman up and down: he had an asexuality that approached annunciation of total disinterest, there was nothing to fear that way. And in grades nine and twelve she *had* represented Sacred Heart High in sprints.

"I will if you promise not to call me that anymore."

"Deal."

So she mockingly struck his own militaristic pose and recited:

"I met a devil named Adèle, who just adores the door to hell. Her mother was a midnight moth, vis-à-vis a Visigoth!" She flourished the finish, twirling her right index finger once at the blue sky. Then she was blushing deeply, as if reflecting the sun's paling fire.

His face shot forward in a squint: "Who's that? Edward Lear? I've not heard it before, I like it!" Whomever he might learn he liked, he obviously liked her; in fact, Crazy Ray was thinking he could die for love again, if only he were young again.

"I wrote it and, uh, it won a contest here." Sure, why not? She'd never come this way again. Then quickly: "You know my name, what's yours?"

"Ray, and Crazy Ray's just fine by me, given the standard for sanity around here. But if you really wrote that, Mary, I hope you're writing more of the same."

"Crazy like a fox, I bet. But I have to go … Ray. Nice talking with you." She took a couple of steps, stopped and turned back. "Was it William Butler Yeats wrote *your* poem?"

"Yeats! That sad lunatic? No, it was Ireland's greatest writer, and maybe the world's. Can you riddle me that, Mary-Mary?"

"Duh, Alice O'Munro?" She mugged dumbly. He got it, mimed tiny applause. She thought her parting words would be the end of it: "My dad loves the Beatles too."

He was oddly offended, even aggressively so: "What's not to love? ... No-no, don't go. Here, wait a minute, listen. And he hurried to the boombox and cranked the volume. The opening piano chords of "Let It Be" (the whole of which she sometimes played for her father) filled the air and echoed off the houses beyond the iron fence. He held up his forefinger, holding her back, let the song play a minute longer, then turned it down.

He sighed deeply at her. "Genius, that McCartney, singing an elegy for his dead mother, mother Mary, *Mary*."

It was like her face had been tasered, she wanted to dash, but couldn't, because she knew she'd regret it, her weakness. She managed a clichéic, "You think?"

"I do think, Mary McGahern. And I can see you're moved, so apologize if I've touched a painful wound, which you are too young to suffer already, even if no one is. I'll say nothing more."

"No, please. Seriously, Ray, you think 'Let It Be' is about Paul McCartney's dead mother?" She could keep it together.

"I do. I have a Beatles theory. I think the dead mother is the source of Paul's inexplicable genius. John Lennon's too, the pair of them a unique accident birthed in the accidental deaths of mothers Julia and the sudden death by cancer of McCartney's mother Mary—*when they were both about the same age*, mid-teens. That's a synchronicity woven in their stars, and ours, *deo gratias*. Do you know that word, Mar—"

She'd flinched again, turned and walked off smartly, she had no further choice in the matter.

He made to chase after, caught himself with a smirk of knowing what he did and didn't know, and called: "God, but you are one beauty, girly! And I'm not talking about your beanpole model's looks, or about only that anyway, so don't let it go to your head! But be extra careful in this quite contrary world, Mary-Mary! And do remember: pain and suffering make us most fully human! And are likely the source of nonsense poetry!"

Without turning—she'd better not—blinded she waved a blind hand overhead: "Thank you, Not-so-Crazy Ray! You too!"

Crazy Ray returned needlessly to reorganizing his book hoard, first brushing along the upturned spines with the back of his fingers like gentling fond pets. He paused over some in mild concern, remained stuck on one, deeply puzzled again—*Where in the hell* …—then perplexed and tugging at his beard till it hurt. And Crazy Ray had what he thought a sane thought: Stop hallucinating, Raymond old boy, that's what you're doing, or they'll cart you off to The Princess again.

Good advice, Mr. Ray, as she was not looking forward to her long-postponed meeting with Dean LaRoque. Late Friday afternoon had certainly not been her choice, that's where the smarmy Dean had already out-manoeuvered her. So, do be careful, extra careful, thank you … Crazy Ray.

Mary pushed off on her knees from the butt-paining concrete step. She then felt rashy cool down there, the stiff denim didn't help. She put her hands on her pelvic bones (which had gotten too prominent) and looked all round as if searching for something that she'd missed. What was it she's feeling? … Appetite? Yes, she felt hungry now. Could the legendary effects of a contact high be real? Crazy Ray's whole corner had smelled of marijuana, which she'd never liked; there was a brand called "skunk weed," and that's what all marijuana smelled like to her (the association with Faucher never helped). Whatever, she shouldn't let pass the urge to eat. There was a modified Tim's counter in Macdonald Library, and she had an instant craving for her (and Dad's) old favourite, which they'd always had after Saturday morning visits to the town library: a BLT on brown, toasted. She would email an apology to Dean LaRoque claiming a medical emergency. She'd just have to chance not running into him … who *was* everywhere unfortunately.

About to take the same route as Professor Flynn, she was arrested by activity in Crazy Ray's distant corner. A car had pulled alongside the frozen gate. There was a long pause, and Mary couldn't say what made her delay. She could tell that Crazy Ray was also watching the car … a shy customer? Someone got out, a darkly lanky figure. Without clear identifying evidence, Mary thought of Detective Kiran Gurmeet. It *was* Detective Gurmeet squeezing through the gate. Had Professor Flynn called the police? Not wanting to be involved in any way, Mary turned away and moved off at a clip. She absolved herself thinking she was only still following Crazy Ray's own advice.

Hungry again, she also felt the world livelier as she made her way across Laurier Avenue to the Grande Allée of the undead campus, having had to wait for only one car to pass before crossing against the red light. How account for it, this livelier world? Was it that the slapstick show of Professor Flynn running from Crazy Ray and the hurled rock had enlivened the dormant campus? She should check up on the Professor before heading to Tim's: he'd looked a wreck in class and now was acting very oddly. But on what pretense visit the Leader's office? … The madman had said his blasphemous poem was Irish. She could recite it. Professor Flynn, do you know the source? But what if Dean LaRoque should show up there? He could; he really seemed to pop up everywhere he wasn't wanted—the pop-up dean. And she was starving now.

Anyway, the distracting internal debate was forgotten, for she had already made the left turn towards the library—Film&WordsWork being off to the right—and climbed the concrete steps to the concrete plateau from which yet another flight of concrete steps reached to the generous terrace of Macdonald Library. As she rose on that final flight and gained a sight line, she saw a slumping figure sitting on the brown platform that supported a bronze statue of John A. Macdonald. Professor Flynn, head in hands, in as brown a study.

Mary instantly forgot why she had come; she forgot all about her excited appetite and the enlivened world, forgot even her ever-insinuating romantic troubles; her mind was instantly focused on the pathetic figure of the needy professor—*so* reminiscent of her dad at times, during the worst times—and what she could do to relieve whatever troubled him. Was she such a daughter that all the men she liked would remind her of her father? Though Jimmy was noth—forget Jimmy. Like, forever.

Professor Flynn didn't notice when she sidled up and stood quietly. Before taking in the statue, she read the plaque that said simply "John A. Macdonald (1815–1891) Canada's First Prime Minister." Above, the twice life-sized Macdonald posed with right hand on hip holding back his frock coat; his left hand held forth a scroll. Did Canada have a Declaration of Independence? No, of course not. It likely represented the British North America Act, the BNA that Macdonald had secured, granting the newborn Dominion of Canada a peaceful and orderly independence. She knew that from her father's history lessons, not her high school's, where Macdonald's achievements were roundly vilified. So no surprise that the dark scroll was covered in red paint, which the spattering below testified had been applied so generously as to drip. The head was also splattered in red, looking as though the effigy had recently suffered serious blunt trauma.

"Professor Flynn?"

He didn't startle but straightened calmly in his seated position and looked up at her. "Mary McGahern," he spoke in a deep and troubled sigh. "No surprise to find you the only student who still uses the library."

Well, not exactly, she kept to herself. "Are you not feeling well, Professor?"

"No, I'm not, Mary, not well at all. But no cause for alarm. This happens to me from time to time."

Was he drunk? *Stoned*? Him too? What else *could* he have been doing with Crazy Ray? "Should I call for help, or your wife for a ride home? With the lovely name, *Jieun*. I love the way you're always bringing her into lectures. But can I call Jieun for you, Professor Flynn, if I may."

He stared at a spot somewhere along the concrete landing. "Jieun left me long ago, Mary. We're divorcing, she told me so only last week. She'd read through my emails, I don't blame her, the way I'd been with her and the family. So I admitted to something, confessed it. Jieun walked out, came back only to tell me that she herself had also been having an 'emotional affair' for the past few years. I shouldn't be saying any of this to you but what the hell." Aware as if for the first time that he was really addressing student Mary McGahern and not dreaming it, he nevertheless continued talking from some delusional place he couldn't escape.

Jesus Christ! Walk away! She didn't need this! Walk away!

"I know I shouldn't be talking to you like this, Mary. But something tells me that we might not meet again anyway, and I need … well, I need someone like you to hear me out. What did I do? What to deserve this?"

She was stunned, dumbfounded. She found a pathetic voice: "I don't know what to say, *Professor*."

"Did you know," he began, lifting his brow at the statue, "that it won't be Macdonald Library for much longer? Which it has been for over the century of Bytown University's brief history. But as of January first next year, this will be The Tecumseh Digital Resource Centre. Before then, a crane will have come and unceremoniously hiked John A. further into historical infamy. In his place will likely appear a statue of Tecumseh that *likely* would shame a self-respecting cigar-store Indian. Oh, what's the point." He drooped.

Talk! You need to talk. "That really is a shame, Professor. It's the sort of thing that drives my father right round the bend too. It's so *in*discriminate, and Dad says that's what education is all about, *discriminating* finely. Or should be. He says what's being done is called *presentism*, insisting the big bad past bend a knee to the enlightened present—the very opposite of what education should do! ... He says, I mean."

"Your dad. He comes into your conversation like Jieun into mine. I like him, Mary, and hope for your sake that he continues more substantial than Jieun."

"What?"

"But it's not the honouring of the great Shawnee chief that bothers me, Mary, nothing of the sort, of course not. If not for Tecumseh you and I wouldn't be here today *as* Canadians in an independent Canada in its capital Ottawa, which, in case you've not heard, is unceded Algonquin-Anishinaabeg land." He grinned horribly. "But not to joke: if not for Tecumseh—whose motives, granted, were his own—but if not for Tecumseh there *is* no John A., at least not as the first prime minister of the new Dominion of Canada. What I hate are these revisionist idiots thinking they are better than John A. Macdonald and can sit in judgement of him. *Why?* What's their justification? Because they've had the courage and vision to create *not* a new free nation but"—and he commenced mincing much as Evander regularly performed in their seminar—"safe spaces and trigger warnings and grief counselors and political leaders with no more sense of real historical grief than a plague has."

She laughed in a puff. He might be okay. She remembered her father's history of the War of 1812 and thought to distract Professor Flynn further. "What about Laura Secord, *eh* Professor?"

Aware that he was being teased Ray smiled horribly tight. "You're right, of course. We'd likely not be here without the *heroine*-ism of Laura Secord either. Or for that matter of Mrs. Macdonald darning John A.'s winter woollies. You remind me what a patriarchal pri ... *professor* I am, Ms. McGahern, and for that I am grateful."

"That's not what I meant to do, Professor, just pulling your patriarchal leg a little. But Macdonald did have D.C. Scott establish those horrible residential schools. My dad says that wasn't literally *genocide*, but it sure was a disgraceful attempt at cultural genocide. Scott himself said as much, and without much remorse."

"I know, Mary. The past can suck and do so big time. But so can the present, just as big a suckee. And the sucking future will judge us as we judge, and in its turn be judged. In the long run, the long historical view, we're all suckers. A little respect, please, that's all I'm saying; a little recognition of historical contingencies, past, present, and future. Natives aren't the only peoples with elders deserving veneration. *And* a little humility, *s'il vous plait.*"

"My dad says much the same." She shifted her vocal register to something lower and supposedly male: "What will our great-great grandchildren think of us, sitting around reading books, barbecuing burgers and drinking beer, while all around us the victimized are starving and Pluto is squealing for freedom like William Wallace. Pluto's our old boar."

Jake snorted, made to speak, caught himself and derailed his train. "Do *you* know what a remarkable girl-woman-person you are, Mary McGahern? You must get sick of hearing that?"

"Not yet."

Jake puffed nasally. "And what a student you are! I wish I'd known your dad, your parents. I wish that one day I could have gone fishing in your ... Big Pond, was it? Your remarkable father and I would hook that magical trout again!"

"But you *can*, Professor, I wasn't being just polite. And I know you and Dad *would* hit it off."

"I know all that too, Mary. But I'm exhausted. I think I'm finished. You make me want to qualify what I'm saying here, *because* what I'm saying could very well be nothing more meaningful than an old man's dithering regrets. I'm just another codger who thinks the whole show closes with him, that *his* world, the very best old world, is going to hell in a handbasket. Because my best self truly believes that the young will find a way, *their* way, they always do, whether I approve or not. You're the proof of that, Mary." He laughed self-consciously at himself for the sermonizing tone. Then thought, *Hell*. "Seriously, I'm challenging you, *charging* you, Mary McGahern, to be one of those who lights the way."

What on earth ...? It was only then she noticed he was holding a rock in his hand, which rested in his lap. The rock Crazy Ray had thrown at him? Or not a rock, too smoothly finished, too flat and shiny where it was broken. She spoke with a worried face: "Why did Crazy Ray throw that ... rock at you, Professor? Uh, I was sitting on the steps of Coriveau Hall, where I was waiting for an appointment with Dean LaRoque, and I saw the madman threatening you and then throwing *that*," she pointed.

He turned it so that she saw the half-faced Buddha. "All I'd wanted to do ... well, all that should have concerned him, was I wanted to return it. Someone I know had taken it, stolen it, and I didn't want that person getting into more trouble for another theft, which could provide extenuating evidence at a trial. Apologies for being so mysterious about it, Mary, but I have to keep confidence. Anyway, instead of taking it and thanking me, Crazy Ray started ranting and threw it at me!"

She controlled a small sputter, he'd sounded so childishly hurt. "But he *is* a madman, Professor. Don't let *him* get you down so."

Jake tried to stare down the broken Buddha, looking lost again. Till he said quietly, "Mary, watch Dean LaRoque."

"I hear you, Professor, but not to worry on my account: the Dean and I will *not* be having any more 'mentoring meetings' for my"—she nailed further LaRoque's febrile intonation—"invaluable freshman—*or* young woman's, *or* woman's—input!"

That got a hard-won chuckle. "Mary, please forgive my presumption, but I really do need to say this to you. You're just about the most promising first-year student I've ever met in some forty years of university teaching. But you're disappointed here, I know, you have to be, what smart student wouldn't be? And you're either thinking about quitting or soon will be."

"But I never—"

He held up a weak traffic-cop's hand: "Please. Indulge the old professor. Thank you. And please don't think of this as unasked-for advice; I still like to deceive myself that I'm principally a teacher, so take this as a lesson and, not to be all melodramatic, maybe my last meaningful one. But don't quit, Mary. Don't give up. Even if I seem to be. There *is* a torch, and I ask you to accept it—to believe it's in your sacred keeping." He snatched breath and forged on: "Feel that breeze, Mary? ... It'll soon be an even colder wind blowing across campuses everywhere—the whole western world. Dark days are coming, coming back, again. It could even be another Dark Ages, when free inquiry will again be banned by a new irrational religion … worship of the Great Good God of *Caring* as the *sine qua non* of civilization. Your people are Irish, Mary McGahern. Well, the Irish, their scholarly monks, saved civilization through the first Dark Ages because they cared about learning. Now it's your turn. No joke."

"I don't know, Professor. I wasn't planning on quitting, but I can't promise either. Besides which, there are other ways to higher learning."

His eyes closed in a small smile. "Everything you say, Mary, confirms my estimate of you and your potential. Your performance in our seminar today lifted my spirits like you could never know. And that's what determined me to say these things to you next time we met alone. I just didn't think the opportunity would come like this." He gestured with the broken Buddha, like a priest with his thurible, swinging his arm round at the campus generally, towards the library, then over his shoulder at the statue of Macdonald. He looked directly at her, and she met his look.

"More advice, Mary, because you might need it. You are brilliant, and if you continue your education, you will grow more so. But don't let your head rule your heart. Smart people, like all my colleagues, make every decision according to the dictates of their considerable intellects. I don't say that ironically. And almost to a person they make a mess of their lives. I've done it too. Have you ever noticed that situation with people, your friends say? That really smart girls can hook up with absolute losers? And vice-versa of course. Brilliant people with the emotional IQ of a psychopath. Mary, no one ever *thought* her way to true love."

Mary was now feeling a touch frightened, but not of Jake Flynn; rather, given her romantic situation, by the scoring penetration of his advice. And she'd once heard something like from Mom! She thought she was saying it for his sake, if not really knowing *what* she was promising not to do: "I won't."

Suspecting he was being humoured, Jake smirked. "I think I know who made you so intelligent, Mary: your home-schooling, anti-TV, contra-computer, Luddite father, if I may say so respectfully. But you're not standing here listening to me because you're so smart." They both smirked. Then Jake abruptly: "Who filled you with so much love, Mary?"

"What? Well my da ... Mom."

He looked down at the broken Buddha in his hands. "And what did you do to deserve it?"

"I'm sorry, Professor, but I don't ..." She was looking down on his considerable tonsure. "You're right of course: nothing."

He stood and, from some height above her, held out his hand. She reached for it and shook, her hand warm, his cool, even cold and waxy. Her eyes teared because the only other time she'd felt such a hand was holding her mother's in the coffin. Why was her life suddenly all leave-takings?

"In this plaguey correct world we could be arrested for what we're doing, Mary." She sniffled and snorted. He smiled genuinely: "*And* for shaking hands."

She got it and laughed.

"I have to go now. But please indulge the old professor in pontificating a little more like a ... a *born eejit*." They laughed lightly. "Seriously, Mary."

"Please, Professor, that's why I'm here."

Everything she said made him smile. "This poor world will not keep faith with you, Mary McGahern; it can't, don't I know it. Nor will the world that's coming, that's arrived actually.

Judge it, yes, that will be your life's work, I hope, in whatever form you eventually do it. But do so compassionately. And forgivingly, forgive it and those who will break your heart, Mary. Don't begrudge the gift of love, that love your father and mother freely gave you; pay it forward, as they say." Looking down affectionately, riskily he placed his hand on her shoulder, so thin, whose slightness made him pinch his mouth: he had no right to burden her like this. "And be strong, Mary, be tough, like your mom. Will you carry the light onward for me and your parents, Mary?"

Such language, such fancy metaphors, such fine speech! But he wasn't joking in the least, or being at all ironic, no, of course not. Dry-eyed she nodded: "Yes, I'll try my very best, I promise you, Professor Flynn. And thanks for everything."

With a smile of ambivalent satisfaction he walked off steadily. Without breaking stride he dropped the chunk of Buddha through the swinging lid of a recycle bin—which swung high to the far side, hesitated … then back out the near side, if lessened, swinging again and again diminishingly, till it returned to stillness.

A mildly mesmerized Mary was working at light speed to process all that had just happened. So occupied by distracting thoughts, she forgot her hunger and the favoured Tim's food and turned towards her residence.

Well along the Grande Allée heading to Brant Rez she finally looked up and took in the unusual sight of a human figure … which she believed she recognized. Little Alice from the seminar, from the back. Unthinking, she picked up her pace and called, "Alice?"

Alice turned, poked her head and squinted dramatically, then threw up her slight arms in mock-surprise, and smiled pleasantly. "Why, if it isn't Mary McGahern, poet extraordinaire!"

As she came up Mary laughed a touch guardedly. "What about Alice … I'm sorry, Alice, I forget your last name, Professor Flynn took attendance only our first class."

"Pham." She waited expressionless, even a touch guardedly herself.

"Then: and if it isn't Alice Pham, slayer of gay Evanders and brilliant reciter of 'Leda and the Swan'—by heart!"

Alice smiled but with an immediate turn-down of her tiny mouth. "I'm gay too, Mary."

"Well, I'm not. And now that that's out of the way, would you like to go for a coffee? I'm starving too, I just remembered, for one of Tim's superb BLTs if not for the love that dare not speak its name." Alice snickered. "*Have* you eaten, Ms. Pham? Up for a BLT?"

Her cute face lit up like a bronzed sun. "Now that's a poem I could sink my teeth into, better even than your moving rendition of 'Among School Children'."

"The girl confirms her questionable taste!"

Alice bowed her shining black head and tittered delightfully into the edge of her hand, in a manner that made Mary wonder if she herself could be a lesbian, or at least give it a try. Further evidence in favour of the experiment? She was a dead loss romantically as a hetero. … No, stick to what you thought in the seminar, girl, seriously: a potential friend, Alice, possibly a first university friend. Make your next move smoothly, Mary, naturally.

So she proceeded in what she feared was too non sequitur, "My heritage is Irish and my—"

"*Really*, Ms. McGahern," in a put-on prissy voice. "Just what makes you think your personal history is relevant to our relationship? If we're to be friends, it must be so only to change the world for the better!"

They bowed slightly in laughter and touched each other's arms as if needing support. Alice continued: "I'd just love to meet Evander's partner, wouldn't you? We'll have to arrange an end-of-seminar party just to force the legendary boy out into the open. I'd not be surprised if Evander pays someone to play the part—maybe some needy *sex-worker*!"

Mary stood tall and looked about as if searching for someone; from her height she pointed at the top of Alice's head and called: "Thought police! Over here, please, we have homophobic hate-speech of the first order!"

"Police!" called Alice, hands covering her head as if for protection. "Help! Safe-space emergency! Mary McGahern is being too tall, I'm feeling awfully uncomfortable."

And they were laughing again. This time Mary was first to find self-control. "Come along then, Ms. Missy." She all-bossily took Alice's upper arm and moved her back the way they'd both just come. "As I was about to say before being so *un*critically interrupted: my Granny McGahern had an expression for what we're doing, wandering lonely as two little clouds; well, one little and one magnificently statuesque." Alice gave a shaking-head snort. "She called it *arsing about*."

Alice frowned reflection, then—"Arsing about! I love it! But stop, please, you really are going to hurt me."

They were back at the concrete climb to Macdonald Library. "Can you come up with an equivalent expression in Vietnamese?"

"Hmm. ... *Lang thang về*. Maybe, likely too literal. It's hard to translate idiom, especially when it has a present participle like *arsing*!"

"C'mon, I'm dying for some *thang* to eat."

"I'll let that pass. Are you sure you're a poet?"

Silly, two silly girls again, soon sitting at a table near the modified Tim's counter, with BLTs and barbecue chips and sharing an oversized ice tea; saying silly things and laughing so much together they were often spraying chips and sputtering bits of bacon, and not caring how they looked, if actually pleasantly aware of how carefree they were for the first time in a long time and wishing only there were more people about to witness their fun and blooming friendship. But what an extraordinary coincidence they discovered—*synchronicity*, Alice said, which was Jung's term for *happenstance*; Jung who influenced the loony part of Yeats's great brain—but *what* a synchronicity then: they both had rooms in Brant Rez!

Mary couldn't stop smiling and feeling like the skin was too scant for her face, and as if that face was facing a small space heater on high. Alice was an angel. Look at that hair, like an ebony slide, it made her own feel mousy. No, wait, not an angel: Alice was the spirit of Big Al come to save her. Though she would think and reflect so only later alone tossing and turning on her rez cell's narrow bed. In the moment she knew herself to be … yes, to be falling in love. But not in that way. Naomi was her BFF. Alice would be her—yes, Anne—*her bosom friend*, a kindred spirit. She just knew it!

And love and Jimmy …? On that racking rez bed she was finally fortified to face the question, strengthened more by Alice's promising friendship than by Professor Flynn's advice. She would never get the visit to his Western residence out of her head, her failed rescue mission to hell. What he said. And the picture, literally the horrifying video of him hanging upside-down over a silver keg. Bosch hell. Could she ever see him the same as before? No. Why do people drink? *Poison themselves with alcohol?* Name one good thing that has ever come of drinking like that?

Together returned to the residence foyer, only Mary had mail, the first real mail she'd received there. The dimensions and pale mauve colour of the envelope meant a card inside—holy fuck! It was her birthday last week! "It's my—" Shut up.

"Hmm," said Alice with rising brow. And with ironic China-doll intonation: "Secret lover boy?"

"No chance," said Mary plainly, glancing at the return address. "Home, my dad, likely just wishing me well." She lowered the envelope to her side, signalling it was not going to be opened in Alice's presence.

They parted ways after arranging breakfast together at the only open campus cafeteria. "I mean, if you have nothing better on offer, I won't be offended if you don't—"

"For fuck's sake, Mary, I'll be there." Walking away Alice turned back and called, "Have you finished *Dubliners*?"

"Almost, but gotta re-read 'The Dead'; loved 'Araby,' reminded me of a Canadian story I love called 'One's a Heifer'; tomorrow I'll tell you what 'Araby' is about and you can tell me what *Dubliners* is *all* about!" But smiling and turning away Mary had made herself think again of Professor Flynn, and worried if their seminar would ever meet again.

In her room, at her desk, she carefully tore the envelope. It was a Gary Larsen cartoon-card of cows. Dad was a big Larsen fan, especially of his cow cartoons: the wall of his workbench in the barn was covered with them, not pinned but nailed there. This one was titled "Cow Poetry," and it showed a Holstein standing erect on hind legs in front of a cow audience sitting in chairs (one of whom held a cup of coffee poised), and reading a silly romantic poem titled "Distant Hills," which ended cursing the electric fence. The literate cow wore pince-nez like Yeats's.

Mary smiled and smiled, a good start. Starting inside the

cover and filling the card's white space, the message in Dad's neat black hand:

Hail Mary! That's what I said loudly (not too) on entering your mother's maternity room a half-hour after you were born (I'd been tending the stock). I've often suspected—I should have addressed it long ago—that like your hero Anne Shirley you sometimes thought that I wished I'd had a son. I never had a preference, but when I entered that room and saw you on your mother's breast, I knew you were all I'd ever wanted, daughter. My two girls forever!

Belated Happy birthday, sweetheart! You are now legal! Finally I have an adult child (joke). But I want to be serious here. For the only time in a long long time I wish I had a telephone again. Even a computer. But for me this is better. I am SO sorry for the way I was at your last visit. Because I ended up missing you entirely and I'm sure ruined your whole week off. Here's my birthday present: I promise never again to drink more than one Big Rock beer a day. Will you come home for a weekend visit soon, please. I might throw in the b-day gifts of a laptop computer and a phone plan.

Love,
Dad

PS. As for cow poetry, a little birdie named Naomi showed me your prize-winning poem. I laughed till it hurt. Brilliant!

PPS. When I finally got off my sodden ass and sobered up (permanently), I was up for some Fall ploughing for the first time. This was rendered tolerable by my deeply depressed hired help.

She'd been tearing-up since the hospital-birth scene, but snapped out of it: *What?* What's he talking about? He never did Fall ploughing or tilling or cultivating or anything? When the final cut was in and all the corn and soy sold or stored, and what cattle and pigs were ready for the slaughterhouse shipped, he was all done for the year. Time to read all day and drink all evening, at most to tinker with machinery. Just about every farmer did fall ploughing, but never him. Hadn't they ... Hadn't Dad talked this over with ... oh, fuck! Hadn't she heard him and *Jimmy* talk about fall ploughing last August? *What* "deeply depressed hired help"? What was going on?

She turned to the computer.

From: Mary McGahern <mmcgahern022@ubytown.ca>
　　　Mon. 14 Nov. at 18:30
To: Naomi Starling
Cc:

Hi, Naomi. Oh my Bff, I am heartily sorry for having offended thee, say but the word and my conscience shall be healed. (Are you too fallen now to recognize my blasphemous conflation of the Act of Contrition and the pre-Communion prayer? I'm impressed with myself for remembering them!) But I'm avoiding here, girlfriend. All seriously, Naomi: I am *so* sorry I didn't return to your lovely place in London or at least stop by Fanshawe on my way to the train station (and by the way, I think the Fanshawe campus impressive). Of course to see you but at the very least to thank you. I don't blame you for not emailing me. All I can say by way of excuse is that it was a very bad scene with Jimmy at the Western U residence. Maybe someday we'll talk about it. But please email back and tell me I'm forgiven.

Thanks for telling my dad about "Adèle." If you write back and forgive me, if you play your cards right, doll, there'll be another poem like that coming your way (in gangsta voice; is there a gangsta emoji?).

I'm thinking of going home for a visit next weekend or the one after. Any chance you'll be visiting the megápolis? Maybe we could get together? I hope so. Tim's French Vanilla on me! How are you and Mike getting on? Like a house on fire? A whorehouse, I bet (joke—I refuse to use emojis!).

Your BFF,
Mary

From: Naomi Starling <mar171@fanshawe.ca>
      Mon. 14 Nov. at 19:45
To: Mary McGahern
Cc:

Oh all right, I suppose, you're forgiven, especially if you
promise me more poems like Devil Adèle. I did miss seeing
you again over break week and you meeting Mike. Mike was
here for two days Saturday and Sunday and Dad made sure
he slept in the guest room, at least he didn't put a padlock on
it. But we're good in London, VERY good and a whorehouse is
about right, dear. Guess who seems to be permanently back in
Leitrim Falls?

Your Bff
Naomi

From: Mary McGahern <mmcgahern022@ubytown.ca>
      Mon. 14 Nov. at 19:48
To: Naomi Starling
Cc:

Please spell it out for me, Naomi. I can't pretend here to a
cool sophistication I don't possess, not on this subject (or any
other, she thinks). As I think you know.
Thank you.
Mary

From: Naomi Starling <mar171@fanshawe.ca>
     Mon. 14 Nov. at 20:00
To: Mary McGahern
Cc:

Somebody's sure grown a hair-trigger finger for email! Just kidding, girl. Jim Collins didn't go back to university after break week, though he never came home for that week either. But looks now like he's back in Leitrim Falls and stuck at home with his drunken old man and tit-useless mom. Cruel of me I know. I AM going home this weekend—for Faucher and Adèle's wedding!Didn't you get your invitation? An oversight I'm sure. NOT. But because Mike can't make it, some clinical assignment counselling Sarnia's young retards, Mike's trapped with them in a high school gym for the whole fucking weekend—in *Sarnia?*. I actually talked Jim into 'escorting' me! I ran into him at Tim's the other day late, he looked a mess, I think he'd actually come from helping your dad with some farm work, he was sitting alone over a coffee, very sad too, so I tried to cheer him up for your sake. He was getting pissed off at me for pushing about the wedding but I finally won him over by saying your name a lot. Anyway, if you don't make it, I'll let you know how the wedding goes. I hope you do, for my sake ... and maybe for Jim's? And yours?

Your bff
Naomi

THIRTY

HAIL MARY 1

Mary McGahern had only ever gone to one football game. It was in the fall of grade twelve, her first year back in the regular school system. Not only was she needing to fit in but she couldn't resist Naomi, her new and only girlfriend, or friend period (maybe Jimmy Collins). It was the championship game, first appearance in a long time for their Sacred Heart Army, and first time ever played in Leitrim Falls. Those aspects of the event meant nothing to Mary, always with farm work to do, but the new friendship with Naomi meant a lot.

Mary had enjoyed herself, though she could hardly follow the game at all. She gauged the results of the play by the home-crowd responses around her, the wild cheering, the groaning and smacking of foreheads, the licensed cursing, noises which were fairly balanced between the supporting sides until the end.

She most enjoyed the gay sense of a fair day and the gift of late-October sun-warmth, the rare odour of cigarette and, especially, cigar smoke, which reminded her of Granda McGahern. For once there was no skunk-weed smell.

She even appreciated the cheerleaders, girly-girl silly as they always were, the boy-fools too: the inappropriately provocative dance moves, the boys' pants almost as tight as the sexy football pants, the girls on top of shaky pyramids, girls being tossed and caught, plaid mini-skirts flying. She *didn't* like that Adèle Pélletier had a lot of say about the formations and dances, but Naomi explained that Adèle was "captain" of the cheerleaders. It looked to Mary that Adèle struck the provocative poses for longer than the others, that her pants were flimsier than the others', that they frequently got stuck in her ass-crack and that she seemed to have no self-consciousness about plucking them out. She didn't yet know Naomi well enough to indicate these things. So she just assumed that those talents were part of what enabled one to captain the cheerleaders. Besides which, Naomi had eyes only for Rick Maclean, number sixty-six, a "wide receiver" she called him, and he did seem mostly apart from the main action, off by himself and just running up the field, turning around and trotting back to the "huddle." A few times he obviously did something well, caught the thrown ball, because Naomi would grab Mary's shoulder and jump up and down and scream in her ear.

Naomi didn't have to be asked about bossy Fred Faucher, who was both quarterback and team captain (Mary did have a vague understanding of what a quarterback was, though the word always made her think of a butchered hog). Fearless Fred (as his jock friends called him when he wasn't present) was everywhere, shouting into the air above the crouching line of teammates, where he would stand before every confused scrambling with his hands positioned like the middle boy (chubby Wayne Rocca, the centre, Naomi had explained) was about to deliver a turd to him, and screaming at his teammates and pointing to where they should go and even smacking their helmets when the play obviously hadn't gone his way. Perfect Faucher.

Unasked, Naomi had pointed out Jim Collins and said his number, and remarked his much less important role compared to her Rick's. She said, "But our brave Army need, like, every available male body, though I expect Pélletier could play better than some of the boys, what with that bum she could bump those Spartans to the clouds!"

Regardless, Jimmy looked pretty good in his tight white pants. Still, Naomi had a point in downplaying his role, for all he appeared to do was take his place in the crouching line only when the *other* team had the ball. And his play, like that of all those in the two facing lines, consisted of nothing more than running back and forth from a "huddle," crouching and, at a shout, running into the opposing croucher. Reset and repeat. Mary had to fight to maintain interest; it helped to pick out Jimmy in the melee of each clash and try to figure out if what he had done had helped or hurt the Army team. Impossible. Next day at his locker she would ask him if *he* knew what he was doing? She believed she could do that now with Jimmy. She turned a smiling face to the warm sun.

Regardless of her general disinterest, she felt the crowd's excitement as the big newly installed digital clock at the end of the field flipped down to forty-five seconds remaining, with the score tied at seven (as it had been for over an hour), Sacred Heart's ball at mid-field. Naomi, becoming more and more of a friend through the long afternoon (victory!), was frequently checking Mary's face and providing play-by-play commentary that Mary pretended to care about and understand.

"A first down's no good, no time left, so Faucher has three plays to score, *any score* and we win—touchdown, field goal, even a single point! Murphy has a good leg, we don't need to get that much closer! *All* we need is a little better field position for a punt through the end-zone and the single point. We can't lose, Mary! We can't lose!"

Mary ordered herself to do it, so shouted, "Let's go Army!" And Naomi gave her a quick half-hug.

Jimmy wasn't in the game, as she knew he wouldn't be when their team had the ball, though at least he now stood permanently along the sideline with his teammates, if not as jumpy as they. The bum of his pants was dark with dirt, and expressionless he watched the field as might her father a moving line of black sky on a once-promising morning.

A play played out in the usual butting confusion and Naomi, watching intently, said to Mary out the side of her mouth, "Good, but we still gotta get closer to be sure the punt's not run back *out* of the end-zone. I just couldn't *stand* overtime, could you?"

"Couldn't stand it, Naomi." Good, the distracted Naomi missed the careless irony. "Go Army!"

Another play brought the hometown crowd permanently to happy feet, and Naomi to screaming hoarsely in Mary's ear: "Beauty! Faucher picked up a good fifteen yards calling his own number! The single point's a sure thing now, Mary! Twenty-five yards? Murphy can boot it over the score board from there! We're gonna win! We're gonna win! ... What ... the ... fuck? Why's Murphy turning back? *What* is Coach Howley *doing*? Wait, no, Howley's sending Murphy back. And the stupid ref throws a flag on us! Oh, fucking great, delay of game, tack ten yards onto the punt. Way to go, Faucher! Whatevs, it'll still be an ... easy ... point. *What the* ...? Faucher's waving Murphy off the field again?"

An eerie silence descended, clichéic and true, until broken by a lone father's voice roaring, "What the hell, Howley? Send out your punter! Murphy!" He was joined by a chorus calling "*Mur-phy, Mur-phy, Mur-phy* ..."

Although she had never watched a minute of football, not even on the TV they'd had for a while, quarterbacking Faucher's repetitive play had become easier for Mary to follow: he would pull the ball from under Wayne Rocca's fat ass, run back sideways in the wrong direction (towards his own goal?), stop suddenly as if realizing his mistake with the football held carelessly in one hand beside his head, and often get buried in the red pile-on of Perth Spartans. Or Faucher would give the ball to someone else, who'd get clobbered trying unwisely to run through the collapsed lines of mixed crouchers. Or Faucher would manage to throw the unprotected ball away just before the clobberers reached him, and sometimes *still* get clobbered, which would have him jump up and shout at the referee. Seen so by Mary (Faucher often clobbered), the game had become almost enjoyable to watch. Of course, no one ever gave the football to Jimmy, and though he repeatedly collided with a Spartan player holding the ball, he was able to wrest the ball away only a couple of times; his teammates patted his bum a lot those times, and many times besides, which made Mary wonder.

So she could almost understand what was playing out at the very end of the championship game, if still needing the help of Naomi's woeful explanation being shouted above the crowd's now-hysterical screaming "*Punt—punt—punt* ..." As usual, Faucher took the ball from Wayne Rocca's bum and again scooted back sideways like someone dragging a bad leg, stopped dead and again held the football vulnerably aloft, but this time threw it the full distance to the end of the playing field, into the "end-zone," yes; there, a couple of players from each team, green Sacred Heart sweaters and Spartan red, were waiting near the goal posts, towards which the ball was wobbling in loopy descent ... but instead of hitting one of the players or landing on the ground, it bounced of the horizontal bar and shot straight up into the air, quite high against the lowering sun, so that everybody else would have been squinting too; the four players who'd been waiting were instantly scrambling for position when a fifth in the ruby-red of Perth's St. Michael Spartans came flying in from nowhere, sailing above the jostling group and snatching the ball just before it dropped within their reach, landing on his feet and striding off powerfully to the right sideline where he swerved to dash in a sprinter's straight line past both shocked teams' benches. Only Faucher himself, wearing number one, the last Army player between the Spartan player and a touchdown, could try to tackle, which he missed badly, his head bouncing off the other player's pumping knees; he recovered to look up as the opponent danced into and about the Sacred Heart end-zone. Faucher dropped his face and lay on his belly pounding the sod with his fists.

Walking back to town, Naomi lamented angrily: "Give Faucher some credit, he got those yards that positioned us for the punt for a single. But that must've been what made him think he could do anything, stupid fucking Faucher! A Hail-Mary pass for God's sake! Can you believe it? A fucking Hail-Mary for a touchdown when all we needed was the sure-thing single point!"

Mary let her simmer for a spell, then asked, "It's really called a Hail-Mary?"

"Yes," said Naomi, irritated as speakers are when their main point seems missed, but willing still to explain. "A quarterback—*a coach actually*—does it when it's his *only* last shot to win, floods the end-zone with receivers, throws the ball up and hopes—*prays* that is—that one of his players comes down with it. It's an act of pure desperation, a Hail Mary, *not* the play when *all you need is one fucking point!*"

So Monday morning Mary understood the terminology when Faucher was feverishly excusing himself for the loss: "We'd had *two* punts blocked, no fucking way Murphy is reliable from thirty-five yards out, c'mon he'd already had a fucking field goal blocked from the forty! The ref *robbed* us with that delay-of-game! And don't forget the punt blocked from the—"

Walking past Mary said normally, *without* having planned it: "BLOCK block-block-block." And into the silence declaimed: "Hail Mary, full of grace, but the Lord was not with thee, Fred." Surprised Faucher stared. Some of the posse spluttered, and Adèle said, "Cunt."

Mary heard the slamming clang of locker metal; Jimmy had melodramatically crucified himself face-first against his locker, was slapping its neighbours and then lightly banging his forehead against his own door. Standing beside him as he regained control, she decided not to bother asking if he knew what he was doing in the game. Instead she pictured him in his football pants. Nice.

For a long time afterwards, pretty well till Christmas break, unlocatable "Hail-Marys" greeted Faucher's entry into packed gym or cafeteria.

THIRTY-ONE

HAIL MARY 2

Okay then, here goes, on a wing and a prayer.

From: Mary McGahern <mmcgahern171@ubytown.ca>
     Mon. 15 Nov. at 17:05
To: Jim Collins
Cc:
Subject: Hail Mary

Are you there to receive this?
M

By six she knew it was over. But she wouldn't budge, she couldn't.
Waiting at the computer she remembered what Professor Flynn
had advised, though it was her head, not her heart, helped her

remember. They work together, Professor, they have to. So she waited on, because she knew in her heart that whether Jimmy answered or not, and whatever he answered, it would never be over. Not for her. And not forev—

Ping.

From: Jim Collins <jcollins181@uwo.ca>
        Mon. 15 Nov. at 18:12
To: Mary McGahern
Cc:
Subject: Re: Hail Mary

I'm here, Mary. And I mean back home in Leitrim Falls living at my parents' house, as you may have heard, still with access to my Western email, for now anyway. I've been too ashamed to write you, believing you'd never talk to me again, which I thought because you didn't write in all this time, though I know I had no right to think that. I'm not ashamed because I've quit university and am back home not knowing what to do, but because of the way I was when you came to London, obviously. I'm deeply ashamed of the condition you found me in, but more ashamed still of what I said to you that finally made you leave. Unfortunately I remember *that*, or maybe that's the way it should be. And I know Ava showed you the vid of my kegger party. I could die for shame. ... Mary, I'm so sorry. I wasn't thinking of you at all but only of myself—my old man, *my* mother, not yours and you. If you had never contacted me again I'd only have thought better of you, which is saying a lot, which is saying everything. And you'd be better off. And that still stands. If you like, I'll stay away from your farm which, with your dad, are the only things keeping me going.

Jim

From: Mary McGahern <mmcgahern171@ubytown.ca>
　　　Mon. 15 Nov. at 18:14
To: Jim Collins
Cc:
Subject: Re: Hail Mary

What took you so long to answer? What about Ava?
Mary

From: Jim Collins <jcollins181@uwo.ca>
　　　Mon 15 Nov. at 18:30
To: Mary McGahern
Cc:
Subject: Re: Hail Mary

I was working with your father all day, Fall ploughing and stuff, believe it or not. *No after-brew*. And I needed time to choose my words (we're not all literary geniuses). But Ava? I don't know what you mean. Just what did that lost girl say to you anyway, Mary? Ava's a lesbian, if that matters, a very 'popular' lesbian. Sometimes it seems that everyone at Western is gay, except for the sluts (males included). Not that there's anything wrong with that (not funny, I know). But even had Ava been hetero and beautiful and all over me, I'm forever in love with someone else (seriously, McGahern, punky blondes are not my type). I'm still a virgin, Mary. ... Can you ever forgive me? Please come home for a visit. Give me just one more chance to show that I love only you, and forever.

Love,
Jim

From: Mary McGahern <mmcgahern171@ubytown.ca>
    Mon. 15 Nov at 18:32
To: Jim Collins
Cc:
Subject: Re: Hail Mary

Me too, Jimmy.
See you Friday.
Love,
Mary

From: Jim Collins <jcollins181@uwo.ca>
        Mon 15 Nov. at 18:34
To: Mary McGahern
Cc:
Subject: Re: Hail Mary

Full of grace.
Love,
Jimmy

THIRTY-TWO

DOUBLING DOWN

TIDINGS
Newsletter of the
Film&WordsWork Undergraduate
Student Association

As president of the Film&WordsWork Undergraduate Student Association (F&WUSA) we are pleased to present another gratuitously and gloriously nonsensical poem by our Double Trouble poetry champ, Mary McGahern, whom we rightfully claim as our discovery (despite Leader Flynn's appropriative delusion to the contrary), though we strongly suspect that she was, like North America for Columbus, there before we discovered her. At Professor Turnbull's suggestion, we solicited the submission below, and were successful with a sweetened offer she could not refuse (classic movie reference): a $25 Tim Horton's gift card, which came with a Seasonal Special gratis 15 Timbits (for those who measure out their lives in doughnut balls—that's a "Prufrock" reference, a poem; and yes, we're now into the Xmas season). We had briefly considered making the free Timbits part of the payment, but the repast disappeared before Ms. McGahern's verse magically appeared in our inbox. We have been asked if Mary McGahern is just (?!) a student and not rather the "beard" of some frustrated professor-poet (<u>note bene</u>: your editorial board does not endorse sexist tropes; <u>note melior</u>: the suspicious have bandied the name of a certain Professor Bartholomew von Blüger, which *is* patently a professorial pseudonym). We have also been asked if Mary McGahern is a real name or a nom de plume. We can assure our readers that it is indeed a plume and can further reveal here that the poet's real name is "Mary Christmas." Which, inclusivity to the contrary, we wish us each and

every one with this the year's final
issue of your newsletter—and voilà, this
compact gift from our resident laureate:

Loose Lucy

Who's afraid of Alfredo the train?
Not I, not naughty I!
I stay my stay at the station
and watchfully watch for his one blind eye.

I stay my stay at the station,
Loose Lucy sluicing her juices,
Yet stay my stay quite stately—
then brake him caboose to cabooses!

– *Mary McGahern*

THIRTY-THREE

VIRGIN MARY

Mary and Jimmy got together at the McGahern farm late the Friday of her return home for the weekend. They sat at the kitchen table, where they'd only ever met for meals. The table was yellow arborite, ageless to Mary, solid as a barn beam. Their hands were mostly warm in their laps or awkwardly attempting casual display atop the cool table, briefly, then withdrawn and hidden again. Throughout the visit her father came and went, pretending he was paying them no mind, if offering twice to make tea, talking in passing to Jimmy about the little that was left of the fall's work, telling Mary he'd loved *The Untilled Field*, wondering if he could give them a ride anywhere, or Jimmy home, uh, whenever of course. His transparent fussing did help some, as they were being strange with each other, unnaturally polite as old high school acquaintances met on Main Street, which made her—both of them—more self-conscious and worried worse. Things would never be the same between them, and they both knew it.

But awkwardly they did manage over eighty-five minutes to make up a relationship of a kind, and despite their last emails Mary was fearing that renewed friendship—the sickening 'good-friends-still'—might have to be enough. She wouldn't allow apologizing Jimmy to abase himself too much, because intuitively she knew that his doing so would make for a troubled friendship later, and maybe even none at all. Besides, she'd never have countenanced his humiliation anyway, for she knew he had his demons to deal with, and possessed a core of self-sufficient pride that she'd always love about him, however much at a distance. Yet even with her reasonable mind half made up to such a lovelorn future, she worried the situation unreasonably, as did he, she could feel it. They'd not even touched when they met. They'd never kiss again. And if she permitted such reflections to continue, she'd cry outright. So they too talked only of the farm, the work done and to be done, and failed miserably joking about Faucher's and Adèle's wedding the next day.

Out at the road, he threw no stones telling her to go home. Childish, that could never happen again. As he was turning away forever in the much-cooled evening air, with the centre of the bike's handlebar balancing in his left hand, she reached for his upper right arm and held him back; drew him infinitesimally closer as she leaned in, because she was the one who had to forgive. Their eyes met for the first time since he'd arrived, his lost and desperate then brimming, communicating more than anything he or she had said. In reality they endured it only a moment, that stopped time that decided two lifetimes. They kissed and, all awkwardness gone in muscle memory, kept kissing, hardly heard the bike fall away behind him. Then held each other nose-to-nose and belly-to-belly till a warmth arose between them. With a hand flat on his chest she pushed him off.

He said again that he'd already told Naomi he was definitely not going to the stupid wedding because, he reminded Mary, work had to be done next day, what with her father having to be at Canopy all weekend and the weather quickly closing down.

She stooped for a pebble, straightened and pitched it at his chest. "Go home, Collins, *home*. ... Tomorrow then."

Throughout Saturday they merely talked and touched in brushing by, and both were again strangely self-conscious at lunch, then more so at supper, aware as they were that the house was empty and above them a bed.

When after supper it got unbearable Mary said, "I feel like a walk. Big Rock anyone?"

She returned to the kitchen with the old blanket and tossed a rolled up sleeping bag at him overhand. "Hail Mary!" she called. He tucked it under his arm like a football, bowed a bit and straight-armed the door. "Touchdown!" he called from outside. She shouted after him on the way out, "You were *hopeless*, Collins! You really didn't know *what* you were doing out there, did you?"

Walking away he called to the sky so full of stars they'd both already forgotten Ottawa and London; a country evening, with farm buildings standing out and starry sky so strikingly present they looked unreal, weirdly three-dimensional like a Christmas card with propped figures. "I failed to help Fred Faucher attain Leitrim Falls hero status, so he could propose straight out to that devil Adèle as is done only in girly romances! She had to get pregnant!"

She all but squealed, "A learned reference to *Sunshine Sketches of a Little Town*! You read it! My-my." She then called at his back, playing the scold: "You think you're so clever, Jimmy Collins. I know it was Dad made you read it. Who do you think you are?" She caught up and bumped his shoulder.

"I am"—he cocked his head and crowed at the sparkling sky—"Alice Munrooooooo!"

Shared language, shared laughter, their way: they were good again, almost wholly so.

For a mid-November early evening there abided some gracious warmth. Big Pond was a second evening sky, a dark mirror pricked further with new stars every minute, like an eternal creation. But coolness came suddenly into the air, as it will at that season and time of day, making Big Rock feel warmer than it was. Mary spread the blanket and they sat, flapping themselves for warmth.

She laughed in a way she'd never before with Jimmy. And then talked similarly: "Are we nuts or what? What're we doing out here this late? And a sleeping bag? What was I *thinking*?"

For answer he pulled the string binding the rolled-up bag, brushed with the back of his hand and it ran out diminishing as it went. Breathing as *he'd* not before, he unzipped it and inserted his hand into the warm lining, flipped back the top. They looked at each other and ceased the strange behaviours.

They lay close together on half the padded plaid bag and she covered them with the other half as best she could. They kissed and hugged and paused to hold each other tightly. Jimmy smelled of open air and fields, of clean sweat and a day's work done. Mary smelled lightly of her favourite perfume, the Lily of the Valley she still had from her mother and hadn't used since. They managed awkwardly to get out of all their clothes for the first time: they'd sat up and she'd caught him lightly with an elbow to the eye socket, he'd said "ouch," she'd not apologized;

turning away to slip from a sleeve he'd knocked her over sideways and hadn't helped right her.

Hurrying some but without further awkwardness they were soon complete lovers. She was thinking throughout, of course: *That hurt, it fits! … It's stopped hurting, yay!* She relaxed, only then noticing his slightly turned face detached and intent as she remembered it from that day in the truck.

It's done?

He thought: *Look at us!* And from above just beamed into the face he loved.

He dialled it down, relieved some of his weight on her, and grinned: "Did you feel Big Rock move?"

She frowned a grin and flexed her body in a laugh, which tickled his. "Maybe, I'm not sure. We'll have to do this again some time."

In response the length of his body rippled laughter on her. When their breathing normalized, she said, "Does it bother you that I'm taller?"

His head jerked. He first tried fakery: "You *are*? … Okay: no. I mean yes, but not worth thinking about. Does it bother you?"

She put a hand flat on his chest above her as if holding him off: "Look how powerful you are through here? You could have snatched the ball from Faucher and scored a touchdown!"

"You're too much, Mary. Luck like this can't last for me." He moved off her.

Then lying sideways in each other's arms Mary drifted to quiet thoughts of her father returning from work hungry. She welcomed it when Jimmy moved to do it again right away, touching her side where it met her hip, making her shiver (he knew her spots), continuing gently to her ass and pulling her against him in a way he never had.

Aoife commenced bawling.

"Shit, I've gotta go back, sorry." She sat but didn't immediately get up.

"I'm not going back."

She knew what he meant. "If you're not then I'm not."

"Yes, you are, Mary."

In her mind she demurred, then accepted for now. Rolling up their plaid-and-shiny bed she noticed the stain—she shouldn't have lain so long as to drain. Or what the hell, she'd tie it up and stow it somewhere for keeps—and together they started back.

"What will you do then, lover—what a word!"

"I don't know, honestly, *lover*. But I do know that I'll never do again what I did to you, Mary, ever, I'd die first."

"Stop beating yourself up over it, Jimmy, it's over. I love you."

They stopped and kissed. Aoife bawled.

"I love you too, Mary." They kissed some more in the bellowing, till he drew back his head. "By the way, your dad says Aoife's pregnant for sure, but her days are numbered, and for stopping us like she just did I say good riddance."

"*What*! Aoife? No way!"

She walked off, picking up the pace. "I *knew* she was pregnant."

He made a mental note: Shit. Careful there. Make it up. He hurried after and grinning called, "I liked your Loose Lucy poem! Thanks for sending it."

"Thank you."

"What's it about?"

"I have no idea."

"Seriously?"

"Seriously."

"Kinda sexy though, doancha think?"

Advancing determinedly into dim space, she made a face: "Sexy?"

"Well, uh, yeah, sorta. Don't get all mad at me, but is Alfredo the train supposed to be Fred Faucher?"

"*What?*" And sputtered a laugh at the sky now brightened by moonlight. "I was thinking more Thomas the Tank Engine!"

He relaxed. She wasn't touchy about her poetry, had never been about Faucher, that was his delusion, but be careful about Aoife.

She had all the confirming evidence she needed: boys *were* different. And she was different now, as was Jimmy, they were. Better different. No one grows alone. She and Jimmy Collins were lovers, now and forever. Amen.

THIRTY-FOUR

PERSON OF INTEREST 3

Propped for viewing at his corner window, Jake Flynn had his left hand on the jagged top of the broken Buddha. He wasn't conscious of pressing down. uBytown's lone field was as empty as Jake's memory of the night before, starting from his parting with the girl student, but hazy from earlier too. Overnight wind and rain had rendered the trees bare as entangled black sketching against a thick grey sky. Crazy Ray's corner radiated a stark morning-after atmosphere: the site of a picnic, an outdoor concert, cleaned up, with the park bench somehow looking reinstalled. Something lively had happened there but this morning-after, life had lost all power to excite, and the campus' one bucolic scene its usual power to comfort Jake.

He smiled dimly as from nowhere came Crazy Ray's pun on the word "field." What were all those other mad things the madman had said? … Jake forced himself to concentrate, but knew only where he was and wasn't. He'd been here before, a number of times, he tried to reassure himself, only never so deeply in blankness and dissociation, with no glimmer in sight of ever connecting again. Or maybe (because it could help to remember the worst) the night of the first time his big father, with hairy forearm and sledge-thick fist, punched his little mother in the face, knocking her sideways from the chair where she'd sat at table's end, elbow-propped, waiting to satisfy any urging or for the opportunity to support any complaint. Jake, an only child, ten years old, had hid in the basement all that night. No one had missed him. Her response to Dad's end-of-bender rage had been to get drunk with him. In the morning the house felt as hollowed out as Crazy Ray's corner looked, if a mess of bottles and butts and one smeared plate with congealed white grease and bone of T-bone like some prehistoric weapon.

He scarcely heard the scuffle of arrival outside his open office door but hadn't the interest to turn and look. Or he was without the strength to take interest, as his chest, his whole front, had been feeling like an inflated thing losing air. He did turn up his left hand but didn't feel where the stone had punctured his palm. As he stared a bit bemusedly, the blood seemed to coagulate in cinematic fast motion. That helped. Whatever help there may be anywhere. He might now even see who was at his door. Instead he spoke lowly to his palm: "Go away." He should have added *please*, but was able only to think he might laugh or cry or something, anything, please. Then knew he wouldn't say or do anything, and didn't care. Only shut the door. But why move, really?

In the alcove outside the Leader's open door, Detective Gurmeet had shown up with two uniformed policemen, which excited the

Pod foyer's lone occupant, Peggy Dubois, no end. In his open-doored office just along the hallway Professor John Turnbull had sensed something was up, and he startled Peggy arriving to the right of the receptionist's window:

"Whazzup, *Ms.* Dubois?"

She'd been leaning out over the counter and looking to the right in an attempt to answer that question for herself. Flushing, she pulled back and straightened up.

"I don't know, Professor, but ..." She didn't finish because she couldn't, having choked up with wet lower lip and trembling chin. Anyway, Turnbull had already walked off in the direction she'd been looking, if displaying none of her worry for Leader Flynn. In fact, Turnbull was near skipping. The little shit, thought recovered Peggy, and instantly chastised herself. Regardless, she would at least concern herself less, much less, about that woman and man from the Human Rights Office who the day before had made an appointment and come to ask some very peculiar questions about Professor John Turnbull.

"Have you ever witnessed Professor Turnbull touch a student, female or male?" And the overly friendly woman (the good cop, Peggy knew): "Has he ever touched *you* unwelcome, dear? Think now. Anything at all, we'll decide what's relevant."

No. ... But he *was* always making smartass fun of her in front of others, like stressing *Ms.*, a usage she'd never requested. Does that count as harassment? They'd both smiled as does Dean LaRoque at a new student who asks directions to the book store or library, that is as one might smile indulgently at half an idiot-savant.

Detective Gurmeet stopped talking quietly with the policemen when she saw Professor Turnbull scuttling towards her down the narrow hall as might some beaver guarding its den. She knew enough to beat him to the punch: "Professor Turnbull, do you know where I can find Mary McGahern?"

"Ah," his eyebrows shot up on arrival as if themselves skidding to a stop. "The noble savage in the over-civilized court of Film&WordsWork? Did she make an impression on you too, Detective Gurmeet, our very own *l'ingénue*? Or was that all a ruse and she's been up to no good? What's the charge? *Not* our nicked *Ulysses* surely?"

Detective Gurmeet didn't like what she was about to do, but she had to get rid of him and had never appreciated the sawed-off creep anyway. She exhaled and looked aside for a short spell. Returned: "Listen, *Professor*, I'm here on serious police business. But—"

"Indeed, you have two serious boys in blue with you." John Turnbull may have been brought up short, but he asserted an impressive reserve of presence and dignity.

Detective Gurmeet recognized those qualities in him, with some admiration and surprising sympathy, but had to continue. "That young woman, Mary McGahern, is no ingénue in whatever scenario you're fantasizing, Professor. So watch yourself there, because I'm watching you. Now, if you'll excuse us, we have official business here."

The two policemen scarcely shifted in bodily communicating their pleasure. In Detective Gurmeet's distraction they did risk a glance at each other, and their brightened eyes and twitching mouths conveyed what most of their colleagues often said: *Gurmeet was something else.*

She'd unsettled Turnbull. "W-w-watching *me*?"

"And for my money, Dr. English Professor, Mary McGahern knows more about the value of reading than this whole Department of lost boys and girls, with the exception of Professor Flynn."

Turnbull's colour had crept higher still. But he truly was nothing if not self-possessed. "*Pod*, you mean. But what *do* you know, Detective Kiran Gurmeet, about the ways we teach *English* literature today? Your opinion of the so-called value of reading is just more of the old privileged position of the hegemonic white male—"

"Little man, stop for just one moment and actually look at *me*." She smiled wickedly through clenched teeth. "Then fuck right off out of this, *now*, or face a charge of interference."

She turned into Jake's office, and in passing the officers to either side of the door addressed the air she troubled: "*No one*." The door closed.

"Yes, Ma'am," they chorused.

Neither cop would again risk looking at the other, only at Professor Bullshit schlepping off. They both needed to know where the men's room was but wouldn't dare even take turns. Instead they clenched, and the need to pee eventually dissipated with the instant boredom of guarding a tame scene. Good. Because Gurmeet would somehow know what they did. She was something else.

Jake had not acknowledged her entrance or appeared to hear the unusual sound of his always-open door shutting.

"Professor Flynn? … *Jake*?"

Nothing.

"What are you looking at, Jake?"

It was more like the corner itself spoke: "Nothing much, Detective Gurmeet. The campus looks more abandoned than ever, and the ghost of myself reflected in the dim window. Still, better out there than in here, I fear."

"Why's that?"

His head-tipping soft snort seemed to acknowledge only

himself, but he answered again: "Call it collapse. Or whatever you like."

Reasonably said. So: "Would you sit, please, Jake."

"I will if you will, Kiran."

She took the chair in front of the desk and waited. ... Still without looking at her, he took his seat and placed all his fingers flat on the edge of his desk like he was weakly holding on to a float. Finally he raised his indifferent face to her and, exhausted, disappeared like the last survivor of a shipwreck.

She needed to sip air and hold it a moment. It was the absolute absence did it. She'd seen that look returned only once before, in the eyes of the middle-aged man still living at home in the suburb of Troutstream, who with a sawed-off twelve-gauge shotgun mail-ordered through Ogdensburg NY (arriving loaded, incredibly, which had actually been a feature of its sales pitch) had killed both aged parents in their bed; and when he couldn't figure out how to reload, had failed to finish acting out his madness by doing himself in (Detective Gurmeet's report had deduced).

A week had passed before the "quiet loner who kept to himself, but a nice fella" (qtd. *Ottawa Citizen*) had been found sitting on the floor against the foot of his parents' bed, by which time his dehydration was more life-threatening than his catatonia, if neither as impressive as the room's stink. He'd responded once and only once to Gurmeet's exhaustive interrogations, with every question being but a disguised *Why?* His face's first expression since she'd encountered him was a sudden crinkled puzzlement, when he'd said, "What's your secret?" Then disappeared down below where everyone but he, knowing the secret, succeeded in life. She could only suppose.

She hoped that being early with Jake Flynn would make a difference. But how to hook his attention from wherever it was quickly sinking to oblivion? She closed her eyes and called for backup: Dad? Mom? Chief Thu? Meike? Granddad? It was the last who answered this time: *Be confident, Kiri.*

"Do we still have a fishing date, Jake?"

He inhaled sharply, like a dying Cheyne-Stoker startlingly revived, then let it out very slowly. He managed a smile like a child about to cry.

"I dunno, Kiran. You tell me."

In the event that she were to have only the one question, it had to be: "Why'd you do it, Jake?"

"Do what?"

Dear Granddad Gurmeet, he meant it. "Steal the book."

"John Turnbull ... good man ... out of control, klepto ..." was all he got out.

He pressed back in his chair, his head dropped forward, and he seemed to doze, or was simply gone, maybe gone fishing, forever. Or maybe he was narcoleptic, not the kleptomaniac she'd diagnosed him as (with help from the Force shrink and MYCROFT). But she was avoiding: she'd made a mistake; the direct-shock tactic had lost him, cost her whatever had been nibbling there to be landed.

"*Jake!*"

His face returned at the emphatic summons, if again wearing the weak strange smile she'd not seen before on his confidently joking mug; nor were his eyes the compassionate if impish eyes she'd known, as he spoke in a voice she'd not heard from Jake Flynn before (could he be a multiple?):

"They don't deserve it. No mystery there, Detective." A scolding, emphatic hissing whisper on the sibilants.

Clearly he was no longer avuncular Leader Jake Flynn, angling aficionado. At least Detective Gurmeet didn't need to call further on her experience of dangerously troubled men, or for moral backup. "Yes, Jake. You mean the book, the novel *Ulysses*."

To her surprise he came clear (she made a mental note for her future report: timing is everything, earliest possible intervention, shock tactic deployed prudently). She was and wasn't pleased, because a dissociated part of herself—the part thinking of Meike—had been hoping to wrap things up speedily. But here was the old Jake Flynn sitting with her again, pleasantly present and smiling sympathy for whatever might trouble her, prepared to chat at her convenience. Then he looked different yet again, serious-faced, and she knew such rapid transitions were warning bells. As a stern look elongated his firm face, she had to wonder if he knew her at all, or in his mind was she just another demanding colleague or complaining student?

"But don't play the fool with me, Detective. I'm an old hand at that game myself. *Ulysses* is the greatest novel ever written, period. Nothing else, barring Shakespeare's oeuvre, comes close. Dickens? Please, like Victorian reality TV. Never even mind Joyce's innovative techniques, just think the novel's treatment of age-old subjects, those dreaded *themes*: fathers searching for sons, sons for fathers—a non-interest these days, of course, what with the rise of patriarchal phallocentrism and all."

He paused for response, daring her, she gave nothing away. His expression became a frighteningly broad smile like some fool's perverse wisdom, then as quickly was tamped down to intent teacher. "*Think* what that novel does in its seven-hundred-page cosmos of one day! Good God! *And* that man's day ends in Molly's lusty body and lustier mind! The very woman's soul is bared—her *ar*sehole too. And all in a language, a kind of Irish-English, that teasing devils and angels may well speak to one another! But no one cares about *that* anymore? And those who do know the novel—John Fucking Klepto-Turnbull—won't teach it anymore! Because no writing's good for *anything* nowadays unless it can be drafted to start some fucking revolution or other? ... Kiran" (*Ah, he did still know her*), "please excuse my language, all of it. The plain fact is that the world had never seen anything like *Ulysses* for true comedy, and we'll never see its like again, not with the post-literate world being what it is. ... Oh, hell. Do just read it, please, you and ... Meike! The scene of Dignam's funeral if nothing else! Or *read* Bloom reconnoitering Dublin and his ingenuous observations of Catholicism! *Share* Bloom's well-earned vision of his stillborn son, Rudy, grown to adolescence—*see it*! And more and more and ... much much more. Oh, just read it, please, and allow an old professor to die happily knowing he wasn't the last reader. Yes?"

She didn't show that she was shaken. "Yes. I will, Professor." She said warily, "But I'll promise to do so only if you'll answer some questions for me. Deal?"

He fell back again in his chair, exhaling sharply, exhausted, deflated. "While I can, Detective. Shoot."

"First off, nobody's being shot here, Jake, and no one is dying. Right? Jake?"

He closed his eyes and smiled normally. "Fire away anyway."

She glanced down at the pad she'd produced when he first lapsed. "The evening of the day before the book went missing, a Tuesday it was, you went for a drink with Professor Pat Kelly, correct?"

Enlivened some, he held his left fist in his right hand at his tucked chin, opened his eyes but looked only downward. "I did? ... I mean, I did, yes, I remember, all *very* correct."

"Good. You and she mutually decided to end your perfectly innocent ... what? Affair? No. Dalliance maybe. Whatever, I already know that for a fact, Jake. But what happened afterwards? Where did you go when you left the bar? ... Jake?"

He smiled small to himself, likely he would never look at her again.

"*Jake*. We're just talking, okay? This is not an official interrogation. But it *is* important that I know what happened that evening. It'll matter. I can't promise help, but I might be able to help mitigate, *if* you'll cooperate here."

He tightened his mouth, but managed, "I was upset, very much so, I don't mind telling you, Kiran. I came back here. Funny, but suddenly I do remember, like waking from a nightmare into another nightmare. I have these blackouts. I'm like a bad horror movie."

"Pat says you had a few drinks, and that you'd usually have only the one?"

"True, but I wasn't drunk when I came here either. The place was empty. You know how a busy place feels dead at night, how it affects you? Like when you move houses and see the home you've lived in for years empty and awaiting strangers? Was *home* always just this boxy space filled with shit? It reminded me of when I was …"

Grab him. "And here you emptied a whole bottle of whiskey down your throat, or however much there was left?"

He returned smiling sternly: "You're better than very good, Detective Gurmeet. That first day you were here you spotted the empty bottle in my recycle container. I forgot to remove it and got a scolding note from Angus Daly! If mainly because there'd be no more for his weekly shot! Though he says Irish whiskey is runny shite."

"Bushmills."

"Bushmills, a good three-quarters of a bottle! Very good. I recall being so sad having left little Pat Kelly forlorn at the end of our table, walking away like my feet were encased in concrete, but really feeling sorry only for myself, because I knew even as I was doing it that I was drowning my last chance to be loved for myself. That sounds like maudlin TV talk, I know, Kiran. I guess I'm both bad horror and worse TV." He laughed falsely, as he often did with demanding colleagues and complaining students. "When I was a child—"

"Why *did* you end it with Pat Kelly then?"

His irritated face—like he'd been rapped on the knuckles—told her that maybe she should have let him dredge up the childhood memory. And maybe she should have, it might have told her something useful, but she knew she likely didn't have much time with him this alert.

In confirmation he darkened further. "I really don't know why I broke it off. Jieun had … Jieun was …" Then as suddenly (and as worryingly) his brow lifted and his eyes brightened. "Yet I woke up at home the next morning in the sacred marriage bed feeling great, for the first time in a long long time—no hangover whatsoever! And with absolutely no memory to trouble me. No Jieun either, I'm afraid."

"You were under a lot of stress, Jake, I can imagine." For Detective Gurmeet it had become like an endgame with some newly fallen angel: each leading question could be the last. "Jieun, yes. Where would I be able to talk with her?"

"Jieun? Jieun …" He was deflating again. "No, impossible … I'm afraid that's it for fond memories of that night … time … Detective Gur … Kir …"

He'd slumped, as though even that short time existing in the real world with her had completely depleted him, and stared at nothing. Frighteningly his colour turned ashen and his eyes appeared to redden, as if some long-delayed hangover had caught up with him, or he was being repossessed by his demon. She needed to jolt him one more time. She must be cruel, and maybe even to be kind for his sake. Bloodlessly she moved towards her check position.

"*Jake*. Guy your height, you didn't need a stepladder, did you? You had access to the secretariat, got the book-case key from Peggy Dubois' drawer, opened the case and took the book."

The blunt rehearsal as statement of fact revived him some; wearily his head wobbled, but he didn't respond. She continued to believe any attention, even this drowsiness, a hopeful sign, and that a continued sharp focus on the stolen book was the best tactic to make him talk and divulge more.

"You *stole* it, Jake, the *Ulysses*, for yourself, no more bullshit or Bushmills excuses."

That seemed to do the trick. However, when he spoke again he talked like a roadside drunk momentarily sobering for the Law's test, more loudly than necessary, overly articulate:

"And my—our copy was signed in the genius's own hand! Which, granted, *had* done other things." He grinned leeringly, as if at a private salacious joke, which it was, being an allusion whose referent was locked up inside Jake Flynn's soon-to-be locked-up head, she suspected.

"*Do you remember hiding the book among the street person's, Ray's, park bench collection?*"

"Wha ...?" Again it was like some soporific had suddenly kicked in. He managed only, "But it was Turnbull stole ... for John ... saving John ... Crazy ..."

She needed to put emotional distance between them, she required objectivity now. So:

Roger that, buddy. His long face suddenly dropped forward again—such rapid transitions!—where it would remain, a sad clown's slipped mask, as if halted from hitting the floor only by his propping chin. He looked wholly exhausted from the effort of having briefly spoken his truth to legal power, drooping in his chair, finished deflating, flattened from this last performance of the little that remained of his best constructed self in the big bad world. *A big ten-four, Chief.* An actual soft snore escaped, or it may have been a weak groan, again like a dead drunk talking to himself alone at the kitchen table at three in the morning. The knob of his uncharacteristically unshaved chin bobbed then lay still in final agreement with whatever ghosts or furies were insisting on his complicity and compliance—he'd done something evil once, or not done something good—till he jerked with a throttling inhalation, and settled finally. *Over and out, Leader Flynn.*

She raised her voice and enunciated for the guards' witnessing:

"Jacob Flynn, I am arresting you for grand larceny, for the theft of the rare book *Ulysses*. You have the right to retain and instruct counsel without delay. You also have the right to free and immediate legal advice." *Shit, she'd sniffed.* "Do you understand, Professor Flynn? Yes. Do you wish to call a lawyer? No." *Again shit, that "lawyer" had sounded like a yodel.* "Do, you, understand, Jacob Flynn? … Yes, good."

And if you really do, Jake, would you please explain this fucked-up world to me.

She wanted to slap him. She wanted to round the desk and hug and hold him. But didn't move, couldn't. Nor would she risk opening the door till she'd stopped crying and fixed her face.

On the way she thought, *It's true what the pricky boys in blue say about us: we're too emotional for police work.* Passing between the policemen, she said, "Boys, bring Professor Flynn along, no cuffs, gentle handling. And say nothing to me if it's not something funny."

THIRTY-FIVE

THE LAST POD CONSULT

Leader *pro-tem* of Film&WordsWork Pat Kelly sanitized her hands twice on the short walk from her new office to the newish accessible elevator. *Pro-tem for now*, she thought, smiling to herself. She was about to sanitize a third time after exiting the elevator on the fifth floor (she *had* touched buttons, if only with her right elbow), but halted after setting her laptop on the small shelf recently provided for that purpose. She examined the backs of her hands, rocking the right like she was displaying an engagement ring. That hand had been looking the more reptilian, and she was right-handed, so it would also be the hand more on view. The sanitizer fluid needed better moisturizer content, her skin had been desiccated by the alcohol. ... *Poor Jake*, she thought slipping both her small cupped hands at once under the dispenser, which automatically squirted like something spitting. *But he just wouldn't keep up to date despite her—*

Janitor Angus Daly had come round the corner. "Ah, lassie," he greeted her. "Rest easy, the big room's spanking for your grand consult. Your fellow wizards are all gathered!"

She'd always liked that for a man he was not much taller than herself, and older, the permanently ruddy-faced Scotsman who in forty years had still not lost his accent, or more likely he worked the burr for credit among the nasally mongrel Canadians. He would be at least sixty, yet there was something forever young about him, the bugger. When she turned only her head to the right she was nonetheless talking up to his handsome face: "No more *lassie*, Mr. Daly. *Leader, Doctor, Professor* Kelly, if you please. Take your pick." She came fully about and smiled like gritting. "You say the Pod cohort is met in five-o-five then?"

He grinned indulgence: "As I said, Leader Doctor Professor Kelly. Taking attendance is Peggy's job, I believe. What do you hear—"

"Good. We have some extra-special guests today, Mr. Daly. *You* are to meet them downstairs and escort them up, then leave. Go now. And *Leader* will do just fine, Mr. Daly."

He saluted in that British backhand manner: "Will do, lass—Leader! And from the scuttlebutt I've been hearing, you are going to have some surprise visitors too."

"*What?* Who? What've you heard, Angus?"

"Custodian First-Class Daly at your service, if *you* please, ma'am." He tugged a phantom forelock.

There was enough of humanity left in Pat Kelly to laugh at that, though she resisted the impulse, and half-succeeded. She checked the pretty little watch that decorated the dried flesh of her right wrist (an 'anniversary' gift from Jake Flynn; she really *had* felt bad at the time, about what she was doing to Jieun). The flaky-skin problem distracted her, as she noticed that it now showed in tiny hexagonal shapes like some desiccated field. Or like the pictures of Northern Ireland's Giant's Causeway, where Jake had once promised to take her someday ("What about Jieun?" ... "Jieun says she's had enough of travel to last her a lifetime, with me anyway!").

Her sputtered laughter nonetheless encouraged Angus Daly, who dropped his own pretense. "What *do* you hear about Jake, Pat? Am I right assuming he stole the great mick's book? Where'd they lock him up? I'd, uh, like to visit, aye."

She retreated from familiarity: "Leader Flynn is none of your concern, Mr. Daly. And it's *Leader Kelly*. Our guests will be arriving soon. No surprises, Angus. Now off you go like a good boy."

Turning away he said to be heard, "Oh, I'll be surprisin' yeh, cunt."

"What was that, *janitor*?" Silence. She had to hurry, if not without another squirt of sanitizer. But before she could turn into the hallway a voice boomed, resounding as though the empty building itself spoke:

"*Crap*," the word burred, "it's all crap! He's worth any ten of yeh!"

She'd never really liked Angus Daly, and not only because he was always kibitzing with Peggy LaRoque—his daughter-in-law, talk of nepotism!—over matters that were none of their business. And now she was in a position to do something about him. Not only *out* of the Digital Humanities Complex but, given that little sexual-harassment epithet, right out of uBytown! She made a mental note to file that very day with their all-powerful Human Rights Office, that most feared arbiter of campus justice, recently fortified with the sinews of RAPE and DARK. She had already put in a request with Dean LaRoque for a new

Receptionist/Academic Assistant for Film&WordsWork. High time to shake things up around here going forward. Mrs. Peggy Dubois was a drag, *so* old-school, and a Jake Flynn loyalist who was always making cow eyes at him. Or did so once upon a time, because the Leader Kelly Era is upon us!

She smiled impishly at sight of the meeting room door—stopped dead. For the first time in her attendance at monthly Pod consults, Jake Flynn would not be present, neither as sympathetic colleague nor as presiding Leader of inexhaustible patience. She felt hollowed out. She wouldn't cry publicly though. Never again. The last time was after Jake had left her in the bar and the waitress had soothed her, saying "They're all pigs, dear." Confidence, girl—onward!

Self-bolstered, Leader *pro-tem* Kelly surveyed her colleagues gathered round the big ovular mahogany table in the wholly glassed meeting room atop the Digital Humanities Complex. Compactly smug, she felt above the gathering. Yet she noted that her entrance had created no respectful hush. Of course her Pod colleagues were unaware of recent developments, she consoled herself, a solacing which also again reminded her, unfortunately, of absent Jake ... if much less movingly already, she was pleased to observe.

The assembled appeared either lethargic or irritated, per usual, depending on whether they were themselves being overlooked or discussing something with a nuisance colleague. As at any Pod function (at social functions everywhere), just about everyone was searching for more prestigious company, though a Film&WordsWork Pod consult was an unlikely place to find such.

Leader *pro-tem* Kelly turned inward wondering how far she could take them—*lead* them—and, much more importantly, how far they would take her, *as in*: making her *permanent* Leader. After which ... well, there *were* no limits, really, were there, for a woman of her gifts and experience, no glass ceiling she couldn't shatter? She frowned round imperiously at the walls of glass. Dean LaRoque was a sexist pig, *and* an idiot, so provided her a clear path to decanal appointment. And President Montjoy? The man had the academic savvy of a Montreal pimp.

The big room's walls of windows, rather than making the space brighter, allowed the lowering end-of-November sky to give it a twilight atmosphere, until Leader *pro-tem* Kelly arrested the latest entrant, the graduate-student representative to Pod consults: "Please enlighten us, Belinda!"

Belinda startled out of her typical grad-student inwardness, half of it authentic, half posturing. Pat Kelly raised her thinly pencilled eyebrows and nodded at the wall switch. Baffled Belinda finally got it and all the lights turned on—an array of blinding pot lights as would serve to land a fighter jet on the deck of an aircraft carrier at midnight (the designer had called it "ambient lighting"). Having been wrong-footed so in her *faux-funk*, Belinda shuffled out of sight to the far end of the room ... if more determined than ever to intervene at length whenever she pleased. She always did so anyway on serious grad-student business, such as crowded Pod carrels in windowless rooms, access to the printer (a humongous problem since someone had left copies of his/her/their ass scattered throughout the Pod), fee-per-course-taught being less for grad students than part-timers, participation of more faculty for such grad-student events as Trivia Twister, and the like matters of postgraduate study.

Everybody was blinking and shifting and breaking off private colloquies like criminals spotlighted in planning a heist. Dr. Professor Bartholomew von Blüger squinted most strenuously at Professor Kelly, so that his shelved head slid forward a half-inch or so as he shaded his eyes with visoring left hand.

Pat Kelly had recently read in a reliably vetted study of women in leadership roles that the best offence is offence, which naturally is difficult for women. So she leaned in: "Yes, Professor von Blüger? Has too much light broken in?" She snickered but was returned snickering support from only two of the four Jennifers and but one of the two Stephanies (who'd been occupied wondering together what putting their purses on the table would signify. Old-fashioned femininity, ironically signalled of course? Assertion of continuing economic inequity? Or—there was real risk among a scholarly crowd—Elizabethan vagina reference?).

"I suppose so. Where's Jake?"

Attentive then, the others joined in squinting dramatically and goosing their necks like Jake Flynn might be concealed somewhere behind Pat Kelly, loudly mumbling their confusion, with Amari Abara, whose wheelchair was a good two metres from the table, complaining above all, "Do we really *need* all this light? I mean, *really, need?*" And caught his linguistic misstep: "I'm just sayin', knowwhatImean?"

Pat Kelly hesitated … "Are you making a formal motion, Professor Abara?"

Energized he clarified as formally as a prosecutor: "If you are punningly referencing my disability with your word *motion*, Professor Kelly—which *I* will determine—then you will be hearing today from the Human Rights Office, I can guarantee you. How *many* times must I request an elevated table?" He was instantly impassioned: "My ankles are on fire!"

"*Leader pro-tem Kelly.*" Pat smiled butter knives at him. "I will talk with Custodian Daly about our *un*-round table, if ever I can find him when he's wanted, and find him sober."

John Turnbull turned to the Jennifer beside him, whom he still didn't know after some ten years of their being colleagues (though her name was easily remembered), and also spoke loudly: "Jennifer, it's this bloody British parliamentary system of coming to order with its Robert's-bloody-Rules!"

It was Jenn, the seeming meek, who sat beside him, though not so near as not to leave a considerate considerable gap for Professor Abara's wheelchair, should Amari choose to butt up, which with both hands on the chrome-and-rubber wheels he would suddenly, silently, dangerously (to others: knees had been knocked, hands crushed, *others'* ankles raked red) do. Jenn smiled at Turnbull as one does at cub scouts importuning with poppies when one is already displaying a veritable bouquet, which is to say, vaguely while periscoping for rescue by one of her Jennifer colleagues, even a Stephanie would do. Her female colleagues frequently agreed privately that Turnbull was the Pod's number-one pig, and recently, at Peggy's instigation, they'd finally taken action. But no help was forthcoming from a Jennifer or Stephanie, because all were focused again on Pat Kelly, who had cleared her throat at too high a pitch, unfortunately sounding like a puppy wanting petting, or a runt rescue.

Pat avoided looking at the massed cohort, instead selecting the vague space just above their heads (as the "Women in Leadership Roles" piece recommended for neophyte Leaders working on their confidence). "I think we can come to order now, as Ms. Dubois tells me we have quorum." Beside her Peggy Dubois nodded pinch-lipped and kept her head down (somewhat like Pat she had determined not to cry for this heartless crowd, though her heart was breaking for Jake). "Thank you, Ms. Dubois. As *Leader pro-tem* of our Film&WordsWork Pod, which appointment was approved yesterday by Dean LaRoque and the uBytown Board of Governors as an emergency measure—no call to dwell on why!—I call this consult to order."

It would prove a momentous occasion, attributable only in the smallest way, comparatively speaking, to the Human Rights/Sexual Harassment action taken recently by the Jennifers and Stephanies and some others. In keeping with the late-day atmospheric dispute between darkness and light, more accurately as between dimness and a little less of it, this last consult of the Film&WordsWork Pod would play out as something of a Miltonic moment, and portentously for the whole of uBytown.

Everyone was suddenly distracted to the door—as tardy entrants will forever disturb lectures and meetings—by the nearly noiseless appearance of Angus Daly. Disturbing entrances continued as he propped the door on its kickstand and as silently disappeared. His departure made way for Dean Jacques LaRoque, who entered ostentatiously, strode in actually, fairly vibrating with self-importance in his usual too-tight suit (teal-coloured). Then even he immediately lost the Pod's attention, for the first (as events would turn out) showstopper came trailing in the dean's glinting wake. Just about everyone—and none more so than Amari Abara and Pat Kelly—knew every functionary of the Human Rights Office (known by the acronym HR, an appropriation that had shouldered aside those letters' former reference to Human Resources), and it was two very higher-ups who followed Dean LaRoque. The dean took up standing position to the right of Pat Kelly, who was not showing her colleagues' apprehension, while the HR functionaries stood rigidly just to the back of Peggy Dubois, their right hands holding their left wrists at their abdomens as if protecting from an impending kick. The tableau would have been yet more alarming only if they'd been wearing wraparound shades.

Leader *pro-tem* Kelly smiled warmly at the Dean. "Welcome, Dean LaRoque and—"

"Jacques, *please*, Pat," said the Dean. "In the Faculty of Digital Humanities we are all colleagues on an equal footing in one big family." He was fairly jigging in self-importance, until he touched where his phone usually waited in his side pocket, went bug-eyed and frantically patted himself down till he felt it in his interior breast pocket, and sighed dramatically. No one looked as if they found the performance odd.

Pat was looking smugly pleased. "Then, Jacques, would you please introduce our other two guests?" She'd not even glanced at the HR functionaries. Peggy Dubois still had her swimming orbs on them in a walleyed sort of way, worriedly so too. No one told her anything; she knew about Jake thanks only to Detective Gurmeet.

The Dean placed his right hand over his heart (home of the interminably pulsing phone), removed it (the hand) and made a throat-clearing noise into his small fist. "As I expect you all recognize, I am accompanied in this welcome visit by Senior Advisor Tom Alban and Senior Officer Sarah Bleat-Packingham of the Human Rights Office."

Pat Kelly interrupted, determined to continue her introductory remarks before LaRoque got up a full head of steam. She tittered uncharacteristically: "As you can see, obviously, we have *special* guests visiting with our Pod family today. As Leader *pro-tem*, I must regret to say that this visit of HR officials is on unpleasant business which, I say right up front, *I* initiated as Leader *pro-tem*, responsible for the safety and well-being of *all* Pod members." A David winked across at John Turnbull (it was the word "members"). "But before turning to that unpleasant business, I must *invite* Dean LaRoque to please inform us first of the unpleasant situation of our *ex*-Leader, Jake Flynn."

Wrong-footed so, the Dean did his best to put on a face signalling that the mouth would yet deliver some happy news, which the Dean did half-believe, because he wholly believed his news to be good respecting the broader future of the whole Faculty of Digital Humanities going forward (as he always said it redundantly). "Colleagues, friends and special guests," he began again, incapable of appearing anything but smug. "I bring you tidings of great joy and hope for the survival of the Film&WordsWork Pod. But first—"

"*Survival?*" piped Peggy Dubois, who was instantly shushed if not comforted by the light touch on her forearm from Pat Kelly. But all the assembled were making similar noises and faces, with at least two of the Davids (Dave and Davey) wagging seriously frowning heads and strenuously blinking eyes; the third David (David) yawned hippo-widely. At the far end of the table the two Stephanies, working to smile professionally, were only managing to look caught in cross-purpose comedy as they alternately set and reset their purses like undecided chess pieces.

"But *first*," said the Dean, "if I may have your rapt attentions—yes? thank you—I would indeed like to report first on your dear ex-Leader Jake Flynn's condition, or tragic situation rather."

Professor von Blüger, dressed in black shirt and charcoal jacket, with head hitched way back now on its phantom shelf, cringed like he would dispute, or at least beg to qualify, such a vulgar use of *tragic*. But given the weirdness of the moment even he thought better of it.

The Dean proceeded: "As I suspect you all know anyway by now, Professor ex-Leader Jake Flynn was arrested two days ago for the crime of grand larceny, for the theft, that is, of the Pod's rare edition of the *Ulysses* text, in hard copy, the so-called book. Professor Flynn was arraigned yesterday morning and immediately remanded to the Princess Diana Centre for Mental Wellness' *secure* Forensic Treatment Unit for a court-ordered assessment. There, he is currently undergoing observation, with diagnosis forthcoming, we must presume hopefully. That is all uBytown's legal office permits me to divulge for now. Though I will add this on a personal note: through his assigned union lawyer, our dear colleague Jake has requested that no one visit him. *I* and our President Montjoy plan to ignore that order and personally deliver to Jake our—*all* our—best wishes for his full recovery."

The room, momentarily stunned, exhaled what was mostly relief on hearing the penultimate announcement. One of the Davids again winked across the table at another, if looking now only like one suffering from a facial tic (few men can pull off a wink, and Davey was not one of them).

But it was repressed alarm that arrested the room when two substantial men and one stout woman in uBytown's brown Security uniforms walked in and took up position with the two HR functionaries back of Peggy Dubois. The room inhaled and seemed to hold its breath. The taller of the two men handed the woman a document, which she walked over to Dean LaRoque, who could hardly hide his pleasure in receiving it; which is to say, he was again veritably vibrating in self-glorification.

"*Second*: referencing the presence of our worthy HR officers" (he clapped hands lightly alongside his face like a shy flamenco dancer), "I *very* much must regret to say that a few of your Pod colleagues have been charged with various counts of sexual harassment under the auspices of our new RAPE statutes, a policy expeditiously approved by the Board of Governors, which your union also approved just this morning at a special meeting."

As he continued speaking, he seemed to be seeing for the first time the document from which he also began to read: "…

the offenders named below have been suspended with pay and must vacate their Pod offices and the uBytown campus immediately. Yes … hmm … *yes*. In keeping with the right of the accused to face her accusers, we can divulge that the charges have been brought by Professors Jennifer Windsor, Jennifer Orillia, Jennifer Sainte-Urbain, Jennifer Sainte-Justine, Stephanie Weyburn, Stephanie Esterhazy, and Leader *pro-tem* Patricia Kelly, *against* Professors John Turnbull, Bartholomew von Blüger, Amari Abara, ex-Leader Jake Flynn—now that's a shame—and … *me*? *Wha* …?"

He was blinking at the sheet he held tightly, focused now rather than scanning, and when he spoke again it was no longer in vibrating vanity but shock: "*By Martine Marois!* Why, this is an outrage! My administrative assistant would never …"

In the ensuing mood of whispered fragments, the smuggest HR functionary turned to the Security detail and nodded once. The tallest campus cop turned to the squirming room: "Will the named professors *and* Dean LaRoque please remain in their places, and *qui-et!*" He'd had to shout.

Because John Turnbull was still shouting, "What'd I do? What the *fuck* did *I* do? …"

Of course Dean LaRoque, recovering, assumed that the question was for him. "You, John? What about *me*?" He recommenced scanning the three sheets held in his left hand as with the right he held the outline of his phone like his very heart, then let go and was again shuffling the pages rapidly like a card shark distracting his mark. He spoke aloud his findings: "… Turnbull's many instances of unwelcome touching on the persons of, inappropriate salacious jokes to and within hearing of, various female faculty, to wit: Professor Stephanie Weyburn regularly referred to as *Stiff-Heinie*, and Professor Stephanie Esterhazy as *Stout-Fanny*. … Professor Flynn exhibiting gender bias in the tardy forwarding of female faculty applications for tenure and promotion ... Flynn verbally *assaulting* Professor Kelly in semi-private by wondering aloud in a supposed joke if the acronym 2SLGBTQI+ would be made more mystifying in Cyrillic ... But *verbal harassment? Me?*"

And so on and so forth, back and forth, and of course always back to himself, alternating the repeated charge against himself with one referencing another: Professor von Blüger's intimidating manner of dress and overpowering male cologne, Dean LaRoque's offensively tight pants (he blushed and decreased his standing manspread), Professor Abara's rubbing the back of his wheelchair against undisclosed derrieres (Abara shouting: "Am I supposed to see what's *behind* me?"), Dean LaRoque's closing his door on meetings with female students only; Professor Turnbull's standing too close and once scratching himself near the crotch area; LaRoque's standing even closer and repeatedly touching himself (whether welcome or not unstipulated). Three of the four Davids were also named, if for sins of omission, for failing to support female colleagues enthusiastically, for skipping Friday meetings of the various Pod equity and harassment committees, and such derelictions. All wrapped up with Dean LaRoque's *cri de coeur*: "But sweet suffering Jesus, Martine! *Me?* How was I to give you instruction, the way you've barricaded yourself in that corner, *without* approaching your chair! *And* I suffer psoriasis!"

The drift towards round-up was in progress, with colleagues standing and gesturing about in befuddlement, and with the dean just commencing further self-justification when—

A newly arriving Security contingent took a few steps into the crowded narrow space at the front of the room, which startled all to apoplexy. The rear of Professor Abara's wheelchair shot into Stephanie Esterhazy's ass sending her into the chest of John Turnbull, who for all his outrage yet managed to smile welcomingly. Nothing was said till all were settled. Leader *pro-tem* Pat Kelly was still looking a little too smug. Peggy Dubois was weeping openly, unselfconsciously. And it could be observed that the lone unnamed David was looking relieved when not checking his sextant-sized watch.

The tallest of the newly arrived HR functionaries back of Peggy Dubois leaned back, cleared his throat, and addressed the room: "If I may," he began, his voice adenoidal and loud, "introduce a lighter note, somewhat." He became windily nasal as, alone, he appreciated some unspoken joke he'd forgotten to speak. "But in all seriousness, you do need to be made aware that our Indigenous Studies and Reconciliation Pod—home of the Trudeau-Freeland Chair in Métis Studies—has filed a formal complaint with both the university's Human Rights Office and the Federal Government's. To wit: the name of Joseph Brant must immediately be removed from our student residence and all appurtenances pertaining to; ditto the immediate cessation of the proposal to rename Macdonald Library the Tecumseh Library." He looked around taking in their puzzlement and continuing self-absorbed worry. "You might find these proposals counterintuitive. But both appropriative events, the ISR Pod charges, continue Canada's shameful history of exploitation, especially, it has been determined, in light of President Sureau Montjoy's recent DARK initiative. Our ISR Pod colleagues propose that we rename the building the Sir Isaac Brock Library in honour of the warrior who kept our Indigenous brothers and sisters from falling under American jurisdiction, which assuredly would have entailed their literal, as opposed to their cultural or figurative, genocide. If not Brock, they propose a series of names in their native tongues, which I won't insult our generous indigenes by attempting to pronounce here; I *have* been informed that each suggestion contains the pan-Indige-nous word either for *medicine* or *woods*.

"For now, our ISR Pod unequivocally insists that the statue of John A. Macdonald be replaced *not* by one of Tecumseh but by ever-changing art installments supplied by First Nations Artists exclusively, remunerated at market prices set by the National Council of First Nations. The first such ceremonial installation, which President Montjoy *strongly* suggests you all attend, wherever you presently find yourselves, will be not of a plastic art but of a performative nature: for two weeks or until first sub-zero temperatures, whichever arrives first, we will be treated to a daily dramatization of the cooperative Huron-Ir-oquois ritualistic sacrifice of Frére Brébeuf, which will take place daily over the lunch hour on the patio in front of the former-Macdonald library, *beginning today*. We are forewarned that if the Macdonald statue is not gone before then, it will be made to stand in for Brébeuf. ... That wasn't intended humor-ously, Professor von Blüger." He was staring at von Blüger—until Bartholomew retracted in startlement: "I suppose—"

For yet *another* small group was crowding into the growing swell near the front door, the room's only exit. This time the HR functionaries comprised the vanguard, the highest-rank-ing officials: Director Dr. Joel Caicos and his Vice-Director Dr. Elizabeth (Betty) Turkaise. To say that a hush fell over the characteristically chattering professors would be to shortchange the very real sudden urge to pee assaulting all, including the earlier HR functionaries. Director Caicos, the vest buttons of his light-grey three-piece bursting, needed no introductory permission to speak.

"Collègues," he began in the horrible franglais of the place, always tinged with facetiousness for the unilingual English-speakers, "I bring you tidings of good news from the

Office of Human Rights *and* your president, Doctor Sureau Montjoy. I am here in point of fact to announce the first most highly welcomed achievements of President Montjoy's DARK initiative."

The plumper HR functionary of the first wave made bug-eyes at his arrived Director (*someone* had been flung from the loop), while Amari Abara plumped up further in his wheelchair wearing a face that said *At long last, finalement*; he drew his wheelchair one half-revolution closer to the table. *Remarkably*, two more uBytown Security in darker brown uniform slipped into the room, which caused the unhealthily congregated already at the front to shuffle along towards the wall of windows. Respectful nodding was exchanged among the now four-strong Security, with the first comers eager to pay obeisance to the latter two (grinning, nodding like bobble toys, while all the time wearing what-the-hell-is-going-on-here faces).

Director Caicos continued: "Your *collègue estimé*, Professor Amari Abara, has filed the charges of racism arising *naturelle- ment* from the systemic racism against *professeurs* David Swift, David O'Brien, David McCabe, Bartholomew von Blüger, Jake Flynn—well, that one is so much irrelevant for the present times since—*Ms.* Jennifer Windsor, *Ms.* Stephanie Weyburn … and, well, fairly well that is, your entire Pod, so I won't name all names farther. *D'accord*?"

The three Davids were exchanging stares from faces that precluded even an attempt at winking. David calmed quickly, touched his big watch and turned a forlorn gaze on Amari Abara: "Maksim?" he all but bleated. "I thought we had an understanding, bro?"

"Nothing is irrelevant *or* agreeable!" Amari near shouted at the Director, semi-miraculously half-rising in his wheelchair.

"Jake Flynn above all others with his passive-aggressive inverse racism must be held to full account!"

The Director ignored him with a small snort. "In complications of Professor Abara's charge, if somewhat only just so, a student registered as a major in this Pod, who self-identifies himself as Indigene non-binary two-spirit and Black Irish—or Afro-Celtic rather—and who cannot be named of course, has filed the charges of racism, arising from systemic racism, against *professeurs* Abara and Flynn for quote *insisting* he/she/they make presentations in their seminar classes when her/his/their heritage says she/he/they don't/doesn't have to if they don't feel like it, eh? End of quoted quote. And furthermore for interferings with his presentation because he introduced the appropriate 2SLGBTQI+context for discussion of an outdated text. I must have to say, though, that this second charge would more *naturellement* be numbered amongst those respecting President Montjoy's innovatory RAPE initiative. … *Whoops!* Have I betrayed the sex of our accuser? We must never reveal our sex. Irregardless, I think we can *all* take great pride in these first fruits from President Montjoy's DARK initiative—"

"This is an outrage!"—Amiri Abara/Maksim Kovalchuk shot backwards.

Professor von Blüger's lower lip had turned out: "I suppose … so."

Director Caicos patted the air in Professor Abara's direction. "Please, remain in your seats—*mon Dieu*, please do forgive me, Professor Abara, *s'il vous plait.*" But he smiled tightly.

"You will *pay* for that," Amari said coldly, sitting back. "I am *not* just saying. *Do you know what I mean?*"

The HR director demonstrated his Office's way with complaints: ignore such pelting pebbles till the pelter goes away (then count it officially in the tally of "cases handled").

He waited a bad half-minute. "We request," he continued, tilting his big head towards the four-strong Security contingent, "that following this present Pod consult all named RAPE and DARK offenders vacate the campus and remain *à la maison* on the paid leave, you shall be happy to hear confirmed, until the further notices, if you whilst *peut-être*."

The HR functionaries and Security were in a radiant state, whereas the members of the Pod were experiencing the numbing aftermath of a series of shocks—when shock all round turned to stunned alarm as a resplendently uniformed RCMP officer stood inside the doorway, towering over the group there who cowered away, as would anyone at the sight only of jodhpurs and knee-high brown boots, let alone shining scarlet tunic and Smokey-the-Bear hat. Recovering, the press at the door joggled to see past him as he stepped farther into the room.

"Make way, make way, please make way," he commanded the gathering at the front, who didn't resist as he ushered them towards the wall of windows as might a farmwife herd chickens. A few made highly displeased faces, obviously not having been brushed off, and especially aside, in decades. The Mountie followed towards that side of the room, turned on a loonie and actually sounded to have clicked his heals. Professor von Blüger's unibrow snapped to in sympathy.

The Mountie had made way for a fat man with a big balding head and large glasses whose thickness had his eyes goggling about like a fish determined to crack the glass barrier—none other than President Sureau Montjoy himself. His entry made the room inhale sharply, even Bartholomew von Blüger who'd not gasped since his eureka over the ur-significance of *a* and *the*. President Montjoy breasted his way like one whose modus operandi was frank bullying; that is, with no thought to shoulderings aside or toes stepped on. But the entourage that followed carefully—as though all knew their places well—finally put the whole room in a condition of dumbfounded staring surrender to life's utter unpredictability: two Asian men and one woman, all attired in shiny black suits of diamond cut, accompanied by an undeniable air of supreme celebrity, and all still wearing big black Covid masks (no others in the room were so precautioned). Bringing up the anticlimactic rear was a man whom only the more senior members of the Pod recognized.

Leader … already ex-Leader *pro-tem* Pat Kelly made to speak but deflated at the challenge, keenly feeling professional and personal defeat in this her first Pod consult as Leader, which she was conceding would likely be her last. Still standing beside her, Dean Jacques LaRoque tipped forward as though he too would speak, or maybe pass out, but rocked back on his considerable heels instead; then rhythmically squeezing the hidden phone like trying to restart his heart.

President Montjoy cleared his throat and spoke in a voice that must explain a large part of his success: a tone deeper even than Jake Flynn's, so resonant in pitch and timber that his barrel chest must be acting as an echo chamber. His poor English, *his* franglais, had made many wonder, though, how he'd reached the top in the world's only bilingual university:

"Perhaps since, I should initially give you to understand the alarming presence of a representation of our vaunted Royal Canadian Mounted Police." He couldn't hide his derision at the Anglo institution, sneering the name as one responds to another's brazen fart. "If you will then since, *s'il vous plait, Serg*ent Preston, do your duties so's we may advance in our most important uBytown business."

The Mountie did advance one step, smirked slightly at the president, then bowed to read from his pad: "Dr. Bartholomew von Blüger, you are under arrest and herewith charged with committing crimes of hate speech and incitement to violence. Come with me, please, sir."

Professor von Blüger stared blankly at him which, despite the over-charged air, was easy for Bartholomew to do without showing emotion. "I suppose so," he rumbled. "But more details please. I waive my right to privacy. Though you should know that academic freedom protects us in these areas."

The Mountie, just a bit destabilized, instantly resumed his boots' solid standing and said more than he'd planned: "Whatever penalty uBytown levies under its DARK initiative is the business of President Montjoy and his Board of Governors." The president affected to nod. The Mountie proceeded: "But your comments over the past months on your," he glances at his pad, "*Proud Aryan Boys* website, and especially your recent article titled *The Yellow Peril*"—the Asian woman flinched—"are crimes under Canada's penal code, provision three-nineteen, sub-sections one and two: *Public incitement of hatred and wilful promotion of hatred*. You are under arrest, sir. Come along now."

Bartholomew von Blüger sneered weakly and stood, and continued sneering round at his colleagues: "Jake would never have allowed this insult to *my* academic freedom, never mind our freedom of expression and Charter Rights." But he went to the Mountie, who took him firmly by the upper right arm and led him out. From beyond the doorway came the sound of jingling metal and a weak "I suppose so."

Most sat shocked, but for the four Jennifers, who smiled tightly at each other, and the two Stephanies, whose purses had tipped over on the table and were spilling a few feminine items, were sniffling less, so likely already well on the way to supportive wellness, which meant that uBytown's insurer, Canada Life, would save some on PTSD counselling. Only Professor Abara joined his six female colleagues in banked satisfaction, his chair rhythmically shooting forwards and backwards like a caged panther.

Nor is it insensitive caricaturing to observe that Professor John Turnbull continued drop-jawed, gaping as might a distracted aging man who'd been pantsed from behind—*not* gaping at the unfolding legal events but at the appearance of his old colleague, Professor Oberon Stangle, who'd left the Pod as ex-Chair when it was still a Department some decade ago.

President Montjoy easily retrieved everyone's attention with a clap of his pudgy hands, which made a sound as of something squishy being squashed, or of an armpit fart. "I know as to the fact that all of this hubbub is since sudden, but such irregular business had to be disposed thereof before introducing our worthy visitors from the east."

All three Asians flinched, if keeping pasted grins emplaced.

"I am expecting too that some of you are cognizant of an old friend of the Film&WordsWork Pod, Dr. Oberon Stangle, when it was as yet the antique Department of English." The president had swept his right arm towards Oberon Stangle, who still sported the signature pea-green tweed cape and matching deer-stalker hat of yore; in step with the president's introduction, he swept the silly hat from a head that Turnbull remembered as darker and hairier. He carefully set the hat like a bargaining gambit on the table beside forlorn Pat Kelly.

President Montjoy proceeded: "As you eventually will be hearing since, Dr. Professor Stangle has a most interesting offer-*cum*-proposal to set before your Pod consult, not to say that the decision is yours any longer as this Pod will be no more anyway. But to let the cats farther out of their sack: because it is presently already the *fait accompli. Mais*, Dr. Professor Stangle, if you will entertain us, *s'il vous plait*?" He gestured as might an acrobat whose partner had landed a triple flip.

With slim fingers Oberon Stangle petted one end of his two-peaked hat—Pat Kelly pulled back—while poising his fine head snootily. "*Mais oui, et merci beaucoup*, Monsieur Montjoy, *mon capitaine*. But before introducing our honoured guests from The People's Republic of China"—the three Asians didn't respond—"let me provide some context, or background, if you will.

"Since leaving this esteemed institution, I have been enjoying a well remunerated appointment as Adjunct Professor of English at an eminent Chinese university, the University of Pingdingshan. Yes, to their shame, or maybe it's ours, some institutions of higher learning still employ the *déclassé* term *university*. From UP I first secured for the University of Bytown a student exchange with their School of Foreign Languages. This arrangement progressed to an exchange of faculty, which has been well utilized *only* by Leader Levine of Bytown's Communications, uh, Pod. Nevertheless, our reciprocal arrangement has evolved to fulfillment, and thus the appearance here today of our delegation." Small smiles and slight bows from the Asians. "But as you can see from the impatient face being made by Dean LaRoque"—no laughter filled his pause—"or should that be *former* Dean? … Regardless, I must for the nonce curtail my speech. In the parlance of the street, here's what the deal amounts to: money. And a lot of it, a portion of which funds will be earmarked to establish a Chair in Renaissance Drama with a focus on Shakespeare"—the Asians smiled more—"and city comedy"—the Asian eyes narrowed some. "I will elaborate in due course, or as our younger colleagues would put it: more to come. For now, I cede the floor back to President Montjoy."

Who was beaming sun flares, and whose English suddenly improved, because he was mainly reading from a file card. "*As* moved and approved by the Board of Governors, beginning immediately the Film&WordsWork Pod will be subsumed by the Communications Pod as an independent sub-Pod, for the present anyway, and will henceforth be known as *Communications in English Language and Literature*."

There was another authentic collective gasp, matched by as pleasant a smile from the Chinese Delegation. President Montjoy's voice deeply resonated in pleasure: "We are encouraged to think that not only will this nomenclature not displease our colleagues at the School of Foreign Languages of Pingdingshan University but will assuredly warm the cockles of their Oriental hearts since." It was like the three Asians had been cuffed on the backs of their heads. "With, I must add, further acquisitions already realized and awaiting only government approval, *our* government's."

The Pod cohort was squinting round the table and room, none really confident that s/he'd heard correctly. A surge of shifting commences. Leader *pro-tem* Pat Kelly looked sideways at the President as a crinkle-faced "Wha …?" escaped her. Oberon Stangle, retrieving his deerstalker for comfort (he used it to cover his left fist), smirked appreciatively. "Shame about Jake," he whispered to Peggy Dubois. "I'd give anything for Flynn to have been here for this." Peggy wasn't listening, but he tipped his head at Dean LaRoque and asked anyway, "Who's the fancy boy?"

Dean LaRoque, who had long since been lost in himself alone, while sneaking peeks at the exit door, was hanging onto the hidden phone now embossed on his breast as if for dear life. But he'd heard something, for he squinted at Oberon Stangle: "Pardon me?"

President Montjoy continued: "I apologize if my news startles. But the precipitous fall in enrollments in Film&WordsWork and the Faculty of Digital Humanities these past years made this amalgamation a necessity of financial exigency. Yes: the sole contractual condition that justifies such radical improvements, including dismissal of tenured professors, which I'm afraid is in the offing. As your union executive was informed yesterday evening. And though not totally overjoyed with the way this exigent adjustment is transpiring—their *fétiche* with process—they are nonetheless on board with a Letter of Understanding—LOU. And they are, as you will presently hear from your venerable association of brothers and sisters, now pleased with another forthcoming announcement: that our new Faculty of English Language and Literature"—the Asians beamed—"has been awarded *fifteen* new full-time tenured positions in Writing! Business English! Report Writing! Practical English for International Students, and Texting Grammatically, and that is only to begin! Starting January, one after Christmas *seasonal* Break, there *is no* Faculty of Digital Humanities at Bytown University." The two Asian men discreetly bumped elbows. Jacques LaRoque had already paled as much as one still living could and was unsteady on his legs—and not from his pants' constriction of blood flow; he had to lean on the tabletop till his fingertips whitened like the big fluffy flakes that had begun falling softly, softly falling on the wall of windows.

President Montjoy graciously agreed to take questions. There were none. The Pod cohort was itching to be off to commence self-protective measures, to, as the legal-political demimonde puts it, "lawyer up."

"In that case, it remains for me only to introduce our honoured guests from the far east, who could well be giving us all lessons in appropriate dress!" Only the woman smiled, and immediately frowned. "First is the lovely little lady"—deeper frown—"who is translator, as none of us speaks even a word of

Chinese and they don't speak much French ... *or* English—for now! So both ways ignorance! Anyway, here she is, Ms. Wen Twei!"

It was delivered in such a way, ending with sweeping arm, that she might have been expected to perform a cartwheel. Prudently she bowed her head.

"And now to our *most* honoured guest, Acting Education Minister of the People's Republic Of China, henceforth referenced as PRC, Doctor Wong Wei! Have I got that correct?" But actually careless of correctness, President Montjoy applauded silently; he then held his hands prayerfully and commenced bowing like a bobbing desk toy. The minister referenced bowed deeply once, with his funereal suit seeming to throw off a dark light. "And last but *certainement* not least, acting *Finance* Minister of the PRC, Doctor Deng Choo!" Nothing, nothing but total discomfort all round. "Are all Oriental politicians only *acting*? I hope not!" At least President Montjoy didn't wait too long. "Perhaps you could be induced to say just a couple of words to us, acting Minister Doctor Choo."

The petite translator had been whispering efficiently to her companions, and the three of them chorused a coughing laugh of understanding and bemused self-consciousness. The translator then checked herself, not for her behaviour but mindfully for accuracy before speaking. She signalled her satisfaction with a nod and spoke: "Ministers Wei and Choo wish to convey how pleased we, the Education Ministry of the People's Republic of China are to be the new owners of the internationally eminent Bytown University. We, the People's—"

What what what wha ... ? Unspoken, half-spoken and unprofessionally articulated from the whole dim room. What had they, the Pod cohort, missed in all the officials' franglais?

Surely not what this sounded like? Most of them were again standing or half-standing between table and chairs. Only the three visitors from the east remained calmly smiling at each other. Or President Montjoy too, he remained kind of becalmed, if frowning at his phone and mumbling to himself: "Connection sucks, *where are we*? China or Ottawa!" Behind this mostly becalmed focal group, the HR personnel had edged back towards the exit. The tall and the short of Security looked like they were looking forward to better things to do.

The female translator raised a commanding forefinger and continued: "We look forward to long and mutually rewarding educational relations … *a* long, excuse please; and furthermore, relation*ship*. Despite rumours to the contrary, we never doubted that we would be chosen over honourable Saudi-Russian bid who, with peak oil passed, paid for your lovely accessible elevator, with help from good Dr. Abara, and funded Pod of International Relations. We will take much care."

Only Professor Abara joined the paused and grinning Asians, surprising his colleagues with a smile … before recalling his new troubles under the RAPE initiative.

"And now, as your eminent President Montjoy has informed us, we must enable the vast majority of you to acquiesce to the orders to vacate the campus, which we hope will be only temporary before your return to the Department of Communications in English Language and Literature in the Faculty of Communications in English Language and Literature—in open and fair competition for positions, some tenured. We anticipate many international students finding a home for study of English writing there—and maybe great Shakespeare, *a-and* maybe even"—she glanced at her pad—"eminent *Canadian* author of fictional work satirizing capitalist academia *Arcadian Adventures with the Idle Rich*, Stephen … Leacock?" She glanced again at her pad then looked confidently at President Montjoy: "Connection strong now."

President Montjoy pocketed his phone and, turning his back on the Pod cohort, commenced flapping both hands backwards at the HR functionaries and Security: "Be off now! Make way!"

The Pod consult broke up without a motion to conclude (so that officially, according to Robert's Rules, they could well be in session to this very day). Led by one of the Davids, the one with the watch like a sextant, Davey, most of the cohort hurried off as though they finally had something important to do, which they did, if not what they'd been planning an hour before. Only Leader *pro-tem* Kelly lingered, delaying the four Jennifers and two Stephanies as they approached. The six stood determined to avoid the appearance of gossiping, until led out in a suppressed gaggle by their former Leader *pro-tem*.

On his own way to the exit Professor John Turnbull dawdled at the Chinese delegation, then planted himself closely in front of them. All ceased chattering and smiled guardedly as they extended hands and, remembering, reflexively retracted them; they steepled hands at sternums and bowed bobbingly. Professor Stangle stepped in front of the Chinese and extended a flat hand like some faith healer's above Turnbull's head. An ancient routine of theirs, Stangle was pretending to take Turnbull's measure, an insult which Turnbull, having been the famous Stangle's lapdog once upon a time, had learned to accept. The former Department colleague pretended some surprise: "Why, John, you've not grown a millimetre—in fact, you may well have shrunk!" Professor Turnbull, playing his old part, raised vertical hands then spread them measurably (indicating that Stangle had gotten fatter), faking surprise with widened eyes. They both snorted and relaxed into collegial chatter, while the translator returned to whispering with the two ministers.

Leader *pro-tem* Kelly had tarried at the light switch and turned to look over the big mahogany table; the Jennifers and Stephanies dominoed behind her like a comedy routine. She pinched her mouth and shook her head. It was getting darker already, which seemed early this distance still from the shortest day of the year. Then she guessed not and, despite the five remaining occupants, turned out the lights. In the crepuscular atmosphere the snow swarmed increasingly ...looking to be general all over Ottawa (as Joyce concludes of Dublin in "The Dead"). Enigmatically she whispered, "They got what was coming to them, but not us, not us. Come along then, girls."

She led the Jennifers and Stephanies to her *pro-tem* Leader's office, where she briefly explained then solicited the women's support—*material support*, she stressed—for the charges of sexual harassment that she'd brought against former Leader Jake Flynn and Professor John Turnbull, adding that Dean LaRoque will now be appended to the count of those charged. But most desirous was she that they include President Sureau Montjoy himself, though *only* of course if justifiable. Locking gazes she took them in one at a time.

The four Jennifers and two Stephanies looked at each other, scurrying back and forth as though weaving a visual cat's cradle, and it was something of a secular miracle that their wary understanding was communicated wordlessly.

Jenn spoke first: "In my one meeting with President Montjoy, supposedly to discuss my initial contract, he was always looking me up and down like a butcher sharpening his cleaver as he gazed at a split pig." (They *were*, or once were, English literature professors.)

Then Jenny: "I'm like, I cannot *stand* the way Montjoy has avoided meeting with me ... during regular office hours anyway! It's like he never even thinks about me or, like, equity issues!"

Other potentially pending charges were suddenly avalanched from long-banked piles of injustice, such as President Montjoy's ignoring Stephanie Esterhazy in passing her on the Coriveau Grande Allée and then turning, she could feel it, to check out her ass, which *was* getting big, she conceded, she had to lose weight. After Esterhazy was pattingly reassured that it was just her dysmorphia acting up, Professor Stephanie Weyburn remembered: "Lucky you, with me it's my tits, like I'm faceless or something." They were all aghast and continued so through a few further rehearsals.

Pro-tem Leader Kelly summed up: "As Director still of Film&WordsWork's Tenure and Promotion Committee, I would be most grateful for your support, as the Board of Governors, headed by President Montjoy, has made many despicable judgements and comments on the files of female faculty. Now, Jennifer Windsor, meet immediately with select female colleagues of the Faculty of Digital Humanities to discuss curricula, and see what manner of consensus can be reached regarding upper-administration pressure to teach certain texts and not others. Here's a list of possible contacts. For now, though, avoid all mention of John Turnbull, the potbelly pig, Dean LaRoque and, well, former Leader Jake Flynn." She sighed deeply ... perked up and winked convincingly at the space just above Jennifer Windsor's head. "Dear ladies, we have a bigger fish to fry." Or she'd winked at least more easily than had Professor David O'Brien at the Pod consult.

The colleagues were no sooner out the door than her phone rang.

"Pat, Jacques LaRoque here. I'm afraid my return to decanal headquarters was greeted by the bad news, surmountable we trust. But for now the Board of Governors has officially rescinded your *pro-tem* appointment as Leader of the Film&WordsWork

Pod. Another *pro-tem* Leader has been assigned, Tiems Upal from uBytown's Asian Studies Pod. A good man, I might add."

"We have an Asian Studies Pod?"

"We do as of this morning. I am unceremoniously informed that it will be only a temporary *pro-tem* in the transition from Film&WordsWork to the Department of Communications in English Language and Literature in my new Faculty of English Language and Literature, or whatever idiotic antique thing they call it. But of course some of this is now likely moot, including even our own continued involvement; I mean, given all HR's pending charges under RAPE and DARK. *Unless* …"

Her heart skipped. She knew to tame it, as nothing from Dean LaRoque had ever helped her career. "Unless what, Jacques?"

As she sat listening to the scheme that would have her attest with veiled threat to President Montjoy respecting Dean Jacques LaRoque's feminist *bona fides*. Professor Kelly appeared to deflate literally: small already she drooped smaller, her face drooped, her shoulders drooped, and under the white shirt that complemented her baby-blue suit, she felt her breasts droop (so she would make even less headway with Montjoy). At the bottom of her drooping she smiled in some hard-won wisdom remembering how perky Jake Flynn had always made her feel.

"Finally, Pat, and I do so hate to be saying this"—she could hear that he loved saying it, his silly command, his last likely, she hoped—"but I must ask you for now to please leave the key to the Leader's office with Peggy, until we get all this straightened around."

"Peggy's gone home, Jacques. You're as locked-out as I am, *finished*. So peel off your pants and leave the key to the Dean's office shoved up your ass. And as our new Asian *owners* might put it, please to be fucking off."

Back in Rm. 509 high atop the Digital Humanities Complex, John Turnbull turned away from Oberon Stangle and took a half-step towards the Chinese delegation. They stopped talking softly among themselves and, all three raising hands to emplace their masks, turned to him. He addressed the translator:

"Would you please ask the acting Minister of Education to enlighten me respecting Pingdingshan University's policy on sabbatical leaves?"

Oberon Stangle chuckled, "Good old John."

The translator smiled warily at him, which Turnbull took for teasing hope, and instantly, as always with him, of hope for more than highly paid leave to research the allegorical significance of animals in mid-twentieth-century British working-class fiction. She turned to her superiors, who never behaved at all superior, and said what sounded like six words. She clearly received only one in response. Putting on a smile just as previously, she returned to Turnbull:

"Sabbatical not now."

He startled slightly. "Pardon me? But I'm not *applying* here and now for a sabbat—"

She smiled less and bowed shallowly in a way that could yet inspire in the frazzled Turnbull urgings of geisha fantasies. "Humble apologies," she said softly, demonstrating a quick-study mastery of Canadian irony. "*No sabbaticals.*"

Turnbull stretched everything, from bugging eyes to neck to arms wide to up on tiptoes: "Get serious!"

THIRTY-SIX

PLAGUING JAKE 12: THE PRINCESS

The abbreviated form for the Princess Diana Centre for Mental Wellness, "The Princess," persisted among even the most enlightened as local code for "gone bonkers," while with the *hoi polloi* the hospital could still be referenced most crudely as "the Mental." Many Ottawans at all levels in the stratified national capital were familiar with The Princess, but only the most reactionary citizens (usually the oldest) still responded shamefully to the association. The likes of Crazy Ray shamelessly paid periodic visits to The Princess, preferably just before the inhuman winter set in, though Ray particularly didn't always have a choice in the timing, because his madness could act out radically in any season. When his older street acquaintances—no "friends" in that world, only territorial competitors—said that Crazy Ray had gone south for the winter or was staycationing at the Mental, his territory would immediately be colonized, because none was more prized than his corner of the Coriveau Hall field.

Other regular staycationers at the treatment centre, such as the variously stressed federal government workers, could fairly admit themselves seasonally for whatever length of stay their union doctor prescribed and sick leave covered; they too would be whispered about dispassionately even by their most enlightened colleagues as being "in for a tune-up at the Mental."

Yet other inmates were being temporarily held under secure watch on their way to some worse place, usually a more specialized institution for psychotics and/or violent criminals entailing a blunderbussing drug regimen that amounted to chemical lobotomy, which *would* temporarily tame their derangement; such soldiers of misfortune would never be discharged on anything longer than an afternoon pass, and ultimately with little of real life left in them.

Newsworthy events, especially those involving the graphically inventive murders of relatives and children, often featured The Princess as a first stop for the accused. In the absence of murder and the like, the media would settle on whatever high crimes in business and politics (a distinctive Ottawa coupling) happened their way; and when a lawyer finagled a judge into ordering psychiatric assessment before trial or sentencing, The Princess would be invoked for added viewer/reader interest. Then would the accused's usual habits of alcoholism and drug addiction come in handy, jurisprudentially speaking. Respecting legal outcome, the insanity defence rarely succeeded but, failing a solid alibi, was still often mounted, as it could postpone judgement beyond the public's interest or memory. And what with the social normalizing of psychological challenges, an insanity defence could yet be counted on to effect mitigation of sentence.

Jake Flynn's situation matched the latter profiles, so at least fed the insatiable media until something involving Parliament Hill and corruption would come along again as reliably as the long Ottawa winter follows the short Holiday Season. Jake, accused of grand larceny involving a strange object (a book of all things, with media points for that weirdness); obviously unfit for trial (a certified heavy drinker, incipient alcoholic, workplace tyrant, unresponsive at arraignment, rumoured sexual harasser, etc. etc. etc.); a mysterious, or at least unusual, psychological condition/defence (kleptomania) that cried out to be officially, clinically diagnosed (perfect for extended media attention)— Dr. Professor Jacob Flynn was having his moment in the unwanted spotlight.

Even the national media were "all over the story," as the saying goes, from Victoria to Leitrim Falls to Cavendish P.E.I. (*even* as a sign-off bit of criminal colour on the American CNN: *Nutty Canuck Professor Steals Million-Dollar Book From Own College!!!*). And as other sayings go, uBytown's President Sureau Montjoy was *rapide comme un renard* to throw *Jake sous le bus*, if executing the sacrifice with accompanying expressions of compassion.

uBytown's future was safeguarded, though, thanks to the fortuitous occurrence of the "Pingdingshan Endowment," whose eye-popping amount the president tactfully let slip, a few times. For what would be the period of intensive media coverage, President Montjoy claimed to be "not only *un cher collègue* of Professor—of *Jake*, but a close personal friend" (*un ami personnel proche*; he had the Ottawa habit of saying everything important in both official languages, the linguistic gift of talking, so to speak, out both sides of the mouth). Someone also let slip that the president would be visiting his dear friend at the Princess Diana Centre for Mental Wellness, also slipping the exact time. Montjoy would visit only once.

Jake stood at the corner window farthest from the narrow entry to the big empty day room watching unnaturally large and distinct snowflakes drift down—he could *see* the holes in their filigree—fairly arcing in the windless late day ... falling softly, softly falling, on the full parking lot of small cars and SUVs, he thought, parodying the end of Joyce's "The Dead." Was snow general all over the black lots and driveways of Ottawa too? Ha! ... But he couldn't even make himself smile at his faint reflection, because he couldn't make his face do anything anymore, even when internally he was finding things hilarious, a riot.

He *had* said aloud, "I know who you are and I want nothing to do with you" ... Hadn't he? Yes. And rid himself of President Montjoy, Dean LaRouque, Pat Kelly and John Turnbull, the camera-wielding media asswipes, *and* the uBytown legal-office functionary—without signing anything! Something about a retirement incentive and a non-disclosure agreement. But when *was* that? Where did that happen? Did it really happen? And what have I to disclose anyway? I have nothing to declare but my madness! ... Would Montjoy have picked up the literary allusion in his rejection? Of course not. Maybe Turnbull or Kelly recognized and explained it to the president. Highly doubtful though, given the books taught nowadays—*whoops*, the *texts*. Anyway, who cares? Who cares about Gabriel Conroy and Bartleby the Scrivener, two of the biggest fucking losers in literature! Better for today's go-ahead students to avoid those desultory lessons in love and business.

For Canadian content (now he's thinking clearly), how about a priestly eejit like Callaghan's Father Dowling or Ondaatje's mad jazzman Buddy Bolden—two other terminal devotees of the faintly reflecting window? (I never could shake the image of Gregor Dungbeetle strainfully holding himself on tiptoe, like a bug-eyed little boy, to gaze out on the responsible adult world that never had a place for him). But even those characters are too elevated for me, I'm only three floors up. Ha! ... Where *did* I leave *Such Is My Beloved*? My breviary for these *pane*ful meditations. (*Ha* again.) I know I had it with me—for God's sake, don't tell me I left it too on Crazy Ray's book bench! ...

Wait a minute: didn't I see Ray today? I did ... and he had my copy! He stole it! Police! Police! ... *Dear God, don't let me really be crazy, Crazy Jake.* ... But seriously, folks, I really am beneath contempt, the things I've done in the dark. I am a worm driven in dirt, an insect condemned to eat shit in hell. Shit-eater, coprophagite (now, Professor, *there's* a word for the literary wise!). Don't even *try* to laugh, Jake! Crazy Jake. Just don't. ... But if I cannot have my pint of plain Bushmills, then Gregor Samsa's my only man! Nya-nya-nya-ny ... Sweet Jesus, am I really mad I am? *No one* cares for literary references anymore, for God's or Joyce's sake. Literature no more! Unless a life's time wasted between the covers can be used to provide safe spaces for street people! ... Or some such. But seriously, folks, try to name just one safe space in the whole wide world? ... Correcto mundo! There is none! Not even for a cloistered nun poring over Molly's meditations! ... Or maybe there is one, just one. If out of this world. And not really one, none, not even for nuns, if you know what I mean. Nothing. Where no thing lives and no one is.

Who was *he* anymore? What was he really? Just listen to him carry on. Crazy Jake is right. When you no longer are what and who you were, can it be enough to go on just standing at windows for the duration of your meaningless existence? Wouldn't it be better indeed to dredge up whatever vestige of integrity you have left and do the indecent thing? Ha! ... Ha, ha, ha.

It's been so long since I gave up what I thought I believed in, and fighting for it: reading, studying, writing a little. Teaching. Love. Sloth that I am, I just got too lazy to make the effort to believe anymore. The optic heart just wouldn't venture. ... Where's that from? ... Fuck it. And that's why Sloth is one of the deadly sins; it's the beginning of the end, the slippery slope requiring no effort towards the welcoming embrace of icy Despair (the bigger sin). The universal *who cares?* The cosmic fuck it. So get active (or *pro*active, whatever the fuck that is), get serious, at least *get real*. To wit, okay: it *was* I who stole the happy Buddha from Crazy Ray. Why? Isn't it fucking obvious? I *wanted* not to want anymore. And as was my wont I wanted to help save ... somebody—John Turnbull. So I told myself and believed it, of all sort-of people! *And* I stole our rare *Ulysses*, I guess, if not for the reason I gave Detective Gurmeet, whose sleuthing word is what I'm really taking as incontrovertible evidence of my crime and/or misdemeanour, my *mea culpa*. I did it ... copper, but you ain't taking me alive. ... But I really remember nothing of any of that. I do know as assuredly as the Recording Angel that I have no lessons to teach anyone anymore. Because I believe in nothing now, and know now that I've believed so for years ... or at least since Pat Kelly dumped me! ... Nothing. No more joking. Nothing. My remaining faith only in unfaith, as one of our old Canadian poets puts it. Then nothing it is. Because for me, uh, going forward, the mind really is its own place, and if unable any longer to make a something of nothing can make a nothing of something.

Kiran Gurmeet had to shake the elbow she'd gently touched: "Jake?"

He didn't startle, just turned his head, no recognition in his gaze, and turned back to the window. The sun had burned a perfect hole through the heavy cloud cover at some point, if only the one opening, and shining momentarily on the window the beam gave some comfort to the expressionless face—not for Jake but for one looking at him.

Encouraged some, she again recalled dealing a couple of times with this sort of affectless condition, one time as outright catatonia, so knew when she spoke to expect nothing in return. She could probably say anything she liked.

"Jake, we went fishing on the weekend, my partner Meike and me, a bit cold for it, up the Valley at—"

"Did you catch anything?"

She instantly collected herself. "Only the sniffles." She sniffled to demonstrate and in small appreciation of the old joke.

Both of which were lost on Jake. Apparently his question had exhausted his wasted energies, interest, and remnant politeness. There was no use asking him the questions she still had. She believed the answers scarcely mattered anymore anyway. He'd never stand trial.

She touched his elbow again. "Next time we fish together, Jake, just as you promised. Okay?"

This time he didn't come about at all. The parking lot was bordered by a brambly cedar hedge that in bald spots showed a ditch and the glisten of water. Perhaps it harboured carp? Jake howled inside. His transparent reflection was his father. When did I get so old and ugly? We'd better get our lines in before the creek freezes solid, Kiran, he thought to say, and made to say— But her window ghost was gone, and the sun had moved on.

Exiting the building she met Mary McGahern approaching the entrance. They smiled weakly, Mary's more of a pinched mouth, but didn't touch. Without spoken agreement they moved back near the curb, where they stood uncomfortably.

"Hi, Mary. I was in the Department the other day and asked after—"

"Yes, I know, and I know why. That's why I'm here."

Detective Gurmeet put on her own noncommittal face. "I was going to say I asked after you, following up on our last meeting at headquarters about police work."

Mary was mortified. "I apologize, Detective Gurmeet. I was upset when I heard that Professor Flynn was arrested, and then I heard it was by you." She'd shifted from looking past Gurmeet to looking at her. "I know you were just doing your job, but ..."

She held the girl's gaze steadily. "Yes, that is my job, Mary. It's just as well you know that part of the job before we go any further. As with lawyers, we're officers of the court, and we're often charged with doing what we don't like. Strictly *entre nous*, I like Jake Flynn, very much; we'd even planned a fishing date." She smiled both at the memory and for Mary.

Mary smiled back. "Me too, both, the liking and the fishing date! ... Will they," she nodded at the entrance, "let me in to see him?"

"Don't ask and you won't be stopped. He's on the third floor, room 171, but you'd likely still find him in what's signed as the *Margaret Trudeau Sun Room*. A shabby day room actually."

"Thank you. Can I still come and see you some time, Detective Gurmeet?"

"*Any* time, Mary, but only if you call me Kiran." She reached and they shook hands.

Mary said, "We could be arrested, *Detective*, for what we're doing." She felt her vision blur in memory of Professor Flynn's same remark on the library steps.

Gurmeet's head tilted back in unvoiced amusement, then came to rest in pleasant seriousness. "It shouldn't go too badly for Professor Flynn, Mary. The stolen book's been restored undamaged, a good lawyer should be able to mitigate any sentence, maybe even get him off, depending what that über-asshole Montjoy does."

One of the doors' pneumatic device was obviously malfunctioning, and the banging shut startled Detective Gurmeet, who laughed in embarrassment. "Yikes, I bet *that* really settles the unsettled day patient! A real suck-it-up-princess kick in the ass."

She looked absolutely lovely in her awkwardness, what Mary thought a rare loss of control. So she held Kiran's forearm lightly and smiled in a way that made up for the lost sun.

Mary said, "What he must have suffered, I think I saw only very little of it."

"Would you testify in court, Mary? Don't feel any responsibility, any pressure whatsoever. But you'd make a very good character witness, I suspect. I could tell Jake's appointed counsel."

"Unhesitantly."

Gurmeet couldn't quite tone down the affectionate patronizing in her look and laugh. "I'm sorry, Mary, but it's your answer, my partner Meike is the only other person I can imagine answering that way, with that one word."

"A compliment then, thank you. Uh, will you, *can* you, tell me anything else about Professor Flynn? I promise complete confidentiality."

Detective Gurmeet ran through a checklist of recriminations and counter-responses, and then, aware of the professional risk, spoke freely:

"Again Meike-like! Maybe English literature *is* the discipline for you, Mary, you certainly—"

"If there was any English literature to read and study. That was one of the things Professor Flynn despaired over. I think it helped make him mad." She watched and waited, applying no wheedle by expression.

"Okay. Going by what I could learn from his witch of a wife, soon to be *ex*, Jieun, Jake (short for Jacob, by the way) Patrick Flynn was a brilliant boy who had a miserable childhood, both parents alcoholics, died together dead drunk in a car accident when Jake was only twelve."

"How horrible." Mary was tearing up. "Was he left all alone?"

Kiran continued without touching her, because it was better Mary first experienced these truths in herself:

"Yes. He made it all the way through university on scholarships and hard work, eventually holding down a *full-time* job while doing his Ph.D. over some eight years at Carleton University. In therapy for long stretches. But that was all he had, his academic life, then his professorship. His talk of children and grandchildren was pure delusion, if not just lying to make the persona he needed. And the wife, partner … none of those words fits this *Jieun*. Far from the Korean flower he painted her, she is a harridan from the harridans. A wicked witch of a woman if ever there was one and, if we weren't on public display here, I'd use a few choicer words, one of which rhymes with *mucking witch*."

Mary snorted a smile and wholly sucked up the crying.

"One minute with Jieun after saying Jake's name is like throwing meat to hyenas. *She's* the one who should be in the, uh, Mental. She could only ever have added immeasurably to Jake's misery … as he watched his world and professional life falling apart."

Mary bowed her head and was sniffling again, kept it down and spoke downward into the open neck of her green cloth coat: "Then Professor Flynn really did steal the rare book?" She couldn't keep her voice from breaking slightly.

"It's okay to cry, Mary. I do it all the time. Meike calls me a long *flûte à champagne* of tears endless tears. That's probably from a poem."

"You're lucky. He's a poet, your partner."

Kiran laughed in a ringing way she rarely allowed in public: "I know or try to keep it in mind most of the time, which is impossible. And Meike's a woman, Mary." She looked with more intensity.

"This is the second time recently a girlfriend—is that okay?"

"Yes. Second time *what* recently?" Gurmeet was suddenly as alert as a police dog whiffing crack.

"Of a girlfriend telling me she's gay, like pre-emptively or something. Do I look like I'm always coming on to people … Kiran?"

Gurmeet smiled warmly.

Mary felt okay. "It must be a bit awkward, strange-awkward, thinking you always have to disclose your sexual orientation to new, like, girlfriends. It'd be like always needing to say you're really rich or you own horses or something. I'm always waiting for when I have to tell new friends I live on a farm, though I'm proud of that, and my dad's work, *our* work. I mean, being a lesbian isn't like having an STD or anything. It's neither bad nor good, I mean. … Anyway that's what I think. Uh, is that offensive? If it is, I'm sorry."

Kiran laughed remembering Mary's age and placed a hand on her shoulder: "You love someone too, don't you, Mary?"

"Yes."

They both turned faces to the sky, where the sun was again winning its competition with the cloud cover; its pale presence beamed forth, but as soon waned again.

Kiran spoke: "But you must be wondering, or you will be, so here's some *pre-emptive* two-bit psychology, all this being strictly *entre nous*, agreed, Mary?" She didn't wait. "Jake's response to everything uncontrollable—what was happening at the university, his life—was kleptomania. Some sub-brain of his must have figured, *Everything's being stolen from me, why not steal it back?* Abused children become abusers. But it's all really a tangle all tangled up in misery and tragedy and the mystery of the human mind. The front Jake put on his whole life must have drained him at last, leaving him empty as a dessert of dangerous rocks, like Mars, with no fight left in him. He just had nothing left, in any sense, because he was left with nothing."

"I think I get that, Kiran. Maybe I should just turn around and leave him alone."

"No, Mary, I don't think you should. I don't think you would anyway, and I think I know you. Don't worry, you will process the confusion you're thinking and feeling. Have faith."

"I don't think ... Thank you. Will Professor Flynn ... be committed to a psychiatric prison or will he be going to a regular jail?"

"For now, he's here for observation, a pre-trial assessment. That part's fairly routine in a case like this."

"If he's found guilty, how long will he go to prison for? I mean, it *was* just an old book."

"An old book worth at least half-a-million dollars. That's grand larceny. But Mary McGahern, I never thought I'd hear you talk like that about any book ... nice try." She smiled warm humour. Dropped it. "Seriously, like I said, I'm confident Professor Flynn will get off lightly, in the legal matter anyway. I'll be telling the judge that he pretty well led me to the recovered book. And he's obviously been under great strain—that's where your testimony could help—and there's his record of life-long psychiatric care, the drinking, some drugs, the collapsing marriage. The tectonic disruptions at uBytown, so I've heard. His good citizenship. As I said, he'll likely not get any time in prison at all. But he'll definitely be retiring. And we don't know how he'll deal with it all, Professor Flynn: the shame, the publicity, the end of his professional life, if there's enough of him left to *deal* with anything. The local media have been all over the story, as you must know. His dear colleagues will be no more help than a dead rat's fart. Talk of your high crimes and mis—"

Behind her the door slammed again and again she startled. A man in hospital greens—pants, shirt, dangling face mask, tied cap—hurried past disdainfully, looking shivery in the flimsy outfit; he had an already lit cigarette cupped in his right hand and was striding towards the parking lot as though heading for an outhouse with everyone watching.

"I'll take that as my signal to be off."

Kiran smiled and raised her right hand like someone asked to take an oath, then made the motion of one hand trying to clap, as if waving bye-bye to a baby. She clapped the side of Mary's upper arm and was off.

Mary called, "Kiran." She stopped and turned. "Thank you. I'll be taking you up on your generous invitation to visit again. I *am* still very interested in police work." She snorted lightly and, rare for her, did a voice: "English ain't the larnin' 'sperience I'd bin spectin'. May's well study the gen-u-ine article, *crime*." She dropped it blushing. "Especially now that my favourite professor's … Anyway, I *will* see you again, Kiran, I hope."

Walking away, Detective Gurmeet called ahead of herself, "Don't disappoint me, Mary!" Thinking: As if she could.

Mary had to call, "That stupid voice was the character Sam Slick!"

And Gurmeet: "Entertain your favourite professor with it!"

The odour, like a pharmacy installed in a barn, provoked a thump in Mary's heart to match the door slamming behind her because, since her mother's death, she could not stomach the smell of hospitals. Fred Faucher might talk of the stink of chicken coops, and he's right (though Fred should be there when the pricey sheep manure arrives, or after it's sat cooking close to the house for days. *Anybody for another lamb chop? You won't find fresher!* Dad). But Mary would take being buried to the nostrils in sheep shit over the antiseptic medicinal hospital smell, with its frequent additive of shat beds. Scouring, scourging olfactory memories. That dreaded hospital smell still messaged Mary where she lived, as if a cheerleader's black megaphone were jammed against the side of her head: *The world stinks. Life stinks. Live long enough and you'll see for yourself. Smell it? ... Mom stinks. Mom's dying and stinking to the very fucking nostrils of God!*

Following Detective Gurmeet's advice and not wanting to be checked out by the bay-bellied belt-straining security guard, she walked smartly like she knew the place. Ever the good reader, it helped that she could process the signage as she hurried along, finally taking the shallow stairs three at a time instead of the escalator, noticing another guard looking up after her through the Plexiglas staircase, not dawdling between floors over the directional floor art of different coloured butterflies mapping three pathways to mental wellness (which she thought cute), and the one cross-eyed cartoon sheep on the far left failing to look cute ... which was puzzling. This way, mental kids? She climbed through the three floors trying not to think seriously lest she'd turn back, half-holding her breath, fairly bounding up with her hand skimming the rail, unaware what a miracle of body-in-motion she was (the voyeuristic guard had a point, if the wrong one), relieved that the upper regions stunk a little less of hospital smell.

Through a third-floor foyer like some air lock and along a broad orange hallway, she fancied herself entering the set of some old movie that stereotyped psychiatric hospitals (asylums, loony bins, mentals) as containers of the agreeably straight-jacketed, the comically faced, the neurotically adorable, the non-threatening cute. But there to deny such romance emerged a realm of catatonic human statues and suffering mumblers lining garish walls and drifting along the hallway—a starved-looking man was pinned by his ever-charging life's torment, scared to death; a monologuing old woman with Einstein hair had been cheated out of lottery winnings, and such—many shamelessly exposed by loosely tied green gowns, some soiled, some both, so that the depressing hospital smell was again ramped up in an overmeasure of human waste, of all sorts. Regardless of the reality, Mary proceeded through the narrow glass door beneath the sign "Margaret Trudeau Sun Room" still half-expecting to see a short man wearing a bicorne hat sideways and standing in a corner with the fingers of his right hand tucked between a military jacket's buttons. But reality insisted, as is its wont, when she was immediately made aware of only one tall man, in the corner, his back to her (thank God), the crown of his head a bicorneless tonsure. Napoleon she could have dealt with better.

To delay the encounter with Professor Flynn, Mary paused at a shabby white bookcase whose wood was broken and showing its pale brown interior at every join (more institutional shit, figurative this time at least), with here and there the glinting silver of an IKEA screw. Broken bodies, broken minds, broken bookcases, screwed. Dawdling on, she surveyed the case's scanty contents, which sprawled sparsely, and was surprised to discover that all were reference books: a big red-white-and-blue *Webster's Dictionary* on its side—with a book mark inserted!—a three-volume boxed set of *The Canadian Encyclopedia* whose clean white case showed that it was never consulted; a thick dark volume titled *A Guide to Mental Disorder Law in Canadian*   .

Criminal Justice, much dog-eared; what looked like an equally well-thumbed catalogue of pharmaceuticals; and a humongous purple book, the *Diagnostic and Statistical Manual of Mental Disorders (DSM-5)*, which stood up alone in the centre of the middle shelf.

"Can I help you?"

She turned expecting to confront another chubby old guard, but no, it was a young guy, maybe in his early twenties, dressed in better-fitting hospital fatigues than those worn by the shunned smoker outside. A stethoscope necklace dangled from his sinewy neck and broad shoulders; he held a large sheet of shiny-white construction paper, with what looked like a coiled string of blue wool pinched against it, and held scissors at the end of his left arm pointing straight down; so looked all contradictory, like a kindergarten teacher who might stick somebody. But he smiled non-threateningly, no teeth showing.

"Thank you, Doctor, I mean, no thank y—"

"I'm not a doctor," he smirked slightly. "I'm a nurse, a psychiatric nurse, Marcel Tierney. Are you looking for someone? Or just browsing our library? May I recommend for light reading the fifth edition of the *DSM*, a perennial favourite among our recurrent clientele."

Recurrent. She exhaled appreciation through her nose. He was good-looking, ruggedly handsome, with closely shaved chin glistening still, not at all the stereotypical picture of an effeminate male nurse. And taller than she; Jimmy was shorter. She wanted to delay further.

"A weird selection of books, your, uh, library. Look, there's even a bookmark in the dictionary!"

"That would be Frank's doing, Old Frank, our ward logorrheic. Do you know that word? Something tells me you do."

He smiled and she was tickled from oesophagus to crotch. "*Frank?* Parents should never pun in naming a child. I'll be Frank today, you be Frank tomorrow."

He nearly spat his appreciation. He regrouped his professional air, glanced at the bookcase and returned to hold her gaze.

"Our clientele are nothing if not exacting about facts and words, as *every*thing relates to their conditions and treatments. Most are not here voluntarily, whatever the misconception spread by that old *Cuckoo's Nest* movie, which is still the image most people have of a psych ward, whether they've seen one or not. *And* of big-nurse me, *Marcel* you can call me"

She smiled and nodded (*misconception*). "I know the novel only. Kesey. But still, look at this," she gestured at the dishevelled shelves of the bookcase. "It's like some biblio-beast devoured everything that might have been worth reading and then gnawed on the bookcase itself."

He was encouraged too. "Biblio-beast? You're a poet, eh? I write a little. What's your name?"

She returned only slightly pursed lips and brightened eyes.

He pressed on: "Our guests want only to be up on the law and its treatment of them. If you'll pardon my unprofessional language, they're like jailhouse lawyers, our padded-cell counsels. What's your name?"

She laughed mainly for his sake but cut it short. "I'm here to visit Professor Flynn."

He was all business. "I apologize for making light. Professor Flynn is over by the window, his usual station."

"I know, thank you." But then she didn't want him to turn away, not like that, and not only because she felt a guilty attraction. Ironically Jimmy's love had emboldened her with flirting guys. "It's been fun, Marcel," she sparkled. Pointing at the construction paper she smirked: "Looks like you're gonna have some more."

He tipped back his head at an angle, indicating the corner behind him, which she couldn't see. "Maybe, but I doubt it. Books again. For some mad reason, *of course*, one of our most devoted readers wants to make a sign to wear around his neck identifying himself *as* a *reader*—two signs!"

She gave him her best: "Some other time then!"

"I leave you to Professor Flynn then, our star patient insofar as the media is concerned. Let me know if you require anything, anything at all. I'll be just over there," he half-turned this time nodding towards an adjacent corner. He smiled a small complex smile of presumed understanding, pale blue eyes like cameras watching always for anything he could do to help—the perfect nurse—and then did walk away.

Mary watched him into the corner at the far end of the wall along from Professor Flynn—the uniform showing his form to fine effect; she couldn't ever see *him* in jockeys hanging upside-down over a keg of beer. Jimmy was sort of stumpy, it had to be said, even a bit bowlegged … the perfect farmer! The nurse (or his ass) arrived where three red-cloth chairs were looking like they could have come from a house full of big cats, a cat … house—

Holy shit, it's that Crazy Ray! Move along, girl—away, head down.

Professor Flynn was dressed not in the regulation hospital gown that exposes ass but in a hospital-like uniform nonethe-less: navy-blue pajama pants baggy as martial artists wear, and a short-sleeved shirt of the same colour. She shivered for him. He had the fingertips of both hands resting on the wide grey-stone sill, where they played as if with a mind of their own. Head held dead still, his face was elevated slightly to the right, to where the fiery sun was setting now behind smoky clouds like a bombed-out scene.

She was reluctant to surprise him with touch, so said tentatively, "Professor Flynn?"

Calmly he responded, without turning: "I knew you'd come, Mary. I like the sun on my face, which I've had a bit of today. That's not much to want but it would seem to be all that's left to me." His head jigged back as though from his nose's derisive puff.

She didn't know what to say, she'd prepared nothing, which was stupid, so she said, "How are you feeling, Professor Flynn? Or as you always insisted to us, what are you *thinking*?" *Do not snicker like some anxious girl.*

He puffed again and looked at her. "It warms me, Mary. And your question reminds me of a Leacock story, a true anecdote, supposedly, since it *is* Leacock telling it. But once upon a time our poet William Butler Yeats was visiting Montreal and Leacock hosted a lunch for him. At some point Yeats had fallen silent and was looking pensive. A grand dame—of course, it's Leacock—thought to solicit the poet: 'Mr. Yeats, we're all simply dying to hear your thoughts.' And he said, 'I'm wondering what they'll be serving for supper on the train to New York.' I'd always thought it mostly a Leacock fabrication, until just now when you asked me, because that's what I was thinking: I wonder what we'll have for supper today?"

She laughed, and they both seemed to feel it as a sprinkle.

He turned back to face the setting sun. "Can you believe I stole the *Ulysses*, Mary? I can't, but I did. Detective Gurmeet tells me so, and I trust her. I do not recall doing the deed, or ever even touching the book. Certainly I have no memory of secreting it among Crazy Ray's park-bench collection. Don't look, but that's him over there confabbing with our ward nurse, Marcel. Small world, this mad mad world. It's just as well you should know this. It doesn't matter."

She had nothing to say to any of that, feeling awkward only, a discomfort that grew in the silence as she tried to think of *something* else to say—*anything*.

He smiled small at her. "It's a great comfort just having you stand here with me, Mary. Because I know you're not here just from a sense of duty. Thanks very much for that consideration, your visit, but you don't have to wait around any longer. You shouldn't."

It was like he could read her mind. Behind him the sun broke through the grey-black cloud cover in a blaze of red low on the horizon, and into the room as if a visible infrared, as if they were standing in some absent photographer's dark room and couldn't find the switch, the door. Jake turned back and looked directly at what amounted to the top half of a blood-red ball. When she only glanced she had to look away. How was he able to *do* that? This was too weird, a mistake. She *should* go, he'd released her. He was about to say something she didn't want to take away: he was going to hurt himself.

But all he said was "Am I still invited up to Leitrim Falls for fishing?"

She settled instantly and involuntarily touched his upper arm so lightly he didn't appear to feel it. "Of course," she said with a serious laugh. "I've mentioned you to my dad, and he said bring him, bring him, I need a fishing buddy! Uh, soon as you're, like, better, I mean." *Dork.*

"Where was it again? I'm sorry … but my mind. I mean the fishing hole, where you said Dad caught a rainbow trout?"

"Big Pond, on our farm." She felt him moving off, something in the way his body swayed, like preparing to unmoor and slip away in the night. She closed her eyes and kept them tight, no one could see her. She let her mind drop into herself, not thinking, as she'd learned to do for the nonsense poems. When she came back her face was peaceful. She had to reach up to place her hand on his left shoulder.

He continued to stare at the remnant red sun, which had all but sunk out of sight, so at least couldn't hurt anymore. He thought, *It's there all day like it'll never go away, then when it starts sinking it goes like hell.* He said, "Please keep talking, Mary, tell me about Big Pond before you go."

"Sure." *Hold it together.* "It's not very large for the name *Big* Pond, Professor. It's kind of hidden away, past the woods that border our farm's farthest field, so we don't really own it; beyond it there's nothing but scrub growth and untilled fields … same as our book of stories, eh!" *Eejit! Poet! Go down, sink.* "The water's just about always dark, and deep even at the edge, no one's ever fathomed its depth at centre, far as we know. Dad swears it's fed by an underground stream. He might be right because sometimes for no good reason the water will suddenly turn clear and you can see far down all around the edge where Big Pond is growing a whole crop of its own, strange frondy plants, and even a good ways out, until it darkens again and you can see nothing of its depths. But in the times of sudden clarity it also reflects the whole sky in a way you'd not have thought possible, and at night the stars appear infinite in it … uh, if you know what I mean. I'm boring you."

"I can see it, Mary, *infinite in it*—yes, you are definitely a poet!"

Some life in him at least. Then why was she crying? *Talk, keep talking.* "But my favourite place is Big Rock on the far side. It's where I've had the worst best times of my life."

"So far."

She collected herself before echoing: "So far."

He turned and caught the hand that was slipping off his shoulder. "Thank you for coming, Mary, and for that. I really *can* see it."

His eyes, was he blind? They looked like shiny red-reflecting eyes in bad old photos. Had the red sun somehow possessed him? "Can I visit again, Professor?"

"Of course, though I really don't expect to be here much longer." Then suddenly he looked normal, his old professor self. Until he laughed, which sounded like something mechanical breaking sprocket teeth. "You really must go now, Mary."

Without thinking she stepped forward and hugged him, and surprised he took a moment to reciprocate. They stepped apart lightly holding hands, then trailed farther apart.

He tried his best to smile again but couldn't manage it. "Do you remember our talk on the steps of Macdonald Library? I do, for now anyway. You *won't* quit on me, will you, Mary?"

"I promise I won't if you'll promise to get better and come back to teach me, *and* go fishing with my dad."

He remembered how to smile, sort of, and was still smiling long after she'd left him, prolonging an affectless grin just like a true madman. He didn't see her go, having returned to his window that, with darkness descended, was now a more solid mirror.

Jake heard nothing more, even when, on her way to the room's exit, Mary was called: "Hey you, girly!"

She would say just a friendly word and leave, so moved quickly to the corner where Crazy Ray sat, a small paperback book in his left hand, his gnarly thumb marking the place. At ease he had his long legs extended onto the round white table, crossed at the ankles with lower heel resting on the silly sign with the blue wool string and the one word: READER. From the overlapping it appeared there were two signs.

"It's Mary," she said smiling, "Mary McGahern."

"I know who you are and I'm even pleased to see you, especially since you're visiting our old friend over there."

"You weren't very friendly when you threw that rock at him."

"I don't know what you're talking about, Mary McGahern."

"I have to be going, I won't interrupt your reading any further. I hate when people do that to me, like other people shouldn't interrupt but they are the exception."

He turned the front cover towards his long morose face distended farther by the mad prophet's beard and started like he'd never seen it before. But he spoke without tincture of madness. "Oh this? Your old perfesser friend over there picked it out of my library one day and recommended it to me highly." He articulated the title unnaturally: "*Such Is My Beloved*. By Callaghan, another mad Catholic Irish-Canadian, groping his way in good and evil with a priest for the main character, of all God's creations! I'm not expecting a happy ending. Why? Because I already finished it and started over. So a self-styled spoiler alert!" He laughed and slapped the arm of his chair, where the upholstery cord was exposed like a frayed nerve. The table lamp rocked dangerously.

She bucked up her courage and pointed: "What's with the signs? The blue strings?"

He put his feet to the floor and leaned forward with a face on him like he'd been challenged to a knife fight. But he wasn't fighting mad, at least not with anything external; he wasn't even angry, just couldn't control his face. "That's work inspired by your old perfesser there. Jake complained that nowadays most of his students want to be writers." Without warning he sang loudly, extending the phrase and echoing himself in falsetto: "*Paperback writers* ... But that none of them can write for beans, because they don't read for beans! So we're going to wear the signs round our necks, like the labelled condemned, only as proud of our crime. They'll ride a little high up. The nurse wouldn't allow me too much yarn, not so much as could be doubled—give a man enough rope, if you get my drift!"

She was still embarrassed from his sudden singing. "Will you do me a favour, Cr … Mr. Ray?"

"I might. If you will read me another of your poems? Because you *are* the real thing, Mary-Mary—no call for blushing—and you need to believe that. And something tells me *your* nonsense will fit swimmingly here!"

"I don't have one at the moment, but I'll make you a deal: I'll bring one with me next time *if* you promise to look after Professor Flynn."

"It's a deal Mary-Mary-quite-contrary. I like Jake anyway, we're two of a kind, Perfesser Ray and Crazy Jake! … Even if he did involve me in his troubles with the law! Still, I like him all right. Jake's different from the others, he tried, if more the fool for that. But I'll watch him for you like a lost lamb, *if* you truly promise to bring, *and* recite for me, your next nonsense poem. Nonsense only—the true poetry!"

Another deal? What was she, a drug pusher before Break Week? *Go.* She certainly wanted to get away but needed to confirm it. "*Seriously*, Mr. Ray."

He sobered up. "Seriously, Mary McGahern. You look after me poetry-wise and I'll look after Jake, don't you fret."

As fretfully she stepped into the hallway, she heard him sing unabashedly: "Let me take you down …"

Yes?

"… nothing is real …"

Nothing? But not a bad voice after all, at least for that weird song, one of Dad's faves. She liked "Penny Lane" better.

THIRTY-SEVEN

PLAGUING JAKE 13:
DEUS EX MACHINA 1

Turned out the old uBytown HR (Human Resources) had done employees a good turn insisting the union negotiate with Canada Life for private-room hospitalization coverage. At the time the majority complained that the union had bargained away more useful benefits, such necessities as additional daycare spaces and parking and gym privileges and, academically, lower enrollment ceilings for the burgeoning new Communications courses and a guarantee of continuing low enrollments for the necessary seminars in Faculty of Arts courses. But sleeping in his cool room—he thought he wasn't sleeping at all—Jake Flynn decided that privacy in such an unexpected situation was worth it, he would tell his colleagues at the next Department of English meeting. But then privacy *was* the thing he prized most in his discrete family, social, and work lives. Or maybe not so clever, the contract value of private-room hospital coverage: because he'd heard from some emaciated high school teacher poring over a fat tome in the Sun Room that when one was remanded for psychiatric assessment, the city picked up the tab, *including* for private occupancy. "Joke's on you, Mr. English *Professor*!" A madman, another. Why had he continued talking with him once he'd learned what he did, or had done, for a living? Professor Flynn had always found high school teachers to be little better than their students—now *his*—when it came to reading, what they read (*Harry Fucking Potter*), if they read at all. *Read!* ... Where was he again?

He wasn't really sleeping in a guarded psych ward, was he? He couldn't be. Please. But he wasn't awake anywhere either. Maybe he was like Lampman when in fine visionary frenzy, the half-and-half visionary state of imminent epiphany! ... Yet he was normal enough to recognize when his rational mind intermittently dissipated and slipped into the illogic of dreams, such as the absurdity of thinking *he* was in the Mental! That was just the normal way of falling asleep, losing your mind. He imagined it so quiet that he could hear a police guard snoring in the hall, like a cello overture: "Let me take you down ..." And then the guard was singing softly, softly singing—a cop singing! High-pitched, falsetto, a girl's voice, was the cop female? Yet another Beatles song, he heard them all day in the Day Room, as he used to open his window to hear them all day from Crazy Ray's corner of Coriveau's lawn: "... *And I love her* ..." Just the ticket!

He rolled his smiling head to the left and looked into the far corner where the singing was coming from, where the window was meshed on the outside with flat strips of twisted black metal tightly woven, admitting only the pale light of fresh snowfall ... faintly fallen ... fallen faintly ... Below the window someone was sitting sideways in a chair but turned so that he couldn't see the face. Had they moved a guard into his very room! ... She had long dark hair straight to the base of her back. He said, "Who are you? What are you doing here?" She turned her face to him. It didn't match the young body, the long slim torso, it wasn't even female, or male, the face, but old, very old. He recognized his father and his mother. The heavy brow, the dark eyes of no-way-out. Or he was thinking absurdly again on his way to welcome sleep, dreaming he must be. In answer it raised the left arm and pointed an elegant finger to the window of snowlight, crooked it once, and the little light lit up the room. He felt an overwhelming love for them, for the first time in his life, which made him turn his face into his left hand and sob. He forgave them their black secrets and dark doings, which had lived on in him. Returning to his logical mind he realized such late love must pay a price, which he was prepared to pay. Was he drugged? Yes. Was that a cheat? Didn't matter. As the old joke had it: No matter, never mind. Ha! When he looked again it was gone. No wonder. Angels have no sense of humour.

He rolled from the bed, wondering why it was, even for him, so high. Good practice, this jumping off, he grinned like the devil.

He knew the room's door would be unlocked, though it wasn't supposed to be. He knew the guard would not even stir, which he didn't. The whole third floor reverberated quietly as an empty tank, so that even the hospital slippers urged him on as in raving nightmares, *sh–whisper–whisper–sh–sh* ... He knew too that he'd find something suitable in the Sun Room, and he did. Table lamps aren't battery powered! Though it took *some* yanking! But worth it, better than cloth, much better—or braided wool!

His sign was on the sill right where he'd left it. She was there too, of course, standing in his corner, still pointing at a window, the one where he'd stood for three days staring at the sun till blinded. Her long hair was now so fair it was made of light. He put on the sign. It still hung too high on his miserable streaky self, though he'd specifically asked Ray to adjust it. **READER** displayed just below his chin, which would look foolish in photos. This window had no security grill, because that wouldn't look right to family, to media. He dropped his pyjamas like shirking dirt. He should at least be wearing underwear! He knew not to joke, angels and all that. If she looked at him he'd never do it, he just couldn't, so she didn't. He felt her slender hand on his back, boosting. Then she was gone.

He was on top of things—he had to watch his head—looking out the toppermost of the poppermost window, which wasn't as clean as the lower. But the night sky had cleared nicely. The stars were their myriad light-pricking selves in wondrous heavens. They were always so exceptional, those points of light, inconceivable balls of combustion trying vainly to heat and light the equally inconceivable black. Surely that was a joke could make even an angel smile!

"Are we good to go, Ringo?"

Peace.

"Are the stars shining brightly, Paul?"

Yes, sir.

"Is the sky dark, George?"

Affirmative.

"And, John, will this love of mine never die?"

You're joking, mate.

So he began to sing, in a voice that no man or angel would call the music of the spheres. He pulled the top louvered window inward, pulled harder at its limit till it broke fairly easily from unused hinges. With the top space freed, the window below came away as if built for that very purpose. Only a solid traversing piece of frame remained intact, again as if constructed to his purpose. He double knotted the electrical cord to it. Tested the noose and slipped it on like a Sunday tie. Singing still, his last squawk was "… die."

THIRTY-EIGHT

DEUS EX MACHINA 2: TRAIN OF THOUGHTLESSNESS

Light of … no, not the shorter string of VIA train coaches approaching but an endless run of brown CN freight cars, he could tell from the whiter beam of headlamp taking way too long to grow larger. Fuck. *Go*, he should go—he had stupidly stopped *inside* the level crossing's barrier when all the clanging and flashing commenced—and there was still plenty time. Who's afraid of Alfredo the train! He who hesitates etc. But what if the old truck stalled? It had been lately. He might have a couple of beer in him—don't tell Mary!—but he wasn't a complete drunken eejit yet! He'll get a new truck, on lease, like every other stupid farmer. Jim Collins was helping him make the operation profitable again, had more than earned his low wages. We'll fix that. Still better keep on at Canopy though. Mary and Jim. Mary's face when Jim broke it off, the pain was too much since her mother died, so he'd drunk, stupidly, not thinking that it was as bad for Mary. C'mon-c'mon, fucking CN trains! *Go already.* No. He settled himself humming the song that had so affected him during Mary's and Jim's breakup, Dionne Warwick killing "Anyone Who Had a Heart." A child's heartbreak was just too much to bear. Then sang in a voice that should never sing aloud. He *was* good and drunk. Careful.

He rested his forehead on the top of the steering wheel and sobbed twice, one each for Mary and her mother, his Carol. How do people who love one another hurt each other so deeply? He'd hurt her mother too like that, one time, thinking he had to go off to a U.S. college, quit the family farm for good, go away to be a writer, of all things. He'd sat all night in the loft, at times sweating so much he believed he could hear it pop and fizz on his back. He was a born eejit, as his mother, who loved Carol and knew what he was planning, had called him, she who had never interfered in such matters. Alone he came slowly and dimly to realize that he'd bought into someone else's story. Almost equally painful, he knew himself not to have the talent to become a real writer. With the sun streaking through the gaping chinks of the barn to create beams of bright dust, and with the cows lowing for relief below him (his responsibility), he'd stopped sweating.

Mary had a gift, maybe just a small talent, like his own had been, or maybe not so small, or small at all. He'd make sure she didn't quit it till she knew. That thought settled him in his impatience with the eternally slow-coming train, though the white headlight *had* doubled at least. They're good together. They could handle the farm together when he's gone, but for a long time still *with* him there of course ... old farmer Seán enjoying his well-earned rest on the porch of a summer's evening, surrounded by the grandkids he watched over for them, with Mary and Jim returning hand-in-hand from Big Pond. He could see it—

Or could have further if the truck's cab and creation itself instantly wasn't blinding white light.

THIRTY-NINE

NEWS FROM HOME

Returned to Brant Rez from the Princess Diana Centre for Mental Wellness, Mary was handed a message by the uniformed reception person, which was unusual, because usually she'd have been told "There's somethin' in your box, McGahern." She'd never taken to the stout woman and didn't like her now openly watching as she read the three-word message: "Call Jim Collins." *Call?* She was dissociated for seconds, the whole residence thing wholly unfamiliar again, the receptionist an irrelevant nuisance. ... Oh, it's just Jimmy's email not working, that's all. Or his phone? Then how *call?* She'd call his home's land line. But that didn't make sense either. She'd call Da—

"Mary?" It was Alice, who'd come up beside her and immediately seen that something was wrong.

Mary turned with the message pinched tightly in her right hand. Alice knew it had to be bad news, and private. She stepped forward and hugged Mary. "I'll talk with you later, okay? Call me, please, if you'd like to talk with someone, I know I would you, friend." She waggled the old-fashioned thumb-and-pinky sign—"Call"—and was off.

Mary watched her walk away and smiled distractedly. *Call?* … She remembered *her* new phone, which she'd not yet learned had to be kept with her at all times, and continued in a daze to her room, where she had blunt trouble making the stupid phone work.

"Mary, there's been an accident." That's all Jimmy got out before he was crying.

He must be alone. "An accident. Yes. Jimmy, stop. Take three deep breaths, exhale slowly."

She heard him take two and wished she could touch him. That's what Dad hated about phones: nothing but the sound of bad news.

"It's my old man, Mary. He …"

"Your father was in an accident. Is he hurt bad?"

"He's dead. Mom too, she was with him. But it's worse even than that." And he was crying jerkily again.

"Oh my God, Jimmy, I'll be home on the next train."

Then he was stone-cold controlled: "Mary, are you sitting down? I know that sounds melodramatic but forget all that shit, this is real. Are you?"

"Yes." She continued standing, the front of her thighs butting against the desk, her right fingertips grazing the hieroglyphs of its gouged surface.

"He was drunk of course, my stupid goddamned fucking old man! They'd phoned Mom from Shea's that he was out of his head and unfit to drive. She Ubered to the pub but he wouldn't let her drive the truck. … Oh, Mary …"

"*Both* of them, *dead*? Oh, my God, Jimmy. Poor you—I've gotta go right now and grab the next train, I think there's one—"

"For fuck's sake! *No*! It's worse, way worse. Your father's dead too!"

She hadn't heard what she'd heard. "What? I don't get it. Is this some sort of sick joke, Jimmy? If it is—"

"Shut up. *Please*."

As Jimmy talked she knew without hearing what she heard, before he'd spoken two sentences she was trembling. The phone slipped from her grip, caught the edge of the desk, hit the floor and went dark. She dropped beside it, crumpling more than sitting, and couldn't reach for it till her vision came back. Then it wouldn't work. She sat on the floor stabbing the phone with forefinger of her shaking hand, harder and harder. Then it did work. She and Jimmy cried, both inhaling jerkily like hurt children, till he managed to get the story out, with Mary's contribution being the repeated "I don't believe it—I cannot *believe* what you're telling me, Jimmy—I don't believe you! ..."

Mary's father's truck had been stopped at the railway crossing on Laird Street, between Burke and Rideau, for some unknown reason inside the barrier. At high-speed Jimmy's father had crashed the barrier and rammed the truck just as the CN freight train arrived, which took the smashed truck down the track some ways before the train derailed like a twisting rope, with its seventh car flattening the cab of Collins' truck. The three had been killed instantly, though not officially declared dead till after arrival at the hospital.

FORTY

THAT THEY MAY FACE
THE RISING SUN

How does one do such a funeral? *Funerals.* Seriously. A loved body without life is as dead as dead gets. What more is there to say? Nothing else matters, or *will* matter ever again. And whether covered with planks and surrounded by indoor-outdoor green carpeting, or a stereotyped grave accessorized by a top-hatted undertaker leaning on a spade, a hole in the ground awaiting that loved one's body is a hole in the ground, waiting patiently. Nor does the scene need leafless trees, grey skies or cold rain. Such a black-and-white cinematic funereal atmosphere neither helps nor hurts, period. Because nothing matters anymore. Nothing. Only death matters, everywhere, waiting, saying nothing, over and over, ad infinitum, patiently waiting.

The fact is, death un-matters. How *could* you ever have thought otherwise, even while rolling in life and love and the like, you who have lost parents (well, not really *lost*: they died), a friend or two, a younger sibling, a beloved? You should have kept that knowledge as close as memory of their love! Remembered that when it comes to the death of a loved one, the only unholy hole is in the heart, which no little backhoe can backfill and tamp out of sight, ever. How *could* you have forgotten that? Yet you did, for a time, for a spell (and maybe you had to, okay). And this: there is no grown-up answer to death? Remembering that fact might have helped some little some, if still never have answered the absence of all feeling but annihilating emptiness. Because even a permanently lodged memento mori also means fuck all in the end. Remember that.

It did matter some little bit, if still not at all in the moment, that Mary and Jimmy had each other. Qualified so because there's something about death's severing finality that makes even a blooming romantic bond almost as meaningless as everything else. Forging the ties that bind? Mutually supportive love? Nothing helped because nothing mattered to either. Nothing could touch them where they lived.

Overcooked cynicism? Consider this: *Adèle Faucher (nee Pélletier) brought her newborn to the graveyard for the burial of Jimmy's parents.* She may have been thinking that a new life would provide some circle-of-life consolation. *That's* what people are capable of respecting another's feelings when it comes to dealing with death. Lost the baby, dear? You're still young enough, you can always have another. ... Didn't you have twins anyway?

It took months before Mary even half-regretted looking deadpan at Jimmy and whispering, "Should we throw little Freddie in the hole?" Neither laughed nor smiled. Mary had spoken only for Jimmy's sake and only because Adèle had stood there as if waiting for a thank you for your thought-fulness. But Adèle had not got what she deserved (that's a funeral for you), and to her credit she walked off in comparative dignity, with Freddie in a canary-yellow carrier happily bansheeing against her swollen front. Only after half a year was Mary even bothered to be relieved that no one believed Adèle's graveside story, which, when she could work up the interest to do so, Mary always denied in some trumped-up umbrage. She and Jimmy eventually learned to love it, that story, near shitting themselves the first time they recalled it together out by Big Rock.

"When she finally processed what you'd said, I thought she was going to *fall* into the grave, with that ugly baby—he does look too much like fat Fred! But that *was* über-cruel, Mary my dear." "Yeah, I think so too: *perfect*. Did you catch what she hissed at me before leaving? 'I read your fucking poem, *cunt*.' *Pome*. Thank you for coming, Adèle dear, your thoughtfulness means more to Jimmy and me than we could ever express."

Okay: holding onto each other and shaking with laughter and crying together was some comfort also, but the only such, and it was the first time only after a very long time had passed. … Though comforting too in its way was the next turn, when through snotty laughter they commenced accusing each other of being the really horrible person. Their way anyway.

Leitrim Falls had turned out for the Collins internment, which was actually the first thing pushy new-mother Faucher had observed to Jimmy, using the sensitive, 'sophisticated' euphemism. Back at the McGahern farm, where no one was invited, Jimmy had refused the Harp and fussed checking off the many chores that hadn't been done and had now to be done. The strangely still farm more than any other setting, more even than the graveside, had been the first place to express the changed world's true mournfulness.

When he and Mary came round to talking sensibly, Jimmy had searched for some fond memories of his parents. He'd managed to dig up admiration for his mother's always having made Christmas on no budget whatsoever, especially in the final years of the farm's failing, before the sale to Canopy Growth. But he followed that with remembering how his father always had had enough cash to drink himself stocious through every Christmas. So first efforts towards comforting each other had proven useless. Sex? Whatever people say about sex being the natural response to death, sex was unthinkable for these two, for days anyway. Two-and-a-half days.

Only Jimmy had attended her father's cremation. Mary refused the offer of a religious service for the atheist (though in lighter moods Séan McGahern could be argued by his daughter into professing a guarded agnosticism). There was no family plot or wife's grave to bury him alongside. Mom had been cremated too, and Dad's reasons for doing so still convinced Mary to honour his wish for himself. At first she'd been shocked when he said he was having Mom "incinerated"—*her* accusing word for it—but came round and eventually was grateful that she never had to think of her mother's body decomposing beyond what it already had by the end (which also is what had them promise to have the other euthanized; she'd asked Dad half-teasingly, "But how will I know you're in your right mind for consent?" He'd grown serious. "Okay, here's my *compos mentis* test: Ask me why the Reverend Dean Drone is the real villain of *Sunshine Sketches*. Here's the answer …"). Contrarily, the image of pale blue flames made Mary think of a spirit freed from the dirt that buried others in their own dirt. Her father had asked for nothing else, so it was her idea to have him cremated with a favourite book on either hand: his first edition of *Sunshine Sketches of a Little Town* and *That They May Face the Rising Sun*.

She'd had to insist on being present for the final event, which the director had discouraged, but relented because he knew these cool quiet types were the ones who could suddenly break into hysteria. Gazing somberly as the cheap container slid glacially into the oven, Mary said with remarkable self-possession, "Why he loved that *Sunshine Sketches* I will never know. It's one of the silliest fucking books I've ever read. Oh well, at least the sunshine and Jesus won't find him with rotting feet."

The attendant *tch-tched* and turning away *tsked* loudly at his monitoring devices, but only once.

Then when the oven door closed with a soft thump and a click, Mary commenced crying quietly, and turned onto Jimmy's shoulder, into his arms, still thinking what a fucking cliché she and they and the whole fucking scene was—even without cold rain and grey skies and a fucking hole in the fucking ground! "Us too!" was the only thing she said aloud. Having made it through the graveyard scene the day before without contributing a tear, Jimmy said, "Shouldn't that be *we*?" But then he was as big a wreck, so she held him too, there in the cold cremation chamber, till they created their own uncomfortable heat. Was any of that—the stoicism, the anger, the crying, the inappropriate nerdy joking—comforting? You'd have to ask them.

Whatever their answer might be, there *was* some minuscule comfort to be had from Alice Pham's having waited a day before emailing Mary minimally the news of Professor Flynn's death by suicide at the Princess Diana Centre for Mental

Wellness. Mary asked for more detail, which Alice provided in the clipped style of a telegram:

Hanging from window of Mental's common room. By electrical cord. Outside. Stark Naked. Sign reading **READER** hanging round his neck. Bizarre. Nurse says Crazy Ray to blame. Detective Gurmeet Investigating. Pic in *Citizen* with dick blurred out. Please hurry back so we can talk. Love, Alice.

She showed the text to Jimmy, who didn't really care when a dead-voiced Mary said, "I worried he might kill himself. But you're right, who cares?"

Still, they cried and cried and cried, caring, it sounded, for the whole world's woes.

FORTY-ONE

CHILDISH THINGS BACK IN PLACE

TIDINGS
Newsletter of the
Film&WordsWork Undergraduate
Student Association

In this time of deep and abiding loss
for the Film&WordsWork Pod, we again
turn to poet Mary McGahern, if this
time sadly for consolation. That may
strike as counter-intuitive, our having
solicited something elegiac from a
so-called "nonsense poet," but we found
ourselves in dire need and didn't know

where else to turn (*pace* uBytown's cadre of eager grief counsellors). We do believe, though, and trust that you will agree, that we were correct in our rationally intuitive solicitation of our Pod's poet laureate (which we assume the authority to crown her). Unfortunately our coffers, unlike our coffins, are empty (Ooooo, apologies), so we were unable to offer Ms. McGahern an honorarium this time, which she graciously agreed to, since we didn't bring up the matter (ah nonsense, there is thy comfort). Nor can we pretend to offer exegesis of the poem below, in which the McGahern nonsense still abides and, in persisting so, by definition resists rational discourse. That said, we will take the liberty of suggesting this to our suffering classmates, professoriate, and administrative staff: thank God daily (or whatever deity to whom you pray, or for that matter thank Angus Daly) that, whatever else you have to answer for in this vale of tears, at least you are not the original of McGahern's nemesis, that devil Adèle!

Yet we continue in dire distress, my fellow classmates and professors. Not only have we lost our fearful Leader Professor Flynn in climax to a personal tragedy about which no one had any intimation (seriously *requiescat in pace*) but we also have literally lost our Film&WordsWork Pod to the Communications Pod. *And*, if the rumours prove to be true, we will soon have fairly lost uBytown itself to China's Pingdingshan University. If such a bi-national arrangement eventuates, we expect soon thereafter to be advertised far and wide as Canada's and the world's only officially tri-lingual university!

In closing this last number of *Tidings*, let me say seriously on a personal note what an honour it has been serving as your president, the last, of the UF&WSA and as your editor here, also the last. Yes, this *is* the last issue of *Tidings*, as together we suffer the end of so much else besides. *Pax et amor*, and R.I.P.

– Spencer Mellon, President, UF&WSA

Madam Forget, Kindergarten Teacher
(*in memoriam* Jacob Flynn, University Teacher)

I wanted one crayon from Adèle's packed pack,
the purple perfect purple.
Mad damn Madam made me give it back.
I'd lied.
And when for shame I cried
and thought I'd die,
her boosting hand was on my back.

I'm just me, I mean me!
And mean Adèle hurt me
by accident on purpose.
Madam said, "I bet we'll feel better,
let's write her a letter
letting her know that she hurt us."

I brightened: "Maybe a poem would be better!"

I will never forget Madam Forget,
she taught me not to totter;
Oh I was no angel, no perfect pet,
just some mother's dotty daughter.

And I'm still just me, still mean old me.
She'd said, "You're the purply perfect girl for me!"
So I will never forget Madam Forget...
Adèle will, and never regret it.

– *Mary McGahern*

FORTY-TWO

ONCE A HEIFER

Aoife's noisy labouring had upset the whole barn, with cows bellowing and stomping and kicking boards; with chickens running in circles and pecking at each other, even their own chicks. Pluto was grunting continuously, which may well have been calming his harem of sows, who, standing apart in the corner of the inside sty with heads together and tails out, appeared to be discussing among themselves the trials of giving birth. The rooster had flown into the rafters, which was exceptionally strange even in such disruption.

Exhausted from a long night—planning, figuring, planning—Mary and Jimmy had no idea how much of the upset they'd slept through. Aoife had passed from moaning to lowing to bellowing before either of them came fully awake from troubled dreams. They'd recognized no signs of imminent labour the previous day and the heifer wasn't due to birth for well over a month yet. But spoiled Aoife had always been on her own clock, and in the early morning Mary found her in troubled labour. "Something's wrong," she said evenly to Jimmy. "And getting worse by the minute." He put down his coffee and went back with her.

Despite their weeks of mutual reassurances regarding their capabilities in running the farm themselves, neither had any idea what to do about a normal delivery, let alone this increasingly troubled one. Jimmy's farm had had little stock, and Mary had been kept away from the seasonal birthings. She'd known of course that Aoife had finally conceived and was well along, because Aoife would always be her pet (to Jimmy she said "her special charge"), yet she'd done nothing preparatory, neither in her mind nor talked to the vet. In the chilled and steaming barn she got down on her knees beside the prone cow—which posture alone was alarming in a labouring cow—and felt her swollen belly like she knew what she was doing. But it was only what she'd once seen her father do, his mouth pinched and head shaking (before she was scatted off home). Jimmy perked up at her seeming expertise, then instantly lost heart when she stood and, slapping the dirt off her thighs, said matter-of-factly, "I think you have to reach up inside and see where the calf is."

"*Me?* Wait here. I'm calling Doctor North."

"Good idea."

But neither was as steady as each tried to appear for the other's sake. Alone, Mary remembered their neighbour's, old man Gibson's, advice respecting farm animals: "If you're going to have livestock, you're going to have dead stock." And hugged herself. The disturbed barn was unusually steamy from the animals' excited breathing, the upper air like a magician's trick of crisscrossing swords of light. She set about feeding the stock. It was taking Jimmy forever to return.

By the time the vet arrived, Aoife had exhausted herself and retreated through bellowing to a pained lowing, then a moaning. He felt the belly with reassuring expertise, put on the long yellowish glove and groped up inside Aoife, which re-energized her to bellowing, and in Mary encouraged hope.

He said, "Impossible to say for sure, but I *think* the problem's we've got twins."

She asked, "Is that a big problem?"

"Yes. *That* and, going from your timeline, the young lady's at least a month early. But maybe with the help of God we can get her to deliver these premature Christmas calves."

That did and didn't make sense: it was well after Christmas, and Mary feared that the calf—calves were coming way too early.

He looked up from his knees and ordered Jimmy to his car to retrieve the chain and come-hither mechanism: "As a precaution." Jimmy seemed to know what was wanted, better than Mary anyway. She stood dumb. The vet remained kneeling at Aoife's rear and for a long half-hour felt and patiently massaged her belly and occasionally reached far up inside her; that looked impossible but neither he nor Aoife appeared to mind the striking violations. He'd been using the same glove and his left shoulder past the glove's covering was soon coated with mucus and blood. Soon Mary was again feeling a mounting panic in concert with Aoife's renewed, exhausted moaning.

The vet, his look progressively darkening, spoke across his right shoulder as he was again blindly feeling inside the distressed animal: "It's twins all right, but they're positioned oddly. I feel ... yes, only the one pair of hooves." He closed his eyes. "They're not moving, no matter what I do, so be prepared. And they seem ... yes, to be lying head-to-tail? I don't ..."

He withdrew his arm, peeled off the messy glove, and looked only at Jimmy. "Son, I need you to drive into town, tell my Mrs. it's a caesarian, she'll know what to bring, and hurry on back here."

Mary found a small voice: "Is Aoife going to die?"

"If we don't perform the caesarian, and the quicker the better, this young lady *will* die and likely take her premature calves with her, if they're not dead already. Take my car, Jim"— he expertly tossed the keys, which Jimmy fumbled—"cops know it and won't bother you, waste no more time."

The vet *tch*-ed when Jimmy took too long finding the keys in the straw and dirt. Their jingling brought Mary to attention, that and the air of urgency.

"Wait, Jimmy, I'm coming with you."

"Sure," called Jimmy moving off.

"*Mary*," the vet stopped her. "No. I need you here to keep her settled. If she panics and tries to stand and bolt, it will all be over."

Jimmy hadn't paused, and neither did Mary. She knelt at Aoife's head and petted and cooed. Dr. North sat back on his haunches at her rump, lips pinched, gazing unfocused at the floor as if searching from some other key.

The vet talked aloud to himself more than for Mary's information, calculating that some six hours could well have passed since Aoife began labouring. That was no good. Mary's throat thickened. He gave himself freedom of the house, found old blankets and fresh sheets where Mary had said he would, and boiled a bucket of water, which took far too long ("A watched kettle never boils": Granny McGahern). He also emptied the coffee pot, bringing the second mug back to the barn, which

Mary refused. With a dismissive smirk he sipped the burned brew himself leaning back against a beam post, and his relaxed posture calmed both Mary and Aoife some. Another slow half-hour dragged by before Jimmy and the vet's wife arrived breathless with the alarming collection of bottles and surgical instruments. Mary was ignored when she asked if the boiled water was still hot enough.

Dr. North and his wife, Lorna, scarcely looked at each other as with her practised assistance he began the procedure. Mary was ordered to get Aoife up, who had to stand or there was no use even trying. Aoife obeyed only when shouted up by Mary, who then had to halter the heifer and hold the rope with all the strength in her left hand only, while with the other alternately gripping one horn and petting the distraught animal's soft pulsing neck and rock-hard face (the only animal she'd let herself humanize since long ago the pet lamb had gone to slaughter). Aoife kept her legs, which fortunately took all her strength and attention. Throughout what followed, the Norths talked to one another in a kind of code, with only one word spoken at a time: "There ... there ... that ... more ... good ... brush ... razor ... rinse ... *wash* please. Scalpel." Lorna's was the far greater assistance, of course, but Jimmy helped too, fetching from the nearby supplies and carrying out whatever directions she gave. He even smiled tightly to himself as the activity began to encourage his confidence.

Mary was enjoying no such reassurance. She was unapologetically shouldered aside (still gripping the halter) when a syringe whose size alone made her not look again was jabbed into Aoife's velvety neck; then three times more along the back's ridge, the spine, and twice deeply atop the rump. A space on her side near the rear was soaped and washed and shaven to a frightening extent. Then washed again, and yet again with a reddish disinfectant. His wife handed him the scalpel and stood near as, without hesitation, the vet nicked deeply then bit by bit opened a slit like cutting through cured leather. The aperture didn't look large enough. So he enlarged the opening exposing the sac, and stood back when he cut it … But nothing gushed, even surprisingly little blood trickled. Wearing a fresh glove he reached far into the opening, and farther, up to the armpit with the side of his head against the cow's back as he appeared to be peering off into a far corner of the barn, like he was doing nothing more than fumbling blindly for something at the bottom of a canvas hockey bag. His face took on an increasingly worried expression—every feature slowly widening and rising till his eyes were plainly startled—but he was too much the old pro to voice his alarm. His wife saw it though, and her own face turned blank. And Jimmy saw her; he took a step backwards and looked at Mary, who was preoccupied.

The vet's hand finally emerged from Aoife with one hazy hoof encased in grey membrane, which he cut open while hanging on to the vibrantly coloured reddish-and-white hoof. He continued cutting the membrane as the leg emerged inch-by-inch—it stuck, and he again widened the passage just a touch; the leg came along, then stuck again and wouldn't budge. The vet whispered only for his wife, "Very odd … scalpel." He widened a good half-inch more—and instantly the calf slipped into Lorna's and Jimmy's waiting arms like some huge fish. *Calf*, singular. They laid it on the floor. Vet and wife gazed at it expressionlessly, until the vet looked at his wife and shook his head. She turned down her mouth. Jimmy was staring in what would be cartoonish alarm if it weren't so shockingly real.

After a minute of dead silence, Mary looked back: "What's going on? Aoife's gone very—oh my god!"

For the calf had two perfectly formed heads branching from a normal body and single neck. Despite neither of its snouts having been cleaned, it breathed noisily some and tried repeatedly to rise but could not lift due to the weight of the two heads, or couldn't for long before both heads would thump down again. Mary let go of Aoife's halter and horn and the cow, with a gaping wound in her side like a puptent's poorly closed entrance, was too shocked and exhausted to move.

Mary went to Jimmy's side and, saying nothing, joined in the dull horrified staring. When she dipped to touch it the vet calmly ordered, "Don't touch."

He regrouped. "Leave it be, dear, it'll die shortly, which is for the best. Right now I need to suture and clean your cow or she'll die too. And you need to keep her calm."

He got to work, moving at speed: expertly locating, suturing and tucking away innards, sewing up the insides first with what looked like an oversize hooking needle, tying off the sutures twice and snipping the excess thread with scalpel, moving with impressive skill always from inside organs to outer layers. Until the wound was closed almost seamlessly, washed and rinsed, and finally sprayed with disinfectant that left a mauve-coloured patch like something ethereal, even a birthmark.

Mary and Jimmy said nothing throughout, mesmerized as much by the display of the vet's skills as by what had actually happened: Aoife cut open gapingly, gone into as though no more than some insentient container, relieved of a two-headed calf, then sewn up like nothing more than a torn sail ready again to set forth.

Dr. and Lorna North went and stood by the young couple, whom they knew well. Still wiping his hands on his own hanky now, the vet spoke first: "More trouble for you two young folks, I'm afraid. Trouble *on* trouble, as Lorna and I know, and you have our condolences. I'd say *our prayers* only neither of us are believers that way. You have been much in our thoughts though, neighbours." Lorna added, "Our deepest sympathy."

A drawn-out nothing, if also a settling—till the cock startled them crowing from his unnatural rafter perch and clumsily flapped down among his hens.

His wife touched her husband's side, and he continued: "As for this," he paused but didn't bother gesturing. "You know, we've all heard of these freaks, but for the life of me I never thought I'd see one. I've read the odds are one in millions. Some *have* survived, but it will die if left alone, and soon, absolutely untouched, and I advise you do that, better all around. Unless you want your place turned into a freak show. Lorna and I will be spreading no word."

The four of them looked. The calf with its two perfect heads could have been dead already. To confirm, the vet crouched and touched its neck for longer than might have been expected. He stood and, spritzed by his wife, recommenced wiping his hands on the clean cloth she provided. "It'll be dead within the hour."

Mary was still whispering: "What about Aoife?" She sniffled and leaned into Jimmy.

Lorna North saw rising distress and spoke evenly: "The best thing for now is that you remove the calf and let Aoife rest. We'll come by tomorrow early and see how she's doing. But maybe best to prepare yourself for the worst, honey, I'm sorry to say." She was moved, but she exuded only cool comfort.

She began collecting and packing up the instruments and empty bottles. She looked plainly at her husband, who still stood gazing down with Mary and Jimmy and didn't move to help her, likely unaware of his oversight. She said, "Oh yeah, John. John?" He reacted. "On the news after you left, they said yet a newer variant of the corona virus has been found in Toronto again, another recombinant strain, again fast-spreading, no doubt more lethal than the last. They're racing like hell to retool the vaccine, but federal government's already talking nationwide lockdown. We'd best get home. And you kids need to get this freak out of here and buried. John, for God's sake give it something and let's skedaddle."

Which he did with his oversized syringe. One head then the other jerked slightly, lay still.

With so much in the air, to Mary the barn smelled almost as bad as a hospital. Gratefully outside she and Jimmy watched the couple drive off. Then she said, "Come on then, we'd better bury it, doctor's wife's orders."

There'd been an edge of anger, he watched her worriedly.

They half-carried half-dragged the weird carcass out behind the barn. Jimmy ran back round the front for the small tractor, picked up the backhoe bucket attachment and soon had excavated a grave. Using the bucket's teeth like a rake, he rolled the freak creature into the hole, backhoed the dirt and tamped it down.

They stood close by the warmth of the throbbing machine— even diesel smelled better—themselves idling awkwardly as if each expected some kind of ritualistic speech of closure from the other, which wasn't forthcoming of course. Instead Mary finally took a step away from Jimmy, turned up her hands and talked in an alarmed crescendo:

"Did it have two brains too? Would each have lived differently, if given the chance? We should at least have *tried* to keep it alive! Aoife would have been satisfied and loved it! Me too! You can't just pull out a baby and let it die and act like nothing happened! How will I explain it to Aoife? And now Aoife might die too! What will I—"

He'd smothered her in his arms and answered only, "Mary."

She finally settled and answered only, "Jim," the first time she called him *Jim*.

FORTY-THREE

EPILOGUE: MARY AND THE CROW 2

The animals are fed and bedded down. Aoife has been coming along well in her private stall, though she'll never be pregnant again. It is still deep winter, Groundhog Day in fact, with no sign of spring in sight if also no snow on the ground. But they are still crazy even thinking of walking to Big Rock … which would sort-of be in character since they'd taken to calling each other Crazy Mary and Crazy Jim. Then crazily they just went, if sanely in long duffle coats and wearing hats and scarves and gloves, and with two sleeping bags.

It's not so bad. Big Pond looked coldly warning as it came gradually into view like an open black eye. Lately it seemed the whole world was warning them to be extra careful. At first they sat on the rolled bags, crushing them comfortably, with backs against the rock which retained some heat from the sunny day.

They talk sitting up, their feet drawn up. But as they register the warmth from Big Rock penetrating their backs and radiating though them, they let their feet slide till they're sitting with legs straight out. In the growing dark they could readily be mistaken for disobedient children hiding.

The evening air is so sharp that when breathed it rouses the throat, tasting of nothing but crispness. Sky to sky on either hand could be artificial for the abundance of stars. Neither of them says you never see it like this in the city. It's just where they grew up. It's where they fell in love. So they know it in their hearts to be anything but artificial, it's all just so breath-takingly real. Or it's both real and art, a cosmic aesthetic as local as a cowpie mandala. Of course they never think any of that, being only eighteen. They don't need to.

They are now often comfortably quiet together, a surprising development for such a talkative two. When Jim does speak he's picking up a conversation:

"No, I'm not going back. I have all your father's books, which are more than I'd read in a lifetime."

"Fine. Like I said, then I'm not going back either."

Jim twists to her and pleads with gesturing palms: "Mary, we've been through this. University is not for me. It's even dangerous … as you, uh, know. But you *have* to go back, like we agreed."

"I agreed to nothing. You're reinventing history to suit yourself. *I'm* going back to uBytown and leaving you here to run *my* family farm yourself?" She snorts derisive finality.

He ramps up the intensity, stiffening his hands: "We did agree. But let's not argue again. I'll stay here and work the farm, you'll help when you can."

"Let's not argue and you argue? No offense, Jim, but you could never run the whole operation by yourself. You need me here full-time." Yet her voice is fairly flat given the seriousness of the subject and the spillover intensity from previous arguments.

Jim works the slight advantage he detects. "You forget, I pretty well ran our place by myself the last couple of years, with only a little help from Mom. You weren't around for grades ten and eleven. I loved the work, I was a joke, never washed and looking like a bum."

"And now? You're the Harry Styles of the sty?"

He is diverted in laughter. "That's good, I keep forgetting you're a famous poet now."

"Ha-ha, very funny. By the way, Mr. Smarty-pants, *did* I mention that one of my professors emailed inviting me to submit a whole book manuscript of poems? He's a big shot in publishing, Professor John Turnbull, owner of Rideau Books."

"Mary, seriously, congratulations. I've been bursting with pride, no irony. What'd you answer? *Do* you have more?"

Now she blushes and tones way down. "I could have." But confidently.

He wants to kiss her but will wait. "And no, you never mentioned it. But see what I mean? You *have* to stay in university ... which is probably why you didn't tell me. Please, I'm dead serious, Mary."

"What about expenses: new Deeres, maintenance, truck, diesel for everything, seed always going up, crop insurance, fertilizer! What about *money*, Jim?" She doesn't care about money, her spirits are warming and urging, like a Japanese sky lantern wanting to lift off into the sparkling sky. "Everything keeps getting more expensive in the stores, and like Dad always said, we get no pay raise?"

He senses he's convincing her. "You forget again, conveniently, my dear. I now have all that money from the sale of our place to Canopy. Even my old man couldn't drink away what he got for the farm, the land that is. In fact, he hardly made a dent in it, for all the good the money did him ... or Mom. But I—*we* have more than enough to see us through a few years. I can afford to hire help whenever I need it. We're both legal age. We can do it, Mary: slowly, small, scale up, together. We can do what we want. But you have to go back to uBytown."

She's turning dreamy. "We'd need to rent a lot more acreage, because you need about twice what *we* own just to hope to break even, let alone ever make a decent living. We've both been there, Jim." No, we don't need anything but each other. Yet she still needs to hear him defend the crazy idea again, one more time.

"Like I've been saying: we start where we are, we scale up slowly. I know how it works, and I've done some reading on the internet. Smaller farms are actually doing better than the big boys, the *agribusinessmen*," he all but spits.

"What about the big girls?"

He smirks. "Okay, the big farmer boys *and* girls have made a deal with the devil, so that their operations live and die by government subsidies, and mostly they're dying. We can do it, Mary, human-scale, I just know we can."

"We can." She believes it, for the first time wholly endorsing the plan. "Maybe two heads *are* better than one." She pats his.

Which he doesn't like. "Jesus, sometimes you scare me, McGahern."

Big Rock is still issuing some warmth, but out from it only a few feet the air feels cold. They slide the sleeping bags from under, unroll like magic carpets and flip them open. They walk their asses down. Lying face-to-face they pull the flaps across.

He says, "This really is crazy, Crazy Mary." But he already has his pants off.

Unbuttoning she says, "I love making love, did I ever tell you that? What a lovely surprise it's been, not at all what the sluts made it look like, like a game, a competition, even Naomi. And of course I mean only with you, Crazy Jim."

He jokes in a tough-guy voice: "Happy to oblige, baby."

"Yes, it *is* how babies are made."

"Really?" Then just a touch more seriously: "What would *we* ever do with a baby, Mary McGahern?"

"Love it to death."

He frowns, impatient, but also considering his response. "A baby? I don't know if I'm up for that."

She reaches. "Oh, I think you are. No condom again?"

She holds him and doesn't use a poetry-recital voice, just normal talking: "*The best lack all conviction, the worst are filled with a passionate intensity.* That makes you the best *and* the worst."

"Huh?"

"Never mind."

He likes that even less than the earlier head pat.

She sees. "It's from a poem by William Butler Yeats."

He grins. "I like it … I think."

At first they touch as much for comfort as arousal, the routine of their love still fairly new. When he rolls across and rises above her the sleeping bag slips from his muscled white back. For a spell they are oblivious to everything but themselves, at first as couple, then self-centredly. Their faces display pleasure and strain as they find their love's rhythm. They strain further to hold on—when he finishes. Again a bit early for her. He slumps, lowers his head alongside hers and lies lightly on her. She loves this part, the deflating, his not withdrawing. She's close to finishing, so cups the crown of his head and pressing against him reaches climax.

"I love you, Mary."

"I love you too, Jimmy."

She settles and releases him.

Sudden sound like the dull thump of wind on a window, the black wings beating still above the startled Mary, whose head tilts farther back. She's no longer staring at the stars from beneath Jim. Her eyes roll back and for a short spell she looks calmly entranced. Her thighs loosen. She smiles small within herself, knowing things no one could know, the McGahern gift. The farm will survive in their care. Nothing will be broken. Granny and Granda McGahern and Mom and Dad will never be gone. In that moment she as good as conceives.

"What the hell was that?" But he can't bend upwards enough to see.

She knows without seeing. "Big Al, Crazy Jim."

From close above the call issues from the crow into the night's clean crisp air:

"*Fuck ... Mary.*"

ACKNOWLEDGEMENTS

The opening chapter, "Leave Taken," was published in the *Arlington Literary Journal*, and the fifth, "Mary and the Crow," in *The Bookends Review*. Both are much revised.

It is a bonus in publishing for a writer to have a publisher and editor who are themselves writers. I am grateful to Matt Joudrey and the team at At Bay Press. Thank you to editor Doug Whiteway for his usual excellent work. And I am grateful to those who saw the manuscript through its final stages, copy editor Priyanka Ketkar and proofreader Danni Deguire.

Gerald Lynch was born on a farm at Lough Egish in Co. Monaghan, Ireland, grew up in Canada and lives in Ottawa. *Plaguing Jake* is his eighth book of fiction. The *Dying Detective* (2020) was the concluding novel of a trilogy comprising *Omphalos and Missing Children.* These novels were preceded by *Troutstream, Exotic Dancers,* and two books of short stories, *Kisbey* and *One's Company.* He has published numerous short stories, essays, and reviews, as well as having edited a number of books. He has also authored two books of non-fiction, *Stephen Leacock: Humour and Humanity* and *The One and the Many: Canadian Short Story Cycles.* He has been the recipient of a few awards, including the gold award for short fiction in Canada's National Magazine Awards.

OUR AT BAY PRESS
ARTISTIC COMMUNITY

Publisher • **Matt Joudrey**

Managing Editor • **Alana Brooker**

Substantive Editor • **Doug Whiteway**

Copy Editor • **Priyanka Ketkar**

Proof Editor • **Danni Deguire**

Graphic Designer • **Lucas c Pauls**

Layout • **Lucas c Pauls and Matt Joudrey**

Publicity and Marketing • **Sierra Peca**